continued...

Berkley Prime Crime titles by Laura Childs

Tea Shop Mysteries

DEATH BY DARJEELING
GUNPOWDER GREEN
SHADES OF EARL GREY
THE ENGLISH BREAKFAST MURDER
THE JASMINE MOON MURDER
CHAMOMILE MOURNING
BLOOD ORANGE BREWING
DRAGONWELL DEAD
THE SILVER NEEDLE MURDER
OOLONG DEAD
THE TEABERRY STRANGLER
SCONES & BONES
AGONY OF THE LEAVES
SWEET TEA REVENGE
STEEPED IN EVIL

Scrapbooking Mysteries

KEEPSAKE CRIMES
PHOTO FINISHED
BOUND FOR MURDER
MOTIF FOR MURDER
FRILL KILL
DEATH SWATCH
TRAGIC MAGIC
FIBER & BRIMSTONE
SKELETON LETTERS
POSTCARDS FROM THE DEAD
GILT TRIP

Cackleberry Club Mysteries

EGGS IN PURGATORY
EGGS BENEDICT ARNOLD
BEDEVILED EGGS
STAKE & EGGS
EGGS IN A CASKET

Anthologies

DEATH BY DESIGN
TEA FOR THREE

THE TEABERRY STRANGLER

Tea Shop Mystery #11

LAURA CHILDS

BERKLEY PRIME CRIME, NEW YORK

THE BERKLEY PUBLISHING GROUP
Published by the Penguin Group
Penguin Group (USA) LLC
375 Hudson Street, New York, New York 10014

USA • Canada • UK • Ireland • Australia • New Zealand • India • South Africa • China

penguin.com

A Penguin Random House Company

THE TEABERRY STRANGLER

A Berkley Prime Crime Book / published by arrangement with Gerry Schmitt & Associates, Inc.

For information, address: The Berkley Publishing Group,
a division of Penguin Group (USA) LLC,
375 Hudson Street, New York, New York 10014.

ISBN: 978-0-425-24020-5

PUBLISHING HISTORY
Berkley Prime Crime hardcover edition / March 2010
Berkley Prime Crime mass-market edition / March 2011

PRINTED IN THE UNITED STATES OF AMERICA

13 12 11 10 9 8 7 6 5 4

Cover illustration by Stephanie Henderson.
Cover design by Lesley Worrell.

For my old Mission Critical Marketing gang

ACKNOWLEDGMENTS

My thanks to Sam, Tom, Niti, Bob, Jennie, Dan, Moosh, Asia, Elmo, and the fine people at Berkley who handle design, publicity, and sales. A special thank-you to all tea lovers, tea shop owners, bookstore owners, librarians, reviewers, magazine writers, websites, and radio stations who have enjoyed the ongoing adventures of Theodosia, Drayton, Haley, and the rest of the Indigo Tea Shop regulars.

The poem "My Fragrant Cup of Tea," from which Drayton so freely quotes, is from the book *Tea Poetry*, compiled by Pearl Dexter, editor of *Tea: A Magazine*.

1

A back-alley crawl had certainly *sounded* like a tantalizing idea to Theodosia when she'd first conceived it.

A blue-black Charleston evening in early March. Candles flickering up and down the narrow cobblestone alleys that snaked behind Church Street's charming shops. And shop-keepers in historic costumes throwing open their back doors to invite visitors in for tea, Charleston cookies, steaming mugs of crab chowder, and special prices on antiques, oil paintings, giftware, sweetgrass baskets, and leather-bound books.

And, as far as Theodosia Browning was concerned, entre-preneur and historic district booster that she was, the event had been a rousing success.

Hordes of folks, locals as well as tourists, had thronged the back alley, dashing from shop to charming shop. And a whole lot of them had dropped into her tea shop, too. She'd doled out more fresh-brewed cups of Darjeeling, tea sandwiches, and miniature quiches than she could remember serving in a long time.

But now, as the back door of the Indigo Tea Shop snicked shut, Theodosia peered down the length of the alley and suddenly had second thoughts about venturing out alone.

For one thing, the hour was late. Almost ten o'clock. And where visitors had swarmed up and down her alley some forty-five minutes ago, now there didn't seem to be any foot traffic at all.

Spooky, Theodosia thought to herself, as palm trees thrashed in the cool wind and dim, yellow gaslights glowed faintly in the mist. She wondered, just for an instant, if she shouldn't run upstairs and snap a leash on Earl Grey. Let her frisky guard dog Dalbrador prance along beside her. Or perhaps she should pop her head back into the warm, fragrant tea shop and ask Drayton, her master brewer and right-hand man, to accompany her.

"Silly," Theodosia murmured. "I'm only going a few doors down."

Pulling an old-fashioned cloak around her shoulders, the cloak that had served as her costume this evening, Theodosia gathered up her basket of tea and scones and set off down the alley. She was headed for the Antiquarian Map Shop, just down Church Street. The owner, Daria Shand, was a dear friend and probably in need of a little sustenance by now.

Theodosia felt the first drops of rain hit her shoulders and immediately thought, *Frizzies.* With masses of curly auburn hair to contend with, Theodosia sometimes projected the aura of a Renaissance woman captured in portrait by Raphael or even Botticelli. Smooth peaches-and-cream complexion, intense blue eyes, and the calm, often slightly bemused look of a self-sufficient woman in her mid-thirties. A woman who possessed a fair amount of life experience, but still looked forward to a wide-open future.

Flipping her hood up, resigning herself to the steady rain, Theodosia picked her way carefully along wet cobblestones. The squall that had been threatening for days had finally blown in from the Atlantic. Thank goodness it had held off this long.

She was passing the Cabbage Patch gift shop when a gust of wind flipped her cape up and threatened to send her airborne like the Flying Nun.

Theodosia fought the elements for a few moments, feeling like an umbrella turned inside out, then finally got her cape and basket righted. Glancing up as rain spat harder, she suddenly stared down the dim alley and beheld a bizarre scenario.

Theodosia's first, fleeting impression was of two people locked in a lover's embrace. Three seconds later she realized a nasty struggle was taking place.

A struggle? Really? Or were her eyes playing tricks on her?

With rain streaming in her eyes, the two figures appeared more like ethereal blue-black shadows, dancing and twisting in some grotesque embrace. But as their dance turned even more macabre, one figure grasped the other by the neck, forcing the other to drop to its knees.

Oh no!

A sharp burst of lightning lent bizarre special effects, leaching color from the landscape and giving the floundering figures the appearance of a slow-moving film negative.

"Stop!" Theodosia yelled. "Don't . . ."

Her plaintive cry was drowned out by a sharp crack of thunder that rattled nearby windows then continued to grumble ominously.

One of the figures was completely down on the ground now, unmoving, while the other bent over it, flailing like mad. Then, as if suddenly cognizant of a witness, the figure straightened up and gazed down the alley at Theodosia.

Theodosia's heart played a timpani beat in her chest as she sensed anger and rage, and she feared this person might turn on her. Instead, the figure spun and darted off into the pounding rain.

Dropping her basket, Theodosia sprinted for the downed figure.

Panic triggered by recognition shot through her like another bolt of lightning. It was her friend Daria Shand! But not the tall, reddish-blond beauty she knew and loved. This Daria's face was a grotesque mask of purple, her eyes half open and pupils staring into nowhere. And seemingly not breathing!

What to do? Call 911 or chase after the assailant?

Calling 911 won out, of course. And as Theodosia knelt in the alley, pummeled by wind and rain, clutching her cell phone, pounding frantically on Daria's chest, trying to recall her long-ago CPR training, a wave of helplessness washed over her.

Was there nothing she could do? But Daria still hadn't drawn a single, strangled gasp, and the words *crime scene* were swirling sickly in Theodosia's brain.

Minutes later, two shrieking squad cars, red-and-blue light bars pulsing, rocked to a stop in the alley. They were followed by a boxy orange-and-white ambulance.

"Help her!" Theodosia screamed, though she feared Daria was beyond help. Probably, she was in her Creator's hands now.

Theodosia was caught in a swirl of activity then. EMTs working over Daria, more police officers arriving to cordon off the area, an officer firing questions at her, taking notes, trying to get a firsthand account.

At hearing all the commotion, Drayton and Haley came running down the alley from the Indigo Tea Shop, fear and concern etched on their faces.

And a familiar burgundy Crown Victoria slid to a stop in the alley.

"Tidwell," Theodosia murmured when she caught sight of the car.

Detective Burt Tidwell, overweight, articulate, and perpetually suspicious, headed the Robbery-Homicide Division of the Charleston PD. He was prickly rather than gracious and routinely brusque with everyone who got in his way. Though his suit coats rarely buttoned over a stomach that sometimes resembled an errant weather balloon and he could sometimes look the buffoon, Tidwell was as predatory as they came. Smart, canny, a dogged investigator.

Pulling himself from his car, Tidwell donned an enormous black rain slicker and lumbered toward the victim, who still lay in the exact spot she'd fallen. At that same moment, the back door of the Antiquarian Map Shop burst open, and a bearded man in a blue-and-white-checkered shirt suddenly cried, "Daria! Is that Daria? What happened?"

"Who are you?" Tidwell asked in his big cat growl.

"Her boyfriend, Joe Don. Let me through. Let me see her!"

Tidwell raised a hand, and two uniformed officers immediately barred the way.

"Later," Tidwell told him. "Questions first."

"That's not right," Theodosia said, speaking up. "He's her boyfriend. He has a right . . ." She stared at Tidwell, anger and grief on her face, thinking he looked for all the world like a bloated vampire in his dark, shiny rain slicker.

"And you are here, why?" Tidwell asked her in a clipped voice.

"She discovered the victim," one of the officers told Tidwell.

"And only doors down from your little tea shop," said Tidwell, turning his unblinking gaze upon Theodosia. "How very convenient."

"Be serious!" snapped Theodosia. "She was my friend. A good friend!"

"My sincere apology," said Tidwell, though he didn't sound one bit sincere. Or apologetic.

Theodosia shook off Tidwell's insensitivity and took a step closer to where Daria still lay. "It just doesn't make sense," she mourned. "Why would someone want to kill Daria?"

Tidwell leaned in and peered at the lifeless body that lay sprawled like a rag doll cast aside. And in a flat, almost impersonal tone, murmured, "Maybe they thought it was you."

2

❧

"*I simply loathe* Tidwell's suggestion of mistaken identity,"
sputtered an outraged Drayton. "Why on earth would
someone want to kill Theodosia? The notion's utterly
preposterous!"

"Calm down," cautioned Haley, as she rubbed a silver
teaspoon against her white chef's smock, polishing it to a lus-
trous patina. "That was just Tidwell running his yap again.
Trying to be the hotshot homicide detective."

"Which he is," said Theodosia. She was putting the finishing touches on an arrangement of tulips, lilies, and orchids in
a tall, straight-sided glass vase that had been wrapped with
a piece of white birch bark and then a snippet of raffia. The
effect was artful and pretty, but did nothing to alleviate the
sadness she was feeling.

It was just before nine on Tuesday morning at the Indigo
Tea Shop, and Theodosia, Drayton, and Haley were setting
up for the day. Although they were all doing their darndest
to pretend it was another normal day, they all knew in their

hearts it was not. One of their own, a fellow shopkeeper and friend, had been brutally murdered. So that nasty reality hung heavy over their heads like a dark shroud.

"I can't fathom what the killer's motive might have been," said Drayton. Setting a pink Royal Doulton teacup onto its saucer with a gentle clink, he pinched the tiny handle between his fingers and arranged it just so.

"Passion," said Haley, pulling a pack of matches from the pocket of her chef's jacket and lighting one of the tea lights. "It was probably a crime of passion. That's what they said in the newspaper article."

"But passion can also translate as rage, obsession, or even lunacy," said Drayton. He straightened up and gazed solemnly about with hooded gray eyes. A stickler for perfection, Drayton always dressed with great care. Today he sported a classic Harris tweed jacket with trademark bow tie, which made him look aristocratic in bearing and every inch the southern gentleman he was.

"Maybe there's a serial killer loose in Charleston," speculated Haley. She pushed a hank of long blond hair behind her ear and stared at Drayton with guileless blue eyes.

"Don't even *think* such a terrible thing," Drayton admonished her. He turned toward Theodosia, who was now seated at the small table by the fireplace, checking her reservation book. "Our dear Haley has quite the runaway imagination. Chalk it up to youth, I suppose."

"Maybe so," said Theodosia, glancing up. "But Haley's probably just being realistic."

Drayton pursed his lips and let his tortoiseshell half-glasses slide down his aquiline nose. "Excuse me, you're implying you and I are idealistic?"

Theodosia managed a weak smile. "Most of the time we are." She gazed around, studying the cozy interior of the tea shop. "We work in an environment where people flock to us for good conversation, excellent food, and a refined atmosphere."

"And that's exactly what we deliver," said Drayton, a touch of pride in his voice. "There isn't a lovelier, cozier tea shop in the entire city."

"In the state," added Haley.

"And we serve jasmine, Darjeeling, and Earl Grey tea, just to name a few," said Theodosia. "And Haley's prodigious baking skills turn out the most marvelous sweet potato scones, cranberry muffins, and banana bread you'd ever want to eat." She smiled. "And between our tea and baked goods, the atmosphere is so deliciously fragrant it's like a dose of aromatherapy for your soul."

"Hmm," said Drayton, frowning slightly. "I *suppose* I see where you're going with this. We do exist in a slightly rarefied atmosphere. You might even say the entire historic district's that way. Antiques, gorgeous mansions, cobblestone streets bountifully lined with live oak trees."

"You wouldn't want the Indigo Tea Shop to change, would you?" asked Haley. "Dump our old-fashioned ways and switch our name to Tea Biddy's or something equally silly so we can hustle customers in and out with to-go type food?"

"Goodness, no," said Theodosia. "I don't ever want to change a thing. All I'm saying is we should probably be a little more cognizant of what's going on. Realize that even our own little slice of Charleston can be a dangerous place."

Drayton's brows beetled together. "Is the back door locked?"

Haley shrugged. "Dunno."

"You see?" said Theodosia. "That's what I'm talking about. Vigilance should be our new watchword."

"Right," said Haley, peering at Theodosia. "But you're the one who's always on top of things. You're our watchdog, so to speak."

"She's right," said Drayton. He hesitated slightly. "Case in point, you were able to give the police a fairly good account of last night."

"But not as much as was reported in today's *Post and Courier*," said Haley. "They made it sound like you could *identify* the killer."

"Which I can't," said Theodosia.

"That might present an awkward problem," suggested Drayton. "If some maniac out there thinks you can."

Haley wrinkled her nose and fixed Theodosia with a serious gaze. "Have you . . . um . . . been able to remember anything more? I know you told the officers and Detective Tidwell about everything you saw. But have you come up with anything else?"

"Like a clue?" asked Drayton, edging closer to Theodosia. "You've got a pretty solid record when it comes to crime solving." He ducked his head, having just uttered the words Theodosia probably didn't want to hear.

"I saw the struggle," said Theodosia, nodding. "Although at first I thought it was Daria with her boyfriend. Being . . . I don't know . . . romantic, I suppose."

"But it was someone else," said Haley, in an ominous tone. "So . . . what else can you recall?"

Theodosia closed her eyes and tilted her head to one side. Tried to think back to last night. Conjure up the memory of darkness and rain-spattered cobblestones and two shadowy blue-and-black figures locked in a life-and-death struggle. An image that bordered on film noir. *And what else?* she wondered. *What else did I see or hear or think? Maybe . . .* She wracked her brain, trying to dredge up something, anything. *Maybe a faint minty fragrance?*

"Mint?" came Theodosia's whispered reply.

"Mint?" said Drayton, sounding dubious. "Seriously?"

Theodosia slowly opened her eyes, as if returning from

a hypnotic trance. "I had the strangest feeling that's what I smelled last night. The closer I got to Daria."

"Pretty strange," admitted Haley.

"Maybe," proposed Drayton, "there's a simple explanation."

"Like what?" asked Haley.

"A mint plant growing nearby," said Drayton. "After all, this entire area's overrun with flora and fauna. There's a reason Charleston's backyard gardens are so famously intriguing."

"Probably that's it," agreed Theodosia, exhaling slowly.

"Should we be doing something for Daria?" asked Haley. She seemed quiet and thoughtful now.

"Maybe send flowers to Daria's mother," said Theodosia.

"Don't you think we should wait until we know funeral details?" asked Drayton, always a stickler for proper etiquette.

"No, let's go ahead and do it right away," said Theodosia. "Daria's mother is a dear friend of Aunt Libby, so . . ." Her voice trailed off. Aunt Libby was Theodosia's only remaining living relative. A tiny, dynamic woman who lived at Cane Ridge Plantation out by Horlbeck Creek. The plantation where Theodosia's father had grown up, where her parents had been married. Now Aunt Libby watched over the low, flat fields that stretched to meet piney forests and cared for her myriad flocks of birds.

One of Theodosia's fondest memories was watching Aunt Libby tote heaping buckets of thistle, black oil seed, and cracklings down to the lake for all the migratory waterfowl that showed up. Of course, once they discovered what a fat deal they'd lucked into, they stayed on like a pack of mooching, shirttail relatives. But Aunt Libby adored them all. Her dear creatures, as she called them.

"I'll order the flowers from Floradora," said Haley. "Theo, you just stay put and compose your thoughts. I assume Detective Tidwell will be dropping by soon. He *said* he would, anyway."

"He'll be here," said Theodosia, though she wasn't sure what more she could offer Tidwell by way of details or faint impressions. She'd racked her brain all night for another nugget of information to feed him but had come up dry.

"Changing the subject," said Drayton, pulling a tin of Assam golden tips tea off the display shelves of an antique highboy fashioned from native cypress. "How are your move-in plans shaping up? You're charging ahead, I assume?"

A few months ago, Theodosia had been fortunate enough to come into a windfall of money. And had decided to move from her apartment above the Indigo Tea Shop to an adorable little English cottage a few blocks away, a former carriage house that bore the name Hazelhurst. A down payment had been made, agreements spelled out in writing, but she *still* didn't have a specified closing date or move-in date from the churlish owner.

"There are a few problems." Theodosia sighed.

"Always are," said Drayton. "No real estate transaction ever goes smoothly.

"Apparently," said Theodosia, "the wiring's not up to code. Which is why the lights keep flickering and the housing inspector has requested the sellers to replace a buried cable. I suppose I'll have to call Maggie and have her run interference." Maggie Twining was Theodosia's Realtor.

"Maybe your cottage is haunted," said Haley as she crossed the tea room floor, a pot of Darjeeling tea in one hand, a plate of fresh-baked cinnamon scones in the other. "That would sure explain the flickering lights. And let's face it, your place wouldn't be the first home in Charleston to have ghosts and supernatural beings wandering around."

"Charleston is supposedly one of the most haunted cities in America," agreed Drayton. "Although I can't say I'm a true believer in that particular spirit world."

Knock, knock, knock!

"Oh!" said Haley, suddenly startled.

"It's the *door*," said Drayton.

"Tidwell," said Theodosia, dreading his visit.

Burt Tidwell, looking bearish and slightly smug, sailed across the floor, dodging tables like a chubby matador, and plopped himself down at the table alongside Theodosia. Then his head swiveled toward Haley, his nose twitched eagerly, and his beady eyes fairly gleamed. "Miss Haley," he asked, "are those items, perchance, fresh-baked?"

So, of course, Drayton laid out a plate, teacup, and silverware for Detective Tidwell. While Haley ran back and grabbed tiny silver dishes filled with Devonshire cream and strawberry preserves.

"A feast," declared Tidwell, tucking into the scones and preserves while Theodosia poured him a steaming cup of Darjeeling.

"I'm glad you have an appetite," Theodosia remarked in a droll voice. She herself did not. Fresh in her mind's eye was the heartbreaking image of Daria's crumpled, lifeless body. *Tragic,* she thought. *Simply tragic.*

"I count on your lovely tea and baked goods to fortify my body as well as my spirit," responded Tidwell. "Preparation for all the difficult work ahead."

"And what is the work ahead, if I might ask?" said Theodosia.

"First course of action," said Tidwell, poised with a tiny butter knife in his big paw, "is the homicide last night. Determine motive."

"How's that coming so far?" asked Theodosia.

"A number of interesting ideas are spinning in my head," said Tidwell. "You don't know this . . . of course, you wouldn't . . . but quite a nasty struggle had gone on *inside* the Antiquarian Map Shop."

"Really?" said Theodosia, grimacing. She hated to think of poor Daria, bravely fighting off her attacker, while maps were flung everywhere and files and bookshelves overturned in the process.

"Place is a huge mess," said Tidwell, munching away. "Maps strewn all over the place. Old family records, too."

Theodosia nodded. Besides selling antique maps, Daria had amassed a fine collection of historic documents, old letters, photographs, and family records.

"Some of the documents had been ripped to shreds," said Tidwell. "Like someone had gone utterly berserk!"

"A maniac," Theodosia said in a low, hoarse voice. Of course, it had been a maniac. He'd strangled Daria, hadn't he?

Tidwell reached for a second cinnamon scone.

"Why would someone want to rip up maps?" Theodosia asked.

"No idea," said Tidwell, popping a bite into his mouth and chewing appreciatively.

"But you will get a handle on this, right?" Theodosia sounded more than a little hopeful. After all, Daria had been a good friend. And her murder had occurred dangerously close to Indigo Tea Shop turf. What Theodosia considered *her* turf.

"Solving last night's homicide is a foregone conclusion, Miss Browning," Tidwell assured her. "My detectives are working numerous angles even as we speak." In Tidwell's former life, he'd been an SPIC, a special agent in charge, with the FBI. Old habits died hard with Tidwell, and he still subscribed to the get-your-man-or-else dictum.

"When do you think you'll have something?" asked Theodosia. She was itching to hear about suspects and suppositions.

"Soon as I get a few questions answered," replied Tidwell. His bright eyes bored into her.

"I don't know what else to tell you," said Theodosia. "I

pretty much told you everything I could think of last night. I only played a small part in last night's tragedy."

"Tell me what you know about Jason Pritchard," said Tidwell.

"Daria's assistant?"

"Correct."

Theodosia thought for a few moments. "He always struck me as a nice enough fellow." She didn't know Pritchard well, since Daria had only hired Jason a few months ago. "Daria had been running her shop, building her map and document collection, pretty much doing it all herself," continued Theodosia. "Then she hired Jason and his presence seemed to allow a certain degree of breathing room for Daria." She glanced down at the table, rubbed an index finger over one of the deep scratches. "Gave her the luxury of dropping by here for lunch, taking days off, that sort of thing."

Tidwell gave a slight nod and his jowls sloshed from side to side. "So you knew this fellow Pritchard?"

"Not so much. Daria once told me he had a fairly good eye. I know for a fact that he was running all over the county, hitting auctions, digging through estate sales, to find various documents for the shop. Building the inventory, I guess you'd call it."

"And Pritchard wasn't present last night," said Tidwell.

"When you talked to the boyfriend . . . Joe Don Hunter?"

Tidwell gave a quick tilt of his head.

"Joe Don seemed to say that Daria had already sent Jason home for the evening," said Theodosia. "That she'd been ready to close up shop."

"So the story goes," said Tidwell.

"Do you know . . . where was the boyfriend when Daria was attacked?"

"Over at the Chowder Hound, getting take-out."

"And you know that for sure?" asked Theodosia.

"He dropped his order directly on my Thom McAn

loafers when I told him how Daria was killed," said Tidwell. "Smelled like crab chowder to me."

"Hmm," said Theodosia.

"But enough questions for now," said Tidwell. His chubby hands gripped the table, ready to push himself out of the groaning captain's chair he occupied, which, luckily for everyone, had been constructed of sturdy Carolina pine.

"Actually," said Theodosia, "*I* have a few questions."

3

Tidwell's furry eyebrows raised high above his beady eyes, then waggled like two errant caterpillars. "Oh?" came his baritone voice, the tone slightly disapproving.

Theodosia plunged ahead. "Last night you speculated that the killer might have thought Daria was really me, given that we're about the same height and both have curly reddish hair. You implied that Daria's murder might have been a case of mistaken identity. Do you still believe that?"

Tidwell settled back in his chair, assuming a reluctant pose. "I suppose it would all depend, Miss Browning, on what *involvements* you've had lately."

Theodosia thought for a moment. "Quite a few, actually. We catered the Friends of the Symphony reception last week as well as a tea for the Dorchester Club. This week we're helping the Featherbed House participate in the annual Bed-and-Breakfast Tour, and we'll be catering a book signing at the Heritage Society on Saturday night, although I haven't quite got the menu planned for that one."

Peering through eyes that were narrow slits, Tidwell looked colossally bored. "That's not quite what I had in mind. I was talking about your *personal* involvement."

"You mean something I might have, uh, meddled in?" Theodosia gazed about the tea room, saw that it was rapidly filling. Friends from the neighborhood come for their morning cuppa and scone, eager tourists who were out exploring. Thank goodness Drayton was escorting guests to tables with his usual cordiality and efficient aplomb.

"You do tend to plunge right in and sort through our local mysteries," murmured Tidwell. The corners of his mouth twitched ever so slightly.

"Not lately, I haven't," Theodosia protested.

Tidwell dropped his head and stared at her.

"Not for a while," she amended.

Now a smile fluttered across Tidwell's face. "You still seeing your two boyfriends?"

Theodosia's face flushed bright pink. "I don't have two boyfriends! I have a current boyfriend and a former boyfriend."

"Do they know that?" asked Tidwell. "Are they clear on the order of things? The order of the universe, *your* universe?"

"Of course, they are," Theodosia shot back. "Exactly what are you implying, Detective Tidwell?"

"Nothing, I'm just mildly curious."

"Surely you've heard the old . . ."

"Adage," responded Tidwell. "About curiosity killing the cat?"

"To say nothing of personal-bordering-on-rude questions," said Theodosia. "Certainly not very gentlemanly."

"Apologies," said Tidwell, a mischievous grin slashing his broad face.

Theodosia decided turnaround was fair play. She leaned in close to Tidwell and in a cozy, conspiratorial manner asked, "What was the weapon used to strangle Daria?"

Tidwell shook his head abruptly, as though a swarm of gnats was suddenly buzzing around him. "Can't say. Forensics lab will have to make that exact determination."

"Plastic cord? Wire? Something else?" she prompted.

"No idea," said Tidwell.

"Feels to me like you're stalling," said Theodosia.

"Not I," said Tidwell, sounding righteous as he sprang from his chair. "In fact, I'm off to question the victim's shop neighbors. Just think of me as the shark that never sleeps, a predator that moves relentlessly forward." He bobbed his head with formality now. "Thank you for the morning repast of tea and scone."

"Scones," Theodosia said, putting a touch of sibilance on the final *s*.

"Now who's being rude?" muttered Tidwell, as he crossed the tea room, deftly dodging customers, then yanked open the door and disappeared down Church Street.

Drayton was at Theodosia's side in a heartbeat. "Not the font of information you'd hoped?"

"Tidwell's playing his cards extremely close to his vest," said Theodosia, thinking it was a mightily straining vest ready to pop a few buttons.

"The important thing," said Drayton, "is that he's working the case."

"I have to believe he'll do his best," said Theodosia. "He always has before."

"Ah," said Drayton, a slight gleam in his eye. "With your capable assistance, he has."

"I'm not getting involved," said Theodosia, glancing across the tea room to the front counter, where Haley had just snatched up the ringing phone.

"That's what you always say," said Drayton. "But you do possess certain investigative skills."

"That's right," said Theodosia. "I'm Charleston's own little Nancy Drew."

"No," said Drayton, following her across the tea room, "you're better."

Haley held out the phone, waggling it back and forth. "It's your aunt Libby," she told Theodosia. "And does she ever sound upset."

Theodosia grabbed the phone from Haley. She knew Aunt Libby was far too stoic to be upset, but she also knew that Aunt Libby would be deeply concerned. A delicate balance of yin and yang.

"Aunt Libby," said Theodosia.

"Theodosia," began Aunt Libby, "when Sophie Shand called me this morning, I couldn't quite believe it! Daria murdered? An absolute tragedy! And now I've got the Charleston *Post and Courier* spread out in front of me spilling the entire dreadful story in gruesome detail."

"Oh dear," said Theodosia. She hadn't looked at the paper yet. She could only imagine how sordid the murder sounded. The paper had a new police beat reporter, Nick Van Buren, who seemed to revel in true crime.

"And you were right there!" wailed Aunt Libby. "An actual eyewitness! I can't believe it, I don't want to believe it!" This was followed by a few genteel sniffs and a blowing of her nose. "Sorry," she said, finally.

"Nothing to be sorry about," Theodosia told Aunt Libby. "We're all feeling just awful here at the tea shop."

"You realize Sophie is one of my dearest friends," said Aunt Libby.

"I know that."

"To have her own daughter murdered . . ." Aunt Libby let loose a low sob, then struggled to clear her throat.

"I know you'll be there for Sophie," said Theodosia. "Give her a shoulder to cry on." Aunt Libby may be a tiny bird herself, but she was a tough one.

Aunt Libby seemed to gather her words as well as her

emotions then. "I'll do more than that," she responded in a firm voice. "In fact, I've already assured Sophie that you'll stay as involved as possible in the investigation."

"I'm not sure I can do that," said Theodosia hedging. "Better to let the police handle things."

"No," said Aunt Libby, and now there was a certain, decisive *tone* in her voice. "You're a very smart girl and an outstanding amateur detective."

"The real detectives don't think so."

"What do they know?" shrilled Libby. "Anyway, I pretty much *promised* Sophie that you'd keep a careful watch of this whole dreadful thing. Especially since you already have a close working relationship with that particular detective. Tinkwell? Is that his name?"

"Tidwell," said Theodosia.

"Of course," said Aunt Libby, "Tidwell." She paused, allowed herself another small sniffle. "So . . . you'll help?"

"As much as I can," said Theodosia, somewhat reluctantly. *As much as I'm allowed,* she thought.

"Thank you, dear," said Aunt Libby. "I'm feeling better already. In fact, I'm going to call Sophie and tell her you're our own personal avenging angel who'll watch over the investigation."

Oh dear.

"I'll talk to you later, dear. All right?"

"Good-bye, Aunt Libby," said Theodosia.

"Oh," said Aunt Libby. "One other thing?"

"Yes?" said Theodosia, spinning on her heels as the bell over the front door let loose a merry jingle.

"See what you can find out about that Jason Pritchard who worked for Daria, will you?"

Theodosia stared at Jason Pritchard, who was standing in her doorway, and said, "Sure thing."

*   *   *

It took Theodosia a couple of seconds to switch gears. Then she said, "Jason . . . hello." Not because they were friends but because she was startled to see him.

"Miss Browning," Pritchard said, his face beginning to crumple.

"Call me Theodosia," she told him, plucking at his shirtsleeve. "And let's get you to a table. You look a little peaked."

"I feel a lot peaked," said Pritchard, once they were seated. Tall, blond, and slightly ethereal, Pritchard looked like he hadn't slept well. His navy polo shirt looked hastily ironed, his khaki slacks just plain rumpled.

"Drayton?" Theodosia lifted a hand and Drayton was beside her in two seconds flat.

"A pot of tea?" Drayton asked, taking in the situation with a single glance.

"Strong tea," said Theodosia. Then she turned back to Pritchard. "Are you okay?"

He shook his head. "Not really. Daria . . . I can't quite believe it!"

Drayton arrived with tea and an apple muffin, set it down discreetly, then hastily departed.

"Have you spoken to the police?" Theodosia asked him as she poured out a cup of tea. Nice, strong Ceylon tea, from the smell of it.

"Last night and again this morning," Pritchard told her. "They came to my apartment last night to tell me about Daria." He frowned and shook his head angrily. "Didn't show any respect for her at all, just jabbed away at me with a thousand different questions."

"What did they want to know?" asked Theodosia.

Pritchard hung his head in a defeated gesture. "They

asked if I knew any reason why someone would want to kill Daria."

"Did you?" asked Theodosia.

"No!" Pritchard cried. "Daria was a neat lady. I *liked* working for her."

"What other questions did they ask?" prodded Theodosia.

Pritchard took a bite of muffin and chewed thoughtfully. "What time I left the map shop, what stops I made on the way home, what time I arrived home." He swallowed hard, then took a tiny sip of tea to wash it all down. "Tea," he said, as if noticing it for the first time. "Don't usually drink this stuff."

"It's pretty good."

Pritchard nodded. "It's okay."

"What else did they want to know?" Theodosia gently prodded.

"Oh," said Pritchard, wrinkling his nose. "They wanted to know who Daria was dating, who her friends were, was she having family problems, was the business solvent. That kind of stuff."

"And do you know, *were* there any problems in those areas?" asked Theodosia.

Pritchard shook his head. "Uh-uh. Not that I know of. I mean, I *worked* for Daria. We didn't exactly chitchat about our personal lives. We kept that stuff separate."

"A business relationship," said Theodosia. "And that's quite appropriate. But . . . I also get the feeling there's something you want to ask me. Or tell me. You didn't just show up here by chance today, did you?"

Pritchard gazed down at the table. "No."

"So, go ahead," said Theodosia. "I'm listening."

Pritchard lifted his eyes and gazed earnestly at Theodosia. "Daria talked about how smart you were," he said in a halting voice. "She really thought the world of you."

"Okay," said Theodosia. She settled back in her chair, giving the young man room to continue. He did.

"Daria said you were real cagey at figuring stuff out. That you helped solve a big kidnapping case last fall."

"Not really," said Theodosia. "I was only peripherally involved."

"That's not the way Daria told it," said Pritchard. "She was pretty impressed."

"I sense you still have a question pending," said Theodosia.

"More like a request," corrected Pritchard.

"Excuse me?"

"Request for help," said Pritchard. "Like I said, I was interviewed by the police again this morning."

"They're just doing their job," Theodosia told him. "Looking for little slivers of information that might shed some light on this whole sad mess."

"No," said Pritchard, "I get the feeling they want to pin Daria's murder on me."

"What?" said Theodosia. "Oh, I can't believe that."

"Here's the thing," said Pritchard, somewhat reluctantly. "I haven't always been the nicest guy in the world."

Theodosia gazed at him. Where was this going? What was Jason Pritchard about to reveal?

Pritchard drew a deep breath and seemed to gather his courage. "Daria took a chance on me when she hired me. I did some stupid stuff when I was a kid." He gazed at her, smiled, and said, "You probably think I'm still a kid, since I'm only twenty-six."

"Some people are still kids at sixty-six," said Theodosia. "Maturity isn't always about numerical age."

"Thank you," said Pritchard. "But to get back to my . . . well, I guess you'd call it a sort of confession. The thing is . . . I have a police record."

Theodosia's gaze never wavered.

"I was an idiot. Committed felony crimes that would have sent me to Allendale for a few years, if I hadn't been under age. Drugs and other stuff. Anyway, I've been on my best behavior since, especially working for Daria. Taking history classes at the College of Charleston and trying hard to learn more about antiquities."

"Very commendable," said Theodosia.

Pritchard squinted at her. "So I was hoping you might run interference for me with the police. Because I'm . . . I'm innocent! Heck, I'm even gonna try to keep the shop going!"

"The family asked you to do so?"

Pritchard nodded vigorously. "The sister did, yeah."

"Okay," said Theodosia. "That's a good sign. It means they have faith in you, that they trust you. The fact that the police are eyeing you is another matter."

"That's why I need *your* help," said Pritchard. He gazed at Theodosia with such earnestness, it touched her heart.

"I'll do what I can," she told him. "But until Charleston Robbery-Homicide comes up with a solid suspect, they could be rough on you."

"But you'll see what you can do?"

"Yes. Of course."

"Thank you," Pritchard told her in a hoarse voice.

"I'm also doing this for Daria," responded Theodosia. "If she believed in you, then I believe in you."

Pritchard swiped at his eyes with the back of his hand, then struggled clumsily to his feet. "Daria always said you were kind. To people . . . as well as animals."

"Daria was a good friend," said Theodosia, her eyes suddenly glistening with tears.

"Got to get back to the shop now," said Pritchard. "Try to keep things going." He turned, gave a sad, slightly hopeful smile, then added a little wave.

"Jason," Theodosia called after him, "when you said you were in trouble with drugs and other stuff . . ."

"Yeah?"

"What exactly was the other stuff?"

Pritchard's eyes slid away from her. "Forgery."

4

"Seafood quiche," said Haley. "Plus a mixed green salad, cheddar and chutney tea sandwiches, and tuna roll-ups." She stood at the massive industrial stove they'd shoehorned into the world's smallest kitchen, stirring an enormous, simmering pot of vegetable soup. "And my vagabond vegetable soup," she added.

"That's lunch," said Theodosia. "And it all sounds wonderful. What about afternoon tea?"

"Orange blossom bars and apple tea cake," said Haley. "Plus we still have cinnamon scones from this morning. Oh, and I'm going to whip up a batch of almond-flavored Devonshire cream. One of my new inspirations."

Theodosia laid out a series of floral bowls on the counter. "Don't forget, Drayton's friends from the Historian Club are coming at twelve thirty."

"That'll be a cinch," enthused Haley. "They get scones, soup, special ham and pear panini sandwiches, and cake for dessert."

"Did Drayton have a chance to mix up a pitcher of green tea sparkler?" asked Theodosia.

"I think he did," said Haley. "I hope he did . . . but you know Drayton."

"What about me?" asked Drayton, suddenly looming in the doorway. "What sin of omission am I guilty of now?"

"The sparkler?" asked Haley.

"Always jumping to conclusions," chided Drayton. "It's already brewed, mixed, and sparkling away in the cooler."

"Then we're all set," said Haley. "No *problema*."

"There rarely is," intoned Drayton.

Lunch was busy, busy, busy with a half dozen reservations, a yellow horse-drawn jitney dropping off a tour group, and at least a dozen take-out orders. And just as everything seemed to reach critical mass, Drayton's friends from the Historian Club came pouring in. Five men whom he proudly seated at the large round table in the center of the room. Drayton was the sixth guest, but rarely would he connect with his chair, so eager was he to impress.

Drayton, being Drayton, had set out the good Saint Dunstan by Tiffany silverware, Fraureuth porcelain dinnerware, and Heisey cut-crystal water goblets. He'd also appropriated a gold linen tablecloth and Theodosia's nicest floral arrangement to serve as the table's centerpiece.

Now, white tapers flickered, glasses clinked, and good cheer seemed to prevail. One of the club's members, Lyndel Woodruff, had just published a book titled *The Battle of Honey Hill,* so they jabbered excitedly about the new release as well as the upcoming book talk and signing event at the Heritage Society this Saturday night. Drayton had asked Theodosia to handle the catering, and she'd willingly agreed. Her current boyfriend, Parker Scully, proprietor and head chef at Solstice Bistro and Tapas Bar was out of town all week, attending a restaurant convention in Las Vegas, of all places. So, as far as her personal life went, Theodosia was free as a bird.

"A toast," proposed Drayton, hefting a glass. "To Lyndel and his newly published tome."

"A toast," intoned the others, also hoisting their glasses.

"Thank you all," said Woodruff, looking enormously pleased. He was a tall, thin man with a nervous air and a perpetually florid face. But Woodruff was a true scholar and professor, having taught American history for more than thirty-six years at the College of Charleston, much to the delight of several generations of students. Now that he was retired, he'd been able to do research and finally write his book. "And I hope you all enjoy my talk this Saturday night." Woodruff glanced around, a trifle embarrassed, then added, "At least I *hope* you'll be coming."

"We wouldn't miss it," declared Drayton, circling the table, pouring refills of green tea sparkler.

"Understand you folks had some excitement around here last night," piped up Jack Brux. Brux was a pinched-face, narrow man who ran an antique shop down on Royal Street and was working on a book himself. "A rather nasty murder," Brux added.

Drayton blanched white. "Terrible thing," he said, shaking his head. "Daria was a great friend. Used to come in every afternoon at three on the dot. Order her favorite chamomile tea and the scone du jour."

Woodruff shook his head. "Pity about her shop being torn up like that."

"Very strange," agreed Brux.

Woodruff gazed across the table at Brux. "You're a real map fanatic, Jack. What do you make of it?"

Brux grimaced. "Crazy person," he said. "Have to be crazy to strangle a defenseless woman, then trash a shop like that. All those valuable maps."

Theodosia set a plate of apple tea cake on the table.

"I understand the Antiquarian Map Shop carried some extremely rare maps. One of a kind items."

"Indeed they did," agreed Woodruff. "A few pieces weren't even marked for sale." He gazed across the table at Jack Brux. "You tried to get her to sell you that Waccamaw Neck map, but she never would."

Brux bobbed his head. "That's right. Told me it was for display purposes only," he said in a petulant tone. "Even when I wanted to borrow it as reference material for my book. Now maybe I've got a chance. Depending on who takes over management of the shop."

Theodosia caught Drayton's eye and frowned. It worried her that Brux would talk like that.

"The estate, I suppose," said Drayton.

"Which is basically the owner's mother," said Brux. "And I don't imagine she's going to want to run the place."

"You never know," said Theodosia. "I wouldn't rule anything out at this point."

Once lunch was finished, dribs and drabs of customers oozed their way in for afternoon tea. A few were locals, many were tourists who'd spent the morning and early afternoon tromping the historic district, gazing at the grand dowager homes that lined the Battery, wandering the cobblestone alleys and pathways that meandered past old cemeteries, churches, Charleston single houses, and quaint cottages.

"Excuse me?" said one newcomer. "The tea you have listed on your board as Earl Green? What is that?"

Theodosia straightened up from behind the counter, touched a knee to a box of tea lights, and shoved it back into the cupboard. "It's a blend of Chinese black tea and green tea, along with a touch of high quality silver tips and bergamot oil."

"It's good?" asked the woman. She was tall and thin, her

dark hair worn in a blunt pageboy style. Silver Tiffany bracelets clanked on both wrists; a giant vintage starburst brooch,
in shimmering tones of pink, orange, and amber, was pinned
to the lapel of her tailored tweed suit.

"Earl Green is extremely mellow yet big on aroma," said
Theodosia. "I think you'll enjoy it, but if it's not to your liking, I'll gladly fix something else."

"You're very kind," said the woman, "And I *do* want to try
the Earl Green. A cup to go, please." She gave a perfunctory
smile. "Since I'm here, I should probably introduce myself."
She stuck a hand across the counter, her jewelry clanking
once again. "Cinnamon St. John."

Theodosia smiled with surprise. "Oh my goodness, you
own the new . . . shop. Down the street. Um . . . fragrance
shop, am I right?"

"Jardin Perfumerie," said Cinnamon, a touch of pride in
her voice. "Just a hop, skip, and a jump down Church Street."
She wrinkled her nose, hunched her narrow shoulders, and
gave a tight little shudder. "Right next to that dusty old map
shop. Thank *goodness* we weren't open last night!"

"A tragedy," said Theodosia, not really wanting to go into
detail.

"Now that we've finally met," said Cinnamon, "I'd love it
if you dropped by for a visit. See what we're all about."

"I've actually heard a little about your shop," said Theodosia, pouring hot water into the single serving glass teapot,
watching the tea leaves unfurl in their "agony of the leaves"
dance. "Brooke, from Heart's Desire, mentioned it just last
week."

"Oh sure," said Cinnamon, nodding, "I've met Brooke.
Such a dear. She came in and bought scented candles. That
poor map shop lady was in, too."

"I didn't realize your shop was officially open," said
Theodosia.

"We're not," responded Cinnamon. "My aunt Kitty thought

a quiet opening would be best. Let folks wander in while we're unpacking for a few quick, casual sales. Meet the neighbors, get our feet wet in the business, that type of thing."

Theodosia poured the cup of fresh-brewed Earl Green into an indigo blue cup and snapped on a white plastic lid. As she leaned forward and slid it across the counter, she inhaled sharply and wiggled her nose. For some reason, she'd just caught a whiff of the scent she thought she'd smelled last night.

How . . . strange.

"That's a rather, um, interesting scent you're wearing," said Theodosia, feeling a little flustered, trying to fight an unsettling sense of déjà vu. "I assume it's one of the fragrances you carry?"

Cinnamon gave a wide smile. "A custom scent, actually. Something my aunt Kitty and I concocted during one of our wilder moments. A blend of lavender, lime blossoms, and mint. I call it Chant du Cygne."

Theodosia instantly understood the translation. "Swan song," she said.

Sitting in her office, leafing through catalogs, Theodosia was supposed to be scribbling up any number of orders. They were low on tins of tea for their retail area. And she knew she should be ordering tea cozies, tea towels, and probably some more of those adorable miniature bone china teacups. The tiny cups had proved to be enormously popular. One customer had created a giant grapevine wreath for her sunporch and decorated it with silk flowers and more than a dozen of the miniature teacups.

But Theodosia, elbows on her desk, feet doing a tippy-tap on the floor, was having trouble focusing. Just couldn't seem to get it together. For one thing, Daria's murder hung heavy over her head. Her heart was sad, which made her brain feel fuzzy as well. She also hadn't slept very well. The closing on her cottage seemed to be creeping along at a snail's pace and she felt at odds with things. Maybe, she decided, if she went over to the cottage tonight to make a few quick sketches and take detailed measurements, it would give her the *illusion* of speeding things along.

Yes, she decided, that was probably a fine, constructive way to handle her case of ennui. Remain positive and keep looking forward instead of glancing back over your shoulder. Turn wishful thinking into reality.

"Theo?" Haley stood in the doorway, clutching a silver tray. "Do you have a minute?"

Theodosia pushed aside her catalogs. "Always. And I hope that cup of tea is for me."

Haley slid into the office and placed her tray on Theodosia's desk. "Drayton brewed you a cup of silvery tip pekoe and I added a few chocolate samples. For your . . . um . . . critical review, shall we say."

Theodosia took a quick, fortifying sip of tea, then said, "I take it these are your entries for tomorrow's Chocolatier Fest?" The Chocolatier Fest was an annual event held at Charleston's upscale Dorchester Club. Chefs, bakers, and candymakers from all over the area entered their finest truffles, trifles, candy, and cakes, hoping to take home the coveted Silver Cupcake Award. Haley had entered last year but only placed fourth with her green tea truffles. This year she'd definitely set her eyes on first prize. More power to her.

"Okay," said Haley, plopping down on the cushy, brocade chair that sat wedged across from Theodosia's desk. "Here's the thing. Last year I was close but no cigar. This year I have a strategy."

"Bribe the judges?" said Theodosia, deadpan.

"Hah," said Haley. "Good one. But those guys are

unbribeable. They're all snooty French pastry chefs from New York or Boston."

"Okay," said Theodosia. "Then plan B."

"Multiple entries," said Haley. "I checked and it's allowed. Up to four entries per person."

"Awful lot of work," said Theodosia. "Especially since you want everything to be as fresh as possible."

"Has to be done," said Haley. "In fact, I plan to stay here tonight and slave away like a mad scientist. Stay all night if I have to."

Theodosia took another sip of tea and glanced at Haley's tray. "Looks like you already did."

"Nah," said Haley, "these are just my prototypes. I'm conducting a highly unscientific taste test to see which ones are best."

"And you're asking Drayton and me for an opinion?"

"Sure," enthused Haley. "You're the most unscientific people I know."

"Thank you," said Theodosia, gazing at the tray. "I think." She reached out, inched the tray toward her, and eyed Haley's chocolates. Of course, everything looked superb. "So what do we have here?"

"First," said Haley, "truffles." She poked an index finger at a chocolate dollop dusted with ultra-fine cinnamon. "That one's a champagne truffle. The one next to it's a tea truffle."

"You entered tea truffles last year."

"I know, but this time I used a much better grade of tea."

"Let me guess," said Theodosia. "You pinched some of Drayton's expensive gyokuro? From the stash he keeps in his secret spot under the counter?"

Haley bobbed her head happily.

"Good girl."

"So take a nibble," urged Haley.

Theodosia took a tiny bite of the champagne truffle, nodded, then took a small nibble of the green tea truffle.

"They're both great," she said, still chewing. "But the green tea truffle's better."

"That's what I think, too," said Haley. "Now try the chocolate bourbon ball."

Theodosia did. And loved it. As well as Haley's white chocolate fleur-de-lis-shaped bonbon and a gooey chocolate praline that was so sticky it had the potential to rip out dental fillings.

"This nutty little blob here," said Haley, pointing at the final piece, "is a gopher. Similar to your standard chocolate, pecan, and caramel turtle, but made with black walnuts instead."

Theodosia took a nibble and let it melt in her mouth. "Wonderful. To die for."

"Wait," said Haley, looking pleased, but holding up a hand. "Gotta tell you about my final idea. I haven't exactly *made* it yet, but I've got a gem of a receipt that my granny gave me."

"What is it?" asked Theodosia, smiling. Receipt was the old southern term for recipe.

Haley assumed a beatific expression. "A bittersweet chocolate pavé."

"I'm intrigued," said Theodosia, not quite sure what a pavé really was.

"Here's the thing," said Haley. "Pavé is basically a rich, dense, mousselike chocolate dessert. I mean, we're talking triple decadent."

"Death by chocolate," said Theodosia.

"Almost," agreed Haley. "Once the pavé is cooked, coddled, and baked, it sets up all nice and firm. Then it's sliced and topped with fresh berries or fruit puree."

"Good heavens, Haley!" exclaimed Theodosia. "And you want me to tell you which dessert to enter? Every one is fantastic!"

"I know," said Haley. "But you still have to pick four."

Theodosia thought for a minute. "Okay, then I cast votes for the green tea truffles, bourbon balls, gophers, and your granny's chocolate pavé. But only if you have time."

"Oh, I'll make time."

"You're going to end up owning your own patisserie," said Theodosia, meaning it.

Haley grinned back. "I already do. Kind of. You always give me free rein on everything that has to do with baking. Almost everything," she amended.

"It's called trust," said Theodosia.

"So . . ." said Haley, flushed with excitement, "you're still coming with me to the luncheon tomorrow, right? I mean, just in case I win I gotta have a cheering section."

"I'll be there to cheer even if you don't win. Count on it."

"I'm gonna make everything tonight," said Haley, half mumbling to herself, "then drop it off first thing . . ." She nodded to herself, then suddenly swiveled her head, frowned, and said, "What?"

Voices raised in discord suddenly drifted toward them. One distinctly Drayton's, the other . . . ?

"Oh no!" exclaimed Haley. She jumped up and headed for the door, arms akimbo.

Theodosia rose, too, a prickle of worry suddenly gnawing at her.

"Oh man!" said Haley, stopping abruptly in her tracks and taking a reluctant step backward.

Then Drayton's voice, tight with anger, said, "*Excuse* me, but I told you she was . . ."

And that's the exact moment Jory Davis, Theodosia's ex-boyfriend and rat fink extraordinaire, popped his head into her office and said, "Hi there."

5

Hi there. The words registered in Theodosia's brain, sounding bright and innocent. Even warm and friendly. The reality of the situation was considerably more complex. Jory Davis had been Theodosia's boyfriend for a number of years. Then, one day, he'd announced to Theodosia that he was up and moving to New York. Marriage was part of the package deal he extended to Theodosia, but so was dumping her tea shop.

Big decision for Theodosia? Heartrending to be sure. Better to dump the boyfriend.

Which she did.

But like trying to strike a deal on a used car, nothing was ever quite final. Jory had popped back into her life again for a few days last October. Then they'd been incommunicado. Until now. Until he poked his handsome, inquisitive face into her office, oblivious of a scowling Haley and a downright frosty Drayton.

Drayton didn't bother mincing words. "What are *you* doing back in town?" he asked in his brusque-bordering-onoratorical tone. "I thought you were back at your law offices in New York, defending hedge-fund scoundrels and corporate raiders."

"I'm here to wrap up some business," said Jory, trying to brush off Drayton and edge his way over to Theodosia.

This time Haley picked up her tray and conveniently stepped in to block Jory's way. "Oops, sorry. Didn't mean to whack you with my tray."

"That's okay," said Jory, rubbing his arm. "But I would like a word with Theodosia, if you don't mind. In private."

"She's awfully busy," Haley told him. "Maybe you should come back another time."

"Or better yet," added Drayton, "call."

"Yeah," said Haley, giving Jory a cheesy, fake-bright smile. "A *quick* phone call would be even better."

"It's okay, Haley," said Theodosia. "Drayton?" She raised her brows at him, feeling like she was calling off Cerberus, the proverbial watchdog of hell.

"Thanks," said Jory, nodding at Drayton and Haley. "Thanks for your hospitality."

"You don't have to be sarcastic," said Theodosia, once the two of them were alone. "They're just watching out for me."

"Couple of tough gatekeepers you've got there." Jory grinned.

"Good friends," said Theodosia. "And Haley wasn't just making excuses, I am busy. So . . . what can I do for you?" Theodosia sat back down, stared at Jory across her desk. Tried to remain cool and confident in her own skin.

Jory plopped down on the chair Haley had recently vacated and crossed his legs, looking like he wanted to settle in for a while. "I heard you had some trouble here least night."

"Trouble," said Theodosia, her brows knitting for an instant. Then she was back to cucumber cool. "Is that what you call it? In that case, yes, we had some very nasty trouble last night."

"Theodosia," said Jory, "I didn't come here to fight, I came here to make sure you're okay."

"Not to worry," Theodosia said, lightly. "I can take care of myself."

"You sure about that?" Jory seemed bound and determined to elicit some sort of emotion from Theodosia, even though she remained reserved and slightly aloof.

"Quite confident," said Theodosia.

"I bet you're getting involved," needled Jory. "It's a murder mystery, after all. Isn't that your specialty?"

"Not really."

"I don't believe you," said Jory. Now his eyes sparkled with a hint of mischief.

Theodosia raised her shoulders an inch. "Believe whatever you want."

"Listen," said Jory. "I'm only in town for a couple of days. I was wondering if . . . well, are you still dating that restaurant guy?"

"Yes. Of course, I am," said Theodosia.

"Are you seeing him tonight?"

Theodosia fixed Jory with a polite but level gaze. "I'm sorry, that really isn't any of your business."

"Would you go out to dinner with me tonight?"

"No, thank you."

"Greetings again," said Drayton, bustling into Theodosia's office with a fresh pot of tea and a teacup for Jory. He made a perfunctory bow, handed Jory his cup and saucer, and said, "If you don't mind my asking, Mr. Davis, I was under the impression you were engaged to a certain young lady."

"Not anymore," said Jory, staring directly at Theodosia.

"How unfortunate," said Drayton, pouring a cup of tea for Jory. "Might I inquire as to what became of the young lady?"

"No, you may not," interjected Theodosia. She glanced at Drayton and gave a meaningful look.

Jory let loose a low chuckle. "It's okay. Drayton does have your best interests at heart." He took a sip of tea, then winced. "Puckery," he said.

"Brisk," intoned Drayton. "That particular tea is an acquired taste, I might add."

"Beth Ann and I broke up a few weeks ago," Jory explained to both of them.

"I'm sorry to hear that," said Theodosia, even though she was suddenly secretly relieved. She'd met Beth Ann at the Opera Society's Masked Ball last autumn, and the woman had seemed a little too brash, a little too coarse for Jory's taste. Of course, that was predicated on the fact that Jory's sensibilities hadn't changed in the few years he'd been gone.

"So unfortunate," murmured Drayton. "Just when we were hoping you two would stroll off into the sunset and live happily ever after." Smiling like a friendly barracuda, he glanced at Theodosia and added, "I'll be within shouting distance if you need me."

"Thank you," said Theodosia, as Drayton slipped away. Then she focused her full attention on Jory. "So it just wasn't in the cards."

"I guess not," said Jory. He peered across his teacup at Theodosia. "Does that change anything?"

Theodosia shook her head. "Not really."

For the first time, Jory looked thoughtful. "It's over, isn't it? I mean, with us?"

"It has been for a long time," said Theodosia.

"I worry about you," said Drayton. He stood holding a gray plastic tub of dirty dishes, looking fretful and a little forlorn. Only a few afternoon customers lingered in the tea room.

"Don't," said Theodosia. The afternoon sun was pouring through the leaded glass windows, bathing everything in a pure, white light. Making her heart feel lighter, too.

"Jory can be very . . . persuasive," said Drayton.

"Trust me," said Theodosia. "Our relationship is over. Finished, *fini, finito.*"

"You're sure?" asked Drayton, doubt still clouding his face.

At which point Haley popped out of the kitchen and joined the conversation. "You mean, like, capital O-V-E-R?" she asked.

"That's right," said Theodosia.

"Because," said Drayton, "and I realize I have no right to say this, but I'm just going to blurt it out anyway . . ."

"Blurt away!" enthused Haley.

Drayton pulled himself up to full height and said, "I don't believe Jory is good for you."

"It really isn't a case of good or bad," said Theodosia, "it's just a matter of moving on."

"Timing," pronounced Haley. "And the timing's so right for Parker."

"I think so," agreed Theodosia.

"You going to marry him?" asked Haley.

"Haley!" said Drayton. And then, in a small voice, asked, "Are you?"

"He hasn't asked," said Theodosia.

"We just springboarded into a whole new decade," said Haley with a laugh. "Maybe *you* should ask *him.*"

"You know," said Theodosia, edging back to her office, "I would if I wanted to."

And drifting back to Theodosia were Drayton's whispered words to Haley: "Well, I guess we know where Theo stands on *that* particular subject."

Some twenty minutes later, Theodosia headed down the block to the Antiquarian Map Shop. Aunt Libby's heartfelt plea and Jason Pritchard's earlier request had been swirling around in her head all day, like a wildly spinning centrifuge. She'd developed a mental itch where Daria's murder was concerned and was suddenly determined to scratch it.

But when she arrived at the map shop, Theodosia was surprised to find not only Pritchard but two other people there as well. A mopey-looking young woman with mousy brown hair who sported a most unflattering, gray shirtwaist dress. And the handsome but sad-looking Joe Don Hunter, the man she'd seen last night, wearing jeans, a white T-shirt, and a buckskin-colored suede jacket.

"Miss Browning!" said Pritchard, popping up from behind a glass counter where any number of priceless documents were on display.

"Theodosia," she said, stepping into the store. "Call me Theodosia."

"Oh my," said the woman, coming forward to greet her. "I'm Fallon, Daria's sister. Nice to finally meet you. Your aunt Libby is one of my mother's dearest friends."

"Of course," said Theodosia, taking Fallon's outstretched hand in both of hers. "And my sincere condolences."

Fallon bobbed her head in acknowledgment. "And this is Joe Don Hunter. Joe is . . . was . . . Daria's boyfriend."

Theodosia shook Joe Don's hand, too. "Mr. Hunter, I briefly saw you last night and . . . well, I'm so very sorry about Daria."

"Thank you," said the boyfriend. His voice was low and gravely and he spoke with a catch in his throat. "And I'm just plain Joe Don."

"Theodosia's agreed to help us," piped up Pritchard. "Do some . . . I'd guess you'd call if freelance investigating."

Fallon and Joe Don both stared at Theodosia with puzzled looks.

"Oh, not really," said Theodosia. She held up a hand, scrubbed it in the air as if to erase Pritchard's remark.

But Pritchard seemed not to hear her. "Daria always told

me that Theo could solve any kind of mystery there was. So I asked if she'd help us, and she very kindly agreed."

Fallon turned bleary, basset hound eyes on Theodosia. "Really?"

"The thing is," said Pritchard, jumping in again, "Theodosia was *here* last night."

"Must have been awful," said Fallon, touching a hand to her heart.

"Did you get a look at her attacker?" Joe Don asked suddenly. "Do you think you could ID her killer?"

"I'm sorry," said Theodosia. "But it was awfully dark and . . ." She let her voice trail off.

Joe Don shook his head. "Doggone it. That would have given us *something* to go on."

Fallon seemed to be struggling to put her words together. Finally she said, "Your aunt Libby did tell my mother that you were a first-class amateur detective."

"Aunt Libby tends to brag a bit," said Theodosia.

"But she said you've helped in other instances," pressed Fallon, looking almost hopeful.

Theodosia gave a tight nod. "Yes, I suppose I have."

"So what can it hurt?" Pritchard asked the other two. "If we huddle up and try to give Theodosia a few details."

"I think it's a good idea," said Joe Don. "Better than sitting around waiting for the police to do something."

"I agree," said Fallon, wiping away a tear. "In fact, it's heartening that one of Daria's friends would step forward to help."

"We all loved her," said Theodosia. She didn't know what else to say.

"So," said Pritchard, "what can we tell you? What do you want to know?"

Theodosia edged up to the glass case, set her bag down, and pulled out a spiral notebook and her black Montblanc pen. It had been a departing gift from her marketing firm colleagues when she'd resigned her position as account exec to purchase a dusty little carriage house and venture into the land of entrepreneurship and free-market economics. Also known as the tea and catering business. "Tell me what was going on in Daria's life," said Theodosia.

Fallon's gaze fell on Pritchard. "Jason?" she asked. "You worked with Daria. You were here every day."

"She seemed fine," said Pritchard. "Business was a little slow, but she had some hotshot collector in Savannah on the hook, a guy who was negotiating to buy at least a dozen maps."

"Has he purchased the maps yet?" asked Theodosia. "Put money down? Paid for them? Taken them into his possession?"

"Uh . . . not yet," said Pritchard. "I should probably call him," he added.

"You probably should," agreed Fallon.

"Anything else going on in Daria's life?" asked Theodosia. "Problems with money, issues with other customers?"

"Not that we can think of," said Joe Don. "Just before you got here, we were kind of noodling those kinds of ideas around. Didn't come up with much of anything."

"Tell me about last night," said Theodosia.

"The back-alley crawl," said Pritchard. "It was amazingly effective. We got a ton of people coming through here that ordinarily wouldn't venture into a store like this."

Lots of people, lots of suspects, thought Theodosia. Someone could have seen Daria, a woman who was not unattractive, and allowed a bizarre, murderous fantasy to caper through his or her twisted mind. Then what? Returned to fulfill that awful fantasy? Theodosia grimaced at her own dark thoughts.

"What time did you leave?" Theodosia asked Pritchard.

He scratched his head. "Probably . . . nine thirty?"

"And you went directly home?" said Theodosia.

Pritchard nodded. "Uh-huh. And that's where I was when the police came banging on my door."

"Okay," said Theodosia, putting together the time line in her head. "And Joe Don, you were here helping out, too?"

"Yes, ma'am," said Joe Don. "Until I went to grab some take-out from the Chowder Hound."

"And that was around . . . ?" asked Theodosia.

"Nine forty-five," filled in Joe Don.

And I came wandering along about ten, Theodosia thought to herself.

"Still lots of folks on Church Street when I came back," added Joe Don.

"Wait just a minute," said Theodosia. She let her gaze wander about the store. Maps hung on all the walls; sepia-tone and hand-drawn maps were displayed in old-fashioned glass cases, as were vintage photos and ephemera such as old letters and papers. Three large wooden flat files held even more maps. A large library table stood in the center of the room, the perfect place for unfurled maps.

"When I spoke with Detective Tidwell," Theodosia continued, "he told me someone had completely trashed this place. And theorized that the struggle had probably started in here."

"It *was* an absolute wreck," agreed Pritchard. "But the crime scene guys took most of the ripped up maps along with them. Well, first they photographed everything, then they gathered it all up in big plastic garbage bags and carted it away."

"Interesting," said Theodosia, wondering what Detective Tidwell hoped to glean from those shredded and tattered pieces. "So you cleaned up everything else?" she asked Pritchard.

Pritchard nodded. "Did my best. Plus Fallon came in around noon and helped."

Theodosia turned her attention on Joe Don Hunter. "And you just happened to drop by?"

Joe Don looked like he was ready to burst into tears. "I didn't know what else to do," he said in a strangled voice. He swiped at his eyes with the back of his hand, the strain of his girlfriend's murder definitely showing.

"As far as the shop goes," said Theodosia. "What do you think the future holds?"

"I'd like to keep it going," said Pritchard. "Maybe even . . . buy it?"

"Can you afford it?" asked Theodosia. She knew she was being blunt, but they'd asked her for help. Direct questions were part and parcel of any kind of investigation. Even her kind.

"Not really," said Pritchard, looking glum.

Theo turned to Fallon. "Did Daria leave a will, or did she have a partner we don't know about?"

Fallon gave a tight shake of her head. "I have no idea," she said in a squeaky voice. And now tears were streaming down her face. "I just . . . don't know."

"My apologies," said Theodosia, "I didn't mean to push the boundaries of decency on this."

Fallon dabbed at her eyes with a Kleenex. "I'm just so . . . ah, dear . . . so *confused*."

"We all are." said Joe Don.

Theodosia asked a few more perfunctory questions, but nobody seemed to have any answers. Or offer any insight.

"I'm sure you all did your best," Theodosia told them. "Okay if I go out the back door and look around?"

Fallon looked stricken. "Just be careful," she said, her voice husky.

Theodosia slipped down a short hallway, past Daria's small office, and let herself out the back door. Thick and heavy, painted Williamsburg blue, it was a wooden door probably constructed of cedar or pine. Probably installed when the brick building had been constructed more than a hundred years ago.

Standing on the narrow cobblestone walkway that snaked along the back of the building, it was hard for Theodosia to believe this was the exact spot where she'd seen Daria struggling for her life. Now a cool, refreshing breeze wafted down the alley, riffling the leaves on a thick stand of palmettos.

Theodosia glanced down at the cobblestones, looking for something, anything, that might yield a clue. But saw nothing. Probably, if there'd been a button or fiber or something dropped during last night's struggle, the crime scene team had already pounced on it. So not much to go on.

Half closing her eyes, Theodosia slowly walked down the back alley, keenly aware of the dampness and the sound of her own footfalls. How was it no one had heard anything? How could no one have seen anything?

Then she was jolted back to the here and now, realizing *she'd* seen the struggle. She was the sole witness.

Too bad she couldn't keep that little nugget under wraps.

Circling back around the block to Church Street, Theodosia strolled along, thinking about Jason Pritchard and Joe Don Hunter. Both claimed to be close to Daria, both seemed heartbroken. And yet, each one of them had had considerable opportunity.

Ah, but the big doozy of a question was, did either have motive?

It didn't appear they did. Not yet, anyway.

Finding herself directly in front of Jardin Perfumerie, Theodosia peered in the large front window. And was utterly delighted by a spectacular array of perfume bottles and crystal atomizers that glinted in the afternoon sun. One tall, obelisk-shaped bottle caught her eye. She leaned in closer, trying to read the label. ARISTOCRACY. Interesting.

Then, in a spur of the moment decision, Theodosia stepped to the front door, where a tiny CLOSED sign hung, and rapped her knuckles sharply against the glass. She fully expected Cinnamon St. John to come scurrying from the back, tug open the door, and welcome her with a big, neighborly howdy-do.

But none of that happened. So Theodosia pressed her face to the window and peered in. Saw only a dim light in the back of the store where shadowy figures glided back and forth. Seemingly ignoring her.

Strange.

6

⚜

Tucked among splendid historic district mansions, Theodosia's cottage was a dream come true. Built in the Cotswold style, the storybook English cottage featured a sharply pitched roof, gingerbread trim, leaded bow windows, and a corner turret on the top floor. Just the sort of thing you'd see in a Currier and Ives print or described in *Anne of Green Gables*, although that was supposedly set on Prince Edward Island.

"What do you think?" Theodosia asked Earl Grey as they paused on the sidewalk, staring at what would soon be their new home. The charming little place sat hunkered back from the street, shielded by a wrought-iron fence and over-grown shrubbery, with darkness wrapped around it. Theodosia smiled to herself, knowing that once her blue-and-white Chinese lamp glowed in the window, it would be a homey, welcoming beacon.

Earl Grey tilted his head and responded to Theodosia's question. "Grrrr." *Great.*

"Hazelhurst," whispered Theodosia. The little cottage

even had a name. "Lovely, isn't it?" she asked Earl Grey. "I think we're going to be very happy here." Pushing open the wrought-iron gate, stepping briskly along the brick walkway, it *felt* like they were both going home. Felt warm and cozy and just right.

"There's even a backyard for you," Theodosia told Earl Grey, as she fumbled with the lock box combination. She spun the dial, didn't get it quite right, so she flipped the dial back to the top and started over. This time the little lock box gave a reassuring click and an old-fashioned skeleton key tumbled out.

"First order of business once we move in," said Theodosia, "is to install better locks. Honestly, anyone could get inside using this kind of key. I see huge entire rings of these old keys for sale in antique shops for, like, five dollars."

"Rarrr," said Earl Grey. *Right.*

Pushing open the arched door, Theodosia flipped on an overhead light and stepped across the threshold. "Well? This is it. Your first look-see. Sure hope you like it."

Earl Grey's toenails clicked against the floor of the small brick foyer, then he wandered slowly across the polished wooden floor. He glanced around the empty room with watchful eyes, then walked over to inspect the brick fireplace that was set into a wall of beveled cypress panels. He stopped, touched the tip of his fine muzzle to the fireplace screen, then turned to stare at his beloved Theodosia. Earl Grey's limpid brown eyes shone like bright oil spots and his long tail swished eagerly. Then he tossed his head in a gesture that was part proprietary, part approval, and dashed off to explore the kitchen.

"Excellent," Theodosia murmured. "I think I've just been awarded the Canine Good House Seal of Approval." She dropped her suede hobo bag on the floor, slipped off her jacket, and went to work.

First order of business was to take accurate measurements.

Theodosia had an inkling that her blue-and-persimmon Chinese rug would fit perfectly in the living room, but she wanted to know for sure. Ditto her chintz sofa, damask chair, and rosewood coffee table. She already knew the walls were more than adequate to display her small collection of oil paintings. In fact, there was enough wall space that, finances permitting, she could continue to indulge her passion for collecting with a few more pieces of early American art. She also had her eye on a Louis XVI–inspired fruitwood secretary that was on display in the Legacy Gallery down on Royal Street. She figured it would fit comfortably against one wall and more than adequately showcase some of the finer pieces in her antique teacup collection. The Royal Winton chintz teacup for sure. And the James Kent hydrangea pattern and the Crown Ducal peony chintz.

Theodosia spent a good thirty minutes pacing the rooms, spinning out her metal tape measure and jotting down room dimensions. She worked methodically, starting in the living room, moving on to the small but jewel-like dining room with its cove ceilings, Georgian paneling, and French doors, then moving upstairs.

Because of the pitch of the roof, there was one nice-sized bedroom upstairs along with two much smaller rooms. The bedroom had a cozy turret corner that would be perfect as a reading nook. Theodosia took measurements, figured that everything she had would fit quite well and then some, and decided to ignore the two other rooms. She already planned to turn one room into a small study and outfit the other as a walk-in closet. Never enough closet space, she told herself, no matter what size your house.

Just as Theodosia was measuring the turret window, dreaming about swags and valances and maybe even velvet portieres dusting the floor, Earl Grey came padding upstairs.

"Almost done," she told him, jotting a final number.

"Then we'll go explore your little domain." As they walked downstairs together, Theodosia paused on the landing. A faded print that she'd passed off earlier as a run-of-the-mill birds and bees print hung on the wall. But now, upon closer inspection, she noted the grace of the drawing, the careful attention to detail. Could it be an Audubon print, left or forgotten by one of the former owners? Theodosia decided she'd have to look at her contract again, see if maybe that little item might be included.

Continuing down the stairs, she turned and went into the kitchen. The counters were junky, the cupboards not much better. Updates would have to be made, new appliances installed, but that could all unfold over time. No hurry. Better to settle in first and get a feel for things. Old houses had a way of whispering truths and history to their owners, of telling them what needed fixing and what parts were best left untouched, original, and charming.

"Cold in here," said Theodosia, snapping on the light over the sink, frowning as it buzzed and blinked, then cut out entirely. "Don't tell me . . ." She flipped the switch again, and this time the light came on and stayed on. For the time being.

That's when Theodosia noticed the open window.

"What on earth!" she cried, as Earl Grey stared solemnly at her. "Was this open when we came in?" Then she answered her own question. "Had to be. Nobody here but us guys, huh?"

Strange, she decided. Perhaps the owner had been airing out the place for some reason? Or maybe Maggie Twining, her Realtor, had been by?

Worry nagging at her, Theodosia stepped over to the window, pushed firmly on the sash, trying to slide it down. The window was old and warped and stuck obstinately in its track. Grunting and tugging, she struggled with it. And suddenly, amidst the squeaks and groans of the window, Theodosia heard a distinct thump in the backyard.

What?

Followed by a loud pop and a patter of footsteps. At which point every light in the place winked out.

Whoa. Now what's going on?

Abandoning the stuck window, Theodosia dashed for the back door, ready to career out into the backyard. Until fear jabbed a talon in her and Theodosia decided maybe the best course of action *wasn't* to rush out quite so hastily.

Grabbing Earl Grey by the collar, Theodosia decided to enlist him as a first line of defense as well as a par excellence guard dog. Plus dogs had nocturnal vision, right? So Earl Grey should be able to see what was going on.

Hanging on to his collar, Theodosia stepped slowly out into the yard. Ordinarily, it was a perfect little Charleston garden, made even more picturesque with magnolia and dogwood trees, a tangle of vines crawling up the back wall, and a tiny fountain that pattered prettily into a small fish pond. Utterly idyllic. Except when things went bump in the night!

Creeping ahead stealthily, Theodosia and Earl Grey crossed the tiny postage stamp–sized patio, aware of the scent of plum blossoms and damp grass. Five, six, then seven footsteps in, they hit a muddy patch of garden. Theodosia pulled a foot from the sticky stuff, wondering why there was so much mud, then remembered how hard it had rained last night.

And just as Theodosia touched her fingertips to the wrought-iron back gate, she heard the distinct grating of shoes on cobblestones. Of someone coming up the dark alley. Heading directly for her!

Crouching into her best kung fu position, Theodosia improvised by landing a hard, sideways kick on the wrought-iron gate. The force of her kick weakened the rusty hinges, causing the gate to fly open and crash loudly against the brick wall. Quick as a wink, she dashed into the dark alley—and ran smack dab into Jack Brux!

"You?" she cried, while Earl Grey danced around Brux,

making anxious doggy chuffing sounds and nipping at Brux's heels.

"Get that dog away from me!" Brux yelled. He was startled, angry.

"What are you *doing* out here?" Theodosia demanded. "Why are you skulking around in my alley?"

"*Excuse* me?" said Brux, his face contorting into a disapproving snarl.

"I asked what you were doing here," Theodosia repeated.

Brux stared at Theodosia, incredulous. "I live down the block," he rasped. "A better question might be what are *you* doing here?"

"I live here, too," responded Theodosia. "Well, I'm *going* to live here, in about two weeks. Look, there was just an intruder in my backyard."

"Not me," snapped Brux.

"Did you see anyone?" she asked.

"No," came his terse reply.

"Strange that you just happened to come bobbing along out of nowhere," said Theodosia, her blood still simmering. She wasn't a huge believer in coincidences.

"This isn't nowhere," Brux snarled at her again. "I just *told* you, I live down the block."

But he still wasn't getting through to Theodosia. "My lights went out. You know anything about that?"

"I suggest you call South Carolina Electric and Gas," said Brux, practically spitting his words at her.

"I'm actually thinking about calling the police," responded Theodosia.

"Not on me you're not," cried Brux. Illuminated from above by a flickering back-alley gas lamp, his face looked harsh and deeply lined. Even threatening. "And maybe you should put your dog on a leash," he added in a sniping tone. Jack Brux spun sharply to see what Earl Grey was up to now, and suddenly, in the space of about two seconds, his face morphed from angry pink to pale white. "Oh my heavens!" he suddenly breathed.

"Is . . . is something wrong?" Theodosia asked. Maybe she'd been too aggressive after all, maybe she'd unwittingly pushed Brux into some kind of cardiac arrhythmia!

But Jack Brux continued to stare at the gate leading to Theodosia's yard, where Earl Grey now stood. Brux's lips seemed to be moving, but he wasn't making meaningful sounds.

Puzzled, Theodosia turned to see what had caused Brux such palpable shock. And saw Earl Grey standing there, paws gobbed with sticky black mud, clutching a bone in his mouth. A rather large bone.

Theodosia took a quick step closer and peered at Earl Grey's find. That's when her face turned a few shades paler, as well. *Oh, sweet mother of pearl!*

No way was she a medical professional. In fact, she hadn't been a particularly astute student when it came to biology. But even to Theodosia's untrained eye, the bone Earl Grey held in his mouth looked hideously like a human femur!

"*Give it to* me, boy," Theodosia urged. "Come on, hand it over." Theodosia crept closer to Earl Grey.

Thinking they were playing some wonderful, new game, Earl Grey immediately dropped into pounce position. Head down, muddy paws outstretched and quivering, back end up in the air. Bone still firmly clenched between his jaws.

"C'mon, boy," said Theodosia, getting more and more flustered.

"Dumb dog," muttered Brux.

Theodosia spun around, held up a single index finger, and hissed to Brux, "Don't." Then she finally pulled it together and remembered the proper command she and her dog had been taught. "Drop it."

Earl Grey promptly dropped the bone. It clunked loudly

and hollowly on the pavement and rolled a couple of inches toward her.

"That's a good boy," murmured Theodosia. "Let's take a look at what treasure you found." She moved closer and poked gingerly at the bone with the tip of her shoe. Ugh. It sure looked like a human bone.

"What are you gonna do?" asked Brux, peering nearsightedly. "Call the police after all?"

"Not sure," said Theodosia. She stared at the bone again, trying to recall the myriad of technical diagrams in her college biology book. The bone certainly *looked* like a femur. Or maybe it was a tibia. In any case, the bone appeared to be human remains. So that meant alerting the police.

Five minutes later, a black-and-white patrol car slid to a stop in the alley.

Two officers, both young and good-looking, one white, one African American, got out, hitching up their black leather utility belts as they exited.

"I found a bone," Theodosia told them in a tumble of words. "At least my dog did. Dug it up, I think."

The African American officer, whose name tag read Darby, spoke first. "Take it easy, ma'am, we get a lot of these calls."

Theodosia grimaced. She knew they were being polite, but the ma'am thing just made her feel old. Which she wasn't. At least she didn't think she was. If sixty was the new forty, what was mid-thirties? The new mid-twenties? Hardly.

"Ma'am?" Officer Darby said again. "We're gonna have to take that bone with us. You want to put your dog inside the house? He looks a little vicious."

"He's a therapy dog," Theodosia told them. "I take him to senior citizen homes."

"Still, what breed is he?" asked the other officer. Officer Lomax. "Maybe like . . . a Doberman?

"Dalbrador," said Theodosia. "A cross between a Dalmatian and a Labrador. And he does have a name. Earl Grey."

"Cute," said Darby, relaxing some.

Lomax gazed at her and suddenly snapped his fingers. "I recognize you. You're that tea lady. I saw you on TV a couple of weeks ago."

"I did a demo for Channel Four," said Theodosia.

"And my girlfriend went to your shop," continued Lomax. "And now she's forever brewing tea and making me tiny sandwiches with the crusts cut off."

"Really?" asked Darby. He sounded like he wouldn't mind a sandwich with the crusts cut off. Or any kind of sandwich, for that matter.

"And you see your girlfriend's activities as a *good* thing?" asked Theodosia. She wasn't sure whether Lomax was pro–tea sandwich or anti–tea sandwich.

"Oh yes, ma'am," Lomax said earnestly. "I particularly like the sandwiches with chicken salad and chitney."

"Chutney," said Theodosia.

"Right," said Lomax.

Darby popped open the trunk and grabbed a pair of latex gloves along with a black garbage bag. "So," he said, "let's bag up that bone."

Jack Brux, who'd watched the whole exchange, asked in a peevish tone, "Can I *go* now?"

7

❧

Come Wednesday morning, Haley, in particular, was stunned by Theodosia's story about the bone. "And you actually think it's a *human* bone?" she asked.

Theodosia nodded. She'd waited until they'd set all the tables for morning tea before breaking the somewhat bizarre news about Earl Grey's late-night find.

Haley jabbed an elbow at Drayton. "Pretty weird stuff, huh? Really creepy."

"The thing is," said Drayton, looking thoughtful and not one iota creeped out, "finding human bones around our neck of the woods really is quite commonplace."

"That's what the police told me," said Theodosia. Although the notion still unsettled her.

"Think about it," said Drayton. "The first English settlers arrived here, at what was dubbed Charles Towne, in 1670. Since then, our fair city has endured the Revolutionary War, War of 1812, War Between the States, and various floods, periods of pestilence, and deadly hurricanes. It's no wonder this entire place isn't one big bone yard."

"Well, that's a happy thought," said Haley.

"Then let's change the subject to something more upbeat," said Theodosia, as she folded a linen napkin into a bishop's hat arrangement. "How did you fare with your chocolate endeavors last night?"

Haley brightened immediately. "Got 'em all made! Even the bittersweet chocolate pavé, which turned out to be quite spectacular if I do say so myself."

"Glad to hear it," said Theodosia.

"Anyway," said Haley, "I dropped everything off at the Dorchester Club early this morning and filled out my entry forms in triplicate." She gazed eagerly at Theodosia. "You're still coming with me to the luncheon, right? It starts at one o'clock."

"Wouldn't miss it for the world," said Theodosia.

Drayton cleared his throat. "Since you two are planning to be in absentia for a few hours, I assume Haley will have prepared a no-fuss lunch? Realize, of course, it will be up to dear Miss Dimple and myself to serve it."

"Haley?" said Theodosia.

"Three easy entrées," replied Haley. "Chicken salad in tomato tulips, spring pea cream soup, chilled and served with cornbread, and ham and Gruyère sandwiches. No muss, no fuss." She grinned a wicked grin. "Think of it as tea time for dummies."

"You don't have to phrase it quite so inelegantly." Drayton blanched. "We're not exactly neophytes at serving customers."

"Hey, all I did was figure out a few things I could make and prep beforehand, so you could focus on plating the food and being your charming selves," said Haley. "Sorry. Didn't mean to ruffle any feathers."

"Haley," said Theodosia, "you'll prep the tomatoes, as well?"

"Sure thing," she said, tossing back her long blond hair and giving Drayton another snarky look as she headed for the kitchen.

"I wish you could come along to the Chocolatier Fest," Theodosia said to Drayton. "I've got a good feeling about Haley's entries."

"How could you not?" responded Drayton. "Our entire kitchen smells as if a giant, chocolate neutron bomb had been detonated. Or perhaps it's the same aromatic, lingering scent that hangs over Hershey, Pennsylvania?" He leaned down, opened a cardboard box, and carefully lifted out a small glass jar.

"Your scent jars came," observed Theodosia.

Drayton turned the small apothecary jar in his hand, studying it. "Yes. Finally. Now we'll be able to give our customers the joy of sniffing our fresh loose-leaf teas before they make their selection."

"I think you had a wonderful idea," said Theodosia, as Drayton continued to line the jars on the second shelf of a mahogany highboy. "It's basically sampling, which makes the whole tea-buying experience highly interactive."

"Sniff, sniff," said Drayton, pleased that she was pleased.

"How many teas are you thinking of putting on display?" Theodosia asked.

"I ordered twenty-four jars, so I think we should put out a full complement of teas."

"What about labels?" asked Theodosia. "We'll have to have labels."

Drayton held up a hand. "Please."

"Oh," Theodosia said. "Really?" Drayton was a skilled calligrapher and often volunteered to do elaborate hand lettering for menus, place cards, and special invitations. "Because if you're pressed for time, I could whip something out on my computer."

"Better I do the labels," said Drayton.

"You are a stickler for quality control," allowed Theodosia, her lips twitching at the corners.

"Someone has to be," replied Drayton, in complete seriousness. "Makes for a far more ordered and pleasant world. Would you . . . ?" He tilted his head back, gazed down his nose, looking suddenly thoughtful.

"You want to fill the jars now?" asked Theodosia. "Before the morning rush?"

Drayton pushed up his left sleeve and peered at his antique Piaget watch, which perpetually ran a few minutes slow. "I think there's time. You think we have time?"

"We'll fill as many as we can in the time we have," said Theodosia.

"Always so practical," said Drayton.

"Someone has to be," grinned Theodosia.

Theodosia dashed to the front counter, gathered up as many tea tins as she could comfortably grasp, then carried them over to Drayton.

"Thank you," he said, sounding pleased and happy. Theodosia had noticed, more and more, that Drayton had evolved into a very task-oriented person. Give him a menu to hand letter in bâtarde alphabet or small tea jars to fill, and he was happy as a clam.

"Drayton," said Theodosia, watching him pour Nilgiri tea leaves into a jar, enjoying a small contact high from the slightly sweet, almost fruity aroma. "What do you know about Jack Brux? Do you think he's an okay guy?"

Drayton tapped the tea tin against the jar, eyeing the amount he'd just poured in. "Brux has always been a hard-working champion for the Heritage Society," said Drayton. "If that's what you're asking."

"It is and it isn't," said Theodosia. "To your knowledge, does Brux have a nasty temper? Or even a violent streak?"

Drayton's head jerked back and he stared at her. "You think he killed someone and buried them in your backyard? That your dog unearthed one of his poor victims?" He sounded deadly serious, but his eyes twinkled merrily.

"No," said Theodosia. "It's just that Brux strikes me as being somewhat ill-tempered. At least he was last night, when I ran into him."

Drayton let loose a snicker. "He *can* be awfully salty. Brux once removed his shoe and banged it on the table at a Heritage Society committee meeting to protest the admittance of a new board member."

"What?" asked Haley, who'd just wandered over to inspect Drayton's lineup of jars. "He took off his shoe? Like that old story about Khrushchev at the UN?"

"That wasn't a story, dear girl," said Drayton. "It really happened."

"What was the fuss about, anyway?" asked Haley.

"Cold war," said Dayton.

"Cold war?" asked Haley, looking slightly puzzled.

"And I'm not talking Celsius or centigrade," said Drayton. "Back in the day, particularly during the fifties, we were all terrified the Russians were going to drop a bomb and blast the bejeebers out of us."

"Duck, roll, and hide, huh?" said Haley, giggling. "And throw a few cans of Spam in the old bomb bunker?"

"Bomb shelter," said Drayton. "And, believe me, Haley, you wouldn't find it all so amusingly anachronistic if you'd lived through that era."

"S'pose not," said Haley. "Hey, those scent jars are terrific. And look how you managed to pour equal amounts of tea into each jar. You know, Dayton, besides being a certified tea taster, you've got a heckuva fine eye."

And with Haley's final pronouncement still hanging in the air, the floodgates of commerce suddenly opened. A half dozen eager customers pushed their way into the Indigo Tea Shop, and just like that, the joint was jumping.

Then a familiar yellow horse-drawn jitney clip-clopped its way to the front door and disgorged another dozen or so passengers. So, in the space of about ten minutes, the tea room buzzed with customers.

"Busy," murmured Drayton as he strutted past Theodosia, clutching a teapot in each hand.

"Right behind you with the scones," said Theodosia. Popping into the kitchen, she slid six plates onto her silver platter, each plate holding a cream scone along with tiny glass dishes filled with Devonshire cream and strawberry jam.

A few minutes later, when Haley's pecan pie muffins came out of the oven, all gorgeous brown and smelling of cinnamon and toasted pecans, Theodosia delivered those to waiting customers as well.

When most of her customers were finally sipping tea and happily spooning extra helpings of sinful Devonshire cream onto their scones, Theodosia took a moment to gaze about her tea shop. This, of course, was the golden hour. When the rich aroma of Chinese black tea hung redolent in the air, tea kettles chirped merrily, and Drayton glided from table to table pouring refills and charming customers with amusing stories. This little picture of contentment always reassured Theodosia that she'd made the right choice in giving up a well-paying job in the hustle-bustle world of marketing.

"Theodosia?"

Theodosia pulled herself from her brief reverie and quickly turned toward the front door. "Brooke!" she exclaimed, at seeing the smiling face of one of her fellow shopkeepers from down the block. "I didn't hear you come in." Brooke Carter Crockett was in her mid-fifties and petite, with a sleek mane of silver-white hair. Since Brooke had taken up yoga, she also seemed more lithe and had an aura of contentment about her.

"You look great," said Theodosia. As sole proprietor of Heart's Desire jewelry shop, Brooke dealt in the purchase and sales of elegant estate jewelry and was also recognized as a craftsman of contemporary pieces in gold and silver.

"Thank you," said Brooke. "I had a little downtime this morning so I thought I'd drop by for a proper tea. Not just grab a cuppa to go." She glanced around. "Don't know if you have a table, though . . ."

"Over by the fireplace," said Theodosia. "See, that couple is just getting up to leave. I'll turn it around in a heartbeat."

"Perfect," declared Brooke.

Drayton, on seeing Brooke come in, sped over to do the honors himself. Cleared away dirty dishes, wiped down the scarred wooden table, laid out a fresh placemat along with flatware, plate, teacup, and linen napkin.

"This is the life," said Brooke, settling in. "A handsome fellow to do my bidding." She winked at Drayton, giggled when he blushed slightly.

"I understand you paid a visit to the new perfumery down the block," said Theodosia, sliding into the captain's chair across from Brooke.

"Last week," said Brooke. "Then I had to fly to Atlanta for the big jewelry show. When I returned yesterday, it was the first I'd heard about Daria's murder." A faint line insinuated itself between her brows. "I pored through all the newspapers and got caught up." Brooke leaned forward, looking grim, and rapped her knuckles against the table. "Must have been awful for you. Since you were the one who witnessed the assault and can supposedly ID the killer."

"The only problem," Theodosia told her, "is that I really *didn't* get a good look at the attacker."

"That's not how the newspeople painted it," replied Brooke. "They made it sound like you were very much involved."

"An unfortunate overstatement," said Theodosia. "Journalistic puffery."

"Does that worry you?" asked Brooke. "That the killer *thinks* you might be able to identify him?"

"It does bother me a little," said Theodosia. "No, actually, it bothers me a lot."

Drayton was suddenly at the table with a cream scone and orange marmalade, as well as a freshly brewed pot of tea. "I have something new for you to try," he told Brooke. "A lovely tea from the Dooars region in India. Even though Dooars is the fourth most important tea-growing region, it's simply not as well known as the Assam Valley or the Darjeeling region." He lifted his teapot, a lovely pink–and–green bone china pot done in the shape of a cabbage. "But the tea they produce in Dooars is rich and slightly fruity, with just a tiny hint of malt." He poured out a steaming cup. "Try it. Enjoy it."

Brooke took a sip and nodded almost immediately. "Oh, I see what you mean. I can taste the fruit and there's also a tiny hint of astringency in the finish."

Drayton beamed. "You have a very refined palette."

Brooke smiled back at him. "I had a very good teacher."

When Drayton finally moved on, Theodosia asked Brooke about her visit to the perfumery.

"Cute little place," Brooke told her. "Loads and loads of inventory, really amazing stuff. You'll have to drop by and meet the ladies."

"I already met one of them," said Theodosia. "Cinnamon stopped by yesterday. She seemed nice enough."

"Ah," said Brooke, "but the real power behind the throne is Miss Kitty, her aunt. Did you by chance meet her?"

"Haven't had the pleasure," said Theodosia.

"Oh, you'll cross paths," said Brooke. "And believe me, Miss Kitty's a real trip. Outspoken, high energy, a world-class talker and promoter. She's already asking me to craft some sterling silver perfume bottle charms to retail in her shop."

"Sounds like a cute idea," said Theodosia. Brooke was renowned for her Charleston-themed jewelry and had created more than a dozen or so tiny charms that were adorable on charm bracelets or could be linked on chains as pendants. Her more recent charms included miniature palm trees, pineapples, magnolia blossoms, wrought-iron gates, sailing ships, oysters, and churches.

Taking a bite of scone, Brooke chewed thoughtfully, then said, "So . . . are you going to get seriously involved?"

"In . . . ?"

"You know," said Brooke, studying her carefully. "The murder. Daria's murder."

"I think I'm already involved," said Theodosia.

"Your buddy Detective Tidwell is on the case?"

Theodosia nodded.

"Then you're already on the inside."

"Not really," said Theodosia.

"You know Tidwell's sweet on you," purred Brooke. "Not romantic sweet, but in a quiet, admiring way. I've seen how he looks at you."

"He watches me like a cat observes a mouse hole," said Theodosia. "It's discomforting."

"Still," said Brooke. "Tidwell is well aware how skillful you are at piecing together clues."

"Only if I can find a clue," said Theodosia, glancing up at Drayton, who had suddenly planted himself at her elbow. "Need help?" she asked, starting to rise from her chair.

"There's a young man here," said Drayton. He gestured toward the front door, where a sandy-haired man, looking rather studious in horn-rimmed glasses, stood waiting patiently. He was young, maybe twenty-seven or twenty-eight, and was dressed in khaki slacks and a matching khaki shirt loaded with pockets and epaulets.

"And we're out of tables," said Theodosia.

"No," said Drayton, suddenly looking more than a little concerned. "He doesn't want a table. He says he want to talk to you about your bones."

8

❧

Tred Pascal was from the State Archaeology Office, hence the
Indiana Jones outfit. Turns out, Tred's boss had received a
phone call this morning from the Charleston Police Department. So Tred had been duly assigned to deal with the bone.
Theodosia's bone. All because the powers that be thought it
should be examined for archaeological significance.

Tred explained all this to Theodosia while sitting across
from her in her office, glancing sideways at dozens of ceramic
and bone china teapots, a pile of grapevine wreaths decorated with ribbons, teacups, and silk flowers, and dozens
of piled-up boxes with stacks of wide-brimmed straw hats
teetering on top.

"Archaeological significance," said Theodosia. The words
sounded stilted to her, especially when applied to a grubby
old bone. And would probably come as a crushing disappointment to Earl Grey, who'd been counting on having his
precious find returned to him.

"The thing is," said Tred, "folks uncover bones all the

time. Digging up gardens, during excavations, that sort of thing. Most of the time they're simply animal bones, but once in a while they turn out to be historically important. Native Americans, early settlers, bones that date back to the Revolutionary War era, Civil War soldiers."

"So I've been told," said Theodosia.

Tred wrinkled his brow, looking concerned. "I did some quick, seat-of-the-pants research. There's a chance your cottage might have been built on the very spot where pirates were once hanged."

"I thought that all happened at White Point Gardens," said Theodosia. "The gallows and the pirate hangings, I mean." That's what she'd always been told. That's what most historic district tours underscored as well. All the ruffian pirates that had been caught plaguing the southeastern seaboard had been summarily hunted down, captured, and hung from a permanent gallows that had occupied a lonely, shell-scattered beach.

"But your place isn't that far away," Tred pointed out. "Maybe the condemned were executed at White Point Gardens, then buried somewhere else. Like in your yard."

"A happy thought," said Theodosia. Who wanted a potter's field in their backyard? Not her!

"What I'd like to do is set up a small archaeological dig," said Tred. "See if anything else turns up."

Theodosia shifted uncomfortably. "You're not serious."

"Even a small dig can yield stunning results," enthused Tred. "I was part of a dig last summer at the Topper Site—"

"Where?" interrupted Theodosia.

"On the Savannah River, over in Allendale County," said Tred, real excitement lighting his face. "The tools and stone implements we unearthed revealed that ancient humans had been present as far back as sixteen thousand years ago. That's three thousand years earlier than previously thought!"

"Wow," said Theodosia. She felt like she ought to be

impressed, but her mind kept circling back to having her backyard dug up. Or should she think of it as prepping the soil for tomato plants? Or perhaps a lovely rose garden?

"Knock, knock," said Haley, suddenly looming in the doorway. "I'm gonna take off for the Dorchester Club now," she told Theodosia. Then she smiled shyly at Tred and gave a warm, "Hey there."

"Haley," said Theodosia, "this is Tred Pascal from the State Archaeology Office. He's here about the bone."

"Cool," said Haley, giving him another shy smile. "Where'd you go to school?"

Tred focused his attention on Haley. "I graduated from the University of South Carolina in Columbia. Department of Anthropology."

"Love the bwana outfit," Haley quipped, obviously feeling playful. "Was that part of the deal?"

Tred blushed.

Haley folded her arms and edged a little closer to him. "And now you get to run around digging up old bones and stuff?"

"Sometimes I do," said Tred. "Most of the time, we're in the laboratory analyzing them. Using carbon dating or electron microscopes." He swiveled his head toward Theodosia. "You still have the bone in question?" he asked.

"Oh, silly me," said Haley, with exaggerated earnestness. "I'm afraid I tossed it into the soup pot."

The look on Tred's face was priceless. "What!"

"Relax," said Theodosia. "Haley's just pulling your leg. She does that once in a while. It's her idea of sport."

"You two are quite a tag team," said Tred, looking a little unsettled.

"Actually," said Theodosia, "the police took the bone last night. Bagged it, tagged it, promised to do the whole CSI thing. Which, I guess, *you're* really going to do."

"So the bone's probably downtown at their lab," said Tred, nodding. "Okay."

"Okay," echoed Haley. "So . . . see you at the luncheon, Theo?"

Theodosia nodded.

Haley grinned at Tred. "Good luck and all. See you around."

"Maybe so." Tred smiled.

"Hope so," said Haley.

"When you said you wanted to set up a small archeological excavation," said Theodosia, getting back to the subject at hand, "what exactly did you have in mind?"

"First," said Tred, "we'd have to determine if your backyard really is worth exploring. According to state guidelines, an archaeological site is defined as an area yielding three or more historic or prehistoric artifacts within a thirty-meter radius."

"Okay," said Theodosia. "So first you'd have to find more bones."

"Or artifacts," said Tred. "Since a site can also be an area with visible or historically recognized cultural features, such as a cemetery, rock shelter, chimney fall, brick wall, or pier . . . well, you get the idea."

"It's really only a cottage," said Theodosia. "A former carriage house. And, technically, I don't even own the property yet. You'd have to get permission from the current owners."

"When were you supposed to close on the property?"

"I was hoping in about two weeks."

"That might not be possible," said Tred.

Theodosia rose in her chair. "Please don't say that. I already started packing. I have a sort of . . . schedule."

"Look," said Tred, "I'm going to do my best to fast-track this whole thing. Take a quick look-see in the next couple of days, then make a determination."

"Based on what you do or don't find," mused Theodosia. "Okay. Hopefully, nothing else will turn up."

"And I'm kind of hoping something does," Tred told her as they walked out of Theodosia's office. Ducking past the velvet celadon-green curtain that closed off the tea shop from the kitchen and back office, they headed for the front door.

Curious at all the hustle and bustle, Tred glanced around and asked, "What kind of food do you serve here, anyway?"

"We're a tea shop," Theodosia told him. "Today we're offering soup, salad, scones, and sandwiches. Plus we can brew pretty much any type of tea you have a taste for." She paused. "Why? Are you hungry?"

Tred nodded. "Famished. But I don't have time to eat right now. I'd like to come back sometime, though." His eyes twinkled. "Are you always here?"

He was flirting with her and she knew it. Funny, she thought he'd been seriously charmed by Haley.

"Most every day," said Theodosia, "since I'm the owner." She paused. "Tell you what. Why don't I package up a cup of tea and a couple of scones to go."

"Takeaway?" Tred looked positively jubilant. "You'd do that?"

"Give me a minute," said Theodosia. She slid over to the counter, poured a splash of Formosan oolong tea into a cup, and dropped two scones in an indigo blue bag. Then, on impulse, ran back into the kitchen and packaged up a nice ham and Gruyère sandwich.

"Tea party in a box," she told Tred, when she handed it to him.

His grin was wide and sincere. "Thank you so much. Once I pick up the bone, do a little lab work, and talk to my boss, I'll let you know, okay?"

"Sure," said Theodosia. "Come back anytime."

* * *

"Problems?" asked Drayton. He'd removed his long, black Parisian waiter's apron and slipped into a camel-hair jacket, the better to meet and greet luncheon customers. Today Drayton's bow tie was a red-and-green tartan, a veritable Celtic-looking butterfly that lent a striking contrast.

"No problems out of the ordinary," Theodosia told him. "Nothing I can't handle."

"Are we still attending the Blessing of the Fleet tonight?" Drayton asked her. The Blessing of the Fleet was a new event for Charleston. This first ever blessing was to be held at White Point Gardens, a lush strip of land right at the tip of the peninsula, where the Ashley and Cooper rivers surged past on each side. Yachts, sailboats from both the Charleston Yacht Club and the Compass Key Yacht Club, and even some oyster boats and shrimp trawlers were going to take part. It was an idea they'd basically pinched from Mt. Pleasant, who did a Blessing of the Fleet on their fishing boats every April.

"Yes," Theodosia told him. "And I'm really looking forward to seeing the sailboats." She knew that two entire fleets would be tacking past, their masts and sails outlined in tiny white lights. Scheduled for dusk tonight, with the crashing Atlantic as a backdrop, the decorated boats were sure to be an awe-inspiring sight.

Reaching past her, Drayton grabbed a cardboard box and plunked it carefully on the counter.

"Don't tell me you're putting out more scent jars?" said Theodosia.

Drayton peeled open the box with a smile. "That shipment of teacup candles you ordered finally arrived." He lifted one out gently. A teacup with a pink-and-cream rose motif, seamlessly epoxied to its saucer, was filled with what looked like pink tea but was really a scented candle and wick.

"These are even more adorable than they were in the catalog," exclaimed Theodosia. "If you put them on display today, they'll probably sell out."

"Then I shall do exactly that," said Drayton.

Theodosia lifted out another teacup candle and sniffed. "Mmm, this one's orange-scented."

"Our shipment should include mandarin, raspberry, lemon verbena, and teaberry," said Drayton.

"Teaberry," said Theodosia, frowning slightly.

"Hmm?" asked Drayton, absently. His tortoiseshell glasses slid halfway down his nose as he studied the design of one of the teacups. "This chintz pattern reminds me of a Shelley pattern."

"You know," said Theodosia, half to herself, half to Drayton, "I'm going to check on something. Satisfy my curiosity."

"Yes," said Drayton, setting his teacup down and giving a perfunctory smile. "Do have a lovely time at your event."

But Theodosia had fifteen minutes to spare before she had to leave for the Dorchester Club. So she headed down the street to Jardin Perfumerie. This time the little shop was open for business when she arrived at their front door. Perfect, she decided, stepping inside a little jewel of a shop that glittered and glowed and proved to be even more fragrant and spicy than when she was brewing a dozen different teas at her own shop.

Cinnamon was there, of course, standing behind a black marble counter that displayed a myriad of dazzling glass bottles. She was just packing up a fragrance for a customer and smiled warmly at Theodosia. A smile that also said, "I'll be right with you."

Theodosia took these few opportune moments to look around. Interestingly enough, Jardin Perfumerie reminded her of an upscale jewelry shop. Lovely glass cases filled with delicate bottles that sparkled like gems. Mirrored walls with glass shelves that held scented soaps, candles, and essential oils. She reached out, picked up a small votive candle in a brocade-decorated glass, and decided it reminded her of a stained-glass window from one of Charleston's fine old churches.

Once Cinnamon's customer had slipped out the door, she wasted no time plying Theodosia with a little soft sell. "I'll bet you'd like us to create a personal fragrance for you," she purred.

"Can you do that?" asked Theodosia. The notion struck her as fun and a trifle indulgent.

Cinnamon came a step closer, her long, midnight blue silk skirt rustling, her long pearl necklace clacking softly and set off beautifully by her white ruffled blouse. She was dressed like a lady of the Belle Époque and was doing her best to play the part. No Junior League suit today; this costume portrayed elegance, grace, and turn-of-the-century glamour.

"We've created hundreds of personal scents," Cinnamon told Theodosia, as she picked up a small glass bottle. Removing the stopper, Cinnamon tipped the bottle toward Theodosia. "Somehow I see you as a clean, woodsy scent. Along the lines of this."

Theodosia took a sniff. Scents of pine, cherry, and sandalwood tickled her nose. "I like it."

Cinnamon narrowed her eyes and cocked her head, as if deep in thought. Theodosia decided Cinnamon had her sales patina down perfectly.

"But maybe a touch more . . . sophistication?" Cinnamon mused. "And perhaps . . ." Now her fingertips danced across the tops of a dozen different bottles. "Perhaps something with a hint of mystery, as well." She selected a bottle, pulled out the stopper, and held it up. "This has lovely top notes."

Theodosia dutifully sniffed again. This time she thought she recognized vanilla. And maybe lavender.

"Vanilla and lavender?" she asked.

Cinnamon looked more than a little surprised. "Goodness but you have an educated nose. That's quite a rarity."

"I do own a tea shop," replied Theodosia. "And, of course, Drayton, Drayton Conneley, my master tea blender, has helped me tremendously when it comes to learning aromas, blending, and scents." Theodosia had the feeling she'd somehow blundered into Cinnamon's special world. Hadn't exactly one-upped her, but certainly demonstrated an equality of knowledge.

Cinnamon snatched the bottle back. "Perhaps you'd enjoy one of our proprietary scents instead. We have several and they're *very* popular." There was just a hint of coolness in her voice.

Theodosia decided to try to warm her up again. "Your shop is really quite amazing. I see you even sell scented drawer liners and room fragrances." She thought these might come in handy, once she moved into her new cottage.

Cinnamon smiled dreamily. "Soaps, candles, essential oils, and more than a thousand different fragrances. From such venerable fragrance and couture houses as Chanel, Bulgari, Tiffany, Dior, and Creed. This one . . ." she pointed at a pyramid-shaped crystal bottle . . . "is Poivre by Caron. A thousand dollars an ounce."

"And a lovely bottle, too," said Theodosia, wondering who would spend that much for a fragrance.

"Baccarat crystal," said Cinnamon. She waved a hand airily. "I could go on and on."

"There's a scent I used to adore," said Theodosia. "Le Dix by Balenciaga? Hard to find though."

"We just happen to have it," chirped Cinnamon. "As well as several of the very popular pheromone-infused fragrances." She let loose a soft giggle. "Should you be looking to make a man fall in love with you, pheromones will do the trick!"

"Good to know," said Theodosia. She pointed at a square,

matte black bottle that sat, looking sexy and a little evil, on an elevated glass pedestal. "Once of your proprietary scents?"

Cinnamon nodded. "I call that one Requiem. A hint of black cherry with top notes of spicy ginger and amber."

"Unusual," said Theodosia.

"Unusual is our specialty," replied Cinnamon.

"What about a teaberry scent?" asked Theodosia. For some reason, the notion of teaberry had stuck in her mind ever since the night Daria had been murdered.

"A wonderful scent," enthused Cinnamon. "So minty and fresh. We have some around here as well as some essential teaberry oil on order. I'd have to check my inventory list for the exact date."

"And you've sold some?" asked Theodosia.

"Probably," said Cinnamon, smiling broadly. "But you simply *must* come back this afternoon when Miss Kitty is in. She's my aunt and the driving force behind Jardin Perfumerie. Miss Kitty worked for Fragonard in Paris at their shop in Saint-Germain-des–Prés. She's even visited Grasse in the Provence region of southern France during their May harvest of *Rosa centifolia* flowers."

"An impressive pedigree," said Theodosia.

"Miss Kitty is extremely well versed in the fragrance industry," said Cinnamon. "So you might want to reserve any questions for her."

"Just one question right now," said Theodosia.

Cinnamon raised her eyebrows in anticipation.

"Is your name really Cinnamon?"

That brought on a somewhat sheepish grin. "My given name is really Cynthia. But I thought Cinnamon sounded a little more . . . um . . . apropos."

9

"I'm so glad you made it!" Haley exclaimed to Theodosia, as they pushed their way through the buzzing crowd of people that had convened in the lobby of the Dorchester Club. "And with five minutes to spare."

Theodosia glanced around at the guests. It appeared to be a crazy-quilt mélange of chefs, bakers, foodies (particularly dessert freaks), ladies who lunch, and Charleston socialites, although Theodosia decided those last two categories were probably one and the same.

"Do we have time to peek at the Chocolatier Fest entries?" Theodosia asked.

In answer, Haley grabbed Theodosia's hand and quickly pulled her past a sea of faces into the Dorchester Club's wood-paneled Fireplace Room. There, a series of tables had been set up to showcase all the cake, chocolate, truffle, and trifle entries.

"Wow," Theodosia murmured, under her breath, as she beheld the striking display. White linen tablecloths had been draped over dark brown silk table coverings. White- and cocoa-colored tapers flickered from tall silver candelabras. And against the back side of each display table were boundless bouquets of chocolate-colored day lilies, gingerbread-colored irises, maroon-brown pansies, and feathery brown and gold ornamental grasses. Some intrepid floral designer had gone all out to create chocolate-inspired floral offerings that coordinated perfectly with the entries.

And what amazing entries they were!

Chocolate truffles with ganache centers and buttercream zigzag decorations. Petit fours and chocolate raspberry cheesecake. Chili pepper chocolates and chocolate lace cookies. Chocolate gelato and chocolate walnut bread. Amazing miniature chocolate bowls that were hand painted to look exactly like porcelain. Champagne chocolate truffles. And a rich chocolate cake displayed in a small, round pillow-top hat box with a wildflower bouquet perched on top.

"I guess chocolate's not just for dessert anymore," joked Theodosia.

"That cake in the hat box?" said Haley, looking slightly in awe. "Over at the Yellow Bird Gift Shop it retails for a whopping one hundred and eighty dollars."

"Awfully steep," admitted Theodosia. Who would pay so much, she wondered, for a cake?

"And see over here?" said Haley, pointing. "A layered chocolate truffle made from seventy percent Criollo cocoa from Venezuela—the best in the world—layered with creamy ganache and infused with real truffle oil." She paused, as if a certain reality was sinking in. "I don't have a chance."

"Yes, you do!" enthused Theodosia. "Your entries hold their own beautifully."

"You think?" said Haley, a little wistfully.

"Look at it this way," said Theodosia. "You took fourth place last year; now it's your turn to move up the ladder."

"What if I slide down a few rungs?" asked Haley, as they headed for their table in the main dining room.

"There's no shame in trying," said Theodosia. "You've given it your best shot; now the decision rests in the hands of the judges." Suddenly catching sight of an overly animated woman in a bright yellow dress, Theodosia added, "Uh-oh, do you see who I see?"

"Huh?" asked Haley, head turning, hair swishing.

"I think Delaine is seated at our table."

"Oh, she is," said Haley. "I peeked at the place cards earlier."

"Delaine's probably going to be bubbling over about her fashion show this Friday. Ah well."

"You weren't planning to attend?" Haley asked.

"Not unless I get my arm twisted," murmured Theodosia.

Of course Delaine spotted them immediately.

"The-o-dosia!" Delaine called, in a frenetic, high-pitched voice. "Over heeeere!"

"Prepare to get twisted," murmured Haley, as Delaine Dish came speedballing at them, taking rapid-fire baby steps in four-inch stiletto heels.

"Long time no see! Long time no see!" cried Delaine, cooing little greetings and peppering them with air-kisses. With her lovely heart-shaped face, inquisitive violet eyes, and dark hair wound up into a psyche knot atop her head, Delaine was beauty with an attitude. A whirling dervish filled with energy, self-confidence, and boundless curiosity. She was also proprietor of Cotton Duck, one of Charleston's finest boutiques. Delaine's shop featured racks of elegant, airy cotton clothing that was perfectly suited to stand up to Charleston's high heat and humidity. She also stocked silk tunics, filmy tops, long evening dresses, scarves the weight of butterfly wings, strands of pearls, swishy skirts, and even a few racks of vintage clothes. Delaine's latest addition included several high-end lingerie lines, including La Perla, Cosabella, and Guia La Bruna from Italy.

"Looks like we're at your table," said Theodosia, trying to extricate herself from Delaine's firm grip. A grip that felt like it would leave talon marks on her arm.

Delaine wasn't having it. "I'm so *happy* I ran into you, sweetie," she gushed. "I wanted to *personally* invite you to my trunk show this Friday afternoon at Cotton Duck." She released Theodosia's arm only to place both hands on Theodosia's shoulders and exert another vicelike grip. "You're *coming*, aren't you? Please tell me you are!"

"If I had to take a wild guess," said Haley, trying hard to keep a straight face, "I'd say she's coming."

"Of course, I'll come," said Theodosia. It was like being captured by terrorists. She'd say anything to negotiate a release.

Delaine let Theodosia go and clasped her hands to her chest in joy. "Thank goodness! Where would I be without my very dearest friend!"

Dearest friend? thought Theodosia. *Lord love a duck, am I really Delaine's dearest friend?* Then she decided that, based on Delaine's over-the-top theatrics, she might be her only friend.

Delaine leaned in and whispered in Theodosia's ear, "Please don't bring up anything about that awful business that happened during the back-alley crawl, will you?"

Her words gob-smacked Theodosia right between the eyes. *Awful business? That's one way to categorize it. Another might be murder.*

"Come, come," Delaine cried brightly, as she shepherded Theodosia and Haley toward their table. "See who else is sitting with us! The ladies from Popple Hill Design!"

Theodosia and Haley slipped into their seats, grateful to be diverted from the slightly manic Delaine, and greeted warmly by Marianne Petigru and Hillary Retton, two lady decorators who, in the last five years, had managed to make Popple Hill one of the top interior design firms in Charleston. Marianne Petigru was tall and thin, with short, spiky blond hair. She was also old Charleston society and knew her way around the Heritage Society, Opera Society, Theater Guild, Art Institute, and the various parties and black-tie dinners that were part and parcel of Charleston society. Her business partner, Hillary Retton, was shorter, dark-haired, and, although she'd been residing in Charleston for a good ten years, was still considered somewhat of an outsider.

"How fortuitous we're all seated together!" exclaimed Delaine. "Our dear Theodosia just purchased that adorable little cottage down the block from the Featherbed House Bed and Breakfast, and she is in *dire* need of a decorating consult!"

"I heard you bought Hazelhurst," drawled Marianne, referring to the name that the cottage bore on Charleston's list of historic places. "A charming little abode." She herself owned an enormous 1850s Victorian mansion replete with multigabled roof, turrets, domed skylight, and all the requisite gingerbread trim. "I just hope your cottage is structurally sound," continued Marianne. "My place may be listed on the historic register, but it's still a futsy old albatross with a mind of its own. It's been seven years since we moved in, and we're still dealing with a bad foundation."

"That sinking feeling," quipped Hillary.

But Marianne just shook her head, almost to the point of fuming now. "You put money into the ground, you never see it again. *Nobody* does. And the fees construction companies charge—positively criminal."

"I think my cottage is structurally okay," said Theodosia. "At least the building inspector gave it a passing grade."

"Thank your lucky stars," said Marianne.

"And it doesn't need that much decorating, does it?" asked

Hillary. "As I recall, there's a small marble entryway and fairly decent wood flooring."

"The cottage is all very Old World," Theodosia told them. "And in fairly good condition. I'll probably need to install new draperies, but that's not such a big deal."

"We can surely help with that," Hillary told her.

"Think about slubbed silk with Parisian pleated sheers," suggested Marianne.

"And you're moving in two weeks?" asked Delaine. "Theo, dear, you really must take advantage of these two decorating geniuses."

"Two weeks will fly by . . ." Hillary snapped her fingers. "Like that."

"Actually," said Theodosia, "there's a slight problem."

"I'm sure it's nothing that can't be fixed," said Delaine in a self-assured tone of voice. "You can always slip an extra twenty to the . . ."

"The State Archaeology Office wants to dig up the back-yard," Theodosia told them.

Delaine, Marianne, and Hillary collectively inhaled, then exclaimed, in unison, "What!"

And so, over chilled strawberry and chocolate soup, goat cheese and pumpkin seed arugula salads accented with white chocolate bits, and chocolate chicken mole, Theodosia related to her rapt audience how Earl Grey had discovered the strange bone, why Tred Pascal had suggested a small dig, and how her long-awaited move might have to be postponed for a couple of weeks.

"That's the craziest thing I ever heard," said Delaine. "Bones." She gave a derisive snort. "Who gives a rat's back-side about a bunch of old bones?"

"Obviously the State Archaeology Office," Haley quipped in a droll tone.

"And you don't want to mess with them," agreed Marianne,

looking serious. "I know a woman who owns an old plantation house over in Georgetown County near the South Santee River. Last year her gardener was using a rototiller and unwittingly discovered some kind of primitive, stone-age tool made from a deer leg. Long story short, she had to abandon her tomato patch for the entire summer just so the State Archaeology Office could take a closer look."

Delaine made a face. "An old deer leg. Makes you want to rethink venison, doesn't it?"

"Or planting tomatoes," said Haley.

"They're only going to poke around in the backyard," said Theodosia. "It's not like they want to excavate five stories down or dismantle the entire house. I mean, how long can something like that take?"

Delaine rolled her eyes. "If I were you, sweetie, I'd put all your moving plans on hold."

"Please don't say that," murmured Theodosia. But Marianne only nodded sagely.

Keeping to the theme of Chocolatier Fest, the dessert the Dorchester Club served was a showstopping assortment of chocolate cakes, cookies, and candies. Waiters brought out three-tiered trays, similar to the ones Theodosia used at her tea shop, filled chockablock with the most delightful chocolate goodies.

"Is that a chocolate-covered orange peel?" asked Delaine, as a waiter placed their tray in the center of their table.

"Agrumelli," said Haley. "Almond paste pillows stuffed with zest of lemon and orange. And that's a honeyed caramel. And it all looks very good." She glanced around, then let loose a nervous high-pitched sound, a cross between a giggle and a sigh.

"It won't be long now," Theodosia told Haley, who was starting to jitterbug in her seat.

"Theo, dear," said Delaine, as she pulled out her makeup kit and reapplied a slick of mauve lip gloss, "have you had a chance to visit that new Jardin Perfumerie that opened down the block from you?"

"Theodosia's not only been there," said Haley, looking slightly frazzled, "they even offered to create a personal fragrance for her."

Delaine snapped the cap back on her lip gloss and managed a surprised double take. "A *personal* fragrance? Really?"

"Might be fun," said Theodosia.

"Well, la-de-da," said Delaine, sounding positively jealous. "Aren't you the indulgent one."

A tap on Theodosia's shoulder was a welcome diversion from Delaine. But when Theodosia swiveled in her chair and saw who it was, she inwardly cringed.

Bill Glass, the publisher of *Shooting Star*, Charleston's local, glossy gossip tabloid, flashed a wide grin at her, along with lots of white, Chiclet-sized teeth.

"Glass," muttered Theodosia. Bill Glass, with his slicked back hair and olive skin, wasn't a bad-looking man. But it was his condescending and cavalier attitude that constantly rubbed her the wrong way. Basically, Bill Glass was Charleston's local version of a paparazzo, a self-absorbed, self-indulgent photographer and publisher who adored rubbing elbows with society and loved it even more when they screwed up. Preferably in front of his camera.

"Some shindig, huh?" he asked Theodosia. "I thought skinny society-type ladies never indulged in dessert. In fact, I thought they only lived on air and water. 'Course, you're not all that skinny."

"What are you doing here?" Theodosia asked, with thinly disguised contempt.

Glass held up his Nikon camera. "Just grabbing a few quick shots. I live for the moment when some society babe tips back too many Cosmos or gets a sugar buzz and dives headfirst into a potted plant. But, hey, that ain't nuthin' compared to the excitement you guys had Monday night." He flashed another callous, careless grin. "Looks like your best-laid plans went awry, huh? Sorry I missed all the excitement."

"Excuse me?" said Theodosia in a cool voice. Glass, as editor of his own mini *Enquirer*, really was a scuzzball.

"The back-alley crawl was *your* idea, right?" Glass asked. "Obviously it backfired big time. Didn't count on capping off the event with a brutal murder, huh?"

"Could you please get away from our table?" snapped Delaine. "You're really quite boring." Even though Delaine was incredibly rude in her treatment of Glass, Theodosia practically applauded her. Served him right.

"Yeah, yeah," muttered Glass, fidgeting with his camera lens. "Maybe I'll run into some of you lovelies later on. Once this happy crap is over I'm gonna hit Church Street and grab a few interior shots of that new perfume joint." He smirked. "Don't mind too much 'cause that Cinnamon St. John babe is quite a looker." As if that wasn't bad enough, he added a nasty sound effect: "Grrrr."

Haley stared at Glass with narrowed eyes. "Do you really think your ridiculous, outdated machismo impresses women?"

"Honey, I know it does," boasted Glass.

"In that case," said Haley, "I think we just determined what type of woman you prefer."

"Shhhh!" hissed Delaine, as a man in a tuxedo stepped to the podium and tapped a finger against the microphone. "They're going to announce the winners." She shot a quick glance at Haley. "Honey, I just hope you're not too disappointed."

"Delaine!" said Theodosia, as Glass scuttled toward the

podium. "Haley needs support, not pessimism." She turned to Haley and gave a hopeful, commiserating smile. "Whatever happens, you'll be just fine, Haley."

Haley clapped her hands over her ears and scrunched up her face. "You tell me what happens, Theo. I'm too nervous to listen!"

10

❦

"You're back!" squealed Miss Dimple. Short, plump, with a perpetual grandmotherly expression on her apple-cheeked face, Miss Dimple was Theodosia's freelance accountant who also adored filling in at the tea shop.

"Not only are we back," cried a jubilant Haley, "but we've returned victorious!" Haley thrust her trophy, a pink-and-chocolate-colored enamel cupcake sprinkled with brilliant crystals, into the air for everyone to see. "Look! We brought home the Silver Cupcake Award!"

"Oh my goodness," exclaimed Miss Dimple, grabbing her hot-pink glasses from the beaded chain around her neck and popping them onto her nose. "Let me take a look at that."

"Well done!" chimed in Drayton as he joined the admiration society. "I never doubted you for a minute, Haley."

"Now that's a trophy!" declared Miss Dimple. "And I love that glittery pink!"

"Yes . . . it is a rather vivid strawberry pink," said Drayton.

"Pepto pink," declared Miss Dimple.

Drayton put an arm around Miss Dimple's shoulders. "I love how you think, my dear."

"I hope lunch went okay," said Haley, setting her trophy on the front counter and quickly checking the tea room where three tables of customers still lingered.

"Using the nomenclature of the day, it was a piece of cake," said Drayton. "Since you had everything so carefully prepared for us."

"We had a fine time," said Miss Dimple. "We served everyone tea and complimentary scones, then I plated in the kitchen, while Drayton delivered the orders."

"Like clockwork," said Drayton.

"But your watch is always slow," pointed out Haley.

Drayton pursed his lips. "Like I said, clockwork."

"So we didn't miss much," said Theodosia. She was relieved the lunch hour had gone so smoothly.

"Only a phone call from your newfound friend, Miss Cinnamon," said Drayton. "She called . . . perhaps ten minutes ago? Apparently her aunt . . . a Miss Kitty . . . ?"

Theodosia nodded. "That's right."

"Ah, yes," continued Drayton. "This Miss Kitty is now in attendance at said perfumery and Miss Cinnamon has cordially extended an invitation for you to come meet her."

"Hello Kitty," giggled Haley, still riding high from her victory.

Drayton peered down his nose at Haley. "But who are we to question a person's name, when it's undoubtedly a pet name or term of endearment."

"I guess," said Haley.

"Huh," said Theodosia. She had a certain curiosity about Miss Kitty. "Okay, if there's nothing crushing for me to handle at the moment, maybe I'll take some tea and scones down to them." She threw a questioning look at Miss Dimple. "We have scones left?"

"Goodness yes, dear," said Miss Dimple. "Do you want me to pack some up for you?"

"I can do it," Theodosia told her, "but if you have time to step in the back office with me, I can give you the receipts for the last ten days."

"Back to reality," said Miss Dimple.

"Your day job," said Haley.

Miss Dimple gazed at Theodosia, Drayton, and Haley, with a beatific smile on her face. "You do realize that working here is my fantasy job, don't you?"

"Sometimes it feels like a fantasy to me, too," remarked Drayton.

"So you're Theodosia!" exclaimed Miss Kitty, in a tumble of words and a cloud of perfume. "Come in, dear, and let me get a good look at you. Cinnamon has told me so much about you!"

"All good, I hope," said Theodosia. She handed her indigo blue bag of tea and scones to Cinnamon and blinked as she beheld the rather amazing Miss Kitty. In her well-tailored purple suit, red silk blouse with a pussycat bow, and at least eight ginormous diamond rings twinkling from almost every finger, Miss Kitty looked like a cross between a saloon girl and a widow who'd run through three or four rich husbands. She weighed maybe ninety pounds soaking wet, with blue-tinted hair that was teased, swooped, and swirled into a creative bouffant hairdo worthy of a Motown singer from the sixties. Her lined countenance was rouged and powdered, her eyebrows plucked into thin apostrophes. And her eyes, dark, dark brown with tiny glints of green in the center of the irises, were the eyes of a magpie. Inquisitive and curious.

Eyes that probably wouldn't miss much, whatever happened to be going on.

"So lovely to finally meet you," said Theodosia, trying to reserve judgment on this animated, birdlike woman. "Cinnamon's told me so much about you, too." As the words sprang from her mouth, Theodosia realized that Cinnamon really hadn't told her much of anything. She'd mentioned that Miss Kitty was the doyenne of the shop and that she'd once worked in Paris. But those were fairly broad strokes. No, Theodosia decided, she really hadn't gleaned any definitive, concrete information about Miss Kitty at all, who, from her piercing, calculating stare, looked like she wasn't born yesterday.

Miss Kitty grasped Theodosia's hand with both of her tiny, bony hands. "Delighted to meet another Church Street neighbor," she purred. "Ya'll have made my niece and I feel so doggone welcome."

"You're from Charleston originally?" asked Theodosia.

Miss Kitty released Theodosia's hand and waved hers in an imperious gesture. In doing so, her rings caught the overhead pinpoint spotlights and sent a kaleidoscope of sparkles dancing across the tops of bottles. "I've lived here before, yes," said Miss Kitty. "Lived lots of different places. Good for a person to move around, broadens their outlook on life."

"I don't know if Cinnamon told you," said Theodosia, deciding to play the whole encounter as straight as possible, "but I'm quite in love with your shop."

Miss Kitty gave a satisfied nod. "It's getting there. Of course, we still have merchandise pouring in."

"I can't imagine where you'll put it," said Theodosia. "Plus, you already carry a galaxy of amazing scents!"

"And I can't wait to add more," said Miss Kitty. She spun slightly, let her fingers fly lightly across the tops of several bottles as she spoke. "Look at this," she said picking up a tall bottle. "Hermès Vanille Galante."

"Very expensive," murmured Cinnamon.

Miss Kitty's apostrophes shot skyward. "Two hundred thirty-five dollars a bottle. And worth every drop." With a touch of pure drama, she swept a hand above a display table, like a hostess on *The Price Is Right*. "And over here, Miller Harris Fleurs de Bois, as well as Narciso Rodriguez Essence, and Badgley Mischka Couture. Which really *is* couture." She gave a self-satisfied smile. "You can't find these scents just anywhere."

"This is Shalini by Maurice Roucel," said Cinnamon, holding up a bottle. "Nine hundred dollars for two-point-two ounces."

"We also carry Eau d'Hadrien by Annick Goutal. Fifteen hundred dollars for three-point-four ounces. Sicilian lemons, grapefruit, and cypress."

"Very impressive," said Theodosia, trying to maintain her neutral stance.

"Of course, not everything is sky-high expensive," explained Cinnamon. "We also offer a fabulous line of French sachets and essences, as well as these handmade soaps in beaded organza lace bags. You see? The bags are studded with tiny seed pearls . . ."

"They're breathtaking," said Theodosia. Could she use something like that for her T-Bath products? Maybe. Something to look into. Amp up the razzle-dazzle factor, which was certainly in generous supply inside this shop.

"Show Theodosia our Egyptian perfume bottles," said Miss Kitty, self-consciously pausing to retie the bow on her blouse. Or was that posing, Theodosia wondered?

Cinnamon handed Theodosia a tall, elegant bottle topped with a fancy gold atomizer. "Leaded glass hand-etched by artisans. And the gold top is from Venice. Very difficult to obtain."

"We were lucky to get our hands on a dozen," said Miss Kitty.

"Our goal here," said Cinnamon, "is to be a veritable perfume emporium. Offer a far greater selection than even the finest department store."

"Like a Middle Eastern souk or bazaar," intoned Miss Kitty.

Theodosia's eyes bounced from glamorous display to elegant arrangement. There truly was a dazzling array of perfumes, apothecary bottles, French milled soaps, bath soap on a rope, scented candles, and couture cosmetics.

"We even offer a series of mix-and-match scents," said Miss Kitty. She picked up three small, colorful bottles. "You can wear these fragrances individually or layer two or three at a time."

"Seriously?" said Theodosia. She'd never heard of such a thing.

"Oh absolutely," said Cinnamon. "You could spray one on the nape of your neck, another on your wrists—well, you get the idea."

Theodosia had to admit she was enthralled. "And the scents are . . . ?"

"We carry spring orchid, red ginger, vanilla bean, champagne musk, and lavender," said Miss Kitty. "Did you know there are two hundred varieties of lavender?"

"I do now," said Theodosia.

Cinnamon smiled. "As I mentioned earlier, we'd be delighted to create a personal fragrance just for you."

"Mmm," said Miss Kitty, narrowing her eyes. "I'm thinking bergamot as a top note, jasmine for the heart note, and possibly sandalwood as a base note." She gave a tiny shrug and her tiny hands flew up. "A thousand ways to go, but the ultimate accessory, no?"

"It certainly would be," agreed Theodosia. "I was telling

Cinnamon this morning that I always considered my tea shop to be a bouquet of scents, but your shop trumps it totally."

"Oh my, yes." Miss Kitty laughed. "And we do try to swoon regularly."

"We've experienced such an amazing rush of customers," said Cinnamon, "as well as so many mail orders, that we're already thinking about expanding."

"Our initial plan was to slowly grow a loyal customer base," explained Miss Kitty. "But now there's a good chance that old map shop next door will be available shortly, so I'm pushing my niece to begin negotiations with the landlord." She wrinkled her nose and added, "Sad about that poor girl who got killed, but it really is an awful place filled with dusty old maps."

Theodosia gazed at Miss Kitty and decided that she didn't seem one bit sad at all. More like . . . opportunistic.

"Of course, the map shop would require *tons* of cleaning," added Cinnamon.

"I've always found the Antiquarian Map Shop quite charming," said Theodosia.

Miss Kitty shrugged. "Probably is, dear, if you're in the proper frame of mind for such things. No doubt it's my learned nose that keeps me from appreciating the . . . shall we say *variances* . . . of the place."

"It's been amazing," said Theodosia, "learning about all your various perfumes. But I'm afraid we let the tea go cold."

"Not to worry," said Cinnamon. "We have a microwave in back."

Miss Kitty grabbed Theodosia's hand and patted it. "It's been lovely to make your acquaintance, dear. We keep hearing from everyone up and down Church Street how plugged in you are to the community and the historic district. And that you're socially conscious and involved in dozens of interesting events. I understand your little tea shop is even catering a book signing at the Heritage Society."

"This Saturday night," said Theodosia. "It's going to be a smaller gathering. After the reading and audience questions, we'll have a candlelight reception out on the patio. Champagne, tea . . . an assortment of sweets and savories."

"Then you must let us donate the candles!" chirped Cinnamon.

"Maybe the Phoenicia cedar candles," said Miss Kitty. "They're so uplifting and warm. Or possibly soy candles or some lovely hand-dipped tapers." With a perplexed look, she turned to Theodosia and asked, "What do *you* think, dear?"

"I'm sure anything you select will be greatly appreciated," said Theodosia.

"The soy votive candles then," proclaimed Cinnamon. "Perfect for an outdoor tea. And here, take one of our silver candle lighters along with you."

Miss Kitty shuddered. "Absolutely *must* use a candle lighter. Matches are so déclassé!"

That was a trip and a half, Theodosia decided as she strolled back to her tea shop. Miss Kitty had been positively manic and Cinnamon also seemed swept up in a perfume delirium. Were they just two crazy ladies who were nuts over fragrance? Or was something more sinister at work here? They did, after all, seem more than ready to snatch up the lease on the Antiquarian Map Shop.

And if they did negotiate for that space, where would the maps go, Theodosia wondered? And who exactly would they go to? She supposed that Daria's mother would sell them at auction. Or would Jason Pritchard find his backer and somehow buy out the inventory? Of course, finding a backer, running a shop, and making enough money to cover a lease were all difficult undertakings. Handling one aspect was tricky enough, let alone all three.

As she stopped in front of the Cabbage Patch gift shop to gaze at a Fitz and Floyd rabbit teapot in their window, Theodosia noticed Burt Tidwell slowly strolling down Church Street. With his hands clasped behind his back, stomach protruding from between his tweed jacket, and beetled brows set in a scowl, Tidwell looked utterly lost in thought.

So of course Theodosia immediately accosted him.

"A return to the scene of the crime?" she asked Tidwell, then grimaced at her own words. She hadn't meant to come across so flippant.

Tidwell didn't seem a bit surprised to see her. "I am, in a manner of speaking," he responded. "I've been conducting face-to-face interviews with various Church Street shopkeepers."

"Have you learned anything new?"

"Possibly," responded Tidwell. "Memory is a tricky thing. Some witnesses can recall *more* information after a couple of days have gone by."

"Any information you'd care to share with me?" Theodosia asked him.

Tidwell assumed a puckish expression. "Not unless you've suddenly passed the lieutenant's test with flying colors and been hired by the CPD."

Tidwell's words didn't dissuade Theodosia in the least. "Any word from your forensics lab yet? And I'm referencing the murder weapon, not the bone Earl Grey dug up."

Tidwell pursed his lips. "Yes, I heard about your bone."

"And the murder weapon?"

Tidwell set his face in a tolerant smile. "My, my, aren't we the eager little investigator."

"What do *you* think the killer used to strangle Daria?" Theodosia asked, plowing ahead. "Twine? Wire? A belt?"

She drew a breath, blew it out slowly. "Take a wild flier here, Detective Tidwell. Stun me with your brilliant speculation."

"I don't speculate," Tidwell said in an icy tone. "I postulate."

"There's a difference?" Theodosia asked.

"There is to me."

Waggling her fingers at him, Theodosia said, "Okay, then postulate."

Tidwell sucked air in through his front teeth and rocked back on his heels, looking for all the world like a large Toby mug. "Possibly a cotton rope," he told her. "Something similar to a wash line."

"Just rope," said Theodosia, her voice tinged with disappointment. Somehow, her mind had conjured up something far more exotic. A leather strap that could be traced to a certain shop. Or perhaps an unusual type of chain.

"Garden-variety rope," repeated Tidwell. He seemed to take pleasure in deflating her.

"Okay," said Theodosia, changing course. "What do you know about Jack Brux?"

Tidwell lowered his head and glowered at her. "And why would you bring up his name?"

"Just because Brux seemed to have a beef with Daria. He tried to buy a particular map from her that she didn't want to sell. And then he was sort of lurking in the alley last night . . ."

"He lives nearby," said Tidwell.

"Still," said Theodosia, unwilling to let it go. "Brux has a nasty temper."

"Did it ever occur to you," said Tidwell, "that you might have badgered the man unduly?"

"Not really," said Theodosia.

"Why does your answer not surprise me," said Tidwell. He withdrew a black leather notebook from his pocket and made a few scribbles.

"Something I said?" asked Theodosia.

Tidwell's jowls sloshed. "Another matter entirely. There's been a rash of truck hijackings lately. Coffee, processed meats, frozen shrimp, fine wines—a trailer can be worth anywhere between twenty thousand and one million dollars these days. Anyway, a request has come down from on high to see if I might possibly put two and two together."

"You?" asked Theodosia.

"I do head the *Robbery*-Homicide division," he snapped. "And now, since I have a great deal of work . . ." He executed an amazingly quick spin for such a large man and lumbered off down the street.

"Hmm," said Theodosia, as she continued down Church Street, pondering the irascible Jack Brux, noodling Tidwell's remark about rope.

It wasn't until Theodosia had her hand on the front door of the Indigo Tea Shop that she remembered the display of soap on a rope at Jardin Perfumerie.

11

※

"*What's he doing* here?" Theodosia asked as she stepped inside the tea shop. She jerked her head toward the small table in the corner where Bill Glass sat nibbling a scone.

"He just showed up," said Drayton, looking like he didn't want any part of Theodosia's problem with Glass. "You didn't want me to be rude to the man, did you?"

"Turnabout is fair play," murmured Theodosia as she headed for Glass's table.

Glass saw her coming and favored her with a smarmy, too-broad smile. "Hello there, Miz Browning. We meet again."

"What are you doing here?" she asked him.

Bill Glass lifted his teacup, waggled it in midair, then set it back down. "Enjoying the lovely food and hospitality of your tea shop. At least I hope there's hospitality aplenty here." Then his voice hardened. "Aren't you the sly one. Not telling me about the bone."

"There's nothing to tell," responded Theodosia.

Glass waved an index finger back and forth in an accusatory gesture. "That's not what I hear. It appears your happy new home may be the exact spot where captured pirates were summarily executed. Death by hanging, that sort of thing." He gave a quick but mirthless grin, his dark eyes drilling into her.

"Why would that interest you?" asked Theodosia. "You publish a glossy *gossip* rag. You speculate on which hostess feuded with which guest. What Charleston society lady is looking a trifle stretched across the cheekbones. Who wasn't invited back to serve as a board member. The really important news of the day."

"You make my job sound so glamorous," smirked Glass, reaching for his Nikon. "Still, pirates and old bones are exciting stuff. Imparts a certain *creep factor* that helps sell magazines." Aiming his camera directly at Theodosia, he clicked off a quick series of shots. "Right up there with sightings of Elvis and UFOs that have crash landed."

"Stop it!" cried Theodosia, holding up a hand as if to ward off evil. "Please don't do that!"

"I can see the headline now," laughed Glass. "Haunted Hazelhurst."

"Don't you dare!" seethed Theodosia.

Theodosia was still fuming when Bill Glass picked up and left some five minutes later.

"Don't waste your energy on him," Drayton advised. "The man simply isn't worth it." He turned toward Haley, who'd crept out of the kitchen to catch the fireworks. "How was it you so aptly phrased it?"

"The man occupies so much space in your head, you oughta charge him rent," said Haley, grinning crookedly at Theodosia.

"Pithy verbiage, wouldn't you agree?" asked Drayton.

"Glass isn't inside my head," Theodosia told them, "he's stuck in my craw."

"Oh, that's entirely different," said Drayton, raising one quivering eyebrow.

"Theo," said Haley, "what if I gave you my award?"

That stopped Theodosia in her tracks. "Haley, what are you talking about?"

"You're one of the kindest, gentlest people I know," said Haley. "But you're working yourself into an absolute frizzle-frazzle over a guy who publishes a crappy tabloid. Think about it."

Theodosia did. For about two seconds. "You're right," she told Haley. "The whole thing's ridiculous. Okay." Her hands fluttered about her head, as if to stir up any residual negative energy. "I hereby banish him from my thoughts."

"Banish who?" asked Miss Dimple, emerging from the kitchen, wiping her hands on an embroidered tea towel.

"I can't even remember," said Theodosia. At which point the bell over the front door tinkled and Angie Congdon strolled in.

"Oh my gosh!" exclaimed Theodosia, putting a hand to her mouth. "The Featherbed House. We're supposed to cater your open house tomorrow night!"

Angie suddenly looked nervous. "You didn't forget, did you?" she asked in a quavering voice. Angie Congdon was the proprietor of the Featherbed House B and B, one of the premier B and Bs in Charleston's historic district. Her short, curly blond hair set off a friendly oval face that flashed a perpetually welcoming smile. Guests loved Angie and passed out recommendations like jelly beans. As a result, Angie's website was filled with glowing customer testimonials.

"I didn't forget completely," said Theodosia. "I just relegated your event to the back burner. Apologies, Angie, now you're cooking like mad on my front burner."

"Mine, too," chimed in Haley.

"Glad to hear it," said Angie, "since I'm unable to stuff a cherry tomato or render a decent pinwheel sandwich if my life depended on it. Which puts me utterly at your mercy."

"Of course, we're doing your catering," Theodosia told her.

"Wait a minute," Haley said to Angie. "Back up. You always manage to lay out a lovely wine and cheese board every evening for your guests at the Featherbed House. *That* requires some culinary skill."

"No, it doesn't," said Angie. "That's just popping corks and cubing cheese."

"Tell you what," said Theodosia, "let's sit down and figure out a few nice appetizers for you to serve."

"Actually," said Angie, "I was hoping you'd serve them."

"No problem," said Theodosia. "Haley, are you up for an extra catering gig?"

"For Angie?" Haley grinned. "Sure. Anytime."

"Take the big table," said Drayton, "so you can spread out and noodle your ideas around. Haley, grab that Brown Betty teapot and help me with refills for our afternoon guests. Then I've got to study my feng shui book."

"*How many B* and Bs are taking part in the open house?" asked Theodosia.

Angie slid a colorful brochure across the table and said, "Eight tomorrow night, fourteen on Friday. Almost every one in the historic district."

"Wow," said Theodosia. "I didn't realize we had so many."

Angie grinned. "Tells you how popular our little sliver of Charleston is, doesn't it?

"The chamber of commerce estimates we get about four and a half million visitors a year," said Theodosia. "So I guess they have to stay somewhere."

"I'm hoping they'll start booking with me," said Angie. "Business has been a little slow lately."

"Lots of businesses feeling the pinch," said Theodosia. "So tell me about open house night. Who, what, when, where, and why?"

"The main thing," said Angie, "is that our Innkeeper's Association wants to really showcase the B and Bs. Get locals as well as visitors to do the walking tour and visit the B and Bs. Then, hopefully, stay with us or make favorable recommendations to friends and relatives. Also, since an awful lot of B and Bs are located in some of our finer old mansions, we want to tell visitors a little bit about the history of the different homes. Impart some fun, historical facts. You know, like who built the place, what's the architectural style, any resident ghosts walking the halls, that sort of thing."

"Your promotion sounds very well thought out," said Theodosia. In her former life as a marketing executive, she knew how important it was to create an event that was newsworthy, able to draw a crowd, and was also promotable.

"That's not all," said Angie. "We'll also be selling our *Historic District Innkeeper's Cookbook.*"

"Oh, you finally self-published," said Theodosia. "Good for you."

"Over a hundred pages," said Angie. "And, believe me, it wasn't easy pulling it all together. Innkeepers can be fairly dysfunctional when it comes to working together and meeting deadlines."

"Lot of that going around," said Theodosia. "Did Drayton give you one of his recipes for the cookbook?"

"Thank goodness, yes," said Angie. "He gave me his recipe for Charleston breakfast casserole. Mostly because I couldn't conjure up a single recipe on my own." She laughed and pushed a fluff of hair off her forehead. "There's a reason Mrs. Klingberg comes in every morning to cook breakfast for my guests. If I had to whip up eggs Benedict or French toast on my own, it would be a kitchen nightmare. Think egg yolks dripping from the chandelier and puddles of pancake syrup."

"Makes for sticky going," agreed Theodosia. "But what you lack in cooking skills you make up for with hospitality and amazing service. Most innkeepers don't go out of their way like you do with coffee and croissants midmorning, wine and cheese in the evening, handmade feather beds, a beautiful backyard patio garden, and arrangements for special walking tours."

"We try." Angie sighed.

"So we'll need finger food for tomorrow night," said Theodosia. "Along with . . . what? Tea? Wine? Cider? Champagne?"

"I think maybe tea and wine," said Angie. "And if you have an interesting tea idea up your sleeve, this might be the time to pull it out."

"I do," said Theodosia. "Or, rather, Drayton does. He discovered the most wonderful pomegranate oolong and everyone who's had a taste has gone gaga for it."

"Then that's our tea," said Angie. "To serve with . . ."

Theodosia had her pen out and was jotting ideas. "How about pimento and walnut tea sandwiches, roast beef and cheddar tea sandwiches, and miniature apple-raisin scones?"

"Wow," declared Angie. "You make it sound so easy." She grinned. "Guess you've done this before."

"A few times," said Theodosia, as she opened the brochure Angie had given her and scanned it. "So your open house starts at seven?"

"Right," said Angie. She hesitated. "And you can bring teacups? I know I don't have nearly enough."

"Not a problem," said Theodosia, thinking about the boxes and boxes of teacups she had stashed in her upstairs apartment. Probably more one-of-a-kind teacups than a crazed tea tippler could go through in a lifetime. They were going along to the new house, so she'd have to locate some very gentle movers.

"Now I have to ask," said Angie, touching a hand to Theodosia's sleeve. "Have you heard anything more from the police? About Daria?" Angie had phoned Theodosia the morning after the murder to express her dismay. Now she, like most inhabitants of the historic district, were waiting with bated breath for news the killer had been apprehended.

"I ran into Detective Tidwell about an hour ago," Theodosia told her. "Unfortunately, he was wearing his typical Easter Island face."

"So no information," said Angie. "But what exactly was the great detective detecting? Do you think he's seriously on the case?"

"He is as far as I can tell," said Theodosia. "And he did share one tiny shred of information with me."

"What's that?" asked Angie, her eyes going big.

"Tidwell said he thought Daria might have been strangled with rope. Basic ordinary clothesline is how he put it."

"Oh," said Angie, looking disappointed. "That could come from anywhere. Plus, isn't it difficult to trace something like that?" She glanced about the tea room and leaned forward, dropping her voice. "And how goes it with the backyard bones?"

Theodosia sat back in her chair. "You heard about that?"

"The rumor mill's been going crazy," admitted Angie. "Hard to keep something like that under wraps."

"Why don't they just run a big fat announcement in the *Post and Courier*?" murmured Theodosia.

Angie bit her lip. "Don't say that. They just might!"

12

"*You're looking awfully* tricked out for a beach party," Theodosia told Drayton as he clambered stiffly into the front seat of her Jeep. Tonight he'd varied his appearance only slightly, donning a navy blue sport coat, gray slacks, and pink bow tie. Very snappy. She, on the other hand was dressed in white slacks and a blue-and-white striped French sailor's T-shirt. *Tres* casual.

"It's not exactly a picnic," said Drayton. "There's a reason they call it the *Blessing* of the Fleet."

"Sure," said Theodosia, "but there's also going to be music, food booths, and probably goofy stuff like face painting and funnel cakes. And the event is being held at White Point Gardens, which is technically a park."

"Shoes," said Drayton, pointing to his loafers. "I made a concession to casual dressing with my choice of footwear."

"You're right," Theodosia chuckled, as she pulled away from the curb. "It's like you stepped out of a J.Crew catalog."

"Where's Earl Grey?" asked Drayton, adjusting his seat

belt. "I thought for sure you'd bring him along. After all, this is one occasion where canine sidekicks are probably welcome."

"Cleo Hollander from Big Paw picked him up earlier and took him over to the Cranston Elder House on Sullivan's Island," said Theodosia. Earl Grey was a trained therapy dog, certified under the auspices of Big Paw, Charleston's very own service dog organization. As such, Earl Grey made regular visits to children's hospitals, senior citizens' homes, and hospices. Most of the time Theodosia accompanied him, taking tearful delight in the sight of a sick child grinning with glee as she cradled Earl Grey's furry head. Or watching an eighty-seven-year-old woman whoop with joy as she tossed a rubber ball down a hallway and Earl Grey came bounding back with the ball only to deposit it gently in her lap.

"Sounds like Earl Grey's enjoying his own social outing," said Drayton.

"He really loves it," said Theodosia. "And he's *good* at interacting with people." When she'd found Earl Grey in her back alley, he'd been a starving puppy huddled in a cardboard box, trying to get out of the rain. She'd worried that he'd never get over the trauma of abandonment, but gentle words and a loving home had more than brought Earl Grey out of his shell. And when he'd begun training as a therapy dog, he'd reveled in the attention and the feeling of being needed. Theodosia had a theory about that. It was almost as though Earl Grey realized what a lucky guy he was and wanted to help bring joy to others.

"You're right," said Drayton, as they meandered past stands of palmettos and live oak trees, then caught sight of the park with its booths, bands, and crowds. "It looks like a carnival swept into town. No dancing bears or sword swallowers, but still plenty of whoop-de-doo."

"A Blessing of the Fleet is supposed to be joyous," said Theodosia, "not a straight-laced, all-day Calvinist prayer meeting. A blessing can be fun, too, don't you think?"

"Of course," responded Drayton, "I just didn't realize it entailed people sipping alcoholic drinks."

"Just beer and wine," Theodosia told him. "See if you can go along with it, okay?"

"Hmph," said Drayton, but Theodosia could detect a slight twinkle in his eyes.

White Point Gardens in Battery Park, the rolling green park that occupied the very tip of the peninsula, was rocking tonight. Musicians in the gazebo played jazz tunes interspersed with a little local folk rock. Red-and-yellow striped food booths featured roast oysters, she-crab soup, Frogmore stew, and country sausage sizzling on charcoal grills along with seared red and green peppers.

"Oh my goodness," declared Drayton, as they wandered through the park. "Frogmore stew. Doesn't that bring back memories."

"Then let's get some," suggested Theodosia, happy that Drayton seemed suddenly happy.

They stepped up to a wooden booth decorated with stars and bars bunting and ordered two plastic cups of the steaming stew.

"I haven't eaten this in years," said Drayton, digging his fork into the rich mixture and spearing a plump shrimp. "I hope the recipe's authentic."

Theodosia peered at Drayton as he nibbled, tasted, and pondered, his nose twitching like a dubious rabbit. "Well?" she asked. "Is it?"

"Fantastic!" roared Drayton. "Really delicious."

"Whew," said Theodosia. "You had me worried."

"I had myself worried," said Drayton, eagerly spooning up more stew. "Do you know that Frogmore stew is named after the tiny hamlet of Frogmore over on St. Helena Island?"

"I kind of guessed it might be," said Theodosia, enjoying the rich mélange of shrimp and sausage and corn.

"Used to be a booming terrapin business over there," added Drayton, as if he had a rousing story to tell.

"I'm not sure I want to know details," Theodosia told him as she bit into a shrimp. "Especially while I'm eating."

They strolled past booths selling sweetgrass baskets, pralines, and fried oysters, eating their stew, getting slightly messy from their small pieces of corn on the cob.

"Look who else is here," said Drayton, arcing his paper cup into a trash receptacle, then wiping his hands on a pristine hanky. "Timothy." Drayton waved a freshly wiped hand. "Timothy! Hello!"

As silver-haired patriarch of the Heritage Society, Timothy Neville stood tall in the community, though he was diminutive in stature. Timothy was descended from French Huguenots who'd come over from France in the late 1600s to escape religious persecution. His ancestors had been ship owners, bankers, and indigo planters. All good things in the South. Timothy himself lived in a huge Italianate mansion on Archdale Street, served on many civic committees, played violin with the Charleston Symphony, and was a decent watercolorist. A talented, well-connected Renaissance man of sorts.

Now Timothy Neville, head up, hooded eyes scanning the crowd, strolled casually over to greet them. He was an octogenarian who could pass for much younger and was a good friend of Drayton's. Like Drayton, Timothy was turned out in a double-breasted navy blazer and gray slacks.

"Did you two text message each other about what to wear?" Theodosia joked.

When they both stared blankly at her, she said, "Twitter?" When they continued to stare, she shrugged and dropped the subject. Oops. Different generation.

"Theodosia," said Timothy, crossing his arms and fixing

her with a purposeful gaze. "I may be able to help shed some light on your mysterious bones."

"Bone," she said, frustration seeping into her voice. "Does everyone know about that?"

"Yes . . . probably," answered Timothy. His smooth, tightly stretched brow twitched into a furrow. "Why? Is there a problem?"

"Only for me, I guess," Theodosia replied. She lifted her shoulders, exhaled slowly. "You were saying . . . ?"

"We have several old maps at the Heritage Society," said Timothy, "that accurately detail various parts of the historic district, including the location of your new home."

"An excellent idea," enthused Drayton, who loved nothing better than to pore over old maps. "Perhaps we'll uncover an important clue." Now he looked positively jubilant. "Maybe even determine that Theodosia's cottage is located on an early settler's graveyard."

"Hopefully not," said Theodosia. "I really wouldn't enjoy living atop the bones of our early residents."

"Oh no?" said Timothy, who also seemed enamored of the graveyard idea.

"But Timothy," continued Theodosia, "you bring up an excellent point about studying maps. Maybe the Antiquarian Map Shop would have something, too."

"They're a fine resource," allowed Timothy. "But . . . do we know who's going to take over as proprietor? *Is* someone going to take over?"

"Probably still up in the air," said Theodosia. "Although Jason Pritchard expressed interest in keeping it going."

"But the direct heir would be the mother, correct?" said Timothy.

"I suppose so," said Theodosia. Then murmured, "Sophie," thinking about how heartbroken she must be. And feeling grateful, once again, that Aunt Libby was her close friend.

Timothy looked like he was clicking off rapid-fire calculations in his brain. "Perhaps Mrs. Shand would be interested in donating the existing inventory to the Heritage Society."

"Perhaps that question should wait until after her daughter's funeral tomorrow," said Theodosia.

"Let's wander over to the shore," suggested Theodosia, once Timothy had moved on. "The boats should be coming along anytime now." She turned to Drayton, saw he was staring blankly into the crowd, and said, "Earth to Drayton. Are you stargazing or just staring out to sea?"

Drayton turned to face her, a strange expression on his lined face. "You remember that young lady Jory Davis was dating? The one he brought to the masked Verdi ball last fall?"

"Beth Ann?" said Theodosia, her voice rising slightly. "How could I forget?" Beth Ann had been tipsy, overdressed, and overly possessive of Jory that night. Not that she'd had anything to worry about. Except maybe how much her head was going to hurt the next morning from all the wine she'd drank.

"I swear I just caught a glimpse of her," said Drayton, his face pulled into a full-on frown now.

"Couldn't have," said Theodosia, though she rose on her tiptoes and tried to peer over the undulating sea of people. "They broke up. When Jory stopped by yesterday, he made a point of mentioning it." *And he was also very interested in taking me out to dinner.*

"Granted, I just caught a glimpse," said Drayton, still looking befuddled. "But I had the distinct impression . . . the blond hair . . ." He waved a hand and said, "Ah, I must have been mistaken. So many people . . ."

"Oh, I'm pretty sure that whole Jory–Beth Ann relationship is kaput," said Theodosia. "And that Jory's here in Charleston by himself."

"Apologies then," said Drayton. "I didn't mean to give you a start."

"You didn't," said Theodosia.

"Theodosia! Miss Browning!" A man's voice was calling to her, fairly demanding her attention.

"Jack," said Drayton, turning, blinking, and homing in on the voice. "Good to see you."

But Jack Brux wasn't having any of Drayton's friendly greeting. He flapped his arms like an angry crow and got right in Theodosia's face. "What do you think you're *doing?*" Brux demanded.

"Ex*cuse* me?" said Theodosia, staring into his pinched, practically rabid face. At such close range, Theodosia saw that he'd gone completely florid. *Whoa,* she thought, *this guy's really on a tear. Not so healthy for the old ticker!*

"I'm not stupid!" snarled Brux. "I know what you're try-ing to do!"

"You do?" said Theodosia. What exactly was she trying to do?

"You're trying to pin that murder on me!" Brux shrieked.

Not one to cower when fired upon by a bully, Theodosia calmly stood her ground. *Doggone that Tidwell, he must have said something to Brux.* "Of course, I'm not," said Theodosia. "But it's no secret that I've been asking around." *Looks like that cat's out of the bag.*

"More like trying to put a bug in that fat detective's ear!" snarled Brux.

"I'll be happy to share that with him, too, if you'd like," said Theodosia, still standing her ground.

Drayton held up a hand. "You're out of line, Jack." But Brux was too angry to listen to reason.

"Go pin your murder on some other poor donkey!" huffed Brux. "And leave me out of it!" Then he turned abruptly and stomped off into the crowd.

Drayton stared after him. "Did I mention that he has a bad temper?"

"The question is," said Theodosia. "Is Jack Brux crazy enough to kill?"

"Look!" exclaimed Drayton. "The boats." They gazed at the harbor where a parade of almost fifty boats, all lit up and sparkling like Christmas decorations, glimmered on the water.

"Beautiful," breathed Theodosia.

"Marvelous," echoed Drayton.

Enthralled by the shimmering vision, the crowd quieted down just as the orchestra struck up "Southern Star" by the group Alabama.

> *Oh, southern star, how I wish you would shine*
> *And show me the way to get home*

As the orchestra played softly and people hummed along, the boats drifted past like floats in a torchlight parade. Theodosia had read somewhere that courtiers at Versailles had constructed elaborate boats to amuse King Louis XVI and Marie Antoinette. She imagined they must have looked something like tonight's spectacle. Twinkling brightly, bathed in white, the waves reflecting the light in a million dazzling points.

A minister stepped up onto a makeshift reviewing stand and read a short prayer, then a high school marching band played a slow-moving version of "Dixie." It was all very lovely, very Old South, and probably a little bewildering to anyone who wasn't from here.

"That was really quite splendid," said Drayton, as they strolled back across the grass toward Theodosia's car.

"I loved the . . ." began Theodosia, then stopped abruptly.

"Jory?" Her ex-boyfriend had suddenly stepped in front of her. This was an unexpected encounter. Or was it?

"Good evening," said Drayton, dropping into the cool, reserved mode he always used when dealing with Jory.

But Jory couldn't have cared less. He fixed Theodosia with an eager smile and said, "I was hoping I might run into you."

"We were just leaving," said Drayton, pretending to stifle a yawn, trying his best to nudge Theodosia onward.

But Theodosia planted solidly in her tracks. "Give me a moment, will you?" she asked Drayton.

Drayton hesitated for a few seconds, then his Charleston manners got the better of him. He managed an abrupt nod and said, "As you wish."

"What's up?" asked Theodosia, when the two of them were alone. Or as alone as they were going to be with a throng of revelers streaming past them.

"You look so cute," Jory told her, reaching out to touch a fluff of her auburn hair. "Like a French sailor."

"Jory . . ." said Theodosia. She really didn't want him to start something here. Or anywhere.

Jory seemed to pick up on her mood and nodded at the distant flotilla of sailboats that continued to bob and glow. "I was supposed to be out there with them tonight." He sounded almost wistful.

"So why weren't you?" Theodosia asked.

"I had my boat all ready to go," Jory told her. "Sails rigged, lights strung. Chuck Strom, the manager over at the Charleston Yacht Club, helped me get it all set up. Then I got a call from my assistant, like an hour ago. He tells me there's an emergency. Which means I have to fly back to New York."

"Too bad," said Theodosia. She knew how much Jory would have enjoyed sailing his J/22 in the regatta.

"I'm actually on my way to the airport now," said Jory. "I

just stopped by for a couple of minutes to sort of drink in the spectacle."

And maybe see me, Theodosia thought to herself.

"The boats looked lovely," said Theodosia, not wanting to toss him too many leading questions.

"Didn't they?" said Jory, but he was gazing at Theodosia.

"You don't want to miss your plane," said Theodosia, taking a step backward. Then she gave him a slightly guarded look and added, "You're flying back alone? By yourself?"

"Sure," said Jory, edging toward her. "Who else would I be going with?"

"Just wondering," said Theodosia. She looked around for Drayton, finally spotted him. "Have a good flight," she bid Jory as she managed a hasty retreat.

13

❧

"*Did you have* a good time?" Theodosia asked Earl Grey. He sat next to her in the front seat, his big head bobbing every time she hit a pothole, which seemed to be in abundance out here on Sullivan's Island.

She'd dropped Drayton off at his home some thirty minutes ago and then driven out here to pick up Earl Grey. Cleo Hollander had assured her that Earl Grey had been on his best behavior and that the residents of Cranston Elder House had enjoyed her dog's visit immensely.

"You're so grown up to come by yourself," Theodosia told him.

As if in response, Earl Grey turned serious brown eyes on her and said, "Grrrr?"

"Very grown up," she emphasized. "Now maybe you should lie down, since you're riding up front, which is kind of a no-no, and you're not wearing a seat belt, which would pretty much be impossible. Okay?"

Earl Grey made one quick circle on the front seat, whacked

Theodosia in the head with his plumed tail, then curled up, nose to hind toes, looking tired but self-satisfied.

"Good boy," she praised him. Theodosia's right hand slipped off the steering wheel and cupped the soft dome of Earl Grey's head, then slid down to tickle a floppy ear. "You just rest your eyes and we'll be home in twenty minutes."

Cranking down the passenger-side window, Theodosia gazed out as they whooshed along Atlantic Avenue. The gentle *cussh* of the waves sliding in, the salty breeze on her lips, stars twinkling overhead, made the place seem like a magical, enchanted island, far away from the hustle and bustle of the city.

Theodosia loved it out here on Sullivan's Island. It was quiet and residential, mostly a mix of old and new beach houses, with a few small shops and restaurants thrown in to give a cozy, small town atmosphere. Long, long stretches of beaches lent a romantic escapist feel, plus there were acres of undeveloped woods and marshland, as well as meandering little estuaries with names like Conch Creek, Crab Pond, and Narrows Creek.

Lots of history out here, too. In the early years of the Revolutionary War, a makeshift fort had been constructed. Builders had used unseasoned palmetto logs, cut from the surrounding countryside, and fashioned into a kind of log cabin fortress. On June 29, 1776, that small fort had proved its mettle when Colonial forces withstood almost constant bombardment from Lord Cornwall's British forces.

Turns out, the palmetto logs used in the building process were so spongy and damp that they miraculously absorbed the impact of the British cannonballs!

To commemorate this Battle of Fort Moultrie, as it came to be known, a white palmetto tree was added to South Carolina's blue-and-white crescent moon state flag.

Flashing past Raven Drive, Theodosia was also reminded that poet and horror writer Edgar Allan Poe had been stationed here in the mid-1800s. As she slowed, made a turn onto Dibbo Lane, she veered close to Gold Bug Drive and Poe Avenue. Probably, she decided, Mr. Poe would have been pleased. This, after all, was where he'd tromped the rain-swept beaches and put quill pen to paper and composed "The Gold-Bug."

Now Theodosia sped past Woody's Clam Shack, a venerable old building with peeling yellow paint and a flickering pink sign in desperate need of a shot of neon. It looked like a dump, but inside, Woody's was cozy and tidy. The menu, painted on the wall and unchanged in years, included specialties such as fresh-caught blue crab, succulent Carolina oysters, and hot, salty sweet potato fries.

Gotta come back here and eat, Theodosia told herself as she glanced into the rearview mirror. A large, dark car seemed to be hanging right on her tail. She braked, as a kind of warning signal, then sped up and hung a left onto Ben Sawyer Drive.

Glancing in her side mirror, Theodosia saw that the same car had followed her into the turn and was, once again, creeping up behind her. A little too close for comfort. She frowned and sped up slightly. The car behind her sped up, too.

"Oh, that's helpful," she muttered. "Climb right on top of me and shine your brights. Thanks a lot."

Earl Grey, who'd been curled up beside Theodosia, snoozing, glanced up with a worried expression.

"Don't worry," Theodosia told him, "we'll lose this jerk as soon as we cross the bridge."

Up ahead was the Ben Sawyer Bridge. It was an old swing bridge, narrow and picturesque, that took a full fifteen minutes to creak open when a sailboat hailed the bridge master and requested passage through the channel. The Ben Sawyer Bridge was slated to be updated soon, but was still sitting in limbo on the highway department's to-do list. Probably, lack of state funds had stalled the repairs, just like lots of other road and bridge projects across the country.

Theodosia felt the first flutter of fear just as she approached the bridge. It was fairly late now, with no streetlights to illuminate the road and not another soul in sight. She goosed her engine, determined to outrun the clown behind her. But just as her foot tapped the gas, the car tailing her slid even closer.

Glancing in her side mirror, Theodosia muttered an angry, "What on earth . . . ?" And was suddenly slammed from behind. Shocked beyond belief, she had only moments to comprehend what was happening as the nasty, crunching impact sent her Jeep careening across the center line and sliding wildly into the incoming lane.

Fighting hard to regain control, Theodosia jerked her steering wheel to the right and tried frantically to brake, even as Earl Grey was suddenly up on all fours and barking his head off.

"No, boy, get down!" she yelled, as a second impact, harder still, caught her left rear fender. Now, the nasty combination of her overcorrection and the second hit sent her careening straight toward the old metal railing!

Bracing for impact, Theodosia hung on to the wheel, praying Earl Grey could brace and fend for himself. She tried to steer away at the very last second, to just graze the metal grillwork, maybe sideswipe it and lessen the impact. But she was traveling too fast and her speed was too great. Her Jeep hit hard with a metallic screech, shuddered mightily for a few seconds, then spun like a child's top into a sickening, heart-stopping one-hundred-and-eighty-degree turn.

Another grating thunk and the car behind zoomed past her, flying at an amazing speed now, this time clipping her front fender! As Theodosia continued to fight for control, Earl Grey was hurled against the dashboard like a rag doll.

And all she could do was let loose a scream. A bloodcurdling "Noooooo!"

Silence. Then the sound of running feet slapping pavement and a man's gruff voice asking, "Are you okay in there? Hello?"

Theodosia sat up suddenly, certain she'd heard a far-off voice reverberating in her head. Then she caught sight of Earl Grey, cowering on the floor, squashed beneath the dashboard where he'd been thrown. Oh no! Her beloved dog was shaking like a leaf, looking both dazed and terrified.

"Ma'am?" came the gruff voice again. Creaking her head to the left, Theodosia peered out the side window. A man with a bushy gray beard, wearing a blue chambray shirt, stood beside her Jeep. Concern seemed to etch his face. "You want me to call somebody?" he asked. "Cops? Ambulance?"

Warily, Theodosia cranked down her window. "Did you see what happened?" she gasped. "Did you get the license plate number of the car that hit me?"

The man gave a vigorous shake of his head. "I only saw your car." He peered at her, a little doubtful she was tracking properly. "Looks like you hit the side of that bridge pretty hard. Let me call someone," he offered again, pulling his cell phone from his shirt pocket.

Earl Grey whimpered, then scrambled halfway onto the front seat. He seemed to be having trouble pulling himself up.

"No," Theodosia told the man. "I have to . . . um . . . get my dog to a vet."

Concern bloomed again on the man's face. "You got a dog in there with you?"

Theodosia nodded.

"There's an emergency animal hospital up ahead in Mt.

Pleasant," he told her. "Open most of the night, I think. If your car can make it."

Turning the key and restarting her engine, Theodosia didn't detect any discernible clank or knock in the engine. She inhaled shakily and asked, "Where?"

"Take the Coleman Boulevard exit."

"Thanks," she said.

Together, Theodosia and Earl Grey limped into the Loveland Emergency Veterinary Clinic. A vet tech in green scrubs met them at the door. "You two okay?" The vet tech was an African American woman with the name KEISHA embroidered on her top.

"Car crash," Theodosia rasped in a dry, hollow voice. "Gotta have my dog x-rayed. He . . ." The tears were starting to come now. "He hit the dashboard pretty hard, and he's limping badly."

"We can surely check him out," said Keisha. She had an aura of crisp efficiency mingled with compassion that helped calm both Theodosia and Earl Grey. "Let me fill out a quick chart on your boy. What's his name?"

"Earl Grey," said Theodosia, rubbing her shoulder.

"Maybe we should x-ray your shoulder, too," suggested Keisha.

"No, just take care of him," said Theodosia. "I'm okay. Really."

Turns out, Earl Grey was okay, too. The clinic did blood work, checked Earl Grey's heart and lungs, and shot hip and shoulder X-rays. A young veterinarian, Dr. Mark Felden, prodded Earl Grey gently, checking his legs, neck, and shoulders for range of motion, shone a flashlight into his still-worried eyes, and did all the tests a doctor can do with a patient who can't tell him where it hurts.

They left with a bottle of Deramaxx and paperwork on all the tests Dr. Felden had conducted. As well as good wishes from Keisha.

By the time Theodosia and Earl Grey arrived home, they were both exhausted. Earl Grey limped slowly upstairs and padded directly to his dog bed in Theodosia's bedroom.

Theodosia did something she rarely did. She sat down at her dining room table and poured a drab of brandy into a cut-crystal glass. And as she sipped the twenty-year-old Napoleon brandy, a gift from Drayton some five years earlier, it tickled fiery and rough in the back of her throat. And served to stoke her inner furnace until she was good and mad.

Obviously, someone had intended to do her serious harm. And in their obnoxiously conceived hit-and-run, had brought harm to her dog! In the South, where canines were hunting buddies, beloved companions, and sometimes even accorded honors in family plots, attacking someone's dog was considered a heinous offense! A reason to fight back!

So, of course, the question that flickered and danced like a searing blue flame in Theodosia's mind was *who?*

Taking another small sip of brandy, Theodosia leaned back in her high-backed chair and gazed about her apartment. It was hard to believe she was going to pack up and leave here in a matter of weeks. She'd lived here, above the tea shop, ever since she'd first opened the place. And her apartment, decorated over the years with furniture, antiques, and paintings she'd managed to acquire from King Street and French Quarter antique shops, had evolved into a comfortable patois that bespoke both coziness and elegance. Moody seascape paintings hung over the fireplace. Her chintz sofa and chair were cushy and just right for cocooning. And a recently acquired highboy of fine Carolina pine held her collection of antique teacups, two Chinese blue-and-white bowls that dated back to the Ming dynasty, and a prized Staffordshire dog.

So . . . sitting here in the comfort and safety of the little home she'd built for herself, Theodosia let her mind plumb the depths of the unfathomable. Who on earth wanted her out of the picture? And why?

The reasonable answer was because she'd been asking questions about Daria's murder. Okay, maybe she had been on the prowl. But that still led directly back to the question—who wanted her out of the way? Or dead?

Was it Jack Brux? Was there a special map at the Antiquarian Map Shop that he was fiercely desperate to get his hands on? Was it Cinnamon or Miss Kitty, who were strange at best and perhaps even obsessive about expanding their shop? Or could it be Jason Pritchard, Daria's assistant. Was he not the trusted right-hand man she'd thought he was?

Or could there be someone else entirely? Someone she didn't even know about? Or hadn't suspected?

On the other hand, and this would be coming out of left field, the attack on her tonight might somehow be related to the mysterious bone Earl Grey had dug up in her backyard!

Theodosia's brain continued to ponder the possibilities, but like a Möbius strip that always led tantalizingly back to the beginning, she couldn't quite fathom a single concrete answer.

Theodosia pulled herself up from her chair and carried the brandy bottle to a small wooden sideboard she used as a bar and display area. Brain still in a whirl, she set the bottle down next to her collection of old hotel silver. A large silver pitcher engraved with HOTEL SHERMAN—CHICAGO. A sterling silver ice bucket engraved with MANSION HOUSE HOTEL, GREENVILLE, SC.

Hesitating, Theodosia reached out and let her fingertips run across the word RESERVED, spelled out in raised letters on a sterling silver table sign.

But no answers here.

The Aubusson carpet whispered beneath her feet as she shuffled around her apartment, turning out lights, checking window and door locks. Then she tiptoed quietly into her bedroom. Earl Grey was curled up tight, sleeping softly, making snuffly doggy snores.

Theodosia breathed her thank-you to the Lord that her pup was all right. And that she was, too. Inside her walk-in closet, she turned on an overhead light and rustled around for a few moments, searching for one particular outfit. When she finally found what she was looking for, Theodosia pulled her black suit from its plastic dry cleaner's bag and hung it on the door. After all, first thing tomorrow morning she had a funeral to attend.

Which, when all was said and done, was depressing at best.

14

⚜

The steeple of St. Philip's Church thrust boldly into the bright blue sky as pink and blue clouds scudded across the far horizon. St. Philip's was one of several dozen historic churches that dotted the cityscape and earned Charleston the moniker of "Holy City." St. Philip's was also a noted landmark, usually remembered as the strangely sited church that stuck halfway out into Church Street.

Theodosia glanced up at the tall, elegant steeple as she drove down Church Street, headed for Daria's funeral. In the late 1800s, a light beacon had been installed in the steeple to help guide ships into the safety of Charleston Harbor. Now, Theodosia was praying she herself might find safe harbor in the church. Or at least peace of mind, so she could hopefully figure out some much-needed answers.

Last night's hit-and-run or smash-and-dash, or whatever it had been, still weighed heavily on her mind as she entered the cool darkness of the church. An organist up in the balcony was playing Simon and Garfunkel's "Bridge Over Troubled

Water" on the magnificent Casavant Frères organ, and the music flowed out smooth and pure. Walking slowly down the center aisle, under high, neoclassical arches, Theodosia was surprised at the large number of people that had turned out for this funeral. The huge showing indicated a heartfelt tribute to Daria, she decided, who'd practically been a fixture on Church Street and a friend to so many.

Midway down the aisle, Theodosia halted and slid into a wooden pew, still mentally running the words of the song through her head.

> *Like a bridge over trouble water*
> *I will lay me down*

Up ahead, sitting together in the first row, two white-haired ladies clutched each other in sorrow. Daria's mother, Sophie, and Theodosia's own aunt Libby.

Craning her head to the left, Theodosia saw the sister, Fallon, as well, looking tearful as she hung on the arm of Joe Don Hunter, Daria's boyfriend. Joe Don's shoulders were slumped and his head bowed forward. He seemed beyond sorrowful, verging on catatonic.

And then the music gently shifted from the more contemporary Simon and Garfunkel into a slow-paced funereal version of Chopin's Prelude in C minor. A few seconds later, Daria's silver casket rolled slowly up the aisle, guided by the hands of a dark-suited funeral director. Her final visit to a church she had known and loved since childhood.

Theodosia watched it all with crystal clarity. The silver casket sliding by on gently clacking wheels. A heart-shaped spray of white lilies, roses, and baby's breath teetering on top of the casket. Mourners turning a sad gaze on the casket, then dipping their heads and wiping away tears. Tragic. All of it tragic.

Reverend Meader met Daria's casket as it slowly rolled to a stop. He put a hand on it, gazed out at the congregation, and began the service.

His words were comforting, eloquent, and uplifting. Still, even though it was deemed a celebration of life, Theodosia couldn't help thinking about Daria's death. If only she'd been a minute sooner. If only she'd screamed louder. If only . . .

Lost in her own thoughts, Theodosia was suddenly aware that the church organ had played a few opening chords and everyone was reaching for a hymnal. She grabbed a well-worn, leather-covered book that sat beside her and paged hastily through it, looking for the song "Just a Closer Walk with Thee."

There it was. She joined the voices already lifted in song and tried to focus on the words.

> *Just a closer walk with thee,*
> *Grant it, Jesus, is my plea*

The words were lovely and soothing. But still Theodosia felt restless. Like she was close to figuring something out, but that something was still unformed and slightly ethereal.

Well, of course it is, she told herself. *Because Daria's killer is a very clever person. And maybe someone who's closer to us than we suspect.* She gazed around the church, eyeing the various mourners, speculating. Still, nothing seemed to gel.

In closing the funeral service, Reverend Meader quoted from a poem by an unknown author.

> *Life is but a stopping place,*
> *A pause in what's to be,*
> *A resting place along the road,*
> *To sweet eternity.*
> *We all have different journeys,*

> *Different paths along the way,*
> *We all were meant to learn some things,*
> *But never meant to stay.*

Then, all too soon it seemed, the casket was being wheeled back down the aisle, closely trailed by the grief-stricken family. Theodosia watched as Aunt Libby, her back straight, eyes dry, her tiny seventy-eight-year-old form seemingly filled with strength, beckoned for her to join them.

Me? She touched her thumb to her chest, unsure.

Aunt Libby gave a quick nod.

Theodosia joined the group and followed along down the aisle. In the vestibule, Aunt Libby gripped her hand tightly and said, "We need to talk."

"Of course," Theodosia whispered back, knowing in her heart what that talk would be about.

And she wasn't far off. Once Daria's casket had been loaded into the long black hearse, Sophie Shand, Daria's mother, turned to her and asked, "Can you help us? Will you help us?"

"Honestly," said Theodosia, accepting Sophie's hand, "I'm doing everything I can."

"Because you were there," moaned Sophie. "You saw . . ." Her voice cracked and she put a hanky to her mouth, unable to continue.

"Take it slow, dear," said Aunt Libby.

"Unfortunately, I didn't see that much," said Theodosia, feeling like a failure. "I've been trying to remember more, and talking to . . ." Now she was the one who couldn't go on. The images in her head were of dark figures, swirling together, dancing a dance of death. But she couldn't pull the face of the attacker into focus.

Aunt Libby, bless her heart, stepped into the breach. "But our dear Theodosia is a smart lady," she told Sophie. "She's unraveled murder investigations before and I have all the faith in the world that she can help figure this one out."

Gulp, was Theodosia's sole thought.

Aunt Libby's eyes burned bright as she gazed at Theodosia. "You're already asking lots of questions, aren't you? You've already settled on a couple of suspects?"

"I have," Theodosia admitted. She didn't have to heart to tell Sophie Shand that's all she had.

"Bless you," said Sophie, staring at Theodosia with red-rimmed eyes. "You're an angel. Heaven sent."

"She'll be our avenging angel," murmured Aunt Libby.

"I don't know about that," said Theodosia. "But I'll try to stay in the loop with Detective Tidwell and keep pressuring him. And I will continue to ask questions." She hadn't realized how strong her conviction was until she spoke those words. *Yes, I will,* she thought. *I can do this. I can figure this out.*

Out of the corner of her mouth, Aunt Libby said, "Your detective friend is standing right over there."

Theodosia canted her head and saw that Detective Burt Tidwell was indeed among the crowd of mourners who had congregated on the sidewalk. In fact, he seemed to be offering condolences to Fallon and Joe Don Hunter. Well, kudos to him.

"Excellent," murmured Theodosia, "I need to talk to him anyway. This just makes things easier." After administering hugs to both Sophie and Aunt Libby, Theodosia dodged her way through the crowd and managed to nab Tidwell as he started to sidle away.

"Detective Tidwell!" Theodosia waved a hand at him, trying to catch him.

Tidwell heard Theodosia's voice and stopped. Didn't wave back, though. He held a rolled up newspaper in one hand and had his other hand jammed in his pocket, jingling random change.

"Who was the woman who sat three rows behind you and couldn't keep her eyes off you?" asked Tidwell, once Theodosia skidded to a stop in front of him.

"What!" Theodosia cried. "What are you talking about?" Whirling around, suddenly unnerved and gripped with fear, she quickly studied the people nearby, thinking maybe the person who'd run her off the road last night was among them. But she saw only a sober group of mourners, talking among themselves. And no one she recognized.

"What did the woman look like?" Theodosia asked Tidwell.

"Average," said Tidwell.

"What was she wearing?" asked Theodosia.

"Black jacket and skirt, like you," said Tidwell.

"You're a detective," shrilled Theodosia. "You're supposed to be hypersensitive to these things. You're supposed to *remember* details about suspects."

Tidwell seemed almost amused. "This woman is a suspect?"

"I wonder . . ." said Theodosia, fretting now. Could it have been Delaine sitting behind her? Or Cinnamon St. John? Would she even come to this funeral? Or was it someone else entirely? The someone who'd tried to do her harm last night?

"I have something to tell you," Theodosia said to Tidwell. When the detective squiggled his furry brows together, Theodosia plunged ahead. Choosing her words carefully, she told Tidwell about picking up Earl Grey last night on Sullivan's Island, being followed by the dark car, then being run off the road. Or rather, almost run off the bridge.

As she told her story, they walked slowly over to her Jeep. "You see," she said, "it's bashed in the back and on the side."

Tidwell took his time to study both gashes. "You were lucky," he said, finally. "It seems as though someone meant business."

"I'll say they did!" said Theodosia. "Earl Grey was even thrown to the floor."

"Were you able to get a look at the driver?" Tidwell asked. "Could you make a positive ID?"

Theodosia shook her head. "No. Not really."

Tidwell's slightly bulging eyes stared fixedly at her for a few moments. "But you harbor a suspicion." It wasn't a question.

Theodosia wrinkled her nose and grimaced. "I do, but I'm not sure I should say."

Tidwell pursed his lips and rocked back on his heels, another sprightly gesture for such an ungainly man. "Spare me your well-bred southern manners, Miss Browning, and just tell me flat out. This may dovetail with our ongoing investigation into Daria Shand's death."

"You think?" she asked.

"And spare me any sarcasm," growled Tidwell.

"Okay," said Theodosia, taking a deep breath. "There are quite a few people on my list that I'm not sure about."

Tidwell slapped the rolled up newspaper against his leg again and waggled his fingers. "Names please."

"Jason Pritchard strikes me as a person with motive," said Theodosia. "Cinnamon and Miss Kitty, who own the Jardin Perfumerie, talk a good game about being sad over Daria's death, but they're frantic to move into her space."

"You think Daria Shand was killed because of a real estate issue?" asked Tidwell.

Theodosia ignored him. Now who was being sarcastic? "And I'm not exactly in love with Jack Brux, our local map fanatic."

"And why," asked Tidwell, "would any of these persons have you in their sights?"

Theodosia stared at him. "Because they're all suspects in Daria's murder? And I've been asking questions about them?"

"Ah," said Tidwell, "we finally journey to the crux of the matter. You *do* ask a lot of questions. And capriciously jump to varying conclusions."

A wrinkle insinuated itself in the middle of Theodosia's forehead. "Wait a minute, are you telling me you have someone else in mind?"

"You might say my focus varies a degree or two from yours," replied Tidwell.

Theodosia was intrigued. "But . . . who?"

Tidwell raised his head and swiveled it like a periscope, his laser gaze scanning the crowd then landing squarely on Joe Don Hunter.

Theodosia followed his gaze. "The boyfriend?" she said, her voice rising in a squawk. "Are you serious?"

"I rarely make jokes when it relates to a homicide," responded Tidwell.

"But . . . why?" asked Theodosia. "Why him?" To her, Joe Don Hunter just seemed like a beaten, broken man.

Tidwell's beady eyes carried a gleam. The wild gleam he got when he was seriously on the hunt. "Why, you ask? Because the man is a treasure hunter."

The words seemed like such a non sequitur, they zipped past Theodosia's brain without registering. "Pardon?"

Tidwell assumed the look of a third-grade teacher who's been forced to repeat a simple recitation. "Did you ever hear of the Kipling Club?"

"Not that I can recall," said Theodosia.

Tidwell's gaze lasered over to Hunter again. Hunter was standing in a crowd of mourners, shaking hands and thanking people for coming. "The Kipling Club is a loosely organized group of about a dozen amateur treasure hunters who also engage in, shall we say, cowboy archaeology."

"What are you talking about?" Theodosia asked. "I mean, the cowboy part."

"Unauthorized," said Tidwell. "Clandestine. In other

words, my dear Miss Browning, these gentlemen, and I use the term loosely, go out and about searching for relics from the past without any authorization whatsoever."

"Weird," said Theodosia, letting her brain wrap around the notion. "And his name's even Hunter," she murmured.

"Occuponomous, wouldn't you agree?" asked Tidwell.

Theodosia let Tidwell's words cycle through her brain for a few moments. "Kipling Club for Rudyard Kipling?" she asked.

"Bingo," said Tidwell. "Give that lady a fluffy, pink panda."

"And you think . . . what?" said Theodosia. "That Joe Don got cozy with Daria because of her dandy map collection? If you ask me, your reasoning strikes me as being awfully thin."

"Then how about this," proposed Tidwell. "Perhaps our Mr. Hunter was on to something. Perhaps he'd found a trove of Civil War relics or something relating to Native Americans or even pirate treasure?"

Theodosia digested Tidwell's statement. He hadn't veered completely off course. The area surrounding Charleston was a hotbed for treasure and treasure hunters. There were antiquities, military relics from Civil War time, and doubloons from pirates who'd plied Carolina waters. Interesting items were forever being discovered. Case in point, the bone in her own backyard.

"And you think Joe Don discovered something?" said Theodosia. "Or Daria didn't approve of his methodology?"

"Possible," said Tidwell. One corner of his mouth twitched. "I've asked Jack Brux to do some forensic work for me."

"What!" Theodosia exclaimed, in an injured tone of voice. Jack Brux? Working *with* the police?

Tidwell remained calm in the face of her turmoil. "We want to reconstruct some of the old documents that were found shredded on the floor of the Antiquarian Map Shop."

He pursed his lips. "It was as if someone wanted to obliterate old maps and documents."

"Who would want to do that?" Theodosia wondered out loud. Then answered her own question. "The murderer."

"Granted, it's a long shot," said Tidwell, "but I have to examine all the angles. Even those that are somewhat oblique." He stared at her, looking a little tired, a little frazzled.

"I suppose," allowed Theodosia, still nervous about Brux.

"And I have other things on my plate, too," he told her.

"The hijackings?" she asked. "How's that going? Any leads?"

"Working on it," he told her. "Keeping an eye on our Interstate Ninety-five and Highway Seventeen corridors."

"You think it's local people?"

"Organized crime most likely," said Tidwell. "When we tightened our borders after 9/11, a lot of former narcotics smugglers turned to cargo crime. Breaking into distribution centers, grabbing trucks right off the highways. And these guys are smart. Once a truck's GPS is dismantled it's almost impossible to find."

"Wow," said Theodosia. "Sounds like big business, huh?"

"On both ends," said Tidwell. "Hijackers as well as the receivers of stolen goods."

"Well, good luck with that, too," she told him.

Tidwell gave an absent nod, then unfurled his newspaper and held it up for Theodosia to see. "Have you seen this?"

Squinting at a grainy black-and-white photo that bore an uncanny resemblance to her soon-to-be backyard, Theodosia hastily read the accompanying headline: Human Bone Discovered in Historic District Backyard. State Archaeology Office to Conduct Excavation.

"Oh dear," she murmured. This was the *last* thing she needed!

* * *

Theodosia was just about to pull away from the curb when she saw Jason Pritchard. She hit the brakes, threw her Jeep into park, and rolled down the window. "Jason," she called. "Over here."

Jason sauntered slowly toward her. "Tough one," he said, when he got closer.

"Yeah," she said. "Tougher than most. How are you holding up?"

He shaded his eyes from the sun and peered into the dark of her car. "Hanging in there."

"You still thinking about buying the map shop?" Theodosia asked him.

"Maybe," said Jason. Where once he'd seemed anxious to keep it going, now he seemed slightly evasive.

"Did you find a partner?" Theodosia asked. "A backer?" She knew how tough it was to start a business, if not purchase one outright. You had to assume a lease, buy the inventory, and get the word out to existing customers. At which point you fought to transition them into becoming *your* customers. There were a million more things to do and a how-to manual didn't exist. You just had to gut it out on your own.

"I might have somebody," Pritchard allowed. "A guy in Savannah who'd be a sort of silent partner."

"The guy that was Daria's hotshot customer?" She remembered Pritchard's words exactly.

"Uh, yeah," said Pritchard. "But nothing's in writing yet. It's still in the planning stages."

"Good for you," said Theodosia. "What did you say his name was again?" Pritchard hadn't mentioned a name, but she was more than a little curious.

"Snelling," said Pritchard, looking unhappy. "Jud Snelling."

"I suppose you've been putting in some long hours at the map store," said Theodosia. "You were probably there last night, right?"

"Yes, I was," said Pritchard. "Why do you ask?"

"Was Fallon there with you? Going through inventory and stuff?"

Pritchard lifted his chin and narrowed his eyes. "Nope. Just me."

"Purchasing the shop means negotiating with Daria's mother," continued Theodosia. "Not easy to do. She'll be emotionally connected."

"I'm not too worried," said Pritchard. Then added, "I'm sure she'll set a fair price."

"Good luck to you then," said Theodosia. "Keep me posted."

Pritchard strolled away and Theodosia watched him. He seemed different now. Not the same guy who'd come into her tea shop, asking for her help. Now he seemed almost . . . opportunistic. Like he'd already dismissed Daria's death. Or maybe wasn't all that sorry.

Also, and this struck her as strange, Pritchard hadn't mentioned a thing about the dents in her car. So he'd either been nervous or self-absorbed.

Theodosia drummed her fingers on the steering wheel, thinking. Then she frowned into the rearview mirror, checked the street, ready to pull out into traffic. The mirror also reflected a sliver of old cemetery that wrapped around St. Philip's Church. A solemn, dark place that was filled with ancient, canted gravestones belonging to early settlers, original signers of the Declaration of Independence and U.S. Constitution, and a former vice president.

The cemetery was also reputed to be haunted. Ghost walk guides in fluttering, dark capes led eager tourists through the cemetery at night, armed with flickering torches and spooky stories. Glowing orbs had been reported as well as photographed. Ghosts of Civil War soldiers had materialized. Voices had cried and whispered.

Thinking about the cemetery made Theodosia assess her own backyard. Had it been a cemetery as well? Was her little cottage going to suddenly assume the reputation of being haunted? Was she going to have to deal with ghost walks and curious tourists and pranksters on Halloween?

And there was something else bugging her, too. Could Joe Don Hunter and his rogue Kipling Club have had their hand in Daria's murder?

15

"Hey!" Haley called from the kitchen as Theodosia slipped in the back door of the tea shop. "You made the paper."

Theodosia dumped her handbag on her desk and traded her tweedy black jacket for a long black apron. "I've already seen it."

"Not this one you haven't," said Drayton, taking up where Haley had left off. He held up a copy of the *Shooting Star*, pinching the corner between thumb and forefinger like it might be infected with bubonic plague. Front and center was a photo of a startled-looking Theodosia superimposed on what was supposed to be her backyard, but looked more like a full-scale archaeological excavation at Karnak.

Theodosia stared at the photo with a mixture of anger and disbelief. "Doggone Bill Glass," she muttered.

"Can you believe it?" asked Drayton. "The man has unmitigated gall. Half the story's a complete fabrication." He scanned the article, pushed his glasses up his nose. "Actually, most of it is."

"Of course it is," said Theodosia. She knew that all Glass's stories were either made up, cobbled together with inaccuracies, or complete and total fluff pieces. Take your pick.

Haley popped her head out of the kitchen again. "Pretty crazy stuff, huh?" She, on the other hand, seemed amused by the whole thing.

"Excuse me," said Theodosia, who didn't come close to finding the situation hilarious, "but is anyone watching the tea shop?"

"Miss Dimple came in again," Drayton told her. "I asked her to work because we're booked to the rafters and she loves working here. Also, our customers seem to adore her mothering ways."

"It's a win-win situation," agreed Haley. She peered at Theodosia, suddenly sensing her prevailing mood. "Uh-oh, you look tired. How'd the funeral go?"

"Sad," said Theodosia. "And a little strange."

"It's a strange world," said Haley, hustling back into the kitchen, pulling open the oven door, and yelping, "Holy cats, these butterscotch scones have gotta come out now before this whole place goes up in a blue blaze!"

Theodosia followed Drayton into the tea room, where it did appear that the very capable Miss Dimple had everything under control. And thank goodness for that!

Drayton slid behind the front counter and grabbed a pot of tea. "Got a surprise for you," he told Theodosia.

"I'm not sure I can take another surprise," she told him. "Or even want one."

"No, no, this is a nice surprise," said Drayton, pouring steaming hot liquid into a pink, purple, and gold Gladstone teacup. "You were so intrigued with teaberry the other day that I went ahead and ordered a tin of teaberry-flavored tea." He slid the cup toward her, a shy smile on his face. "Try it. I think you'll find it an interesting blend of white tea, green tea, teaberry leaves, hibiscus, dried cranberries, and honey. A trifle on the minty side, but quite delicious."

Theodosia took a quick sip. "It is good. Who blended it?"

"Kent and Dinmore, one of our favorite tea purveyors."

"You're thinking of adding this to our tea menu?" They already had a list of more than one hundred fresh-brewed tea offerings, to say nothing of their infusions list and tea-totalers menu of nontea beverages.

"I wouldn't mind," said Drayton. "Would you?"

"You're the master tea blender," said Theodosia. "I leave it up to you."

"But you're the boss lady." Drayton smiled, seeing her humor creep back.

Theodosia gave a chuckle. "Please don't call me that. At least not in public."

"Honey," asked Miss Dimple, scurrying up to them. "I have a table asking for an organic Darjeeling. Do we have that?"

"Is that honey me or honey Drayton?" asked Theodosia.

Miss Dimple grinned and waved a hand. "Honey meaning Drayton," she said. "Isn't he the big, important tea guy?"

"You see?" Theodosia said to Drayton.

"To answer your question," replied Drayton, "yes. And I shall be happy to brew a pot of Darjeeling, although it's going to be from the Ambootia Estate, since we're completely out of Makaibari Estate."

"Uh . . . no problem," said Miss Dimple, hurrying back to her customers.

Drayton reached up and grabbed a tin of tea from the huge array of tins, glass jars, and metal bins that occupied a warren of floor-to-ceiling wooden shelves. "You see? No problem."

"Maybe not with tea," said Theodosia in a low voice. "But more than a few other issues have cropped up."

"Hmm?" said Drayton, carefully measuring out scoops of loose tea leaves.

And so Theodosia quickly related her little episode of last night. Black car, nasty crash, injured dog. Then she filled him in concerning her earlier conversation with Detective Tidwell.

Drayton was stunned. "You've obviously struck a nerve!"

"The question is, whose nerve?" replied Theodosia. She reached for a teapot, pulled out a Staffordshire green spatterware teapot, and stared fixedly at it. Tempest in a teapot? she wondered. Or great big storm brewing?

"Okay, you guys," said Haley, corralling Theodosia and Drayton at the front counter. "I want to take a couple of minutes to go over today's menu."

"Busy day today," muttered Drayton, as he measured Assam tea into an antique Haviland teapot with gold and ivy trim. Besides their regular luncheon customers they had a group of Red Hat Ladies coming in at one o'clock and an afternoon tour group driving up from Beaufort.

"Butterscotch scones," said Haley. "Mediterranean salad, squares of spring vegetable quiche, and lemon tea bread."

"And the tea sandwiches?" asked Drayton, trying to hurry her along.

"Getting to that," said Haley, checking her notes. "Three different kinds today. Chicken salad with almonds, cucumber mint, and goat cheese with sun-dried tomatoes."

"Wonderful," breathed Theodosia.

"I don't know how well goat cheese and sun-dried tomatoes are going to go over," said Drayton.

"We'll just have to wait and see," said Haley, not allowing herself to get rattled. "And, to help you keep it all straight . . ." She reached into her apron pockets and pulled out small index cards. "Cheat sheets for everyone."

"So our customers can order any of the offerings in any combination," said Theodosia.

"Think of it as a free-for-all," quipped Haley.

"Perhaps a la carte might be a more genteel and accurate term," said Drayton.

"Perhaps we should tend to our customers," said Theodosia.

"Or I might do an assortment on three-tiered trays," said Haley.

"Whatever works," said Drayton.

With a large silver tray propped against one hip, Theodosia was serving scones to a table of six when Delaine Dish came parading into the Indigo Tea Shop. She was wearing an exquisitely tailored tweed jacket and had another woman, not so finely dressed, in tow. Pausing at the front of the tea shop, Delaine let her sharp eyes skitter across each table until she finally spied Theodosia.

"Theodosia!" Delaine called in an authoritative voice that clearly rose above the noise and rustlings of the luncheon crowd. "A table, please."

Theodosia finished setting out the Devonshire cream and lemon curd, then hurried to head off Delaine. But Drayton arrived there first, bless his heart and soul.

Upon encountering Drayton, Delaine melted slightly, blowing air-kisses and gushing compliments. Wallowing in his even more lavish compliments, she finally remembered that she had her sister in tow.

"Y'all remember my sister, Nadine, don't you?" she said, giving an offhand wave and causing Nadine to blush.

"Of course," cooed Theodosia. She remembered Nadine quite well. Three years ago, when Nadine had first showed up in these parts, she'd been a practicing kleptomaniac. Had made off with silver teaspoons, a couple of necklaces, and some old coins. Theodosia could only hope that Nadine had long since sought therapy and had somehow overcome her little problem. Or at least reined it in.

"Lovely to see you again," said Drayton, giving Nadine a chaste peck on the cheek.

Not to be outdone, Delaine let loose her big pronouncement. "Nadine's come all the way from New York to help me with my big fashion show tomorrow." She smiled brightly at Theodosia and said, "You're still coming aren't you, dear?" There was an arch tone to her voice.

"I'll certainly try," said Theodosia. She led Delaine and Nadine to a hastily set table while Drayton hurried off to grab a pot of tea.

"No, no, no," said Delaine, plopping into a chair and suddenly raising an index finger in Theodosia's face. "Try isn't even in my vocabulary. I come from a place of *do*ing."

"You absolutely *must* come," said Nadine, grabbing Theodosia's hand. "Delaine's launching her new lingerie boutique."

"I'm calling it Méchante," said Delaine, trying to approximate a French accent.

"Which means naughty in French," said Nadine with a giggle.

"We're showing our new spring and summer fashions interspersed with the lingerie," Delaine rhapsodized. "The event is going to be truly delicious. In fact, I instructed my assistant Janine to twitch all my customers."

"Twitch?" said Theodosia.

"She means Tweet," corrected Nadine. "Delaine's into Twittering."

"All over town," said Delaine. "Just for my show!"

"In that case," said Theodosia with a smile, "I don't dare miss it."

Delaine gave a little shiver. "This is really shaping up to be a big weekend. My show Friday and Lyndel Woodruff's book reading at the Heritage Society on Saturday."

Drayton was suddenly at their table with a steaming pot of tea. "Oh," he said, trying to be pleasant, "you enjoy lectures on Civil War history?" Delaine was a crackerjack fund-raiser for the Heritage Society, but she'd never shown more than a passing interest in their lectures and book events.

"Can't say's I do," said Delaine. "But I try never to miss a nice social opportunity. Nothing like a good mingle."

Drayton raised his eyebrows but held his tongue as he poured tea into their teacups. "This is Gingerbread Peach Tea," he told them. "One of my proprietary blends. Chinese black tea, ginger root, cinnamon, and citrus."

"Oh my goodness," said Nadine. "So . . . you made it yourself?"

"Blended it," said Drayton.

"Delicious," proclaimed Delaine, taking a quick sip.

Drayton looked pleased. "To quote the poet John Milton on tea, 'One sip of this will battle the drooping spirits in delight beyond the bliss of dreams.' "

"Who's drooping?" asked Delaine. At which point everyone broke into laughter and Drayton beat a hasty retreat.

"Delaine," said Theodosia, gazing at her friend's black-and-cobalt-blue tweed jacket, "do my eyes deceive me or is that yet another Chanel suit you're wearing?"

Delaine grinned a Cheshire cat grin, delighted to be called out for her expensive outfit.

"Of course, it is," she told Theodosia, shifting in her chair to best show off her jacket, basking in the recognition.

"Delaine positively adores Chanel," Nadine added, looking a little wistful, like maybe she *couldn't* afford to wear the double Cs.

"Delaine's going to have to join Chanelanon pretty soon," joked Theodosia.

"I *love* it!" Nadine screeched, then proceeded to parody Delaine's slightly patronizing tone of voice. "Hello, my name is Delaine and I'm a Chanel addict."

"I'm not *that* addicted," protested Delaine, looking slightly sheepish.

"Oh yes, you are," Nadine insisted.

"No, dear," Delaine told her sister, a gravely firmness in her voice. "I adore Prada, Dior, and Cavalli just as much. You might even say I'm an equal opportunity clotheshorse."

"Enjoy your tea," said Theodosia, "while I grab you a selection of sandwiches."

Over at the counter, Theodosia whispered to Drayton, "Is Delaine and Nadine's table set with the good sterling silver?"

Drayton nodded. "The Gorham."

Theodosia snuck a peek at Nadine over her left shoulder, then said, "Keep an eye on it, will you?"

16

❧

Twenty minutes later the Red Hat Ladies from Goose Creek came pouring into the Indigo Tea Shop. Calling their chapter the Goose Creek Gadabouts, they definitely seemed gabby and giddy.

Filling three tables, the Gadabouts proceeded to warm Drayton's heart by ordering pots of Lapsang souchong, a nice smoky Chinese tea, as well as a high grade of Earl Grey that was a blend of both Chinese and Ceylon tea along with natural oil of bergamot.

Drayton, of course, had set the three tables using Limoges china and cut-crystal water glasses and created special red-and-purple bouquets using lavender, purple irises, and roses.

And because the Gadabouts were so animated and fun, continually jumping up to look at the T-Bath products and antique teacups that were for sale, Haley decided to change up her serving style, too. Instead of serving separate courses, she pulled out her extra-large, three-tiered serving stands, which were always a showstopper. Scones were placed on top, of course. Three types of tea sandwiches were arranged on the middle tier. And the savories, quiche in this instance, went on the bottom tier. Haley added a few edible nasturtium flowers and the serving stands were ready to go.

Twenty-five minutes later, the bus tour from Beaufort arrived and they did it all over again.

"Haley," said Theodosia, "you didn't tell us your sand-wiches were going to be so exotic." Haley had baked her own bread in narrow heart- and flower-shaped tubes, so when the bread was sliced thinly, the designs were readily apparent.

"Just something I decided at the last minute," said Haley, as they stood in the kitchen, arranging four more three-tiered trays.

"What am I going to do when some big fancy hotel offers you a job as the catering manager?" asked Theodosia. She grinned ruefully, then added, "I'll advise you to take it, of course. You're a very skilled chef and baker."

Haley wrinkled her nose as she carefully arranged quiche squares on tiny silver doilies. "Don't be so sure I'm ready to scurry off. I really like it here. You and Drayton let me run my own show. Any other place there'd be management via helicopter."

Theodosia squinted. "Helicopter?"

"Hovering," explained Haley. "They'd be asking me to try this or telling me to add such and such dish to the menu. Or I'd do a lobster Cobb salad and some stick-in-the-mud bean counter would decide the ingredients were too expensive and tell me I should use canned tuna." She wiped her hands on her apron and stepped back to appraise her lavishly arranged tray. "Anyway, it wouldn't be my call anymore."

"I see your point," said Theodosia.

"Truth be told," grinned Haley, "I'm looking forward to moving into your upstairs apartment. Once you get the high sign to move into your cottage, that is."

"Haley," said Theodosia. "There's something I have to tell you. Something that could possibly affect our safety here. Yours, mine, and Drayton's."

Haley glanced up sharply. "Huh? What are you talking about?"

So Theodosia told Haley about last night. Gave her the 411 on what had happened to Earl Grey and her.

Except for concern over Earl Grey, Haley wasn't all that fazed. "Somebody comes after me," she declared, "I'll give 'em a dose of pepper spray."

"Perhaps a better decision might be to turn and run," said Theodosia. "And scream very loud."

"Sometimes," said Haley, artfully tucking a half dozen ripe strawberries among her tea sandwiches, "you just have to take a stand and fight."

Theodosia didn't know it then, but those words would prove to be prophetic.

Once the tea trays were delivered, oohed and aahed over, and more tea was brewed and poured, Theodosia slipped away to her back office. For one thing, she wanted to see if she could find out a little more about Joe Don Hunter and the Kipling Club. She wasn't quite sure what she was looking for as she typed "Kipling Club" into Google, but she knew she needed more information.

Not much turned up. A couple of references in the Charleston *Post and Courier* about the Kipling Club holding an oyster roast out on Johns Island. Another note in a local shopper.

But wait, here was something that made her perk up. A mention in the *Summerton Gazette* about a citation issued to two members of the Kipling Club, specifically Joe Don Hunter and a Ferris Allan, concerning unlawful use of a metal detector near the Santee Indian Mound and Fort Watson Site.

Theodosia leaned back in her chair and slid off her shoes. Rubbed her toes across the carpet, thought about what the two men might have been looking for. Surely not pocket change. Then . . . what? Civil War uniform buttons? Fossils and arrowheads? Old trade beads? Although those last couple of items wouldn't necessarily register a hit on a metal detector.

On the other hand, what if the so-called metal detector had really been a ground-penetrating radar device? Then Hunter and his buddy could have turned up all sorts of things. Pottery shards, old tools from the Colonial period, even . . . dinosaur bones. It was all out there, slumbering under layers of mud and muck, waiting to be found by anyone with half a brain and a penchant for digging.

Theodosia also knew that type of exploration would definitely be classified as an illegal dig.

So now what? Should I go ahead and confront Joe Don Hunter?

Theodosia spun that notion around in her brain for a minute. Decided that the problem, of course, was confront him about what? Participating in illegal digs? That fact had pretty much been established. Confront Hunter about strangling Daria Shand? That route took her into what could turn out to be either dangerous territory or false accusations.

Because, when all was said and done, good old boy Joe Don Hunter might be exactly what he appeared to be. A fellow whose girlfriend had been savagely murdered. Someone who was caught in the leg trap of hard grief. A person whose extracurricular activities led him into gray areas.

Theodosia's fingers tapped idly on her computer keyboard. So . . . what now? Or rather, who else bore a second look?

Like a cartoon bubble forming above her head, Jason Pritchard popped into her brain again. Which brought to mind the possible backer and new co-owner of the Antiquarian Map Shop.

"Jud Snelling," Theodosia said aloud. "Sounds like an old-timey name. So . . . maybe an older guy?"

Hmmm.

Another quick search brought up the Silver Plume Antique Shop in Savannah, Georgia. Theodosia clicked on the website and found that Jud Snelling was listed as the proprietor and that the shop specialized in Civil War relics, American paintings, old glass and crockery, and fine antique furniture. Very interesting.

Clicking and scrolling through the website Theodosia found several pairs of Civil War–era spurs, a Jefferson Davis hat pin, antique glass ale bottles, and some nice paintings.

At the bottom of the page was the address and phone number for the Silver Plume. She squinted, thinking of a plausible reason to call Jud Snelling. Then, after a few moments of creative brainstorming, punched in the phone number.

Jud Snelling picked up on the second ring. "Silver Plume Antiques."

"Hello there," said Theodosia. "You don't know me, but I'm a friend of Daria Shand's. In fact, I own the Indigo Tea Shop just down the street from her place."

A long silence spun out and then Snelling said, "Oh my. I wanted so much to attend the funeral yesterday, but I couldn't get anyone to watch the shop. I'm so sorry I missed it."

Theodosia drew breath, thinking. Snelling sounded sincere. Then, again, so did Ted Bundy when he worked the hotline at a women's crisis shelter.

She plunged ahead with her plan. "The reason I'm calling," she told Snelling, "is to invite you to an event this Saturday night."

"Oh?" Now Snelling sounded genuinely puzzled.

"Yes," said Theodosia. "A local author and historian by the name of Lyndel Woodruff is doing a book reading at the Heritage Society this Saturday night. He's written a book titled *The Battle of Honey Hill?* Anyway, there's going to be a cocktail party afterward and some of Daria's friends will be there." Crossing her fingers, Theodosia went on with her little white lie. "There'll be a sort of remembrance for Daria, too."

"I've met Woodruff," said Snelling. "And the reception afterward . . ." He hesitated.

Was he going for it? Theodosia wondered. Was that enough to bring Snelling up here so she could take a look at him? Quiz him. Maybe even get Tidwell to speak to him. Informally, of course.

"I'll try to make it," said Snelling.

"Excellent," breathed Theodosia.

"The Heritage Society you say?"

"That's right. You know where Gateway Walk is? The Heritage Society is located at the far end of it."

"Yes," said Snelling. "I've been there a number of times."

"I look forward to meeting you," said Theodosia.

Pleased and a little embarrassed with her ruse, Theodosia wiggled back into her shoes and headed into the tea shop.

The atmosphere out front, to put it mildly, was a love fest. The Gadabouts and the Beaufort tour ladies had seemingly merged into one large, gregarious group. Spirits were running high, tea and lemon tea bread were in constant demand, camera phones snapped playful poses and group photos, and Drayton, standing in the middle of the room, was just about to begin a recitation.

"He's a charmer," Miss Dimple said to Theodosia, as she stood in the doorway watching the proceedings. "Those ladies have been begging Drayton to recite one of his tea poems ever since they arrived."

"I doubt he needed much prodding," said Theodosia. Drayton, as parliamentarian and frequent lecturer at the

Heritage Society, adored an appreciative audience. And this one was so warmed up, he could have read the phone directory and received a shower of applause.

"Look at him," said Miss Dimple. "He loves it." And with that, Drayton stepped to the center of the room.

"Just a small piece," he told the group, "snipped from a lovely poem written by Minna Irving back in 1920 titled 'My Fragrant Cup of Tea.'"

> *I pour the steaming amber drink*
> *In china thin and fine,*
> *Gold banded, bordered daintily*
> *With wild rose flower and vine,*
> *Add cream and sugar or condensed,*
> *And sipping slowly see*
> *A film of far off scenes unroll,*
> *The drama of the tea.*

Applause rang out and Drayton, not one to loosen his grip on an audience, reached over and grabbed a pink-and-white tea cozy. "Thank you kindly," he told the women. "And now, I simply must show you a new tea cozy that the Indigo Tea Shop has added to our giftware section."

"He's really good," marveled Miss Dimple.

"Drayton could sell Ginsu knives at a state fair," responded Theodosia.

"This new wraparound tea cozy fits directly over your teapot and stays there," continued Drayton. "No more pulling your tea cozy off to pour." He popped the pink-and-white-gingham tea cozy onto a teapot, demonstrating for the crowd. "You see? Plop it on and simply pull the drawstring ribbon to snug the tea cozy tightly. Now only the teapot's handle and spout are left sticking out."

A woman in a froufrou red hat raised her hand. "You have other colors?"

"Of course," said Drayton. "Other patterns, too." He set the teapot down and adjusted his glasses. "Gingham, patchwork, and a lovely ticking stripe as well."

"And you sell loose tea?" asked another woman.

Drayton pointed toward the shelves and highboy that stood against the brick. "Thirty-seven different kinds of tea, with many available for sniffing thanks to my new scent jars. And, of course, we also have our T-Bath products, a selection of antique teacups, DuBose Bees Honey, and our wild grapevine wreaths decorated with miniature teacups."

Needless to say, more than a few tins of tea, wreaths, and jars of honey were sold that day.

"What a success," Drayton chortled some forty minutes later as they cleared the tables, loading dirty dishes into gray plastic tubs. "Even though it's more work, I adore having larger groups come in."

"Then you're in luck," Haley told him, with a mischievous grin. "Since we have another group coming in tomorrow."

Drayton let loose an inquisitive, "Oh?"

"That's right," continued Haley, looking even more impish than usual. "Tomorrow's our children's tea."

Drayton suddenly straightened up like a martinet called to attention. "Tell me it isn't so."

"No can do," said Haley with a laugh, "since it's really happening." She glanced over at Theodosia. "Right, Theo?"

Theodosia nodded. "It's been on our calendar for almost two months."

Now Drayton looked exasperated. "The event completely slipped my memory." He shook his head. "I seem to be having more and more lapses the older I get. Probably, I should stay home tomorrow and try to recover my . . ."

"No way." Haley laughed. "You're going to work this tea if it kills you."

"But . . ." said Drayton, sounding genuinely aghast, "there'll be *children* present. I don't generally deal well with children."

"This will be good for you," Haley assured him. "Help you get reacquainted with your own inner child."

"Drayton doesn't have an inner child," Theodosia commented, as she picked up a Crown Dorset Chintz and Cameo teapot and wiped the outside with a dish towel. "He was born old."

"Thank you, Theodosia," said Drayton, looking slightly heartened. "Yes, I've always had an old soul. Although I believe the more appropriate term would be mature. Case in point, my great-uncle Edgar taught me how to play chess at the tender age of three and I'm pleased to say I never looked back."

"Wait a minute," said Haley, not quite buying Drayton's story. "You're telling me you never played cops and robbers? Or mumblety-peg? Or whatever it was people did back in the Dark Ages?"

"Not when I could be reading Dickens," said Drayton. "Or classics like *Moby-Dick* or *Treasure Island*."

"Please!" Haley begged, "just spare me the anguish of recounting how many miles you trudged to school. Or how you had to haul wood to stoke the fireplace or something."

"No fireplace." Drayton smiled. "Central heating."

"Wow," said Haley, pretending to be amazed. "Modern stuff."

17

While Haley bustled around in the kitchen, prepping food for the open house that night at the Featherbed House B and B, Drayton fussed over a fern terrarium.

"That's a lovely arrangement," Theodosia told him. "I hope it's for display here at the tea shop." Drayton had taken a large glass bell jar, filled it with rich black dirt and bright green sphagnum moss, then planted an assortment of ferns. Southern lady fern, netted chain fern, even a cinnamon fern.

"It's actually a prototype," Drayton told her. "If this terrarium turns out nicely, I thought I'd make one for each table."

"Your arrangement is gorgeous," Theodosia told him. "In fact, it's so lush and elegant looking you could probably turn out a bunch and retail them." Indeed, she'd seen terrariums and other botanical arrangements selling for well over two hundred dollars at Floradora, the floral shop down the street.

"Making them via assembly line might take the fun out of it," said Drayton, as he picked up a final shoot of resurrection fern using his long silver bonsai tweezers and carefully transferred it into his terrarium.

"Suppose so," said Theodosia, looking at her watch. "You realize, we're supposed to meet Timothy Neville at four to finalize the food for Saturday night?"

"We've got time," murmured Drayton. He was judiciously placing a small rock into his grove of ferns. Interestingly enough, the addition of the rock suddenly gave the arrangement a sense of scale. Made it look like a believable landscape.

"Then I'm going to . . ." began Theodosia, just as a loud knock sounded on the front door.

She scurried over, thinking, *Must be stragglers. Tourists who don't know we're closed.* "I'm sorry," she called, putting her mouth to the door. "We're closed for the day." She peeked through the leaded glass window, gave a start as she suddenly recognized the straggler, and murmured, "Oh dear."

Turning the latch, Theodosia pulled open the door and let Fallon in.

Daria's sister didn't look much different than she had this morning. Sad, forlorn, a slightly defeated slump to her shoulders. Her black jacket was a little too large for her, her skirt a tad too long. The word *dowdy* bubbled up in Theodosia's mind, then she dismissed it as being mean-spirited.

"Apologies," Theodosia told Fallon as she lead her to a table. "I didn't realize it was you." She sat down across from her, then popped up from her chair. "Let me bring you a cup of tea."

Fallon smiled faintly. "That would be nice."

"Already have one for you," said Drayton, hustling toward them and setting a gleaming cup and saucer in front of their guest. "I hope you enjoy Assam tea?" he asked Fallon. "This one's nice and strong. Help perk you up from the difficult day you've had."

"Thank you," said Fallon, watching carefully as Drayton poured a hot, steamy stream of tea into her cup.

"My deepest sympathies," Drayton murmured to Fallon.

She made a sound in the back of her throat, acknowledging him.

Then Drayton said, "I'll leave you two alone." And melted away.

"This is so kind of you," said Fallon, staring at Theodosia. Her eyes were still red-rimmed and glistening and Theodosia hoped she hadn't been on a daylong crying jag.

"Try the tea," urged Theodosia.

Fallon picked up the cup and gingerly took a sip. "Mmm. Good." She took a longer, more satisfying sip, then placed her cup on the saucer with a tiny clink. Her troubled eyes met Theodosia's kind eyes. "You know why I'm here?" she asked.

"I have a fairly good idea," said Theodosia. "But why don't you tell me in your own words."

"I . . ." Fallon tried, but faltered badly.

Theodosia reached across the table and patted her hand. "Take your time."

Fallon worried her lower lip with her teeth for a while, then said, "Not to put pressure on you or anything, but do you have anything at all on Daria's killer?"

How to begin? Theodosia wondered. *And how much should I tell her?*

"Your aunt Libby was quite outspoken about how clever you are," said Fallon. "And how you've cracked cases before."

"Mostly I just ask questions," Theodosia responded.

"That's not what I've heard," said Fallon, doggedly. "I hear you're famously good at unraveling mysteries."

"Unraveling," murmured Theodosia. But as she pondered Fallon's words, she decided that was a legitimate way to describe her investigatory style. She'd pick up a germ of an idea, tug on a string, and pull something into place. Of course, with more ideas and loose ends popping up, she generally ended up in a tangle and was forced to sort things out. Clues, people, events.

"The police still don't have any idea who strangled Daria," said Fallon. She hunched her shoulders forward and stared forcefully at Theodosia, as if willing her to take up the cause.

"The police, especially Detective Tidwell, who seems to be honchoing the investigation, are playing it close to the vest," Theodosia agreed. "But I doubt they're without ideas. Or suspects."

"After everything your aunt Libby told us," said Fallon, "I think I trust you more. And, of course, you . . ." She stopped. Her unspoken words, *you were there*, hung in the air between them.

"I understand what you're getting at," said Theodosia, any semblance of a smile slipping from her face. "And I'm still beating myself up about that. I mean, I should have reacted quicker. I should have given chase. I should have . . ." Theodosia drew a deep breath. "I should have done more."

Fallon brushed away a tear. "But you are now, aren't you? Asking questions and all?"

Theodosia nodded, tears forming in the corners of her eyes. "Honey, I'm going to give it my all."

Fallon stood up abruptly and came around the table. Slipped her thin arms around Theodosia and hugged her gratefully. "Thank you," she said, tears streaming down her face. "I don't even *know* you and I trust you. No wonder your aunt Libby says such wonderful things about you."

"Well," said Theodosia, sniffling and slightly embarrassed now. "She is my aunt."

"Bless her," said Fallon. "And bless you."

"Is she going to be okay?" Haley asked, once Fallon had left. "She seems to be in a real tailspin. You think she can pull herself out of it?"

"Eventually she will, yes," said Theodosia. Standing in the kitchen doorway, she watched as Haley mashed pimentos and walnuts into cream cheese. Filling for one of tonight's tea sandwiches.

"How about you?" asked Haley. "How are you doing?"

"I'm good," Theodosia assured her. "Don't worry about me."

"But you're going to keep at it, right?" said Haley. "See if you can make sense out of things?"

"I'm going to do that," said Theodosia. "Yes."

"Want me to get you a can of mace?" asked Haley. "There's this really nasty stuff called Stop-Em-Dead. Kind of a cross between mace and pepper spray. I think cops even use it."

Theodosia shook her head and chuckled softly. "That's one of the strangest offers I've had, Haley. Thanks for your concern, but no, thanks. When I go out at night I'm going to put my trust in Earl Grey."

"And in me," said Drayton, coming up behind her. "Don't forget those kung fu lessons I took at Master Kwan's dojo." He suddenly jumped forward, knees bent, arms akimbo, assuming a martial arts pose. "Since I earned my black belt in under two years, these hands are deadly weapons registered in three states."

"What?" said Haley, looking startled. "Seriously?"

Drayton pointed a finger at Haley and winked. "Gotcha!"

"Oh you!" exclaimed Haley, searching for something to throw at him, finally coming up with a half-eaten scone.

"Watch it!" cried Drayton, ducking. "We could sell that as half-price baked goods tomorrow."

"Not from my kitchen you won't," declared Haley.

But still Theodosia and Drayton couldn't get out the door. Because just as they were ready to leave, Tred Pascal showed up.

"Five minutes," said Drayton, looking dour and tapping his watch face. "That's it, then we have to leave."

"Right," said Theodosia, absently. People seemed to be popping up like errant mushrooms today and she was up to her elbows in events. She was starting to feel the frazzle and pictured herself dashing about like one of those old vaudeville performers spinning multiple plates on sticks. Because she *still* had to get to the Heritage Society, work out a menu with Timothy, dash back home to walk Earl Grey, then grab Haley and all the packed-up food so they could hustle over to the Featherbed House. Yikes.

"What's up?" Theodosia asked Tred as they stood by the front counter. She figured if they remained standing she might be able to hustle the meeting along. She was also strategically positioned so Haley could come sashaying out to flirt with the young archaeologist.

"We're going to go ahead and dig," Tred told her. "We talked to the owner of your property and he's granted us permission. Signed off on all the paperwork."

This didn't come zooming like a comet from the blue for Theodosia. "I figured that," she told Tred. "But please, tell me exactly what you'll be doing."

"Well," said Tred, "it's pretty much going to be a controlled dig."

"Controlled," said Theodosia. "Run that by me with a little more detail, will you?"

"We'll probably stake out a twelve-by-twelve-foot area," Tred explained, "since your backyard's not all that big. Then we'll divide it into three-by-three-foot squares and dig each square down about a foot or so. If we haven't encountered anything by that time, we dig down another foot."

"So," said Theodosia. "The digging down part. Exactly how far do you intend to go?"

"Maybe thirty feet down," said Tred.

"What!" shrieked Theodosia.

"Just kidding," said Tred, finally cracking a smile. "No, it'll be three or four feet max. We don't find anything at that depth, we let it go. No sense completely ripping up private property."

"An archaeologist with a heart," said Theodosia.

"No." Tred chuckled. "Just a limited budget."

"You'll be doing this yourself or bringing in students?"

"I'll jump-start things myself," said Tred, "then hand off to reinforcements. Archaeology and anthropology students mostly."

"Okay," said Theodosia. She couldn't launch much of a protest since she didn't technically own the property yet. And she didn't see that digging up the backyard was that big a deal. Frankly, it could serve as the basis for some landscaping of her own. Help make her backyard a little more pet friendly. She'd read a recent article about the importance of adding a doggy woodchip area, planting shrubs to divert dogs from creating a "racetrack" in the yard, and giving them a few rocks to use as hidey spots.

"When do you start digging?" she asked.

"First thing tomorrow," said Tred. "You should be there. I've got a couple of papers that need your signature, too. Can you stop by?"

"I suppose."

Tred picked up a tin of Earl Green tea that was sitting on the counter and hefted it. "I really enjoyed the tea you fixed for me the other day."

"We'll turn you into a tea connoisseur yet," said Theodosia.

He took a step closer to her. "I think I already am."

"Theodosia?" called Haley.

One hand slowly parted the celadon-green velvet curtains, then Haley stepped out into the tea room. "Oh. I didn't realize we had company." Haley said it with such amazing innocence and guile that Theodosia couldn't help smiling.

"You remember Tred Pascal," said Theodosia. "From the State Archaeology Office."

"Of course," said Haley. She threw a warm smile at Tred, lifted her long blond hair off her neck, then let is cascade down over one shoulder. "Really nice to see you again." She put a tiny emphasis on *really*.

Tred colored slightly. "Great to see you, too."

"You coming to the Heritage Society Saturday night?" Haley asked him. "We're catering all the fixin's." Haley reached into her apron pocket and pulled out an invitation. "Oh look, I just happen to have an invitation." She handed it to Tred. "Lyndel Woodruff wrote a book on the Honey Hill battle," she added, as Tred scanned the invitation. "There's a reading and a reception afterward."

"Sounds neat," he told her. "Thanks. Maybe I'll drop by."

"Great," said Haley. "Maybe I'll see you then." She gave a little wave and disappeared between the curtains in a slightly mysterioso manner.

"Before you take off," said Theodosia, delighted that Haley had enjoyed her little moment, "there's something I want to ask."

"Shoot," said Tred, still clutching his invitation.

"You know anything about the Kipling Club?"

"Those idiots!" Tred spit out. "Yeah, I know *of* them."

"I take it they're persona non grata in the archaeology community," said Theodosia.

"They're not even *in* the archaeology community," said Tred. "They're just a pack of treasure hunters, interested in digging up arrowheads, pottery, and fossils so they can cash in."

"That's it?" said Theodosia. "They sell the stuff?"

"Like mercenaries," added Tred.

Theodosia nodded. "Lot of that going around."

* * *

The Heritage Society sat like a medieval castle at the far end of Gateway Walk, an enormous stone fortress that was the designated repository for the historical treasures of Charleston and its surrounding environs.

Hanging on its walls were early American oil paintings by such artists as Henry Benbridge, Jeremiah Theus, and John Wollaston. The cypress-paneled library held thousands of leather-bound volumes, a few of which dated back to Benjamin Franklin's own printing press. The Heritage Society's storage rooms contained thousands of paintings, prints, and maps, as well as early tradeware, artifacts from area rice and cotton plantations, firearms, antique uniforms, old silver, a fine collection of glass plate negatives, and a couple of prints by John James Audubon.

At the front desk, Camilla Hodges, the majordomo receptionist for the Heritage Society, greeted Theodosia and Drayton. She was sixty-something and petite, with a waft of white hair and the lingering scent of Arpège, or something equally old-fashioned.

"Good afternoon, Camilla," said Drayton. "Is Timothy available?"

Camilla grinned up at Drayton, who was quite obviously one of her favorite board members. "He is, and he's been waiting for you. Anxiously, I might add."

"We are a little late," admitted Theodosia. "I hope it's not a problem."

"It probably is," said Camilla, "but that's because Timothy is tightly wired. But . . . we're used to making allowances for that here. After all, he is the heart and soul of the Heritage Society."

Theodosia giggled to herself as she and Drayton marched down a hallway carpeted with whisper-soft Chinese rugs. She could easily conjure up a few other excellent descriptors for Timothy.

"Look sharp," said Drayton, as they pushed their way into Timothy Neville's cavernous office, as if he knew what Theodosia had been thinking.

Turning his famously stern gaze on the two of them, Timothy half rose in his tufted red leather chair, then quietly lifted a hand, indicating for Theodosia and Drayton to be seated. They crossed a wide expanse of carpet and slid into the leather-and-hobnail club chairs that faced Timothy's massive wooden desk. And once again, Theodosia felt a hint of suspicion that the chairs had been purposely lowered to enable the diminutive Timothy to face them precisely at eye level.

"What have you there, Timothy?" asked Drayton. Timothy wore white gauze gloves on both hands and was obviously in the middle of handling the small, framed oil painting that sat on his desk in front of him.

Theodosia pulled herself up straighter, the better to see.

"An early American oil painting attributed to Sir Godfrey Kneller," Timothy told them. It was a small painting, maybe twelve by fourteen inches including frame, of a lovely young woman wearing a pink gown. She was youthful but resolute-looking, with diamond earbobs and long, dark hair pinned up in a twist. The artist had seen to give her cheeks the same rosy glow as her gown.

"Lovely," said Theodosia. Though the oil paint was threaded with hairline cracks, the painting still had a strong presence.

"Only problem is," said Timothy, "Kneller wasn't really the artist."

"Is that so," said Drayton.

"Sir Godfrey Kneller enjoyed some repute as a sort of society artist," explained Timothy, "but most of his paintings were actually executed by Charles Bridges."

"So Bridges was a ghost painter," said Theodosia. "Along the lines of a ghost writer."

Timothy nodded. "Something like that, yes."

"Still," said Drayton. "An interesting piece for the Heritage Society. Since it is authentically old."

"I'm told it dates to 1750," said Timothy.

"Wow," said Theodosia. "And this was a recent gift?"

"Donation," said Timothy. "Someone discovered it in their attic. After it was dusted off, we became the lucky recipient."

"Remind me to check my attic again," said Drayton, who lived in a small, wooden, Civil War–era house.

"Good thing they didn't take it to *Antiques Roadshow*," said Theodosia. Then, focusing all her attention on Timothy, she said, "Have you by any chance located one of the maps you mentioned the other night? One that might shed some light on the location of my house and the . . . er . . . usage of the backyard?"

Timothy's normally tight brow furrowed. "I'm afraid I have not." He waved a hand, seemed to notice he was still wearing his gauze gloves, then pulled them off. "Been awfully busy. So much going on here." He gazed at her purposefully. "But I'll assign someone to look."

"Appreciate that," said Theodosia.

"So," said Timothy. "The menu for Saturday evening. More last-minute planning." He sighed heavily.

Drayton folded one leg over the other, placed both hands loosely in his lap, and responded pleasantly. "Not really. Lyndel's reading is still a couple days away and we pride ourselves on speed and efficiency."

At that Timothy managed a faint smile. "Miss Browning?" he asked, raising his eyebrows in his tight, almost simian-looking face. "I presume, then, you've already prepared a menu?"

Theodosia hadn't, but she wasn't going to give Timothy the satisfaction of knowing she'd come unprepared. "Of course," Theodosia responded. "I was thinking of simple hors d'oeuvres. Shrimp and avocado kabobs, smoked salmon and goat cheese on baguette slices, and crab salad in puff pastries. Finger food."

Timothy steepled his fingers and nodded. "And you're assuming a full bar?"

"I think we should go simpler," said Theodosia. "Hot Russian caravan tea and flutes of champagne. Something top quality like Veuve Clicquot." She knew this was one of Timothy's favorites, since he stocked it by the case in his wine cellar. "And maybe, for a fun twist, some tea-tinis."

"Pray tell," said Timothy, his bright eyes betraying his interest, "what is a tea-tini?"

Theodosia turned her gaze calmly on Drayton. "Drayton?" She didn't have an actual tea-tini recipe in her head at the moment, but she knew she could count on Drayton.

"Glad you asked," said Drayton, leaning forward, never missing a beat. "Firefly Vodka, a local South Carolina distillery, makes Sweet Tea vodka, Raspberry Tea vodka, Mint Tea vodka, and several more."

"Hah!" said Timothy. "Intriguing. Served in martini glasses?"

"Of course," said Drayton.

Timothy mulled over their suggestions for a few moments, then said, abruptly, "I like everything you've proposed. Sophisticated but not overly fussy."

"That's us," said Drayton.

Theodosia nudged the toe of her shoe against Drayton's shin, then added, "We're thinking of serving a dessert, too."

"A sweet," said Drayton.

"Toll House cookie bars," said Timothy.

"Hmm?" said Drayton.

"I have a recipe," said Timothy, looking pleased. "Passed down from my great-grandmother. I'll have Camilla e-mail it to you immediately."

"I'm sure our Haley will adore your recipe," said Drayton, as Theodosia kicked him again.

18

❧

Thursday night at the Featherbed House. Candles blazed, overstuffed couches and chairs beckoned, and an admiring crowd of tourists and locals drifted in and out of the sprawling lobby. Because the Featherbed House B and B didn't just look cozy, it was adorable bordering on splendid.

The geese, of course, were the focal point. Angie Congdon's Featherbed House was famous for its collection of handcrafted geese. There were giant white ceramic geese, calico geese, carved wooden geese, plush geese, needlepoint geese, and even colorful embroidered geese. All clustered in corners, perched on tables, cozied into chairs as pillows, and hung on walls. There were even geese motifs in the colorful rugs that graced the pegged wooden floors.

Theodosia and Haley had arrived at the Featherbed House just in the nick of time, just as the very first guests were starting to shuffle up the front walk for a guided tour. They set up hastily in the lobby, spreading everything out on a large, wooden trestle table set against a white board-and-batten wall. A window in the center of that wall afforded a view to the backyard garden. On either side of the window were geese paintings, trivets, and wall hangings.

"Holy smokes," said Haley, as they watched people pour in, "this Bed-and-Breakfast Tour is bigger than I thought it would be."

"I think there might be a lot of curious neighbors," said Theodosia. "Folks who are dying to get a look inside some of the grander old homes that were big enough to convert into B and Bs."

"You're probably right," said Haley, as she poured cups of pomegranate oolong tea and doled out pimento-walnut tea sandwiches as well as beef and cheddar tea sandwiches.

"Oof," said Theodosia, blowing a strand of hair from her face. "Warm in here."

"But your hair looks great," said Haley. "Really puffed up."

Theodosia patted her hair nervously. When the heat and humidity rose, which it tended to do in Charleston, her auburn hair, always full to begin with, expanded dramatically and formed an exotic halo about her head. "That's called frizz," said Theodosia, patting it again, wishing for some sort of control.

"Still," said Haley, "it's better than stick-straight hair like mine."

"I don't know about that," said Theodosia, sneaking a peek in the mirror, wishing she could somehow tame her mane.

"Anyway," said Haley. "You look great even though you're probably bushed. You've had a busy day and your meeting with Timothy ran long."

"Not so much running long as starting late," Theodosia told her. "But at least we got his menu figured out."

"And you're absolutely positive Timothy wants us to use his great-grandmother's cookie bar recipe?" asked Haley. She looked a little glum.

"Are you kidding?" said Theodosia. "He's already e-mailed it. I took a quick look and there's nothing too tricky, just your basic Toll House cookie recipe."

Haley wrinkled her nose. "I was hoping to make profiteroles and fill them with my homemade sour cream ice cream."

"Mmm," said Theodosia, then decided to pitch Haley on a compromise. "What if you whipped up ice cream cookie bar sandwiches instead?"

Caught off guard, Haley said, "What? Using Timothy's cookie bars?"

"Sure. Why not?"

"So my sour cream ice cream with Timothy's cookie bars," said Haley, mulling it over.

"Sounds delicious," said Theodosia, coaxing.

"I suppose," said Haley. "But . . . hey, are you going to run this idea past Timothy?"

Theodosia grinned. "Sure. And then we'll probably exchange banana bread recipes. What do *you* think?"

"Point taken," said Haley. "And surprises are fun. For most people anyway." She gazed out over the front parlor, blinked with recognition as she spotted two familiar faces in the crowd, and said, "Whoops, look what the kitty cat just dragged in. It's . . ."

"Delaine!" exclaimed Theodosia, as Delaine Dish elbowed her way toward them. "And Nadine. Nice to see you both." Delaine was a vision of sophistication in her hot-pink sheath dress with long, swishing strands of creamy white pearls. Nadine wore almost the same dress in canary yellow, only with black pearls.

"Isn't this an utter madhouse?" complained Delaine. "So many people. *Too* many people."

"It's an open house," said Haley, deadpan.

"Which I'm afraid is also an open invitation to the riffraff."

Delaine sighed, fanning herself with her silver clutch purse and managing to look put-upon. "But I suppose this kind of crowd can't be helped."

"Duh. Angie wanted this crowd," said Haley.

"Are you ready for your big fashion show tomorrow?" Theodosia asked, hoping to steer the conversation in a more positive direction.

"More than ready," declared Delaine. "Cotton Duck is decorated to the nines, the chairs are arranged, runway installed, models have been fitted, and we're absolute stocked to the rafters with new merchandise."

"Now if our show attendees will just buy," put in Nadine.

"Of course, they'll buy," snapped Delaine. "They *always* buy."

Nadine looked puzzled. "But you said . . ."

"Never mind that," said Delaine, "let's take a look around and see if we can find Angie." She screwed her face into an exaggerated smile and waggled her fingers. "Bye-bye," she called to Theodosia and Haley.

"Byeeee," said Haley, rolling her eyes once she was sure Delaine was out of sight. "Are you *really* going to her fashion show tomorrow?" she asked Theodosia.

"I told her I would," said Theodosia. "Why, do you want to come along? I'm sure it wouldn't be a problem."

"It would be for me." Haley laughed. "'Cause her kind of glitz and glam is so not my style. Hey." She put a hand on Theodosia's shoulder. "I'm going to zip into the kitchen and grab a couple more trays of food, okay? We're going through tea sandwiches like jujubes at a Disney flick."

Theodosia straightened a stack of plates and was about to pop a miniature apple-raisin scone into her mouth when she heard a familiar whisper.

"Oh, tea lady. Tea lady . . ."

She knew that voice. It was . . . Theodosia turned to find Bill Glass looking at her, his expression halfway between a smirk and a leer. A smleer? Yeah, maybe.

"Don't you know it's rude to stare?" she told him.

"I'm lining up a shot," he said matter-of-factly, then hefted his Nikon to add credence to his statement.

"Well, please don't," she said. "In fact, I'm not even on speaking terms with you anymore. I saw the crappy article you wrote about me in your silly *Shooting Star* paper."

"But a cute picture of you, wouldn't you say?"

"There was nothing cute about it," said Theodosia, as Glass held his camera up and clicked off a couple of shots.

Theodosia threw up her hands. "Leave me alone," she pleaded. "*Please* leave me alone. Go take photos of Angie and the guests. Especially Angie. This place can use the press. Even bad press like yours."

"Come on," wheedled Glass. "You're lots more fun. I can always get a rise out of you. Besides, you look cute in that silvery dress."

Theodosia blushed, wishing she hadn't worn such a sporty T-shirt dress. "No," she said, deciding to treat Bill Glass like an unwelcome alley cat who'd come slumming around her back door looking for a handout. "No, you run along outside."

"Hey, babe, a couple more?" cajoled Glass. "What can it hurt?"

"Rats," Theodosia muttered, as she capitulated and posed with a pot of tea in one hand. That seemed to do it. Glass gave an approving nod, held up his camera, and took a few more pictures.

"Safeties," he told her.

"Fine," said Theodosia. "Done now?"

"I guarantee you're gonna love . . ." Glass studied the image on his small LCD monitor and scowled. "Huh."

"What's wrong now?" asked Theodosia. "You forget to remove your lens cap?"

Glass shook his head. "Nah, there's like a ghost image or something."

"Angie always told me this place was haunted," Theodosia joked.

"I'm serious," said Glass. "It almost looks like there was someone standing behind you." He looked up and gazed past her. "Funny. There really must have been someone." He gestured with his thumb. "Peering in that window."

Theodosia whirled around. There was a window there, all right, but no one was peering in. At least not now.

Glass was still thoughtful. "That's gotta be it," he muttered.

"Just delete the shot if you don't like it," Theodosia advised him. "In fact, I'd be delirious if you deleted *every* shot."

"Ha-ha," said Glass, giving a shrug, while still puzzling over the image. "I'll just count that as my artsy shot."

Angie Congdon was thrilled with both the food and the turnout. "I had no idea so many people would show up!" she gushed to Theodosia and Haley. "It's amazing what a few flyers can do."

"There were a couple of community event mentions on the radio, too," said Theodosia. "Which was nice since electronic media always garners attention."

"Oh," said Angie to Theodosia. "Did the person who was looking for you find you?"

"You mean Bill Glass?" asked Theodosia, as she hurriedly arranged more scones.

"No, there was a woman," said Angie. "Came in the back way, asked for you by name. I sent her over here . . ." Angie saw the look of concern that suddenly clouded Theodosia's face. "What? Something wrong?"

"Exactly what did this woman look like?" asked Theodosia.

Angie screwed up her face, trying to remember. "She was . . . uh . . . I don't know. Average height. Pleasant-looking." Angie waved a hand in front of her, fanning herself, looking flustered. "And . . . gosh I'm sorry to sound so ditzy and flaky, but there've been *so* many people through here tonight."

"That's okay," Theodosia told her. "Don't worry about it. Go charm your guests. Lead a tour or something."

"Is Angie okay?" asked Haley. "She seems kind of harried."

"Just lots going on," said Theodosia, still wondering who'd come looking for her. Delaine coming back to harass her about tomorrow's fashion show? No, that wouldn't be right. Angie and Delaine knew each other.

"This is the last tray of sandwiches," said Haley. "Of both kinds. After that, we're out of luck."

"After that, we're out of here," responded Theodosia.

"This has been kind of fun, though," said Haley. "Kind of makes me want to go on tomorrow night's B and B tour. Check out some of the other places."

"That's what Drayton said, too," said Theodosia. "He's always wanted to poke his head inside the Rosewalk House B and B."

"Supposed to be fancy," said Haley. "With cool rose gardens and fountains out back. One of those hidden Charleston gardens."

Suddenly, Bill Glass was back and directly in their faces, looking cranky and a little panicked, too. "Did you guys see my camera?" he asked. "I set it down for one second and now it's gone!"

"Gone?" said Haley. She sounded disinterested veering toward bored. "What a shame."

"You don't have to be nasty about it," huffed Glass. "That camera cost me almost a grand." He threw a pleading look toward Theodosia. "Theo? You see anybody glom my camera?"

"Nope," said Theodosia, while all she could think was, *Rats, did Nadine get her sticky little fingers on Glass's camera?*

Forty minutes later the cupboard ran dry. They'd been cleaned out of sandwiches and scones and were down to the last dregs on tea.

Haley dragged the debris back into the kitchen, packed it all up in plastic bins, and together they toted it out to Theodosia's Jeep.

As Theodosia popped open the back hatch, Haley asked, "So when are you gonna get your fender and bumper ironed out?"

"Eventually," said Theodosia.

"You call your insurance agent?"

"That I did," said Theodosia.

"Make a police report?"

"Sort of," said Theodosia. "I talked to Tidwell."

"You think he's gonna bend over backward and file all the paperwork for you?" asked Haley. "Sheesh. He's probably forgotten about it."

"You're probably right," said Theodosia, drinking in the cool air and enjoying the darkness that wrapped around them like a soft, cashmere blanket. "Tell you what, Haley, you take the keys and drive back home. I'm going to walk."

"Really?"

"Sure," said Theodosia. "You head home and relax. Leave everything in back, we'll unload tomorrow."

"You going to wander down the block and take a look-see at your new place?" asked Haley.

"Maybe," said Theodosia. "Mostly I'm just going to enjoy a little quiet time."

"I hear you," said Haley, accepting the jingle of keys, then tossing them up and catching them. "But you take care, all right?"

"Will do," said Theodosia. She watched Haley climb into her Jeep, start the engine, then pull self-consciously away from the curb and proceed up the block. Taillights flared red and the turn signal clicked on, then Haley hung a left and disappeared from sight.

Theodosia exhaled slowly and turned back toward the Featherbed House. Guests still milled about on the front porch, every window blazed with lights. Gazing up at a second-story window, Theodosia noticed what was probably the last tour group going through the place, inspecting the high-ceilinged, elegant rooms that were painted a French palette of pale pink, ivory, and pale blue. They were probably marveling over the mounds of down comforters that graced each four-poster bed, too.

Better out here, Theodosia decided. The air was refreshing and the breeze fluttering in from the Atlantic carried a nip of salt and a dash of coolness. But not unpleasant. Theodosia tilted her head back and lifted a hand to massage her neck. Always the back of the neck. That's where she carried her tension. Probably time to hit the spa for a hot stone massage or some deep tissue work. Or maybe take a walk tonight, depending on how Earl Grey was feeling. It'd feel good to blow out the carbon and get some endorphins percolating.

Looking up at the sky, Theodosia saw puffy low clouds scudding along, with patches here and there where stars twinkled through. She tried to find a constellation, thought she might have spotted Cassiopeia, decided it was probably Orion. Then she let her mind wander, thinking about all the commercial fishermen who sailed the Carolina coast and sometimes ventured into the low-country bayous. How they probably depended on the stars for directional navigation. Or maybe they used GPS these days. Who knew? Still, steering by the stars was a romantic notion.

Theodosia wandered back up the walkway, then followed a stone walkway around the side of the house and into the backyard where dozens of pillar candles sputtered low. It was a lovely yard, moody and evocative at night, replete with lush greenery, patio sitting area, and lovely little pond surrounded by judiciously placed boulders of blue granite that had been quarried and carted in from Winnsboro. She walked slowly to the free-form pond, hypnotically drawn by its dark, luminous reflection. Gazing down, Theodosia saw wriggling fish and something else shimmering at the bottom of the pond.

What was it? she wondered. Some sort of underwater light that wasn't working? Yeah, probably. Or, wait a minute, had someone haphazardly dropped one of Angie's good crystal glasses into the drink? Well, that wasn't good.

Getting down on her hands and knees, Theodosia placed her left hand on a large moss-covered rock for support and extended her right arm. She touched cool water, broke the surface with a minimum of ripples, and watched as tiny goldfish darted away from her intrusion. Reaching all the way down into the bottom of Angie's man-made pool, Theodosia's fingers grazed metal. She hesitated for a split second, then stretched her arm down a little deeper still, closing her hand around something that felt like it might be a transistor radio or cell phone.

And fished out what was left of Bill Glass's Nikon.

19

"*You just missed* seeing your seller," Tred Pascal told Theodosia. Standing atop a mound of dirt, wearing khaki shirt and slacks, he looked like he was ready to dig for the lost cities of Troy, rather than poke around Theodosia's backyard. But it was her yard all right. Birds tweeted and flitted from tree to bush, wondering what was going on. The sun burned down, golden and bright in an azure blue sky, promising another glorious early spring day.

"That's not really a problem," Theodosia told Tred. The seller, a somewhat surly lawyer by the name of Dougan Granville, wasn't exactly on her faves list. He was a little too slick for her taste, wore sharkskin suits, and, she suspected, might even have a bite worse than his bark.

"As you can see," said Tred, slightly effervescent now that they were actually starting work, "we're just staking out a grid."

"Just mind the magnolia tree, will you?" said Theodosia. "Take care with the root system." Drayton, who was a bonsai artist and gardening enthusiast, had once explained to her that the root system of a plant, any plant, mirrored below ground exactly what you saw above ground. And since the magnolia tree was large and bushy, Theodosia could only imagine that the root system was equally complex.

"We'll be careful," one of the student diggers assured her. "We've done this before."

"Okay," said Theodosia. "Thanks." She squinted at Tred. "You've got papers for me to sign?"

Back at the Indigo Tea Shop, Theodosia discovered that Drayton and Haley had already set up for morning tea.

"You don't need me," she told them. "You have morning prep down to a fine science. Tea Shop 101."

"Oh, we need you," said Drayton, as he popped a small pink tea candle into a glass teapot warmer. "When one thirty comes, you're going to be our point man."

Theodosia squinted at him, a crooked grin on her face. "What?"

"Point *woman*," Drayton corrected. "For when, sigh, the *children* arrive."

"It's not only children that are coming," Theodosia told him. "Quite a few of the mothers will also be present. So there will be adult supervision."

"That's an enormous relief," was Drayton's snarky comment.

Theodosia reached out and gave him a conciliatory pat on the shoulder. "Don't worry," she said. "You'll do fine. Just be your own, immutable charming self."

"Are you kidding?" shrilled Haley, as she hurried in with a silver tray that held a dozen cut glass bowls filled with white poufs of Devonshire cream. "If Drayton really acts like himself, the self *we* deal with every day, he'll probably scare those kids to death."

"Thank you, Haley, for your kind and generous words of support," said Drayton, gazing at her with hooded eyes.

"On the other hand," said Haley, "maybe Drayton can lead by example and turn them all into proper little ladies and gentleman." At that she practically dropped to the floor, convulsed with laughter.

"I knew I should have confined myself to bed," muttered Drayton. "This entire day is going to be a veritable *trial*."

"A tribulation," prompted Haley.

"No, it's not," said Theodosia, "but it will be interesting. Think of this as another experience that will add to the fabric of our corporate culture." She glanced around the tea shop, glowing cozy and warm from the sun's morning rays that poured through the multipaned windows. The polished, pegged floor fairly gleamed, the tables sparkled with lead crystal glasses, pure white linens, and a mélange of bone china tea ware. The shelves and highboy that served as their gift area had been restocked with tins of tea, T-bath products, tea infusers, tea cozies, and tea timers. It was all so perfect that Theodosia was summarily stunned when her mind suddenly dredged up a vision of the Antiquarian Map Shop. The way it had looked the last time she visited seemed like a harsh contrast to her lovely shop.

Of course, the map shop was sadly without its owner now. And just as the sun shone brightly into the Indigo Tea Shop, gloominess had seemed to pervade the map shop.

But maybe, hopefully, she could do something to change that. Keep asking questions, continue to snoop around, try to find something that might point to Daria's killer. Somehow put into motion a *resolution*.

"Now what's on *his* mind?" muttered Drayton, gazing out one of the front windows, interrupting her thoughts.

"Who?" asked Theodosia.

Her question was answered almost immediately as the front door crashed open and Bill Glass stomped in.

"Oh," said Theodosia, touching a hand to her chest. "You got my message." Then she hurried across the floor to greet him.

Glass looked tired, cranky, and on edge. His photographer's vest hung on his frame and dark stubble shaded his face. "Yeah, I sure did," he told her. "Where is it?"

"You're welcome," said Theodosia, placing a hand on one hip and raising her eyebrows in a questioning gaze.

Glass bristled slightly, then said, "Yeah, okay. Thanks for pulling my camera out of the drink. Thanks for leaving a message with my answering service."

"You're welcome," Theodosia said again, this time much more graciously.

Drayton ducked behind the counter and grabbed the Nikon from the shelf where Theodosia had stashed it. "I was wondering whose camera this was. Figured it might be one of yours," he added as he handed it over to Glass. "Fine piece of equipment."

"Not if it's ruined," said Glass.

"What's the problem?" asked Drayton, who was a bit of a photography buff himself.

"Theo found it in the drink," explained Glass.

"The pond behind the Featherbed House," said Theodosia, translating.

"You don't say," said Drayton, surprised. He turned toward Glass. "Someone pinched it from you?"

"Guess so." Glass sighed. He peered at the Nikon speculatively, fiddled with the lens. "Doesn't look so good."

"See if you can revive it, will you?" asked Theodosia. "There's something I'd like to take a look at."

Both Glass and Drayton threw questioning glances at her.

"That photo you took last night," said Theodosia. "With the person looking through the window?"

Glass stared at her. "Yeah? What of it?"

"I think that might have been the person who stole your camera."

"*What was that* about?" asked Drayton, once Glass had stumped off. He stood at the counter, measuring spoonfuls of Sumatran black tea into a round floral teapot with a perky handle. Made by Meissen, the teapot had once been part of his private collection.

"Bill Glass snapped a photo of me last night and happened to catch a kind of double image," said Theodosia. "I think someone was watching me through the back window."

"But it was an open house," said Drayton. "One that attracted a large crowd. So it could have been anyone."

"I don't think it was just anyone," said Theodosia. She'd pondered that notion the better part of the night and come to the conclusion that someone had been keeping tabs on her.

"So who do you think it was?" asked Drayton.

"If I could conjure a name and a face, I might get a bead on Daria's killer," said Theodosia.

"Now you're scaring me," said Drayton. He touched a hand to his blue-and-yellow-polka-dot bow tie and smoothed it nervously.

"Join the club," said Theodosia. "I've been jumpy ever since somebody tried to run me into that bridge embankment."

"So . . ." Drayton peered at her sharply. "You've made some assumptions as to the killer's identity?"

"Theodosia shook her head slowly. "That's what's so weird, because I really haven't. I mean, I've voiced a few minor suspicions to you and Haley . . . even to Tidwell . . . but nobody has popped up definitively on my radar screen."

"Maybe they have now," was Drayton's ominous response. "Only you have to figure out who it is."

"Not unless Glass can salvage that camera," said Theodosia. "Or I get a whole lot smarter."

* * *

"Guys," said Haley, clapping her hands together. "We've got a super busy day today, so I want to quickly go over the menu, okay?"

"As you wish, Haley," replied Drayton. He was standing behind the counter, arranging teapots, tea strainers, and tins of tea, off in his own fragrant and heady world of Assam, Darjeeling, Gunpowder Green, Yunnan, and Pouchong.

"For our breakfast cream tea," began Haley, "we have cherry scones and carrot cake muffins."

"And lunch?" asked Theodosia. "Early lunch, before the children's tea?"

"The Alice in Wonderland Tea," said Haley.

"Ooh," said Drayton, "the dreaded tea now has a theme. I think Haley's trying to intimidate me."

Haley ignored him. "Early lunch will be fruit salad with date nut bread, asparagus quiche, and chicken salad with chutney on cinnamon raisin bread. Each can be ordered as an entrée for seven ninety-five, or we can make up a kind of luncheon tasting plate consisting of all three for eight ninety-five."

"So we need to reserve the big table and try to get everyone out by one o'clock at the latest," said Theodosia.

"That's about the size of it," said Haley.

"I also have an announcement," said Drayton. "Concerning tea."

"Do tell," said Haley.

"Today we'll be brewing pots of American-grown tea," said Drayton. "American Classic black tea from the Charleston Tea Plantation here in our own backyard and a wonderful oolong from the Fairhope Tea Plantation in Fairhope, Alabama."

"Wonderful," said Theodosia. "I think our customers will enjoy those brews enormously."

Drayton pushed his half-glasses up with an index finger and gazed balefully at Haley. "And what is it you intend to serve at your so-called Alice in Wonderland tea?" he asked.

"That," said Haley, with a cock of her head and a twinkle in her eye, "is my little surprise."

Twenty minutes later they were buzzing with customers. Most of the tables were quickly occupied and Theodosia and Drayton began pouring tea and serving scones and muffins like crazy.

"Our customers are loving our home-grown teas," Drayton whispered to Theodosia as they swished past each other.

Of course they loved the teas, Theodosia thought to herself. Both teas had been grown on American soil, so a good deal of hard work and love had gone into the growing, pruning, and harvesting process. Plus, tea wasn't quite as natural a fit in this country as it was in places like China and India, where the tea-growing tradition had been handed down for several centuries.

Just as she was brewing a special-request single pot of lemon herbal tea, Theodosia glanced up to see Miss Kitty step through her front door. In her bright purple dress with a creamy yellow pashmina wrapped casually around her shoulders, there was no missing her. Drayton, unsuspecting soul, hurried over to greet Miss Kitty and was immediately swept up in her tidal wave of conversation.

"So excited to finally meet you," Miss Kitty burbled to Drayton as she grabbed onto his arm. "I've heard so much about you and your prodigious tea skills, but . . ." She stopped midsentence and gazed around, her bright eyes burning with curiosity. "What an adorable little shop! And so impressive that you brew such a huge variety of teas. Really amazing. And the aromas . . . all this time I thought my perfumery was rich with aromas, but this is over-the-rainbow heavenly, too!"

Since Drayton's face had acquired a slightly dazed

expression, Theodosia hurried over to intercede. "Miss Kitty, hello."

Miss Kitty threw Theodosia a quick smile. "Hello, dear, I was just chatting with darling Drayton here and telling him what a lovely tea shop you folks have. Really darling, like something right out of the English Cotswolds." She hugged Drayton's arm possessively. "I'm assuming you have a table, dear fellow? It's just little old me this morning, but I simply can't wait to sample your tea and goodies."

"Drayton?" said Theodosia. "The table by the fireplace?" Theodosia figured they should put Miss Kitty where she'd be the least disruptive.

"Absolutely," agreed Drayton. He smiled down at Miss Kitty. "This way, madam."

Haley was suddenly at Theodosia's elbow. "Who the heck is that?"

"That," said Theodosia in a low voice, "is the remarkable Miss Kitty. Cinnamon's aunt as well as the brains, and I assume money, behind Jardin Perfumerie."

"Brains, money, and brass," murmured Haley. "Miss Kitty looks like a lady who's used to getting her way."

"Strikes me that way, too," agreed Theodosia.

"And she's openly flirting with Drayton," added Haley. She sounded just this side of disapproving.

"Drayton can handle her," said Theodosia. "This isn't his first waltz around the dance floor."

Haley giggled. "'Spose not."

"That's one crazy lady," Drayton whispered to Theodosia back at the counter. "It's like there's a cyclone whirring inside her head and random words just hurtle from her mouth."

Theodosia laughed silently, her shoulders shaking as she bent over a pot of tea.

"I mean it," said Drayton, chuckling a little himself. "And she wants to talk to you. Says it's of utmost importance."

"Me?" said Theodosia, straightening up. "I wonder what she wants?"

"Get over there," said Drayton, nudging her. "Find out."

"Did Miss Kitty place an actual order?" asked Theodosia. "Or is she just here for conversation and general snoopiness?"

"Oh no, she ordered," said Drayton. "I'm putting together a plate for her now. So if you could be so kind as to deal with her . . ." Drayton hesitated. "And remain at her table until I deliver her tea and scone." He rolled his eyes. "Perhaps then she might be slightly less flirtatious."

But Miss Kitty wasn't a bit flirtatious when Theodosia approached her. In fact, she suddenly switched into tough-as-nails business mode.

"Exactly the person I need to talk to," said Miss Kitty, reaching a tiny birdlike hand across the table to firmly grasp Theodosia's arm.

"How can I be of help?" asked Theodosia, sliding into a chair, noting that Miss Kitty was surprisingly strong for her age and size.

"A favor," said Miss Kitty, her sharp eyes glittering.

"Ah," said Theodosia, relaxing. Miss Kitty was probably going to ask her to cater Jardin Perfumerie's upcoming grand opening, which shouldn't be a problem at all. Or perhaps ask her to serve tea and treats at a trunk show similar to the ones Delaine staged at Cotton Duck. Although she wasn't sure if perfumeries had actual trunk shows. Maybe . . . scent shows?

"It's about that map store next to me," said Miss Kitty, finally launching her conversational grenade. Her eyes were dead serious now, like a slumbering lizard that *appeared* to be in repose but was really itching to strike.

"The Antiquarian Map Store," said Theodosia. "Is that . . . a problem?"

"I want that space," Miss Kitty spat out. "And since you

have a good relationship with the owner, I was hoping you might intercede for me."

Theodosia leaned back in her chair, trying to digest this request that had zoomed out of left field. "Unfortunately," she said, in a tight voice, "the owner is dead."

20

Miss Kitty waved an imperious hand, as if to brush off the insignificant fact of Daria's murder. "I know *that*. I meant the *new* owner. Whoever stands to inherit the place or is set to purchase it. You seem to know all the local denizens and stand in good stead with them, too. So I'd appreciate any help you can give me." She rapped her knuckles on the table as if to punctuate her sentence.

"I'm not sure what you're asking," said Theodosia, stalling. She knew exactly what Miss Kitty was asking, but her mind wasn't formulating a good response or even a decent-sounding excuse. Weasel words, as Haley would call them.

"For starters," said Miss Kitty, "you could help me negotiate a good price." She took a quick sip of tea and gave a wolfish grin. "The way I see it, that old place is distressed property now, so a sublease at a greatly reduced rate should be easy to negotiate." She pulled her napkin from her lap and touched it to her lips, leaving behind a smear of red.

"Plus we're still in the middle of a tough economy, so . . ." She let her words trail off, but kept sharp eyes focused on Theodosia.

"You know," said Theodosia, turned off by Miss Kitty's rapacity, "you really should be talking to the building's owner about this. Or, better yet, enlist a commercial Realtor to determine if that space is even available, then have them handle all negotiations. Realtors take a commission, of course, but they often have the skills and know-how to strike a much more favorable deal."

"Oh, honey," said Miss Kitty, shaking her head in dismay, "I don't want to bother with commercial Realtors and paying commissions." She spat out the word *commissions* like it was cow manure. "I just want to do a little business deal. Keep it among friends, you know?"

Friends, thought Theodosia. *Really? Because it sure doesn't sound like friendship.* She was thinking of a few choice alternate descriptors, all plucked from the list of Seven Deadly Sins, when Drayton suddenly, blessedly, appeared at the table.

"I have a pot of cardamom tea, per your request," Drayton told Miss Kitty. "Plus a fresh-baked scone with Devonshire cream and some lovely lemon curd." He set his tray down, then raised his eyebrows and stared fixedly at Theodosia. "And I certainly don't mean to interrupt, but, Theo, you do have an urgent phone call."

"Oh crap," said Missy Kitty, looking grumpy.

Saved by the bell, thought Theodosia as she quickly stood, murmured a hasty "excuse me," and dashed for her office.

Tred Pascal was on the line. "I have good news," he told her.

"You didn't find any more bones," said Theodosia. "You've finished and are packing up your tools of the trade, anxious to go home." *Wishful thinking on my part?* she wondered. *No, I'm pretty sure the whole bone ordeal is over. And thank heavens for that.*

"No!" exclaimed Tred, the line crackling with static. "We actually found a few more bones!"

"Please tell me you're joking," said Theodosia, her vision of a perfect end to the digging suddenly shattered. Sitting down hard in her desk chair, she stared at the new issue of *Tea: A Magazine* that lay on her desk. Wished with all her heart she could magically disappear into those pages and transport herself to some far-off, exotic tea plantation that was profiled inside.

"All in all, it's a rather exciting turn of events," enthused Tred.

"Sure it is," said Theodosia, without a single vestige of enthusiasm in her voice.

"Anyway," said Tred, "I just wanted to let you know. Looks like we'll be here for a while."

"Peachy," said Theodosia. "Just peachy."

"You don't look happy," said Drayton, when Theodosia finally emerged from her office.

Theodosia shook her head, as if shaking away a swarm of gnats. "The archaeologists found more bones."

Drayton grimaced. "Unfortunate."

"No kidding."

"Do they think it was an execution site?"

"Don't know," said Theodosia.

"So this means the archaeologists will continue digging?"

"For now," said Theodosia. "Yes."

"How long do you think it will take?"

Theodosia flapped her arms in frustration. "Who knows?" She wrinkled her nose, knowing she should try to relax, try to calm down. Getting upset wasn't going to help anything or anyone, least of all herself. She took a deep breath, hummed a quick *"Ommm,"* and asked, "So, how's Miss Kitty faring?"

Drayton peered over his tortoiseshell glasses with an owl-ish expression. "Bending the ear of everyone in her immediate vicinity. Whether they're interested in chitchatting with the old bat or not."

"She is a tough old girl," said Theodosia. Then thought, *But is there more to Miss Kitty than meets the eye?*

"Drayton," said Haley, flipping her straight blond hair back over her shoulders, "you've got to snap to and deliver checks. Try to move our customers out of here."

"They're paying customers," countered Drayton. "We can't just toss them out on their keesters. Besides, this is a tea shop. We're supposed to exude an air of genteel refinement—remember?"

"But I have to get ready for the children's tea," said Haley with a certain amount of stubbornness.

"We have to get ready," countered Drayton. "Which means we shall simply work around our good customers. That's really not a problem, is it? Or are you so obsessive-compulsive you need to have the tea room completely cleared?"

Haley thought for a few seconds. "Cleared would be better."

"For you," said Drayton. "But not for everyone else. Now try to calm down and focus."

"Focus," repeated Haley, staring straight ahead with a glazed expression.

Drayton squinted at her. "That's right."

Haley continued to stared blankly.

"I'm not in the mood for games," said Drayton.

"But she is," said Theodosia, cruising past them with teapots in both hands. "Drayton, don't you know when Haley's putting you on?"

Haley blinked rapidly. "I am? I thought I was focusing."

"I know what you're trying to do," said Drayton, in a smooth voice. "You're trying to get me all discombobulated, right before the children arrive."

"Good call," shot back Haley.

"There will be payback for this," Drayton warned, a crafty expression stealing across his face. "You won't know when or how, but I intend to repay you in kind for all your craziness."

Haley faced Drayton with a lopsided grin. "Bring it on, big guy."

"Don't you have to check on the cakes, Haley?" asked Theodosia. "Drayton, shouldn't you be setting up the large table?"

"I suppose I better get moving," said Haley. She stuck out her hand. "Sorry, Drayton. Friends?"

"You don't have a trick buzzer hidden in your palm, do you?" asked Drayton.

"Drayton!" exclaimed Haley. "Would I ever?"

"Yes!" exclaimed Theodosia and Drayton in unison.

"Oh my goodness!" said Theodosia, gazing at the carefully set tables. "This is simply amazing!" She'd just emerged from her office to do a final check on the tea room before the children and their moms arrived. "How did you . . .?" she stammered. "When did you . . .?" She looked from Drayton to Haley.

Drayton pointed at Haley. "She did it."

"You helped some," admitted Haley.

Theodosia pushed a fluff of auburn hair from her face and grinned from ear to ear. The four tables that had been set up were adorable beyond her wildest dreams. First off, everything carried an *Alice in Wonderland* theme. So there were oversized playing card placemats, little "drink me" bottles of fruit juice, and small white, fuzzy rabbits capering across the tablescape. Plus *Alice in Wonderland* gift bags for all the children, and pink, purple, and green Mylar balloons bouncing everywhere.

"Where did you find the ceramic Cheshire cat centerpiece?" asked Theodosia, pointing at the fat and saucy grinning cat.

"Borrowed it from Leigh at the Cabbage Patch," said Drayton. "It's actually a cookie jar."

Theodosia turned to another table. "And the cake in the shape of a white rabbit with a fondant pocket watch . . . I know you made it, Haley, but did you decorate it, too?"

Haley executed a slight bow. "Indeed I did."

"And do I really see White Rabbit cups and saucers?" Theodosia asked.

"That's right," said Drayton. "Again, borrowed from our most generous neighbors."

"See?" said Haley. "Once Drayton put his mind to it, he went full steam ahead."

"Only because we made a commitment," said Drayton, holding up an index finger. "When you agree to host a tea party, no matter what the theme or circumstances, you're duty bound to do your best."

"And you most certainly did," said Theodosia.

"Now, if Drayton can only hang in there for the actual party," added Haley.

But ten minutes later, when a dozen little girls and boys came scampering into the Indigo Tea Shop like a group of crazed space invaders, Drayton was the perfect gentlemen.

"That's right, take your seats," he told his youthful audience, as their mothers smiled on. "We have place cards at each setting, so find your name, then settle down."

Amidst giggling, scraping of chairs, and excited exclamations, all the young guests managed to get seated.

"Excellent," said Drayton. "And now, Miss Haley will come around and take your tea order. "Each of you has a bottle of apple juice in front of you, but we're also brewing hot cocoa as well as a very special tea. And I'm pleased to announce our first course will be gingerbread scones."

There were oohs and aahs, much like their adult customers, and then Drayton proceeded around the table with a Mad Hatter teapot.

"Is it really tea?" a young freckle-faced girl with braids asked him.

"A special tea today," Drayton told her. "Warm milk with a hint of vanilla bean and a dollop of tea."

"Will I like it?" she asked.

"My dear young lady," said Drayton, "if it does not please you I shall prepare something more to your liking."

"Thank you," she said in a small voice. "I'll try the tea."

"Good choice," said Drayton.

Then Haley appeared with a tray full of scones. "I hope you all like gingerbread scones," she said. "They're also stuffed with walnuts and apples and dusted with granulated pink sugar."

That brought a round of applause.

"Goodness," said Drayton, watching from the sidelines. "The little munchkins approve."

"You seem surprised," said Theodosia, who'd already had some experience with teddy bear teas and little princess teas.

"No," said Drayton, "I'm stunned."

While tea was being slurped and scones munched, Drayton stepped forward again. This time for an abbreviated lesson in etiquette.

"First point," he told them, "be sure you always settle your napkin into your lap." There were some surreptitious grabs for napkins, then all was quiet. "And when Miss Theodosia brings the tea trays out, be sure to say please and thank you," he reminded them. "Now, most of the foods we'll be serving today are finger foods, so it's perfectly acceptable to eat with your fingers. But, please. Take small bites. Even if a sandwich is small, kindly don't pop the entire thing into your mouth." He gazed around the table, noting the interested expressions. "Needless to say," he continued, "you never talk with your mouth full. And if you want something passed to you, just ask politely, instead of reaching." Firing a stiff glance at two boys who were smothering giggles, he added, "And never, ever, engage in rude discourse at the table—especially such things as a burping contest." He lasered his gaze at the boys. "That means you two fellows!"

Haley nudged Theodosia. "Never engage in rude discourse? He *is* trying to turn them into miniature Draytons."

"But it's working," said Theodosia. "Look, they're raising their hands and asking him questions. They think Drayton's the neatest thing since sliced bread."

"Go figure," said Haley, shaking her head.

Once the detritus from the scones had been cleared away, Drayton poured another round of "tea" and Theodosia and Haley brought out tea trays filled with sandwiches.

"Now you're in for a treat, children," said Drayton. He smiled at Theodosia. "Miss Theodosia is going to tell us what Miss Haley has prepared for us today."

"I think you're going to enjoy it," said Theodosia. "We have peanut butter and jelly tea sandwiches, fruit kabobs, cream cheese and raisin triangle sandwiches, petite cheese tarts, and pretzels coated with honeyed yogurt."

Halfway through the tea, Drayton even did one of his famous recitations for the children. An abbreviated poem he'd picked up somewhere and modified.

> *Let's all sit down together and have a cup of tea—*
> *a nice warm cup of friendship*
> *Brewed with love by me.*

Dessert consisted of the white rabbit cake served with fudge ripple ice cream as well as sugar cookies in the shapes of teapots and clocks.

Afterward, during a rousing game of pin the tail on the white rabbit, when everyone was struggling to keep order, the phone rang.

"Hello?" said Theodosia, turning her back to the tea room. She could hardly hear above the din.

"Theodosia?" came a quiet voice. It was Aunt Libby.

"Hang on, Aunt Libby," Theodosia told her. "I'm going to move into my office." She gestured for Haley to hang up once she'd grabbed the extension, then headed into her office.

"Okay, I'm back," said Theodosia, plopping down into her chair. "Can you hear me?"

"I can now," said Aunt Libby. "But what on earth have you got going there? It sounds like an awfully wild tea party!"

"You have no idea," murmured Theodosia, wondering how they were going to get the crunchy, pink sugar granules out from between the floorboards. Supersonic vacuum cleaner probably.

"I don't mean to put pressure on you, dear, but I was wondering if you'd made any progress," said Aunt Libby. "I was visiting Sophie this morning and she seemed so awfully down. Fallon was there, too. Poor girl isn't faring much better."

"You're such a good friend to Sophie," said Theodosia. "Fallon, too."

"I'm trying," said Aunt Libby. "But it's so difficult not *knowing*. The police tell Sophie they're working the case, but . . ."

"They are working it," said Theodosia. *Just not fast enough.*

"Made any inroads at all?" Aunt Libby inquired in a tentative voice.

"I'm still talking to people, asking around," said Theodosia. She really didn't want to tell Aunt Libby about the accident at the bridge a couple nights ago. It would only worry the poor dear.

"Well, you're a real champ to take this on," said Aunt Libby, encouragement in her voice.

"I haven't done that much," said Theodosia, feeling a tiny twinge of guilt.

"I have faith," said Aunt Libby. "I believe in justice and I believe in *you.*"

"Thank you," said Theodosia. She hesitated. "Still it might not hurt to say a prayer or two."

"I am praying, dear heart," said Aunt Libby. "I truly am."

21

❧

The first thing Theodosia saw when she strolled into Cotton Duck was an elevated runway covered in white Mylar. The second thing she noticed was a knot of ultra-chic, beautifully coiffed women sipping flutes of champagne.

Theodosia had visited Cotton Duck millions of times, but this newly revamped Parisian-looking atelier looked nothing like the Cotton Duck of old. Besides the new earth-tone sisal carpeting, there were tons of green palm trees, low hanging, white-enameled chandeliers, and pinpoint spotlights that drew the eye to the various clothing racks and displays of accessories.

The clothes were the same fluttery evening gowns, feather-light silk tops, and cotton slacks and T-shirts Cotton Duck was know for. Plus new lines of designer pieces, couture handbags, giant status rings, and some very exotic-looking lingerie.

Then Theodosia spotted Delaine in her cadmium-blue-and-yellow short shift dress, flitting from group to group like an overcaffeinated bumblebee and noted that while her shop may have morphed into a cool, sophisticated boutique, Delaine still projected over-the-top enthusiasm.

Catching sight of Theodosia, Delaine threw back her head and screamed, "The-o-dosia!" Elevating the word to an eardrum-bursting pitch. She bulldozed her way through the crowd, grabbed Theodosia's arm in a viselike grip, and hissed, "You didn't dress up. I thought for sure you'd be more dressed up."

"I came from work," explained Theodosia, indulging in a little white lie. Actually, after the kids and moms had all gone home, after the tea shop had been cleared and readied for yet another day, she'd run upstairs and changed into what she'd deemed was a fashionable pair of pale yellow slacks paired with a cream-colored camisole and sporty, cream jacket. But even with the addition of long gold chains, her outfit apparently didn't pass muster with the fashion-conscious Delaine.

"There are serious *society* ladies here today," Delaine told her emphatically. "Come to see my fashion show and view my expanded shop and new lingerie boutique." She pinched Theodosia's arm again. "There's a *reason* I'm outfitted head to toe in Yves Saint Laurent."

"A great-looking outfit," agreed Theodosia, surveying Delaine's lush silk dress. Forty gazillion silkworms had probably given their lives for it. "And I'm sure very expensive."

"You have no idea!" said Delaine.

"But on the plus side," added Theodosia, "you probably didn't have to pay retail."

"Uh . . ." said Delaine, amazingly at a loss for words. Then she said, "Oh *you*. But . . . you showed up, Theo. And that counts for a lot."

"Glad to hear it," drawled Theodosia. "I was beginning to worry."

"There's just a teensy little issue," began Delaine, looking serious now, her voice taking on the tenor of a surgeon addressing the family of a seriously ill patient. "A teensy, weensy problem."

"Okay," said Theodosia.

"One that I hope won't bother you."

"Try me," said Theodosia.

Delaine drew a deep breath. "Even though you are my dearest, bestest, closest friend, I'm afraid we had to seat you in the second row."

"Oh no!" said Theodosia, pretending to be shocked.

Delaine nodded soberly. "I know, I know, Nadine and I hated to bump you, it practically *killed* us, but that's how the seating chart shook out. The thing of it is, it's critical we put the really important customers up front." She looked sorrowful, but firm. "Business, you know."

"I understand completely," said Theodosia, who really didn't care which row she was seated in. Who would have preferred to be elsewhere this afternoon.

"I *knew* you'd understand," Delaine gushed with relief. "I knew that you of all people wouldn't grouse and complain about being seated in the second tier."

"I can live with it," Theodosia told her, because it sure wasn't the worst thing that had happened to her this week.

"You're such a dear," said Delaine, administering a quick air-kiss. "Now you just toddle off and find your seat—your name's on a card somewhere—while I go make nice with the rest of my guests."

"Okaaaaay," Theodosia muttered as she gazed about Delaine's renovated shop. Which, she had to admit, did look rather spectacular.

"We meet again," a male voice murmured in Theodosia's ear.

Theodosia whirled around to find Bill Glass staring at her, a bemused expression on his face.

"What are you doing here?" Theodosia demanded.

Glass shrugged. "Playing photographer again," he said,

touching the Canon that hung around his neck, a camera that Theodosia assumed must be his backup camera. Glass jerked his head at Delaine as she flitted about her shop. "*She* called me. Practically begged me to cover her fashion show."

"First the Chocolatier Fest, now this," said Theodosia. "Is this really in your line of work?"

"Nah," said Glass, "I just hang out to ogle all the great-looking women."

Theodosia raised an eyebrow.

"Hard to get the really hard-core, gritty stuff these days," admitted Glass. "Hard to be timely when everything's splattered all over the Internet within minutes." He sighed. "Seems like more and more I'm falling back on photos and articles about regular, old everyday events."

"That's not completely bad," Theodosia told him. "At least it's honest reporting."

"Just not as much fun," said Glass.

Theodosia reached a finger up and tapped the Canon slung around his neck. "How did your other camera, the Nikon, fare? Ever get it to work?"

Glass shook his head. "Nah. It's completely trashed."

"Couldn't get anything at all?" asked Theodosia. "I was really hoping you could pull up that double image thing from last night."

"Not gonna happen," said Glass. He stepped aside, let the hired DJ in his black leather jacket and matching chain bracelets push by them. "Classy event," he said to Theodosia, flashing a wicked grin.

"We should probably find our seats," suggested Theodosia.

Together they pushed their way through the crowd, eyed an ocean of white folding chairs that each had a name card tacked to the back, then finally located their respective seats. Theodosia's was in the middle of the second row; Glass was almost directly behind her.

Everyone else seemed to have the same idea, because suddenly there was a run on chairs. When the dust settled, a few unhappy guests were left standing, like a contentious game of musical chairs. Bill Glass, as exasperating as he usually was, suddenly scrounged a modicum of manners and offered up his chair.

Then the lights dimmed, a buzz of excitement filled the show room, and the pulsing beat of "Sweet Dreams" by the Eurythmics suddenly blasted from the speakers.

The first model burst onstage to huge applause. Wearing a short black dress with heroic shoulders, she clomped down the runway like she owned it, staring fiercely ahead.

The music pulsed louder.

> *Sweet dreams are made of this*
> *Who am I to disagree?*

The second model swished out in tight white slacks and a belly-grazing shirt, silver chains swinging, large bangle bracelets clanking.

Swinging hips and pouty lips, Theodosia decided. That seemed to be the MO for all these models. Still, they looked elegant yet breezy, showing off the clothes with great panache. Just the thing to intrigue the audience and maybe even stimulate sales.

Theodosia leaned back in her chair, enjoying the show. The music was thumping loud, the models were totally into it, and the guests seemed to be grooving, too.

Four minutes in and twelve outfits later, the DJ segued to a second tune. "Beautiful" by Moby. A little slower, a little more elegant, a little more haughty in atmosphere, but still amped at full volume.

> *Look at us, we're beautiful*
> *All the people push and pull*

Theodosia remembered that particular song from the soundtrack of *The Devil Wears Prada*. It had imparted a powerful statement. Still did for this show. Glancing around, she realized that many of the women around her were making little notes. Probably jotting down what they were going to purchase or special order later. Should she make notes, too? Maybe yes, especially since a swinging black jacket with a diagonal brass zipper had really caught her eye. But good.

Leaning forward, Theodosia reached into her cocoa-colored leather bag that rested in a puddle on the floor. As she did, she squiggled sideways in her chair and her eyes fell upon a woman sitting in the row ahead of her. A woman who looked strangely familiar.

Hmm?

As Theodosia continued to peer down the row, curious, she tried to dredge up a name to go along with that face.

She squinted again and was suddenly gob-smacked with a jolt of recognition.

Oh no, it can't be . . . can it?

Was it Beth Ann? Jory's Beth Ann? The wacked-out girlfriend he'd been previously engaged to? The one Jory claimed was no longer part of his life?

Clearly Beth Ann still was in his life! Because she was here! Sitting front and center at Delaine's spring fashion show. In Charleston. Not Beth Ann's ghost or even a reasonable facsimile thereof, but Beth Ann in the flesh.

The question was . . . why? What was she doing here?

As Theodosia stared with burning curiosity, a million questions zoomed through her brain like chase lights on a movie marquee. Then Beth Ann turned slightly in her seat, twisted her head, and in the dim light, with colored strobes flashing, suddenly met Theodosia's gaze full on.

Startled, caught in the act of staring, Theodosia's initial instinct was to be polite. A smile flickered at her lips and then . . . *ka-pow*! She was knocked back by Beth Ann's cold, icy glare!

What? Why is she . . . ? I mean . . . what is her problem anyway?

Straightening up in her chair, eyes riveted on the runway now, Theodosia fought to compose herself. Not an easy task when someone's shooting chilly daggers at you with their eyes. Or staring at you like they wished you were dead.

Let it go, Theodosia told herself. *Don't worry about Beth Ann.*

But she did worry. In fact, the longer Theodosia sat there, staring at the kaleidoscope of models and colored lights, letting throbbing music wash across her but not really hearing it, the more nervous she became.

Nerves have a curious way of running rampant, of jangling all sorts of emotions and what-ifs. And suddenly Theodosia found herself terrified.

For one thing, since it was quite obvious Beth Ann was camped somewhere in Charleston, then maybe Drayton really had seen her at the Blessing of the Fleet Wednesday night.

And if Beth Ann was still consumed with anger about losing Jory, then maybe Beth Ann was the crazy person who bashed in her Jeep and tried to run her and Earl Grey off the road!

Oh man, this isn't good.

Theodosia jiggled her leg, cleared her throat, and squirmed in her seat as her mind raced crazily.

Could it have been Beth Ann who was peeping in the window last night? Could Beth Ann have stolen Bill Glass's camera because . . . because she was afraid her image had been captured? Yeah, maybe.

Standing abruptly, Theodosia scurried down her row of chairs, in the opposite direction from Beth Ann, bumping knees and whispering "excuse me" all the way. She came out near the end of the runway, ducked behind a stand of klieg lights and then behind a three-panel screen with a trompe l'oeil design of the Champs-Elysées painted on it.

Putting up a hand to still her rapidly beating heart, Theodosia once again asked herself the all-important question, *What's going on?*

Because, just for openers, this had been one wacked-out week. Daria Shand murdered, strange bones turning up in her backyard, her Jeep run off the road by some nutcase, a stalker at the Featherbed House.

Was everything connected or just some of it? If so, how to put the pieces together? The pieces that counted.

Okay, Theodosia thought to herself, let's start with Daria's murder, the night of the back-alley crawl. Detective Burt Tidwell had made the astonishing remark that maybe she'd been the killer's intended victim.

She'd blown it off with a certain amount of anger and angst, but hadn't really taken him seriously.

Until now.

If Tidwell, smart ex-FBI guy and homicide detective that he was, had seen that as a possible angle, then maybe it *was* a legitimate angle. Maybe Tidwell's words had been prophetic; maybe he'd picked up a vibe that she'd missed completely.

Did that mean Beth Ann had murdered Daria Shand? Theodosia wondered. *Fully thinking that Daria was really her?* Possible. But not entirely probable unless . . . unless Beth Ann had been turned into a crazed stalker-killer because Jory jilted her!

Yowza. Got to talk to somebody about this. Have to talk to . . .

"Theodosia!" came a loud whisper. "Why are you crouching back here? Who are you hiding from?" Delaine had slipped up behind her and was peering with great suspicion, as if she'd just caught her in the act of shoplifting. "More important, why aren't you watching the show?"

"I . . . something startled me," said Theodosia, fumbling for words.

"In the show?" hissed Delaine, her voice tinged with disbelief. "On stage?"

"No," said Theodosia clutching Delaine's arm. "Someone here. A guest. A woman who scares the bejeebers out of me."

Delaine cocked her head. "What are you talking about? *Who* are you talking about? I'm sorry, Theo, you're not making sense at all."

"I'll show you," said Theodosia, plucking at Delaine's sleeve and peering around the screen. "*That* woman."

Delaine squinted into the somewhat raucous crowd of fashionistas who were clapping and responding to Rocky, the DJ, on stage. "Can you be a little more specific?"

"Front row, sixth from the end," said Theodosia, waggling a thumb at Beth Ann. "That one."

"Oh," said Delaine, stepping back behind the screen, keeping her voice low. "She's a new customer. But a very good customer I might add. She's already preordered almost two thousand dollars' worth of designer clothing."

"You can't be serious," said Theodosia. Beth Ann had money? She didn't strike Theodosia as having a good deal of disposable income at all.

"Just be careful," Theodosia warned, a cold tingle running up her spine. "That woman is scary-weird."

"Define scary-weird," said Delaine, bunching her perfectly arched eyebrows together. "You mean like she might be over the limit on her charge card or something?"

"No, I mean she's a stalker!"

"Oh," said Delaine, visibly relaxing. "You had me scared for a minute."

"Delaine!" said Theodosia. "Did you just hear what I said?"

"Yes, dear, that the young lady's a stalker." She glanced

at her watch, a fancy, jewel-encrusted Chopard. "Now *please* keep your voice down. My grand finale's set to begin in less than two minutes! Just think, fifteen models strutting down the runway in one glorious burst of glitz and glam!" She hugged herself with glee. "And Rocky's going to play the opening track from *Sex and the City*."

"You're incorrigible, Delaine."

Delaine peered at her. "That's a good thing, right?"

"Sure," said Theodosia.

"Theodosia," hissed Delaine. "In case you haven't noticed, I have a major event taking place! Society women are present! Along with a scattering of trophy wives and wives of million-aires! Do you have any idea how critical these women are to my business? I'm sorry, but it can't always be about you!"

As Theodosia turned in frustration, her eyes fell upon Bill Glass. He'd hurried to the end of the runway, undoubtedly getting ready to line up a key shot. Theodosia hissed and waved a hand at him.

Glass turned, saw her, did a double-take, and touched a finger to his chest. Me?

Theodosia nodded vehemently. Yes, you.

Glass shuffled back to where she was semi-hiding. "What's up?"

"You see that woman sitting there?" whispered Theodosia. "The blond in the front row wearing the red suit?"

Bill Glass peered at Beth Ann, said, "Yeah."

"I want you to take her picture."

Glass made a rude, dismissive sound. "She's nothing special."

"I need to e-mail a photo of her to Detective Burt Tidwell," Theodosia told him. "So please stop being a lunkhead and just do what I ask."

"Why?" asked Glass, challenging her.

"Because I think she might be the one who stole your

camera last night," said Theodosia. *And could be responsible for other strange goings on as well.*

Fumbling for his Canon, Glass sputtered, "Holy shi—"

"Shhh," warned Theodosia, putting a finger to her mouth. "Don't make a big deal about it. Please just *do* it."

22

❦

While Bill Glass dodged his way around Cotton Duck, hopefully getting a few good shots of Beth Ann, Theodosia made
her way to the front door and stepped out onto the street.
With a bright Charleston sun shimmering down through
rustling palm fronds and gently dappling her shoulders,
she plucked her cell phone from her bag and dialed Jory's
number.

When Jory came on the line, she said in a clipped tone of
voice, "This is Theodosia. Where are you?"

Jory was both startled and befuddled. "Excuse me?" he
responded. "What? *Theo?*"

"Yes, it's me," said Theodosia, "and I'm waiting, rather
impatiently I might add, for you to tell me exactly where
you are!"

Now Jory sounded even more flustered. "I'm in New York.
At my office. Why? Where are you?"

"I'm in Charleston where I've always been. Where I will

continue to be. But I have a major news flash for you, my friend." She hesitated, letting her outrage build into a nice head of steam. "Are you sitting down?"

"Yes," said Jory. "What's this all about? I have to run to a meeting in about two minutes."

"You might want to cancel it," Theodosia told him. "Because while you are sitting fat and sassy in your high-rent law office somewhere on the island of Manhattan, your crazy girlfriend is perched ten chairs away from me at a fashion show!"

"What?" exclaimed Jory. Papers rustled, something clunked loudly—a chair going over backward?—and he said, "What?" for the second time.

"You heard me," said Theodosia. She knew she was gritting her teeth and fought to stop before she gave herself a permanent case of TMJ. "Beth Ann is here. In Charleston."

"Doggone," muttered Jory. He sounded confused, maybe even a little outraged. Theodosia was expecting some sort of commiseration, apology, or at least a stumbling explanation, but instead, his next words stunned her. "I knew something like this was bound to happen."

"What!" cried Theodosia, her heart suddenly beating out of her chest. "What are you talking about?" She gripped her cell phone tighter, aware her knuckles had turned white. Wished Jory were standing in front of her right now so she could bonk him on the head. "I want an explanation and it better be good. No, let me rephrase that. It better be stellar." She walked a few paces, moved out into the street where she could scream at Jory without upstaging Delaine's grand finale. Without being stared at by local fashion mavens.

"Beth Ann has been staying at my apartment over on Ashley Street," explained Jory, sounding high-pitched and nervous now. "And I can't seem to get her to leave."

"Excuse me?" said Theodosia. *What on earth is he talking*

about? And, did I hear correctly? He kept his apartment? Or did he get a new one? Was I really in love with this clown?

Jory let loose an audible sigh. "It's a long story."

"Please," said Theodosia, biting off her words. "I have time."

"Beth Ann and I were planning to be married," Jory explained hastily, "and then we unplanned it. But Beth Ann never seemed to comprehend or completely accept the breakup part. And this last time I came down to Charleston on business, she flew down to be with me."

"To be with you," said Theodosia.

"Yes," said Jory. "To try to patch things up, talk me into taking her back."

"And that's when she moved into your apartment," said Theodosia.

"Not really moved in," said Jory. "More like planted herself, like a solid, immovable object."

"Uh . . . did you try asking her to leave?"

"I tried *telling* her to leave," said Jory. "I tried to physically shove her out the door. But I didn't have any luck."

"You should have given her the old heave-ho," said Theodosia. "Like you gave me."

"That's so unfair," moaned Jory.

"Deal with it," snapped Theodosia. She drew breath, let it out slowly, watched a tour bus drive by with a sign on the side panel that said, SEE HAUNTED CHARLESTON BY NIGHT! Maybe there should also be a sign that said, SEE THEODOSIA GO POSTAL! She tried to pull her thoughts together then and regroup. "So . . . you honestly couldn't get rid of Beth Ann?"

"I tried everything," said Jory. "But she stuck like a burr. Still is, I guess."

"Listen to me, Jory," said Theodosia, "this isn't just a case of puppy love gone awry. Or star-crossed lovers. There's a good chance this whole Beth Ann thing has morphed into something more serious. For one thing, I'm pretty sure she's been stalking me."

"I can't believe Beth Ann would do that," replied Jory.

"She would and she is," said Theodosia. *Is he not listening to me?*

"Oh man," moaned Jory.

"The really bad news," Theodosia went on, "is that there's a possibility Beth Ann is involved in a major crime."

"Like what? Give me some facts!"

"I need to speak to Detective Tidwell first," said Theodosia. "But, trust me, I will get back to you."

"You can't leave me like this . . ." said Jory.

But Theodosia thumbed the Off button on her phone before Jory could finish his sentence, then dropped the phone into her bag. She needed more information—and maybe even police cooperation—before she leveled any charges against Beth Ann. But once she talked to Tidwell, pointed him in the right direction, maybe all the components would fall into place. Maybe justice would finally be served.

Stepping back inside the door of Cotton Duck, Theodosia saw that the show had ended and the ensuing party was pretty much a madhouse. Models mingled with customers, clothes were flying everywhere, and Rocky was still up on stage spinning music. Delaine and her assistant, Janine, were nowhere to be seen. Neither was Beth Ann.

And that was good, Theodosia decided. Even though she felt fairly secure, surrounded by gobs of people, she didn't want to mess with Beth Ann. Not at this juncture.

But Theodosia did bump into Bill Glass.

"Did you get the photo?" she asked him.

Glass nodded. "Quite a few. That's what you wanted, right?"

"Perfect," breathed Theodosia. "Now I want you to e-mail them to Detective Burt Tidwell. You know who he is?"

Glass nodded.

Digging in her bag, Theodosia found her wallet and pulled out Tidwell's business card. "Here."

Glass glanced at the e-mail address and said, "Okay. I can remember that."

"Excellent," said Theodosia.

Glass peered at her expectantly. "This is about more than just my camera, isn't it?"

"Yes, it really is," admitted Theodosia.

"You gonna give me the full story?"

"When I unravel the full story," said Theodosia, as someone tapped her on the shoulder, "you'll be the first to know." She spun around, bracing for a face-to-face confrontation with Beth Ann, but it was Delaine's nutty sister, Nadine, who stood there grinning like a manic windup toy.

"Theodosia," enthused Nadine, "what did you think of the show? Wasn't it fantastic? Almost as good as Fashion Week in New York!"

"Really wonderful," said Theodosia.

"You don't sound very enthusiastic," said Nadine, managing a little pout.

"Probably because I'm still too stunned for words," said Theodosia.

"Any piece in particular catch your eye?" Nadine prodded. Theodosia saw that Nadine was holding a small notebook. "Because I get twenty percent commission on any orders placed today."

"I'm kind of in a hurry, Nadine," said Theodosia, starting to back out of the store.

Nadine's pout was back with a vengeance. "It won't take but a second," Nadine told her, sticking like glue.

"No," said Theodosia, and this time she put some backbone into it. "Not now, not today."

Out the door for the second time, Theodosia walked

hurriedly to her car. She climbed in, locked the doors, glanced back over her shoulder. She didn't relish the notion of Beth Ann following her out, trying to engage her in conversation. Some phony little chitchat about bumping into each other, about Jory, about some imagined problem or betrayal. Then—*bap*—just like that, Beth Ann might do something nutty. Or murderous.

But there was no sign of Beth Ann.

Theodosia drove slowly down Church Street, checking her rearview mirror a couple of times, then headed into the heart of the historic district, finally ending up in front of her soon-to-be home.

Sitting in her car, gazing at a riot of green plants tumbling down the brick walkway that led to her front door, studying the wrought-iron fence that pushed up against a tangle of wild dogwood and crepe myrtle, she called Burt Tidwell.

It took a Herculean effort to go through the various gatekeepers and get Tidwell on the phone, but finally she had his ear. Quickly backgrounding Tidwell on Beth Ann, she told him about running into her today, the possible photo of her from last night, then voiced the very suggestion he'd put forth the night of the murder: "What if I really was the intended victim? What if someone mistook Daria, with her curly red hair and gray wool cloak, for me?"

Suddenly, Theodosia had his undivided attention.

"And this woman, Beth Ann, has been in town how long?" Tidwell asked, his voice a low growl.

"A week, ten days," said Theodosia. "Which gave her plenty of time to stew about Jory, lurk in the alley behind my tea shop, and maybe even decide to kill me."

"And end up strangling Daria Shand by mistake," said Tidwell. He said it slowly, as though he wasn't quite convinced now, merely chewing on the words.

"Yes," said Theodosia. "It's all possible, isn't it? I mean, you were the one who came up with that theory from the get-go."

"But now we find ourselves with additional suspects," said Tidwell.

"Well, I know that," countered Theodosia. "Any of which could be the guilty party. Still, I'm putting my money on Beth Ann."

"It doesn't quite work that way," said Tidwell.

"But you'll look into it, won't you?" Theodosia asked, suddenly gripped with a rising tide of panic. "You'll talk to her? Interrogate her?"

"You want me to beat her with a rubber hose, too?" asked Tidwell.

"I want you to *investigate*," said Theodosia. "Do what you do best."

Once again Theodosia thumbed the Off button on her phone, feeling angry, frustrated, and a little bereft. She sat in her Jeep, watching the sunlight seep away, noticing how dark and unoccupied her cottage looked in the muted green of the late afternoon.

Going to change all that, she told herself. Once she moved in there'd be Tiffany lamps glowing, the aroma of fresh-baked scones, and real warmth in the house.

Tromping up the front walk, Theodosia parted a large bush and headed around to the back side of the house.

Tred and another young archaeologist, a young woman, were just packing up their tools for the day.

"Hey," Tred said, when he saw her. "I was wondering if you'd swing by again."

"How's it going?" Theodosia asked.

"Good," said the young woman. "Great." She was tall and

skinny with tightly curled brown hair and the unbridled enthusiasm of a twenty-two-year-old.

Tred, more reserved, shrugged his shoulders. "We went down a couple more feet—nothing."

"That's good news, right?" said Theodosia.

"Maybe for you," said Tred.

23

❧

"Look at the quality of these pieces," marveled Drayton. "A bombé Louis XV commode along with a fine Italian marquetry desk. Both quite distinguished."

They were standing in the library of the Rosewalk House, one of the B and Bs that had thrown open its doors to the public this Friday evening.

"I'm in love with that bronze-and-crystal candelabra," Theodosia told him.

"The collection of leather-bound books isn't bad, either," said Drayton, perusing the floor-to-ceiling shelves. "What does this place charge per night?" he wondered. "Everything is so Old World and elegant."

"What I want to know," said Theodosia, "is who do they get to guard all these goodies?" She glanced at the colorful brochure she'd been handed at the front door, then turned her attention to Drayton. Just as they'd planned, they'd met here some ten minutes ago. Of course, Theodosia hadn't wasted any time filling Drayton in about seeing Beth Ann at the fashion show. Breathlessly, she'd told him about calling Jory, then finding out that Beth Ann, his former fiancée, was ensconced in Jory's Charleston apartment.

Drayton was still mulling over this strange news as he eyed the various antiquities. "Nice rose medallion pitcher," he muttered, then asked, "Are you quite sure Jory was referring to the same woman?"

Theodosia nodded.

"The blond lady he was engaged to?" continued Drayton. "The one who overimbibed in Pinot Grigio at the Masked Ball?"

"Same girl," said Theodosia. "Beth Ann. Specifically mentioned her by name."

"Huh," said Drayton. "Same one. So maybe I did see her that night."

"Maybe so," said Theodosia. "You'll be happy to know she's still as charming as a rattlesnake." *And maybe just as dangerous.*

"And she's holed up in Jory's apartment."

"So he claims," said Theodosia.

"Like some kind of squatter," said Drayton, making it sound slightly sordid.

"Something like that," agreed Theodosia.

"I take it you called Detective Burt Tidwell immediately?" asked Drayton. "Expressed your deep concern? Explained that perhaps . . ."

"First thing I did," said Theodosia. "Right after I got off the phone with Jory."

"What was Tidwell's response?"

"He said he'd look into it," said Theodosia.

Drayton was taken aback. "That's it? That's all?"

"That's it," said Theodosia. "Disappointing, no?"

"Disappointing, yes," agreed Drayton. "If there's a possibility this Beth Ann person is completely unhinged, she shouldn't be wandering around Charleston. Shouldn't be stalking people." He held Theodosia's eyes for a long moment, the subtext being, *she could be stalking you.*

"Exactly," said Theodosia. "Because the very real possibility does exist that she confused me with Daria."

"And murdered the wrong woman," said Drayton. "Just like Tidwell suggested at the very beginning."

"Chilling," said Theodosia.

"If this Beth Ann person is somehow involved in Daria's murder, then she should be cooling her heels in a jail cell. Dreaming up excuses to tell her attorney," sniped Drayton.

"I think," said Theodosia, "that most attorneys are fairly skilled at coming up with excuses on their own."

They wandered through the dining room, which was dramatic and elegant, the walls painted a deep emerald green, tall windows covered in gold damask draperies. A long dining table had a dozen Chippendale ladder-back chairs parked at it.

"How'd you like to eat your toast and jammy here?" asked Drayton.

"It's awfully formal," said Theodosia. Though Theodosia was no stranger to fine dining or elegant surroundings, she preferred the coziness of a smaller space. Still, this was a grand old dowager mansion that had been converted to a bed-and-breakfast, and the guests who stayed here were probably charmed to pieces.

"You want to take the upstairs tour?" asked Drayton, peering at her with slightly hooded eyes that conveyed his disinterest.

"Not if you don't," said Theodosia.

"Good," said Drayton. "Then let's push our way through this crowd and follow the hallway out to the back garden. That's what I'm most curious about."

"The rose garden," said Theodosia, as they descended

curved, wide brick steps and saw the beautifully cultivated rose garden spread out before them. "Wonderful." Lights, luminaries actually, marked the edges of the patio and various paths. Rose bushes of all different species and colors were arranged in a large, pie-shaped pattern with brick walkways between them. An imposing brick wall at the rear of the property was a jungly jumble of small, pink climbing roses. White Greek statuary—modern, not old—had been installed throughout the garden.

"Isn't this grand?" remarked Drayton. "Sometimes I think about selling all my bonsai trees and starting over with roses. Dig up my backyard and cultivate exotic varieties. Perhaps Multiflora or Cherokee roses, all wild and overgrown like you see growing among tumbled-down ruins of an old abbey."

"Have you been reading Bram Stoker again?" Theodosia asked.

Drayton gave a wry smile as they headed for a black wrought-iron table and chairs. "But the thing is, I adore my bonsai, especially the tiny forests and windswept trees. And I enjoy the Zen-like feeling they impart. Hence my new fascination with feng shui."

"Why not grow both?" proposed Theodosia as she slid into one of the wrought-iron chairs. "Yin and yang? Look at my yard. I have a garden, a pond, and an archaeological dig."

"Say," said Drayton, leaning forward. "How's that going?"

"I stopped by earlier and they hadn't unearthed a single T-Rex bone or velociraptor tooth."

"Is that good news or bad news?"

"Good for me, I guess, bad for them," said Theodosia. "I think they were hoping to find a whole trove of bones." She glanced at the rose garden, said, "Those are fairly mature plants, aren't they?"

"Been here a while," said Drayton, studying the brochure he'd been given. "Several dozen years of pruning and cultivating. Of course, new plants are probably being added every year since new rose varieties are constantly being developed." He glanced up at her. "You know anything about the language of roses?"

"What do you mean?" asked Theodosia.

"During the Victorian era," said Drayton, "the use of rose symbolism was extremely popular. It became a subtle form of communication."

"Like text messaging today," said Theodosia.

"Not exactly," said Drayton. "For example, red and white roses mixed together in a bouquet stood for unity. While dark crimson roses symbolized mourning."

"I had no idea," said Theodosia, charmed. Was there nothing Drayton didn't know? "What else?"

"Yellow roses were used to convey jealously. Of course, now they express friendship and joy."

Theodosia pointed to the small bouquet of tea roses on their table. "What about tea roses?"

"Ah," said Drayton. "Tea roses mean remembrance. So they're most appropriate when you have old friends in for tea."

"Ma'am?" said a white-coated waiter, who'd suddenly materialized at Theodosia's elbow. "Care for any refreshments here?"

"What's on the menu?" Theodosia asked.

"Sweet tea, lemonade, coffee, and white wine," said the waiter.

"How about a lemonade–white wine spritzer?" asked Theodosia. "Mixed together in equal parts, shaken not stirred."

"I can do that," said the waiter. He glanced at Drayton. "And you, sir?"

"Same," said Drayton. "Please."

Theodosia smiled at Drayton and said, "What about red . . . ?" as her words were suddenly drowned out by a nearby burst of riotous laughter. Both she and Drayton swung sideways in their chairs, wondering who the noisy guests were, only to find Miss Kitty and Cinnamon swiftly descending upon them.

"Look who's here!" gushed Cinnamon. "Our new neighbors!"

"Why it's Miss Theodosia and Mr. Drayton!" cried Miss Kitty, taking up the cry.

"Please," said Drayton, scrambling to his feet, "join us."

Theodosia hesitated for a moment, hating to spoil the calm of the evening, then said. "Of course."

But luckily, thankfully, Miss Kitty and Cinnamon demurred.

"We're doing this Bed-and-Breakfast Tour on the fly," Cinnamon told her.

"Our own crash course on the historic district." Miss Kitty laughed. "Since this is our new home and we certainly want to cater to its more posh residents."

"I'm sure you do," murmured Drayton.

"We're still planning to come to the Heritage Society tomorrow night," added Cinnamon, shaking a finger at them. "Hoping you'll introduce us to all your friends."

"Oh," said Miss Kitty, lightly touching Theodosia's shoulder. "We dropped the candles off at your shop this afternoon. Since you weren't around, we entrusted them to dear Drayton." She laughed airily as if she'd just made the most wonderful bon mot.

"They're tucked away safely," Drayton assured her.

"Ta-ta!" said Miss Kitty, waving wildly as she grabbed Cinnamon's arm and pulled her away.

"Those two women are genuine characters," said Drayton, watching them scurry across the patio. "An interesting addition to our Church Street merchants."

"I suppose," said Theodosia, watching them go. "I hate to say this, because I can't quite put my finger on it, but it feels like there's something *off* about them."

"They can be a little *too* friendly," allowed Drayton.

"As well as overly gushy and enthusiastic," agreed Theodosia. "But . . ." She stopped, shook her head, murmured, "Something."

"Of course you're put off by them," said Drayton, dropping his voice. "They're also on your suspect list for Daria's murder."

"Not completely," said Theodosia. "There's no real evidence I can pin to them. Just the fact that Miss Kitty, especially, is hot to trot about taking over the map shop space."

"One of them could have argued with Daria?" proposed Drayton. "Things turned ugly? Led to an unfortunate accident?"

"I don't think looping a hank of rope around someone's neck is particularly accidental," said Theodosia.

"Point well taken," said Drayton.

Their drinks arrived, and they sipped them slowly, enjoying the warm, dark evening as sputtering candles illuminated the garden, imparting a dark and moody splendor.

"Do you still see Jason Pritchard as a suspect?" asked Drayton. "Even though Beth Ann is now on the scene?"

Theodosia nodded. "It could be him. It could be Joe Don, the boyfriend, too. Or even Jack Brux."

"I don't think Jack . . ." began Drayton.

"If he wanted to get his hands on a particular map?" asked Theodosia. "And Daria didn't want him to for whatever reason?"

"Brux does have a nasty temper," said Drayton.

"As you said before. An argument . . . things turned ugly?"

Possible," said Drayton. He glanced at his antique Piaget watch, said, "Do we still want to ankle over to the Magnolia Inn?"

"I don't know," said Theodosia. "Do we?" Talking about Daria's murder, analyzing suspects had left her in a bit of a funk.

"It's only a block away, just off Gateway Walk," said Drayton. "Come on, what's the harm? They're supposed to have a lot of lovely, detailed carvings."

"As if that matters to me," muttered Theodosia.

"It matters to me," said Drayton.

"Then we should go," said Theodosia. "And I apologize. I have no right to drag down your evening because I'm suddenly introspective."

"No," said Drayton, "I'd say you're rather *per*ceptive. I wouldn't be surprised if you figured this out yet."

The Magnolia Inn B and B was smaller than the Rosewalk House, but just as lovely. The front parlor featured hand-carved cornices, medallions, and plaster work along with a black marble fireplace and large gilt mirror. Aubusson carpets covered wood-planked floors and the four upstairs rooms, furnished with antiques, all featured canopy beds.

"It's a little jewel," declared Drayton. "And just the right size, too."

"Cozy," agreed Theodosia. It was a place where a weary traveler could relax and really snuggle in. Enjoy morning tea on the back balcony, evening wine and cheese in the parlor.

Apparently everyone else thought it was adorable, too, because every time Theodosia and Drayton ventured into another room, they had to deal with the crush of crowds.

"Because it's located so close to the Battery," said Drayton. "This is the historic district hot spot. Everyone wants to visit these homes and play 'let's pretend I live here.'"

"Plus it's got that neat porte cochere on the side of the house," said Theodosia, "that leads to a little cobblestone back alley." She said it with enthusiasm, then was immediately reminded of the back-alley crawl. Thought about how badly that had ended.

Drayton saw the look on Theodosia's face and said, "Come

on, time to go. We've seen most of the house and you're introspective edging toward maudlin. You're thinking you might have saved Daria that night, when you really couldn't."

"Don't say that," said Theodosia, as Drayton led her outside. "Please don't say that."

"You're a good person, Theodosia," Drayton told her, as they stepped outside onto the front verandah. "You do charity work, garner media coverage for the Spoleto Festival, and take Earl Grey on visiting rounds at countless hospitals and senior citizen residences. And you've made quite a name for yourself with the Indigo Tea Shop. But as talented as you are, you're not a superwoman. There was nothing you could have done."

"But there's something I can do now," Theodosia said, quietly. "I can keep snooping around and asking questions. And maybe, just maybe, figure out who killed Daria."

"It's what you're good at," Drayton agreed. "Just . . . please, be careful."

"I always am," said Theodosia.

He looked at her askance, not believing her for a minute, but was too polite to say so. Instead, Drayton said, "Here. Let's follow the alley to Gateway Walk. Take the scenic tour."

24

❧

Gateway Walk was a hidden, four-block city walk that consisted of lush gardens, ancient slate graves, and a famous pair of wrought-iron gates. It began at Archdale Street, rambled its way past the Library Society, Gibbes Museum of Art, and four different churches, ending in the graveyard behind St. Philip's Church. It was quiet, contemplative, and dripping with flora and fauna. It was also reputed to be haunted.

Old legends spoke of hair that had turned to Spanish moss and now beckoned spookily to unsuspecting visitors. Countless folk had claimed to see a headless torso in a Confederate uniform, aimlessly wandering the serene gardens and secret cul-de-sacs. Glowing blue orbs had been photographed but never explained.

None of that mattered to Theodosia and Drayton right now, as they strolled past the stately Library Society building, heading for the Governor Aiken Gates.

"Lovely here," mused Drayton, their footfalls echoing hollowly on the narrow stone footpath. Flowering white dogwoods brushed their shoulders and the occasional coo of a dove punctuated the silence.

"Maybe the most peaceful place on earth," agreed Theodosia.

"I've always thought," said Drayton, "that I wouldn't mind being buried here."

"Please don't talk like that," said Theodosia. "Don't talk old."

"I don't intend to leave my corporal body for a very long time," chuckled Drayton, "but when I do, I wouldn't mind being in the company of several centuries of Charleston history."

"I suppose you're right," said Theodosia. "The hidden gardens, all the old plaques and tombs . . . very peaceful."

"You know what would be interesting?" said Drayton.

"What?" asked Theodosia.

"If we swung by your cottage to see how the big dig is progressing."

"Not much to see," said Theodosia.

"Still," said Drayton, "I've never seen an actual archaeological excavation."

"Then you're on," said Theodosia. They walked past the Gibbes Museum, crossed Meeting Street, continued past the Circular Congregational Church.

"When we get to St. Philip's," said Theodosia, "let's cut left and . . ." She hesitated and cast a glance over her shoulder.

Drayton picked up her vibe immediately. "What?"

"Someone behind us?" said Theodosia in a low voice.

They continued walking as Drayton took a quick check as well. "I think you might be right," he said quietly.

"Following us?"

"Maybe," said Drayton.

"Maybe not so good," said Theodosia. She grabbed hold of Drayton's arm and, together, they picked up their pace. She knew it might be smart to gain some distance on whoever was behind them. Get to St. Philip's graveyard where they could duck behind one of the larger tombs and figure out what to do—if there was anything to do. Sit tight, hide, or make a dash for it?

Just past a cluster of slate markers that dated to the 1600s was a large marble tomb. They scurried around it, ducked down, and waited, their breathing coming in measured gasps.

They waited fifteen seconds, then thirty.

Drayton finally poked his head up, like a gopher taking a careful look.

"What?" Theodosia whispered.

"Something," he whispered back.

"Something or someone?" she asked, but Drayton just shook his head. Theodosia took a deep breath, then peered around the side of the marble tomb. Her eyes scanned the darkness, flitting across an old gravestone decorated with a skull and crossbones, a stand of magnolias, a statue of a winged angel, its face upturned, its hands almost melted away from the ravages of time.

Finally, she saw something. What looked like a person just standing alone in a copse of dogwood. Not moving, but maybe . . . muttering to himself?

Theodosia nudged Drayton. "Somebody's standing over there," she said in a low voice.

"You think they're dangerous?" he asked.

"I don't think it's Beth Ann, if that's what you're asking," said Theodosia.

"So, what do you want to do?" whispered Drayton.

"What I don't want to do is crouch here all night," Theodosia responded. "Or even just skulk away. It would seem kind of . . . I don't know . . . cowardly."

"Then what do you say we call that fellow's bluff," said Drayton, standing up abruptly. Theodosia followed suit and together they slipped out from behind the marble tomb and tiptoed back down the walk, retracing their steps.

"Careful," whispered Drayton as they drew closer.

Then Theodosia put a hand up, pushed back an overhanging hank of Spanish moss, and did a double take. "Joe Don?" she said, her voice rising in an off-pitch squawk.

Joe Don Hunter jumped as if touched by an electric wire, then rubbed his eyes and stared at them in disbelief. "You?" he breathed.

"What's going on!" Drayton demanded, using his Heritage Society call-to-order voice.

"What are you two doing here?" Joe Don Hunter asked in a quavering tone. He seemed more startled than they were.

"You were following us!" said Theodosia, jumping on him hard. "You were dogging our footsteps!"

Joe Don swiped at his forelock nervously. "No, ma'am," he declared. "Truth be told, I didn't even know you were here."

"You have to have known," said Drayton. "You're not deaf or blind, you knew we were walking ahead of you. What were you planning to do?" Theodosia had to hand it to Drayton, he was definitely keeping the pressure on.

"Following us is fairly suspicious," said Theodosia, adopting Drayton's harsh tone. "Especially in light of the fact I've been looking into your girlfriend's death."

Joe Don's face fell like he'd been thunderstruck. His mouth started to work, but no sound came out. Finally a tear rolled down his face, glistening in the low light, and he finally said, "That's what you think? That I was going to harm you?" He seemed to be in shock. "That I'm the one who killed Daria?"

"You're on the suspect list, yes," Drayton told him, putting both hands on his hips.

Joe Don extended his arms in a pleading gesture. "I wouldn't . . ." he said. "I couldn't . . ."

"Then what are you doing here?" demanded Theodosia. "We'd like an answer."

Sniffling loudly, Joe Don said, "I . . . I haven't been myself these last few days. The police haven't figured anything out about Daria's murder and I feel completely alone and helpless. Confused and . . . what would you call it? Bereft."

"Bereft," snorted Drayton, as if he hardly believed Joe Don knew the meaning of the word.

"I wander around aimlessly," Joe Don confessed. "Just . . . trying to figure things out."

"And this is one of your aimless rambles?" Theodosia asked him. "Down Gateway Walk?" She wasn't sure if Joe Don Hunter was genuinely distraught or if he deserved an Academy Award.

Joe Don gazed around as if unaware of his surroundings. "Yeah, I guess so. I guess that's where I am."

Theodosia and Drayton exchanged glances, then Drayton suggested, not unkindly, "Perhaps you might benefit from some grief counseling."

"Yeah . . . maybe," said Joe Don.

But Theodosia wasn't willing to let him off so easy. She took a step closer to him and said, "Are you still participating in the Kipling Club?"

Joe Don stared at her.

"That's right," said Theodosia. "We know you're in a group of local treasure hunters."

"I am," said Joe Don, grudgingly. "So what?"

"I hope you're not digging up precious Civil War battlegrounds or Native American cultural sites," said Drayton.

"We're not like that," protested Hunter.

But Theodosia knew they were.

Five minutes later, Theodosia and Drayton walked past the Featherbed House, where lights blazed but no crowds had gathered. Just lit up for the sake of the overnight guests, Theodosia figured.

"Did you believe Joe Don?" Drayton asked. "Do you think he's so distraught that he just wanders around aimlessly at night?"

"He did seem confused," admitted Theodosia. "And a little bit lost inside himself."

"I don't know," said Drayton. "Something about him seems fishy to me."

"Maybe Joe Don seems fishy because we're fishing for suspects," said Theodosia. "You realize we still haven't stumbled on one concrete shred of evidence. Against him or anyone else."

"You know," said Drayton, "Beth Ann being in town might be the best evidence of all."

"You like her for the murder," said Theodosia.

"From what I know about Beth Ann," said Drayton, "she strikes me as being cold, calculating, and a trifle unhinged. And the more you talk about her, the more I tend to suspect her."

"Which means I'm probably unduly influencing you," said Theodosia.

"Then again, you always do," said Drayton. They were standing on the sidewalk directly in front of Theodosia's cottage. A thin, silver crescent moon shone overhead, casting faint shadows and icing the landscape with its glow. Hunkered fifteen feet back from the sidewalk, the little cottage was a darkened curiosity, like something you might stumble upon in a forest.

"Can we go inside?" asked Drayton. "Do you have a key?"

"No key," said Theodosia, "but my Realtor gave me the lock box combination. I've been using that to scoot in and out."

"Unbeknownst to the owner?" asked Drayton.

"I think it's well knownst now," chuckled Theodosia.

They strolled quietly up the walk, Theodosia went through her usual fumbling with the dial on the lock box, and then they were inside. She hit the wall switch, bathing the front room in soft light.

"Say now," said Drayton, talking a few steps in, "this is even more lovely than I remembered."

"You think?" asked Theodosia. Lately she'd had the sinking feeling she might never move in. All sorts of problems seemed to conspire against her, barriers to closing on the house, barriers to her actually moving in.

"I really love it," said Drayton. "And I don't say that lightly."

"You do have a critical eye," said Theodosia.

"But this place . . ." Drayton strolled over to the fireplace, ran a hand across the cypress paneling. "This place has good bones. Architecturally speaking."

"That's what I think, too," said Theodosia. She was secretly thrilled that Drayton approved of her new home, humble though it might be. "And I can't wait to start decorating."

"Probably need to purchase a couple more pieces of furniture," mused Drayton.

"That's what I think, too," agreed Theodosia. "Maybe check out some of the shops on King Street." King Street was Charleston's acknowledged antiques district, where red-brick shops with white-washed windowsills stood shoulder to shoulder, bursting with English silver, old family crystal and china, estate jewelry, and antique furniture. Even browsing there became a joyful history lesson of sorts.

"And these window treatments have seen better days," said Drayton. He reached out and gave a tentative tug on a long velvet drapery that had faded from maroon to off-pink.

"You don't have to be coy," said Theodosia. "I know they're tattered. So, yes, I'm definitely going to need new draperies."

"But you can make do for a while," said Drayton, who

prided himself on being practical as well as frugal. "Best not to go overboard and buy everything at once. Better to . . . select a few choice pieces."

Theodosia agreed. She had friends who'd moved into new houses and did all their decorating in one fell swoop, ending up with Country French or Mediterranean or something that screamed mega-mansion. But that wasn't going to happen to her. Theodosia was a big believer in thinking big but taking smaller steps. That was how she'd settled into her tea business; that was how she'd settle into her new home.

Drayton was still peeking and probing, opening closets and nosing around. "And this dining room . . . it looks out over the back garden?" He cleared his throat. "On your archaeology dig?"

"I think at night," said Theodosia, "with a small amount of outdoor lighting, it could be quite spectacular."

"Mmm," said Drayton, frowning. "Outdoor lighting."

"Not tiki torches or anything like that," Theodosia hastily assured him. "I was thinking more like small, solar-powered lamps. Something tasteful and discreet."

"Might work," said Drayton. "And the kitchen?"

"Through there," said Theodosia, indicating an archway.

Drayton ducked through, batting his hand around, searching for a light switch, then finally found it. "This is a decent size, too, but you're—" He stopped suddenly and stared pointedly at the back door. "Did you know you have a broken window?" he asked.

Theodosia was beside him in two seconds, staring at her missing window pane. One of a dozen beveled into the back door. "What on earth!" She leaned forward, put her index finger where the missing glass should have been. Touched only . . . air. "This wasn't here when—"

A loud crash sounded from the backyard.

"Someone's outside!" said Theodosia, fumbling with the

door lock. She pulled, rattled the doorknob, finally bullied the door open.

Now the sound of running footsteps echoed down the back alley.

"C'mon!" she yelled at Drayton, then took off in a mad dash. Skittering across muddy patio stones, Theodosia made a giant sideways leap, avoiding a wide, muddy pit, careened around a clump of magnolias, hopped over a low string, and then was out the back gate and into the alley.

"Stop!" she called. "Stop or I'll call the police!" She paused for a few moments, her heart thudding in her chest, waiting for Drayton to catch up to her.

He finally did. "Did you see anybody?" he asked, breathing heavily.

"No, but at the risk of sounding like a B movie, they went thataway."

The two of them continued down the alley, Theodosia walking briskly, then breaking into a jog, Drayton lagging behind. From behind a tall, wooden fence, a dog barked. A high-pitched, rapid-fire, upset-dog bark.

Then, as the cobblestone alley curved around to the left and plunged into darkness, Theodosia gave a little squeal and ran forward. Right ahead of her, like a crumpled heap of rags, lay a body!

"Theo, don't!" warned Drayton.

But Theodosia was already leaning over the man who was groaning and fighting to sit up. "Drayton! Over here!" she called to him.

Drayton approached with caution.

"It's Jack Brux!" Theodosia told him. "He's hurt!"

"Jack?" said Drayton, hurrying now. "What on earth?" He stared down into the angry, contorted face of Jack Brux.

"This is like a bad second act," murmured Theodosia, grabbing for Brux's arm, but unable to move him. His head, she noted, had a nasty cut and blood, shiny and dark in the moonlight, trickled down the side of his face.

Drayton immediately took an offensive posture. "What are you doing here?" he demanded of Brux.

Brux turned on him like a snarling wolverine. "What am I *doing* here? Excuse me, but I *live* here. Some idiot pushed me from behind and practically trampled me!"

"Are you okay?" asked Theodosia.

"Do I look okay?" snapped Brux. "Because I'm certainly not. My knee is throbbing like crazy and I cracked my head hard on the cobblestones. Does that sound okay to you?"

Theodosia thought Brux sounded pretty much like he always did. Feisty, cranky, and perturbed. But she was willing to give him the benefit of the doubt, especially since he was bleeding profusely. "Ambulance," she murmured to Drayton and pulled out her cell phone.

Drayton knelt down, his knees making little popping sounds. He got an arm around Brux and tried to help him to his feet. "Can you tell us what happened?" he asked in a kindlier tone.

Brux staggered a bit but finally made it to his feet. Now that he was upright, Brux seemed groggy and slower and less sharp-tongued. "I was taking my evening constitutional," he moaned, "when I heard somebody running, coming up fast behind me. I didn't think much of it—joggers come barreling down this alley all the time—rude buggers, all of them, even though I don't know why anyone in their right mind would want to run on cobblestones, but—"

"What happened exactly?" asked Theodosia. She really did want to cut to the chase without too much editorializing from Brux.

"Like I said," said Brux, "I was attacked from behind. Someone slammed me on the head and I . . . I went down." He put a hand to his head, felt the blood, said, "Oh man."

* * *

Four minutes later, the ambulance showed up. The EMTs sat Brux on the back step of their rig, checked him for injuries, and shone a penlight in his eyes. All the while Brux managed to keep up a constant barrage of complaints.

"I think he's feeling better," said Drayton, deadpan.

Five minutes after that, a burgundy Crown Victoria came prowling down the alley and rolled to a stop. Theodosia wasn't all that surprised when the passenger door opened and Burt Tidwell hauled his bulk from the vehicle.

"Just what I needed on what was supposed to be a leisurely Friday evening," began Tidwell, lumbering toward them. "A callout because the two of you are involved in yet another problematic situation." He sighed mightily and stared at Theodosia and Drayton with an expression of supreme disapproval.

"We had no idea—" began Theodosia.

"Of course, you didn't," sang Tidwell. "You never do."

"But you were up late," said Drayton, trying to help the situation and failing.

"I certainly was not," muttered Tidwell. "And if you must pry into my personal habits, I was lying in bed reading *Ulysses.*"

"A fine book," noted Drayton, still trying to inject some note of normalcy.

"Is it?" said Tidwell. "I've been interrupted so many times I've barely made it through the first three chapters."

"Maybe you should think about retirement," piped up Tidwell's driver. He was a young, uniformed officer with surfer-boy blond hair who offered his remark in a lighthearted manner. Theodosia figured he'd soon learn not to attempt jokes with Tidwell.

Tidwell swiveled his giant head like the periscope of a German U-boat seeking out a nice tasty convoy to attack in the north Atlantic. Then his steely gray eyes bore directly into the young man, like a drill bit chewing rock.

"I didn't mean . . ." said the young officer. "Not that I . . ."

Tidwell's lips pursed, his jaw tightened. Theodosia almost expected to see steam come pouring out of his ears.

"Sorry," the officer finally muttered contritely. Definitely a fast learner.

"Harh," grunted Tidwell.

They watched as the EMTs put a couple of butterfly bandages on Brux's forehead, then placed an oxygen cannula under his nose.

Drayton cleared his throat, then said, "Do you think this is related to the murder?"

Tidwell turned and stared at Drayton, almost daring him to continue.

"I mean," said Drayton, "what with Theodosia warning you about this Beth Ann person and Jack being a kind of, er, emotional fellow . . ."

"Don't know," said Tidwell. He looked like he was turning all the facts over in his mind, like a rock polisher sanding away on a few choice agates.

"Drayton and I have been talking all evening," said Theodosia. "And we think it's very possible Beth Ann was the killer."

"You were the one person who saw Daria Shand struggling with her assailant," said Tidwell, in an almost accusatory tone. "Did it look like this Beth Ann person to you?"

"I don't know," said Theodosia, feeling guilty again. "I wasn't close enough to really see."

Tidwell blew out a glut of air.

"What about the documents that were shredded in Daria's shop?" Theodosia asked. She glanced over at Jack Brux, who was being loaded onto a gurney now. "Do you know . . . did Brux ever come up with anything?"

"I spoke to Brux early this afternoon and he mentioned that he might have a couple of things figured out," said Tidwell. He gazed at the ambulance, as an EMT scrambled inside and pulled the back door shut. "But now . . ."

Drayton picked up on Tidwell's thought. "Let's hope that knock on his head didn't . . ."

"Erase his hard drive," finished Theodosia.

25

❧

Theodosia was tired, bordering on cranky this Saturday morning. She hadn't gotten home until eleven last night, then she'd spent some time walking Earl Grey. Even after she finally crawled into bed, she hadn't been able to fall sleep right away, so she'd puttered around her apartment, murder on her mind. Not such a good thing.

Her sleep quota not being met, Theodosia was feeling decidedly depleted. And more than a little frustrated by Daria's murder and the slow-moving Robbery-Homicide Division of the Charleston PD. She was filled with dread every time the phone rang, thinking it was Aunt Libby calling or maybe even Sophie, Daria's mother.

Did she have any news for them? No. Could she impart any comfort by telling them she'd unraveled a clue or stumbled upon a nugget of information? Again, nothing. Basically, Theodosia had bupkes.

It also didn't help that Haley was wandering around this morning, redoing table settings and restless as a kid waiting for the recess bell to ring. Of course, Drayton hadn't wasted any time in filling Haley in on last night's strange doings. Relating tidbits about Joe Don's mysterious ramble in Gateway Walk and Jack Brux getting assaulted. So now Haley was postulating her own slightly wild theories.

"Maybe," said Haley, grabbing tulips and sprigs of dogwood to arrange in large ceramic crocks, "maybe last night's bump and run in your back alley was intended for you, Theo."

"Maybe it was meant for Jack Brux," said Theodosia. "The man's not exactly Mr. Warmth. He's not big into winning friends and influencing people."

"Or maybe it really was an unrelated accident," offered Drayton. "A clumsy jogger, smacking into Brux on his late-night run."

"No," said Haley, "from the way you guys have been telling it, the incident *feels* intentional. Brux was in the alley behind Theodosia's cottage, so I think his assault somehow relates to that cottage."

"There was that broken window," said Drayton, glancing at Theodosia.

"Did you ever think," said Haley, "that your new place . . . what do they call it? Hazelhurst? That it might be haunted?" She gazed at Theodosia with saucer eyes. "What if the ghosts of all the pirates that were strung up there have come back to seek revenge?"

"A chilling supposition," agreed Theodosia. "But awfully far afield, since we don't know if a pirate's gallows ever really stood there. And, frankly, I'm beginning to have my doubts."

"About the spirit world?" asked Haley.

"I believe in all things spiritual," said Theodosia. "I'm just not sure deceased pirates have the innate ability to come back and annoy us." Theodosia was anxious to nip any sort of pirate or ghost legend in the bud. If that sort of tale started to spread, it could take on the dimensions of an urban myth and really lead to problems.

Drayton swiped the back of his hand across his cheek and asked, "Do you think it had something to do with the work Jack Brux was doing? Piecing together the shredded records? Assisting the police?"

Theodosia shrugged. "Possibly. Or maybe Jack Brux was in the wrong place at the wrong time." She hesitated. "Or maybe it was Beth Ann."

"Maybe," said Drayton.

"It's as if someone is stalking us," said Haley.

"Excuse me?" said Drayton. "Us?"

"Folks from the historic district," said Haley. "Think about it. First Daria, then Theo in her car, then Jack Brux last night."

"And the camera," pointed out Drayton. "Somebody did grab Bill Glass's camera."

"And Joe Don was following you guys last night," said Haley. "And Beth Ann turned up at the fashion show."

Theodosia set an antique Minton teacup into its matching saucer. "I hadn't thought of it that way." She reached back, pulled the ties of her black apron snugly around her waist. "Interesting."

"A pattern," said Haley.

They stood for a while, the three of them exchanging worried glances.

Then Drayton swallowed hard and said, "But who exactly is the stalker?"

They got busy then, propping open the front door to let the warm breezes from the Ashley and Cooper rivers swoop in, welcoming guests to the Indigo Tea Shop.

"It's almost warm enough to set up the outside tables," said Drayton.

"But let's not," said Theodosia. "If we do that we'll be deluged with customers who'll want to linger and sip. And we want to close a little early this afternoon."

"Right," agreed Drayton. "Get prepped for our catering gig at the Heritage Society tonight."

"I thought you didn't like the term *catering gig*," said Theodosia.

Drayton shrugged. "What can I do? Haley uses it almost constantly so it's part of my lexicon now."

"What can you do?" agreed Theodosia.

She delivered prune and date scones to a couple of tables, then grabbed a pot of black jasmine tea and made the rounds. As the delicious scent of jasmine filtered up through clouds of steam, Theodosia relaxed. And started feeling a little better. She'd already shrugged off her tiredness, although that could be accounted for by the two cups of Viennese Earl Grey she'd sipped earlier. Nothing like a little caffeine and a hint of bergamot to rev a person's brain and metabolism!

By the time Haley popped out of the kitchen to deliver small plates of French crepes stuffed with chicken and mushrooms in cream sauce, Theodosia was back to her old self.

"You're suddenly so peppy," Drayton commented. "Must be looking forward to tonight."

"You know," said Theodosia, "I am. Everything is so well planned I'm positive it'll go off without a hitch."

"Agreed," said Drayton. "I just hope we get a good crowd."

"Theo!" called Haley. She was standing at the front counter, holding up the phone, looking perturbed.

"What?" asked Theodosia, setting down her tray and grabbing a glass bowl filled with Devonshire cream. "A late reservation? A cancellation?"

"We should be so lucky," said Haley, rolling her eyes.

"Tidwell?" asked Theodosia, searching for a small silver spoon. Maybe he'd discovered something new.

"You're not going to believe this," said Haley.

"Delaine?" said Theodosia, tucking a napkin onto the tray.

Haley shook her head. "Nope. Jory."

"Seriously?" said Theodosia, accepting the phone gingerly, like it might contain spores of the deadly Ebola virus.

"Ayup," said Haley, squirting away.

Theodosia put the phone to her ear and said, "Now what?"

"Theodosia, hello," said Jory, in his best hail-hearty, upbeat voice. "I'm still in New York, but if you don't believe me, you can call my office and check."

"I believe you," said Theodosia, sounding just this side of bored.

"The reason I called," said Jory, talking faster, "is because I need a small favor from you."

"What?" yelped Theodosia. Was he kidding? Or was this his idea of a bad joke?

"Here's the deal," said Jory, starting to sound chattery and a little panicked. "I just got a phone call from Chuck Strom, the manager at the Charleston Yacht Club . . . you know, the marina where I keep my boat?"

She said nothing.

"Anyway, the Coast Guard called Chuck early this morning and said they spotted my sailboat over at Castle Pinckney. They read him the registration number and it's my boat, all right." Silence spun out. "Chuck checked my boat slip and, sure enough, my sailboat's not there."

"That's great they found it," said Theodosia. *Is that what Jory wants? For me to commiserate with him? Because, really, I don't have time for this.*

"It's a lucky break," Jory continued, "but now I have . . . well, I have a problem. And a huge favor to ask of you."

No, no, no, thought Theodosia, closing her eyes and gritting her teeth.

So, of course, Jory voiced the words Theodosia was dreading to hear.

"Is there any way you can you go over to Castle Pinckney and bring my boat back to the yacht club?" he asked.

"You're not serious," breathed Theodosia. Castle Pinckney was a small island in the middle of Charleston Harbor. Basically an abandoned old fort.

Jory plunged on ahead. "I already set it up with Chuck. He's got his Chris-Craft Corsair all gassed and ready to go. He'll take you over and drop you."

"Excuse me," said Theodosia, annoyed beyond belief and letting Jory know it. "But why doesn't your pal Chuck just motor over and tow the boat back himself? Why don't you offer him a big, fat tip or reward or something?"

"Because Chuck doesn't have time to do all that," said Jory. "His cousin's getting married today. Over in Goose Creek. He can make the run over, but he can't mess around with setting up a tow line and hauling it back. Take too long."

"And you couldn't find another soul?" asked Theodosia. "Out of all the members at the yacht club? All those guys who run around in captain's hats and deck shoes with cute little tassels?"

"Nobody I can trust," said Jory. And now his voice turned pleading. "Theodosia, you've sailed my boat dozens of times. You *know* that boat. And I trust you implicitly."

Theodosia exhaled loudly and slowly into the phone. "Well, shoot. This isn't the conversation I thought we'd be having."

"Why did you think I called?"

"Oh, I don't know," said Theodosia. "Let me make a wild and crazy guess. Uh . . . maybe I hoped you pulled your freaky ex-fiancée, Beth Ann, off my case? Or how about this? You called to apologize."

"In that case, I apologize," said Jory. "In fact, I fervently extend a blanket apology for every caddish thing I've ever said or done. Past, present, and future."

"Oh jeez," groaned Theodosia. "You don't . . ." She stopped, shook her head to clear it, thought, *Why me?* "Jory, you know I'd help you if . . ."

"Does that mean you'll do it?" Jory asked in a semi-hopeful tone of voice.

"I suppose I could," Theodosia said slowly. Glancing at her watch, a classic Cartier tank watch from the fifties that had belonged to her mother, she tried to work out the timing on a few things. "Okay, I'm going to have to really book it, though."

"Wait," said Jory. "There's more."

"Don't tell me!" groaned Theodosia. Now her dismay was palpable. And she didn't care if Jory thought she was being rude or not.

"I think Beth Ann might have cut the sailboat's line on purpose," said Jory. "I think she's been stalking me, too. In New York and then flying back and forth, even before she sort of crash-landed in my apartment."

"Why didn't you tell me all this," Theodosia demanded, "when I talked to you yesterday?"

"I don't know," said Jory. "I suppose because I didn't want to assign it too much importance. I thought maybe she'd just . . . go away. Now I really feel terrible. About everything."

"You're crazy, you know that?" said Theodosia.

A long silence spun out and then Jory said, "I'm still crazy about you."

"Don't be," said Theodosia, as she hung up the phone.

Theodosia was still fuming as she motored out from the Charleston Yacht Club with Chuck Strom. This was going to be her last contact with Jory, she decided. They were over, done, kaput. To keep flogging their broken relationship just made it sad and difficult for both of them.

So . . . the thing to do now was concentrate on the job at hand. Get Jory's sailboat rigged, sail it back across Charleston Harbor, then turn her attention to the book signing tonight.

As Theodosia adjusted her sunglasses and leaned back in the Corsair's bucket seat, she had to admit this was an almost perfect day for a sail. There was a fair amount of wind, about twenty knots, just enough to put a chop on the water and make things interesting. And the sun blazed bright in a parfait sky where wispy layers of yellow and pink clouds swirled on the breeze.

Rounding the tip of the peninsula, Theodosia swiveled in her seat, taking in a fine view of the Battery to her left. The green of White Point Gardens looked like a velvet carpet while just beyond it, the enormous Georgian, Italianate, and Victorian mansions stood like grand old matriarchs, sentinels of the harbor.

Straight ahead was Castle Pinckney, a brick and mortar fort that had been constructed in Charleston Harbor, on a large marshy island known as Shutes Folly, just prior to the War of 1812. Castle Pinckney had been occupied by soldiers over the years and had once been home to a lighthouse. Now the lighthouse and buildings were just piles of crumbling ruins, owned by the South Carolina Ports Authority. Boosters of the old fort had high hopes of converting it into some type of park, but funding never seemed to materialize.

Theodosia gazed at Castle Pinckney, then her eyes focused on another island in the distance. Fort Sumter. If they bypassed Castle Pinckney, then shot past Fort Sumter, they'd end up in the surging waters of the Atlantic. Probably no place for a boat this size. Or Jory's sailboat, either.

Strom was shouting something at her. She leaned toward him, listening over the roar of the engine.

". . . Beach over there," Strom was saying. He gestured toward a stretch of shimmering white sand. Theodosia homed in on it, tracked right for about fifty yards, and saw Jory's sailboat, his J/22. It had been washed into a small cove and now its foredeck nosed the beach, while the aft part of the boat bobbed gently, like a cork in the water.

"Okay," she said. Theodosia climbed from her bucket seat, glad she'd changed from her silk blouse and crop pants into boat shoes, red T-shirt, and navy shorts. Using the side rails for support, she made her way to the back of Strom's boat, ready to climb onto the rear swim platform.

Strom waved a hand at her, indicating he was going to back in. Then the boat bucked slightly and they swung into a one-hundred-and-eighty-degree turn, engines churning like crazy as Strom reversed toward the beach.

When they were fairly close, Theodosia nodded, then jumped down onto the swim platform. She counted to three, took a giant leap, and landed in about six inches of water. One heroic stride brought her to the beach, where shale and shells crumbled underfoot.

"You gonna be okay?" Strom called to her. He seemed concerned but anxious to get going at the same time.

She gave an exaggerated nod of her head. "I'll be fine," she called back over the roar of the motor. Strom seemed to hesitate for a few moments, then powered up his engine and swung around. Theodosia watched his boat, with its midnight-blue hull, take off like a joyful dolphin skimming the waves.

Okay, Theodosia thought, as she slogged toward Jory's sailboat. *Now we put my seamanship to the test. How long will it take to rig this boat? How long will it take to sail back to the Charleston Yacht Club?* She stood on the deserted beach, hands on hips, letting the wind whip her hair while she inhaled the salty breeze. Overhead, white gulls cawed noisily, floating on thermals, their wingtips curled expertly upward.

She wondered if the Coast Guard might send a cutter along to check if someone had indeed come to fetch Jory's boat, since they were the ones who'd first noticed it.

Interesting, she thought, that the J/22 had made it here seemingly of its own volition. On the other hand, the wind and water currents had probably just worked in concert with each other. And Pinckney Island wasn't that far from shore.

Standing alone now, motorboats droning in the distance, Theodosia did a quick scan of Pinckney Island.

Interestingly enough, she'd never set foot here before. Theodosia had sailed past it, read newspaper blurbs about how Civil War reenactors had used the place for special weekend events, but she'd never experienced the island up close until now. And like most folks, Theodosia was more than a little curious. Castle Pinckney was, after all, a piece of Charleston history. And Charleston was a town fueled by history.

So, Theodosia decided, wasn't this as good a time as any to take a look around? Wouldn't Drayton, history buff that he was, ply her with a myriad of questions? That said, shouldn't she make a quick reconnoiter before the Coast Guard shouted warnings at her via bullhorn? Before the Ports Authority got wind of her intrusion and tried to have her arrested?

Theodosia worried her lower lip with her teeth and thought for a moment. Ahead and to her right, where Jory's boat was hung up, stretched a large patch of tall marsh grass, green and yellow-gold, dancing in the wind. To her left stood the crumbling brick walls of the old fort, leafy green treetops bouncing and peeking up behind them. Really, what was the harm in taking a look at this so-called "forgotten fort?" She thought for a few moments. Probably no harm at all.

Crunching her way across the beach, Theodosia scrambled up a hill, mindful of sand burrs pecking at her ankles, and approached the crumbling brick wall. It was maybe six feet high, covered with tangled vines, and more than a little intriguing. Following along the wall, Theodosia touched a hand to the old bricks. Pitted and pocked with age, most were loose and unstable, barely held in place by small dabs of earthen mortar. Probably, she decided, a strong wind could blow these walls over. Probably most of these walls *had* blown over when Hurricane Hugo ripped through here in '89.

Still, Theodosia found the place fascinating. This little bit of history and mystery sat so close to a modern thriving Charleston, yet was clearly a throwback to the 1800s.

What could be inside, she wondered, as she ducked into a low, rounded passageway? She'd heard that most of the buildings were rubble. Still, there could be something . . .

Keeping her head low as she scrabbled through the ancient passageway, Theodosia put a hand on each side of the doorway as she emerged slowly into bright sunlight. A low, round stone artifact, possibly a well or cistern, sat directly to her left, while to her right was . . . holy cow! The biggest rattlesnake she'd ever seen!

Oh no! That thing is . . .

26

❧

. . . A monster!

Theodosia gasped as she practically felt sharp fangs sinking into flesh, flinched in anticipation of hot venom searing
through her veins.

But none of that happened. Just as her terrified brain registered the somewhat somnolent reptile and chattered warnings of imminent danger to her front cortex, she dove left,
then skittered a good twenty paces. The mad dash, along
with her body's own shot of adrenaline, had her heart pump-
ing furiously. Pausing near a thicket of dogwood to catch her
breath and reconnoiter, barely conscious of the low stir and
whir of katydids, Theodosia shot a furtive glance over her
shoulder. Much to her relief, no six-foot rattler had launched
itself in hot pursuit. In fact, chances were good that the
snake had been just as startled as she was. Still, Theodosia
knew she'd have to be a whole lot more careful. Oh yeah.

Reaching up, Theodosia pulled hard on a sapling, twisted
the leafy branch low, then snapped it off and quickly shucked

sticky, green leaves. From now on, she'd prod the long grasses ahead of her to alert and dislodge any type of critter that might be hunkered there, no matter what. Even if it proved to be a harmless marsh hen or slow-moving terrapin.

Pushing through underbrush, probing her stick like a professional beater trying to flush a tiger from the bush, Theodosia carefully moved on, finally emerging in a packed earth circle that didn't offer much. Piles of bricks, crusted metal—maybe part of an old cannon?—and a few crumbled buildings. There wasn't even anything left of the old lighthouse, except remnants of the foundation.

Theodosia stood there, feeling like she'd stumbled upon the ruins of some ancient civilization, some secret place where people hadn't trod for a hundred years. Then she realized that was the legacy of Castle Pinckney. An old fort, abandoned for decades, left to molder and die a slow death.

So kind of fascinating, after all, she decided.

Poking her stick out ahead of her, Theodosia moved forward. Creeping along slowly, she still hoped to discover some small vestige of the old fort. Some sort of testament to the War of 1812 or even the Civil War. She stepped over bricks, rocks, and crumbling foundations. But there seemed to be nothing of any real significance.

She wondered if the Kipling Club had ever made its way out here. Maybe they had. Possibly, unbeknownst to the Ports Authority, they'd plundered anything of value.

Theodosia continued to wander. An entire forest of trees had grown up and thrived here, obscuring foundations and making it difficult to determine where buildings and barracks had once stood. As she rounded a clump of magnolias, poking and prodding with her stick, she discovered a sort of wall with narrow rifle slits built into it.

This had to be part of the old fort!

Bending forward, peering through the stone slit, Theodosia wondered what it had been like to see an entire fleet of

British warships hurtling down upon you, Union Jacks fly-ing, cannons pounding, sails billowing. Exciting, to be sure. And terrifying.

She stood for a moment, trying to sear that vision into her brain so she could tell Drayton. Then, amidst the solitude of the ghostly ruins, Theodosia heard the smallest of sounds. A kind of *tink-clink*, like a pebble falling onto damp cement.

Theodosia froze. The notion that someone else might be here suddenly unnerved her. But who? Other clandestine explorers like herself?

Or maybe—and now her brain was working overtime—what if Jory's sailboat hadn't drifted haphazardly and beached itself here? What if a cool hand on the tiller had purposely steered the boat here?

But whose cool hand?

Beth Ann? Someone else? Someone who might be observing her right now?

Quick as a fox, Theodosia darted past the wall and plunged into a sea of tall grasses. Casting an eye toward the sun as she plodded through shifting sands, she adjusted her course and determined she was probably, hopefully, headed in the approximate direction of the beach. And she was right. Three minutes later, she emerged from the weeds and reeds onto the beach, close to where Jory's J/22 sat rocking listlessly.

Time to skedaddle, Theodosia decided. She kicked off her shoes and tossed them into the boat. Then she bent forward, grasped the prow of the boat, and shoved hard.

Nothing.

Digging her bare feet deeper into the sand, Theodosia braced a shoulder against the boat and pushed with all her might. And this time was rewarded with a sudden whoosh, as the boat heaved free of the sandbar.

Okay, she decided, *now we're cooking.*

Pulling herself aboard, Theodosia quickly apprised the

situation. If someone had, in fact, sailed the J/22 over to Castle Pinckney, then they'd done a masterful job of stowing away the sails. Which probably hadn't happened.

With that calming thought, Theodosia pulled open the hatch, climbed into the fore cabin, and muscled the sails onto the deck. Then she quickly set about rigging them. Snapping clips to her mainsail and spinnaker, working as fast as she could. When everything was ready, she gave a sharp tug on the line and the mainsail ripped up the mast, catching air and billowing like crazy the higher it rode. Tying off the line, Theodosia scrambled back to the cockpit and grabbed the till. From there it was a simple matter of maneuvering the J/22.

Five minutes later, Theodosia was skimming across Charleston Harbor. Wind rattled the halyards against the aluminum mast, sails whumped and thumped while other, speedier, motorized boats zipped past her. Gazing down toward Fort Sumter, she could see one of the tour boats making its thrice-a-day jaunt around the harbor.

Trimming her sail, checking her speed slightly, Theodosia rounded the tip of the peninsula, close enough now to see actual Frisbee players lobbing orange discs at each other. She heeled over slightly, completing her turn, and then it wasn't long before she was easing the J/22 into Jory's slip at the Charleston Yacht Club.

Taking down the sails and stowing them was the easy part. She'd done it dozens of times, in happier times, on this boat, and could pretty much do it in her sleep.

With the sails folded and stored, Theodosia tossed her orange life vest down the hatch, then leaned down and coiled the last of the line.

Jory's joke had always been that when you bought line instead of rope, the decimal point moved over a couple of notches. But as Theodosia handled this line, her brain suddenly recalled the cotton rope that had strangled Daria.

Could it have been line from this very boat? Cut by Beth

Ann's own hand? Was Beth Ann the missing link in all of this? Was Beth Ann a zonked-out, crazy-lady killer?

Theodosia let the possibility trickle through her brain again as she walked the length of the dock back to her car and decided it might be a real possibility.

So what now? she wondered.

Popping the locks on her car, Theodosia leaned across the front seat, dug into her shoulder bag, and pulled out her cell phone. Tidwell didn't answer; instead she got his voice mail. But she left what she thought was a fairly tantalizing message. Along with an urgent request to meet her tonight—at the Heritage Society.

Haley was finishing up in the kitchen when Theodosia returned.

"You found the boat?" she asked, wiping her hands on a tea towel.

"Yup," said Theodosia.

"Get it back to the marina okay?"

"No problem," Theodosia told her. She wandered over to the small counter, helped herself to a plump, pink shrimp.

"Well," commented Haley. "I don't know how you're going to take this, but you look like you had a wonderful time."

Surprised, Theodosia quickly swallowed her bite. "Really?"

"Oh yeah," said Haley, peering at her. "Your eyes look bright and your complexion's all glowy. Like you just had an oxygen facial or some other kind of spendy spa treatment."

"A wind-and-sea-salt scrub." Theodosia laughed. "Which I highly recommend."

Haley looked askance. "So you're not mad at Jory?"

"I didn't say that," Theodosia responded. "I'm still furious beyond belief, but I've decided not to let my personal dealings with him compromise activities that I enjoy. Case in point, sailing."

"Okay," said Haley, "I get it. I think."

Theodosia hastily changed the subject. "Looks like you've got everything ready for tonight."

Haley shook her hair back behind her shoulders. "Almost. Got to pack up the avocados and baguettes yet, but other than that we're good to go."

"I take it Drayton helped?"

"Enormously," said Haley.

"Okay then," said Theodosia. "I'm gonna scram upstairs and take a shower and try to get presentable."

"Which means I can load most of this stuff in your Jeep now," said Haley. "Right?"

"Right," said Theodosia, digging into her pocket and tossing Haley a jingle of keys.

But once Theodosia retreated upstairs, once she stepped into the shower and let hot water pound her head, back, and shoulders, once she shampooed her hair and let it air-dry, she couldn't make up her mind about what to wear that night.

Theodosia Browning, being a decisive, organized, and fairly low-maintenance person, always seemed slightly befuddled when it came to dressing up. Probably because she preferred to dress down. Enjoyed wearing comfy crop pants, a slinky T-shirt, and comfy sandals versus a dress and tottering high heels. Not that she didn't love dresses and high heels; it's just that they were so . . . dressy.

Digging in her closet, she pulled out a black cocktail dress and a short, sea-green silk shift with a hand-painted iris on it. Held them up in front of her, checked the mirror, still wasn't sure. Decided maybe she should solicit an unbiased opinion from the pup with the poshest taste around.

"What do you think, fella?" she asked, showing Earl Grey both dresses.

Earl Grey studied the two choices with solemn brown eyes. "Gwrrr," he finally told her.

"The green one?" she asked.

"Rwrrr." Right.

Theodosia studied the green dress again, said, "Maybe we should call Delaine. You think?"

Earl Grey laid down, placed his soft muzzle atop his front paws, and rolled his eyes.

"Just a quick check," she told him, reaching for her phone. "After all, she is a professional."

"What?" screeched Delaine, sounding harried.

"My green dress," said Theodosia. "The one with the hand-painted iris."

"Hmmm?" said Delaine.

"You think it's good for tonight?"

"Gosh, I don't know, Theodosia," replied Delaine. "Do you want to look positively smashing or like a little brown wren?"

"When you put it that way . . ." said Theodosia.

"Wear the green!" shrilled Delaine. "It's perfect. Besides, you bought it at my shop. Remember? The trunk show last summer?"

"How could I forget," said Theodosia. *Why did I call her? Why did I open myself up for such a direct hit?*

"And wear your silver Prada heels," Delaine added, then hung up abruptly.

Theodosia turned and gazed at Earl Grey, who regarded her with placid, unrelenting, doggy scrutiny. "I know, I know, I should have listened to you in the first place."

Earl Grey twitched an ear and sighed deeply. *Humans. Unpredictable creatures.*

27

❧

"Excuse me, excuse me," murmured Haley as she and Theodosia, clutching large plastic bins, elbowed their way through the well-dressed throng of Charleston socialites. Hung with dark oil paintings of long-dead South Carolina residents and defunct rice and indigo plantations, the wide hallway as gallery was the perfect place to hobnob. Edging into the lecture hall, Theodosia and Haley encountered yet another scrum of buzzing people who were chatting and air-kissing. Finally, they made it into the small service kitchen at the back.

"Lots of people here tonight," said Theodosia, depositing her load on the aluminum kitchen counter. She was surprised so many folks had turned out for Lyndel Woodruff's lecture. Then again, Timothy Neville was a master at drawing a crowd and Drayton had been politicking nonstop to alert friends, members, and donors.

"It's hard to imagine so many folks are interested in hearing a lecture on a Civil War battle," said Haley, starting to unpack the food. "I even saw Bill Glass out there."

"Great," said Theodosia.

Haley hesitated. "Or do you think everyone's just here for the social part?"

"Probably a little of both," said Theodosia. Heritage Society events were a place to see and be seen. And Lyndel Woodruff's lecture just happened to fall right between the end of opera season and the beginning of the symphony's three-month run. Which meant that a lot of socially prominent people were on the prowl for a night out. And Timothy did have a way of twisting arms.

"Think we brought enough food?" asked Haley.

"If we run out, then everyone will just focus on drinking," said Theodosia.

"And hobnobbing," said Haley. "These people are really world-class hobnobbers. Hey, do you think that archaeology guy is gonna show?" She draped a black apron over her head, glanced about the small but serviceable catering kitchen.

"Tred Pascal?" said Theodosia. "He will if he knows what's good for him." She smiled at Haley. "Since he knows *you're* going to be here."

"Hah," said Haley. "We'll see how interested he really is."

"I'm going to be on the lookout for Jud Snelling," said Theodosia. "He's that fellow I told you about from Savannah who might be interested in becoming a silent partner in the Antiquarian Map Shop."

"You suspicious of him?" asked Haley.

"Maybe. A little."

"So you're doing some investigating," said Haley. "Besides the catering."

"You could say that."

"What's the plan?" asked Haley. "Do we have a timeline?"

Theodosia checked her watch. "Lyndel's lecture is scheduled to begin in ten minutes or so and, according to Drayton, should run about thirty minutes. Tacking on another fifteen minutes for audience questions, I'd say we need to have our food and tea on the patio no later than eight thirty."

"In that case," said Haley, "we've got oodles of time." She pointed to a metal door. "I can squiggle out that way to the patio?"

"Yes," said Theodosia. "And as soon as Lyndel's done answering questions, Drayton and I will open all the French doors so guests can stroll out."

"And then we do our thing," said Haley. "Got it."

"What can I help you with?" asked Theodosia.

Haley held up a hand. "Absolutely nothing. You just go out and mingle. Have fun. Do your mystery-solving thing. Find the killer."

Theodosia's face assumed a slightly stricken look.

"Oh jeez," said Haley, trying to backpedal. "Apologies. I didn't mean to sound so flippant. Really. I just . . ."

"I know," said Theodosia, "we're all on edge over what's happened this past week."

Haley still looked pained. "Hey, I really am sorry. I know you and Daria were good friends."

"As are we," said Theodosia, giving Haley a quick hug.

Cinnamon and Miss Kitty accosted Theodosia the minute she emerged into the crowded hallway.

"Hello, dear!" squealed Miss Kitty. "Wonderful to see you!"

"This is so much fun!" gushed Cinnamon. "So many nice neighbors in attendance. Can you tell us, do most of these folks reside in the larger, fancier homes?"

Theodosia decided to remain noncommittal, since Miss Kitty and Cinnamon both seemed desperate to cultivate only customers with money. "The Heritage Society stages dozens of lectures and gallery shows throughout the year," Theodosia told them. "Perhaps you'll take a few more in and become members." *And perhaps I sound like the mission statement in their annual report,* she thought. *Oh well.*

"Maybe," said Cinnamon, glancing around, her eyes roving across those women who sported the real bling-bling diamond bracelets and matching earrings.

"Or you might even become donors," added Theodosia. At which point the two women went completely mute. Theodosia gave a sly smile, murmured, "Excuse me," and slipped away. She'd spotted someone else she very much wanted to talk to.

"See you later," called a subdued Miss Kitty.

"Fallon?" said Theodosia, hurrying over to a display of maps, daggers, and antique pistols. "I had no idea you'd be here tonight."

Daria's sister, Fallon, turned from where she was hanging a large map to greet Theodosia. "Theo, hello," she said smiling. "I wasn't planning to come, but then Timothy called about borrowing this map for display." She smoothed the sepia-tone map carefully with one hand. "Jason was going to come at first and then I thought, why don't I come instead?"

"Do you good to get out," said Theodosia. Dressed in a shiny black tank top and a slightly puffed short skirt, Fallon looked less mousey than usual. Quite presentable, in fact.

"I thought coming here tonight would do me some good," said Fallon. Her eyes assumed a slightly haunted look, then she asked, "How are you doing?" She dropped her voice to an even lower register. "I mean . . . with your undercover—or should I call it insider—investigation?"

Theodosia hesitated for a moment, then said, "I think I might be making progress."

Fallon's eyes widened and she leaned in closer. "Seriously?"

Theodosia put a hand on Fallon's shoulder. "Please don't get your hopes up. I need to speak with Detective Tidwell and untangle a couple of things yet."

"He's here?" asked Fallon.

"No, but I'm assuming he'll show up," said Theodosia. "I left a voice mail telling him it was fairly urgent that we meet."

"You really are on to something!" breathed Fallon. "Oh, you are such a love."

"No, no," said Theodosia. "Please hold any and all thanks until we have Daria's killer locked securely behind bars. But do understand that I haven't given up on this, okay?"

"Thank you," said Fallon, her eyes filling with tears. She reached in her small shoulder bag, dug past lipstick, mascara, and an atomizer, and grabbed a tissue.

"Theodosia," came a commanding voice.

Theodosia whirled to find Timothy Neville standing there, looking typically serious and a trifle imperious. "Timothy, hello. Great turnout tonight."

Timothy nodded in agreement to Theodosia, then said to Fallon, "That looks perfect, my dear. Many thanks for the loan of your map. Along with our display, it's a wonderful adjunct to Lyndel's lecture."

"You're welcome," said Fallon, ducking her head, looking pleased.

"And if I might have a word with you," said Timothy, grasping Theodosia's upper arm and pulling her aside.

"A problem?" Theodosia asked.

"No," said Timothy. "Fact is, I believe I've been able to shed considerable light on your backyard mystery."

"Uh-oh," said Theodosia, as they moved down the hallway together. "What's up? Did you discover a long-lost cemetery beneath my cottage? Or worse yet . . . catacombs?"

"Nothing so dire," said Timothy, reaching into the pocket of his snappy houndstooth jacket and pulling out several folded papers. "I had one of our interns do a bit of digging in our library. Studying old newspapers and documents, that sort of thing. Here." He thrust the papers at Theodosia. "See for yourself."

Theodosia unfolded Xerox copies of old newspaper accounts and scanned them as Timothy continued to talk.

"It seems the mansion next door to you was used as a temporary hospital in the final year of the Civil War," Timothy told her. "And your little cottage, Hazelhurst as it's now known, served as the chief surgeon's residence."

"Oh," said Theodosia, glancing up. "A residence?" She frowned. "I was under the impression it was an old carriage house."

"Might have been." Timothy chuckled. "I didn't say the doctor lived in a *first-class* residence. For all we know, it could have been falling down back then." He cleared his throat, still looking pleased. "Anyway, I'd be willing to bet that the bone or bones are probably the result of some poor soul who passed away while under the good doctor's care. Or are, perhaps, remnants from an old surgery or autopsy."

"Did you tell her?" asked Drayton, rushing up. He turned a serious gaze on Theodosia. "He told you?"

"About the doctor's quarters, yes," said Theodosia.

"Good news, wouldn't you say?" asked Drayton. He also looked scrubbed and slick in a navy-blue jacket and dove-gray slacks.

"Will this information get the archeologists to stop digging?" Theodosia murmured, almost to herself.

"We think so," said Timothy. "And you know I'll be happy to intercede any way I can."

"I'll take you up on that," said Theodosia, knowing Timothy's tremendous clout in the community. "And I owe you one."

Timothy gave a breezy wave. "All I ask is that our cocktail party go off without a hitch."

"That I can do," said Theodosia. "Our theme tonight is lovely and low-key."

"In that case," grinned Drayton, "I'd better run out and feng shui the patio. Make sure that we achieve harmonic balance to draw positive energy."

"Couldn't hurt," said Theodosia. She wasn't a big believer in charms, totems, and palm readers, but she was willing to give anything a try once. Well, maybe not *anything*.

Strolling back through the lecture hall, Theodosia noticed that people were beginning to gather in earnest now. She pushed her way back into the kitchen and found Haley arranging shrimp and avocado kabobs on three-tiered trays mounded with crushed ice. "Those look absolutely delicious," she told Haley.

Haley wiped her hands on the front of her apron. "Thanks. I'm gonna stick 'em in the cooler, though, until we need to take 'em out." She smiled. "Plus, I've got smoked salmon and goat cheese generously lathered on baguette slices and . . . what else? Oh, I have to spoon crab salad into puff pastries."

"I can help with that," said Theodosia.

"Okay," agreed Haley. "If you insist. I brought along some of our teeny gold teaspoons so we can add just the right amount . . ." Hearing a sudden whack, she turned toward the kitchen door as it blasted open.

Drayton came steamrolling in, looking unhappy. "There's a huge problem!" he wailed.

"Certainly not with the food," shot back Haley.

"Beverage service?" inquired Theodosia. Although she'd seen an efficient-looking bartender with his ice chests and multiple cases of champagne stacked outside.

"Worse!" wailed Drayton. "You know those marvelous Civil War–era weapons Timothy arranged in the display case in the front hallway? It seems someone's pried open the cabinet door and made off with a knife!"

"That's it?" said Haley. "You had me worried for a second."

"A theft *is* most certainly cause to worry," replied Drayton. He cast a meaningful glance at Theodosia. "Theo . . . ?"

"You think Theo took the knife?" asked Haley, slightly horrified.

"No," said Theodosia. "Drayton's asking in a roundabout way about someone else."

Haley's mouth opened, then closed without making a sound. Finally she said, "Holy shamoly, you mean Delaine's sister?"

"Nadine," said Drayton, sotto voce.

"Don't tell me she's still a practicing klepto," said Haley, almost amused now.

Drayton pounced on Haley. "You think Mrs. Wentworth from the History Club has sticky fingers? Or Philippe Dupree from the Civil War Reenactors Society?"

Or a crazy person from the Kipling Club? Theodosia wondered to herself.

"Uh, I'm guessing the millionaires didn't do it," said Haley.

"I prefer to think of them as significant donors to Charleston's various arts and civic organizations," said Drayton.

"Fat cats," declared Haley.

"Whatever the case," said Theodosia, stepping in, "maybe we should pull Nadine aside and do some oh-so-gentle probing."

"Timothy's having an absolute hissy fit," said Drayton, "so I don't think we should be particularly gentle with Nadine."

"Then just probe her," snorted Haley.

Theodosia took off her apron and tossed it on a ladder-back chair. "I'll go talk to Delaine and Nadine right now. See if I can shed a little light."

"Thank you!" said Drayton.

Theodosia hustled out into the lecture hall where most of the guests had taken their seats by now, scanned the crowd for familiar faces, but didn't see either Delaine or Nadine. She slipped down the aisle and out into the main hallway, where only a few folks, latecomers and concerned-looking Heritage Society staff, still milled about.

Maybe one of the side galleries?

The Heritage Society had a half dozen small galleries where oil paintings, photography, old silver, and antique pottery were displayed. But as Theodosia dashed from gallery to gallery, she could find no one.

So where?

Was it possible Timothy Neville had spotted Nadine with the missing object and was already grilling her? Or stalling her until the police showed up? Maybe he was holding her in the reception area or in his office behind closed doors where a certain amount of discretion could be maintained? Maybe.

Theodosia flew down another hallway and emerged in the reception area. But it was dark, silent, and unoccupied. Two upholstered armchairs were but dim lumps, a single, green glass shade glowed on Camilla Hodge's reception desk.

A slight noise, a whisper really, like footsteps on a carpet, caused Theodosia to whirl about and peer down the narrow hallway that led past Timothy's office. And did her eyes detect a slight movement at the end of that corridor? In the low light, had she maybe caught . . . a brief flash of pink?

Without hesitation, Theodosia hurried down that dim hallway. She paused at the doorway to Timothy's office, put her hand on the brass doorknob, and turned it. Nothing. His office was locked tight as a drum.

Continuing down to the end of the hallway, Theodosia paused, her hand caressing the worn knob of a wooden banister. This stairway led downstairs to the storage rooms.

Should she? Is this where the person she saw—or thought she saw—disappeared to?

Plunging downstairs, Theodosia almost tripped on the narrow, wooden stairs. Steadying herself, she clambered to the bottom only to be faced with another choice. Two corridors led off into darkness, with only twenty-watt bulbs glowing at the far end. Not much charm down here, she decided. Cement floor, cinder-block walls, a couple of locked doors complete with keypads and blinking lights. Obviously, a security system armed against possible intruders.

So if this person she'd been following, supposedly Nadine, had come down here, where had she gone? How had she disappeared like a wisp of smoke?

Edging down one corridor, Theodosia felt both nervous and a little silly. Because, probably, no one was prowling around down here after all. She was just chasing light and shadows, figments of her imagination.

Okay, enough said. Theodosia hurried back upstairs and headed for the lecture hall.

She found Delaine, lounging in an aisle seat, chatting away with Hillary Retton, as the last of the guests filed into the hall.

"Where's your sister?" Theodosia murmured in Delaine's ear.

Delaine turned, frowned, and waved a hand. "I don't know. Socializing, I imagine."

"Socializing where?"

"Wherever," said Delaine, sounding peeved. "Last I saw Nadine she was talking to that adorable man, Barton Palmer. Have you met him? He owns Bubbles, that new wine and champagne bar."

"Okay, let me ask you this," said Theodosia. "What's Nadine wearing tonight? Is it a pink jacket and skirt?"

Delaine tilted her head back and seemed to ponder the question. "I'd say the color was more of a blush rose. Of course, under the absolute right lighting conditions it could be mistaken for primrose."

"Delaine . . . please!" said Theodosia. "We're not picking paint chips at Home Depot, just answer the question. It's important!"

Shrugging her shoulders in an I-don't-know gesture, Delaine hissed, "Shhh, Theo, the lecture's starting."

Glancing around, Theodosia saw that Delaine was right. Everyone had settled into chairs as the grand overhead chandeliers slowly dimmed. Then a bright key light fell upon Lyndel Woodruff as he took long, loping strides to the podium.

Stepping back into the hallway, Theodosia silently closed the door behind her and slumped against the deeply grained wood. She drew a breath and decided to take a look at the pilfered display case. Spinning quickly, she found herself gazing into angry, blazing eyes set into a hardened, female face.

Theodosia cringed even as she reflexively threw up a hand and cried, "Beth Ann!"

28

❧

"Beth Ann," *Theodosia* choked out again, staring at Jory's ex-fiancée, regarding her almost as if she were some hostile spirit who'd magically materialized from the great beyond. "What are *you* doing here?"

Beth Ann lifted her chin in an imperious manner and gazed at Theodosia, hatred blazing in her eyes. "I came to see you, Theodosia. It's time we had it out." She spat out these last words, then took a step forward, doing her best to intimidate Theodosia by invading her personal space.

"Had it out?" said Theodosia, not yielding an inch. "Had *what* out?"

"As if you didn't know. The issue of Jory Davis, of course!"

Theodosia put her hands on her hips. "I don't have an issue with Jory Davis."

"You're trying to *steal* him back," said Beth Ann, seething with molten anger.

"No, I'm not," said Theodosia. "Fact is, I haven't wanted Jory back for a long time."

"Liar!" snapped Beth Ann. Her nostrils flared; red blotches blazed high on her cheeks. Beth Ann was clearly overwrought and looked like she was ready to do battle.

Theodosia shook her head as if to clear away this nightmare encounter. "Listen to me," she said, biting off each word. "I don't want Jory. You can *have* him."

Beth Ann's eyes widened in shock and her resolve seemed to waver. "What?"

"Read my lips," said Theodosia. "You're welcome to Jory Davis. He's yours. End of story."

"I don't believe you," Beth Ann hissed. "You're just saying that to get rid of me."

"No," Theodosia muttered, "there's a better way to be rid of you." She squared her shoulders, turned away, took a few steps . . . then hesitated. Running through her brain was the notion that if Beth Ann was crazy enough to zoom around like the Wicked Witch of the East, spewing venom and nastiness, she might be crazy enough to engineer other things, too. Turning back toward her, Theodosia focused on Beth Ann and asked in a gravelly voice, "What are you doing here?"

Frustration manifested itself on Beth Ann's face. "Talking to you!"

"No," said Theodosia. "I meant here, geographically. In Charleston. Why are you here?"

Beth Ann huffed out an enormous sigh. "Typical of Jory not to mention it, but I've relocated permanently to Charleston. There's a good chance he and I will be married soon."

"Sorry, Beth Ann, that's not the story I heard."

"Don't say that!" screamed Beth Ann. "You're just jealous!"

"Uh, Beth Ann, could you please dial it down?"

"What?"

"Question number two," said Theodosia. "Do you have a car?"

Beth Ann stared at her, hatred radiating from her eyes like a demon possessed. "Of course I have a car," she spat out. "A rental. How else do you think I'm going to learn my way around these crazy, stupid streets?"

"What color is it?" asked Theodosia.

Beth Ann tilted her head to one side and folded her hands across her chest in a confrontational gesture. "I don't know. What do you care?"

"Please just answer the question," said Theodosia. When push came to shove, Theodosia could be just as stubborn.

Beth Ann let loose another deep sigh, as if coughing up an answer was a supreme imposition. "Dark. Navy. Black, maybe. I don't know."

"Okay," said Theodosia. "Now we're making some forward progress." The car that had tried to run her into the bridge embankment three nights ago had been black, so checking out Beth Ann's car was going to be a serious litmus test. If Beth Ann had a bash in her car or a dented front fender, then it stood to reason she'd been the one on the Ben Sawyer Bridge that night.

"What I need to do," said Theodosia, "is take a look at your car."

"What?" said Beth Ann again. "Why?"

"Indulge me," said Theodosia.

"You're crazy, you know that?" said Beth Ann. "No wonder Jory left you."

"Can we just . . . go outside for a minute?"

Reluctantly, Beth Ann followed Theodosia out onto the patio.

"Drayton," Theodosia called. "Could you come here for a moment?"

Drayton strolled over from where he'd been buzzing about, arranging napkins, silverware, and teacups on the tables. "Hmm?" Then his eyes widened in surprise when he recognized Beth Ann.

"Drayton," said Theodosia, "You remember Beth Ann, don't you? We're all going to go take a peek at her car."

"I say . . ." said Drayton.

Cocking her head toward Beth Ann, Theodosia said, "The bridge . . ."

Drayton picked up on her meaning. "Ah . . ."

"What's wrong with you people?" demanded Beth Ann. "Don't you talk in full sentences?"

"It's a southern thing," Theodosia told her. "Kind of a code you're going to have to learn if you intend to live here."

"You people really are crazy," muttered Beth Ann.

Beth Ann's rental was a shiny black Nissan Sentra. No bashes or mashes marred its sleek countenance. Hence, probably no recent bridge crashes.

"Happy now?" asked Beth Ann. She stood off to the side, fingering her electronic key fob. "You want to tell me what this is all about?"

"Not particularly," said Theodosia. She stared down the dark street parked solid with cars. Gaslights shimmered in the mist that had drifted in from the harbor, live oaks arched and whispered overhead.

"Definitely not the one," said Drayton.

"So we keep . . ." said Theodosia.

"Indeed," replied Drayton.

"You're doing it again!" screeched Beth Ann. "Talking in stupid riddles."

"It's just . . ." said Drayton.

"Oh, forget it," Beth Ann blurted in a sour voice. "I'm out of here." She extended her arm and punched the key fob, sounding a tiny electronic beep. Pulling open the door, she scrambled into her car, still railing at them, just this side of hysterical. "I really can't *stand* this place, you know? You people literally drive me crazy!"

Theodosia smiled faintly as Beth Ann gunned the engine all the while muttering to herself and making futile gestures. "She really is off the hook, isn't she?" They watched as Beth Ann slammed her car into gear and screeched wildly away from the curb.

"Now what?" asked Drayton.

"Not sure," said Theodosia. "But I think we just eliminated one suspect."

"So a bit of an upside," allowed Drayton.

They stood there talking for a good ten minutes. About Beth Ann, wondering where Nadine had run off to, and about Joe Don Hunter.

"What if he grabbed the dagger?" asked Theodosia. "So he could turn around and sell it."

"Could have," said Drayton, "though I didn't see him prowling around."

"Still," said Theodosia, "Joe Don had to know about this evening." She thought for a few moments. "Maybe Fallon mentioned it to him."

"Maybe," said Drayton.

They chatted for a few more minutes, then strolled back through the darkness, down a gravel path lined with tall, whispering bamboo plants, and onto the Heritage Society's outdoor patio. With its exotic, almost Balinese feel, the patio was dark, deep, and secluded. Ground-level spotlights tucked into thick stands of bamboo, magnolias, and crepe myrtle cast shadows and heightened the feeling of wandering through an exotic land. A free-form pond brimmed with silver-white Japanese koi while water trickled down strategically placed rocks, emitting a hypnotic, melodious sound.

Wrought-iron tables and chairs were set around the patio;

two larger buffet tables covered in white linen tablecloths had been arranged to hold appetizers, tea, and champagne.

All they had to do now was carry out food trays and teapots and alert the bartender, Theodosia decided, since it was just a matter of time before their guests would come streaming out.

"Ye gadz," squeaked Drayton, glimpsing the lecture hall through the French double doors, "I think Lyndel's almost done with his lecture."

"Let's dash in and catch the tail end," suggested Theodosia.

They slipped through the back door and into the kitchen, where Haley and the bartender were locked in bantering conversation, then emerged in the back of the lecture hall.

"He is finished," Drayton whispered. Lyndel Woodruff was gazing out at his audience, looking pleased with the talk he'd just delivered. Looking a little relieved, too.

"What I'd like to do now," said Lyndel, "is open this up to all of you who were so kind to come here tonight." He spread his arms in a magnanimous gesture to the audience, then leaned forward and grasped the podium.

Off to his left, the hallway door suddenly slammed open and two troopers from the South Carolina Highway Patrol strode noisily into the room, boot heels drumming against old oak floorboards. Dressed in full regalia with insignia and guns, they appeared to have business on their mind. Then, as the overhead lights flashed on, Lyndel Woodruff seemed to falter and wilt at the podium, his face going blush red. A few members of the audience stood up to see what was going on, a loud buzz rose from the crowd.

Not sure what to make of this rude intrusion or how to soldier on with his program, Lyndel Woodruff asked in a quavering voice. "Are there any questions?"

The taller of the two officers, a man with a modified handlebar mustache and grizzled gray hair sticking out from under his Smokey Bear hat, strode to the podium, bent toward the microphone and barked out, "Are Cinnamon St. John and Kitty Devlin present?"

An even louder buzz erupted from the audience as heads twisted and the curious audience scanned the room for the two women in question.

"What's this about?" muttered a stunned Drayton.

His question was promptly answered as Detective Burt Tidwell, flanked by two uniformed police officers, entered the room at a brisk trot.

"You heard the state patrol officers," Tidwell snapped out, his jowls sloshing, his beady eyes roving the crowd.

Seated in the center of the room, Miss Kitty suddenly stood up, followed by a reluctant Cinnamon. A man next to them proclaimed, "This is an outrage!"

"No," said Tidwell, addressing the audience with all the aplomb of a trained Shakespearean actor, "this is an arrest."

"What are the charges?" wondered Theodosia, as she watched the two women being taken into custody by the contingent of officers. Had Tidwell somehow linked them to Daria's murder?

"This is so cool," exclaimed Haley, who'd rushed out to catch the fireworks. "I never saw anyone get arrested before."

"Isn't pageantry exciting?" asked Drayton, rolling his eyes.

"Tidwell must have discovered some sort of evidence against them," Theodosia murmured as the spectacle continued.

Actual handcuffs were produced and placed around the wrists of the two women.

One of the state patrol officers pulled a small, laminated card from the pocket of his khaki shirt and began to read. "Under sovereign authority entrusted to me by of the State of South Carolina, I hereby place you under arrest. You have the right to remain . . ."

With the entire crowd goggle-eyed and standing on its feet now, Theodosia edged up the aisle toward Detective Tidwell. He flashed a single glance at her, but kept his focus on Miss Kitty and Cinnamon. Finally, when the two troopers escorted the two women out, Tidwell lifted a single eyebrow and gazed at Theodosia.

She was beside him in a second. "Why were they arrested?" she asked. "Was it because of Daria's murder?"

Tidwell stared at her, looking almost confused. "No, that's not it."

"Then what?" demanded Theodosia.

Tidwell shook his head as if to dismiss Theodosia's previous statement. "Receiving stolen goods," he told her, as Drayton suddenly flew past them, then veered toward the podium.

"You mean . . . *perfume?*" sputtered Theodosia. "You're telling me Cinnamon and Miss Kitty were involved in the hijacking case you were working on? You *knew* they were receiving stolen goods?"

"I wish I could take credit for such amazing skill and deductive reasoning," said Tidwell. "In fact, we weren't having much luck at all until a disgruntled wholesaler in Miami finally placed a GPS transponder *inside* his last shipment. Guess where we traced it to?"

"Uh, a certain shop on Church Street?" said Theodosia, sounding disgruntled.

"Interesting, yes?" said Tidwell.

But it was disappointment that registered on Theodosia's face.

"Excuse me!" Drayton's cultured voice suddenly boomed from the microphone. "Will you all take your seats please?" He paused. "Thank you, thank you, everyone." As conversation began to die down and people actually took their seats, Drayton continued. "As a Heritage Society board member, I wish to apologize for this unusual and rather inconvenient interruption. However, our guest lecturer, Mr. Lyndel Woodruff, is far from finished." He mustered an enthusiastic grin for Lyndel. "Mr. Woodruff is now ready for the question-and-answer portion of the evening."

A spatter of applause broke out, then pretty soon the entire audience was caught up in the applause.

Drayton stepped back, relinquishing the podium to Lyndel. "Lyndel?"

With renewed energy, Lyndel Woodruff, began to accept questions from the audience.

Drayton rushed to the back of the lecture hall where Theodosia and Haley whispered together. "They were really arrested?"

"Apparently," said Theodosia. She stared out into the front hallway where Tidwell was deep in conversation with Timothy. For some reason, she fervently hoped Timothy wasn't bothering him about the missing dagger.

"Because . . . ?" asked Drayton.

"Receiving stolen goods," said Theodosia. "But I think . . ."

"They had something to do with Daria's death, too?" Drayton asked breathlessly as they slipped back into the kitchen.

Theodosia exhaled slowly, suddenly feeling like the crack in the case hadn't cracked open that much. As if the bad dream might continue. "Building a murder case against them is up to Tidwell now. But if you ask me . . ."

"If you ask me," cut in Haley, "the case is closed. Cinnamon and Miss Kitty murdered Daria." She stared at them mournfully. "The sordid details will all come out eventually."

Drayton looked thoughtful. "But what possible motive did they have?"

"Perhaps," said Theodosia, venturing a guess, "Daria may have *seen* something?"

"Like a delivery!" said Drayton, pouncing on the idea.

"It's possible," said Theodosia, piecing people and events together as she went on. "And then Daria put two and two together," said Theodosia. She paused. "Does that make sense?"

"Makes perfect sense to me," said Drayton.

"Wow," echoed Haley. "Who would have thought a couple of hoity-toity dames who sold bottles of perfume were really serious criminals?"

"You never know what lurks deep within someone's heart," said Drayton. He cocked his head, as if deep in thought, then said, "What about the candles and lighter those women donated for tonight? You suppose those are stolen goods as well?"

"Let's not worry about candles right now," said Theodosia, still trying to cobble together a murder scenario.

"Our little secret," Haley added with a wink.

"If you say so," said Drayton. "But I for one don't care to get busted."

"Busted?" Haley hooted. "Over donated candles? Gimme a break."

"Okay, guys," said Theodosia, knowing they'd better focus squarely on the cocktail party, "let's get back on track. You two double-check appetizer platters while I run out and take a final look at the patio. Once I give the high sign, we'll ferry everything out."

"Got it," said Haley.

Bustling about the patio, Theodosia didn't have to do much to make it any more gorgeous than it already was. The romantic lighting, the pond with its tinkling waterfall, the dense foliage that swayed slightly in the warm evening breeze set a magical scene.

Each of the round, wrought-iron tables also looked perfect, adorned with centerpieces of white roses, sweet peas, and lily of the valley arranged in crystal vases. Tiny white votive candles twinkled in silver julep cups. On the main tables, teacups and crystal champagne flutes were arranged just so, bottles of champagne rested in large silver ice buckets.

Theodosia felt lighter and, strangely enough, more hopeful, knowing it hadn't been Beth Ann who'd tried to force her off the bridge.

So maybe it had just been a crazy person that night? Or a drunk driver in an all-fired hurry? Or perhaps it had been Cinnamon and Miss Kitty after all. They seemed to be the crazy ones in this whole mess. They were the ones who'd been arrested and hauled off in handcuffs.

But were they murderers? Drayton's words rang so true—it was impossible to peer into someone's heart, to understand their motivation, the greed, or the demons that drove them.

Gazing at the main table, Theodosia decided she had to let this murder mystery go for the time being, release it like so many fluttering night moths. Better to light the candelabra, bring out the food, and signal the start of the festivities.

Drayton had generously brought along what he'd dubbed his Phantom of the Opera candelabra. It was an antique sterling silver piece that held a half dozen tall cream-colored tapers and looked absolutely stunning on the food table.

Now, if Theodosia could just find her lighter. She glanced around, trying to recall where she'd put it, momentarily delighted by the flickering white candles she'd positioned on the large rocks that outlined the small pond. Theodosia wandered across the patio, still absorbed. Maybe she'd left the lighter on one of the tables? Scanning the table nearest the door, her senses were suddenly tickled into awareness by a vaguely familiar scent. Something woodsy, like cut grass or cedar?

Only at the very last second was she cognizant of the teaberry scent and someone coming up behind her. Sensing danger before she saw it, Theodosia spun quickly just as Fallon lunged from the darkness like a bloodthirsty vampire!

29

✦

Shrieking like a banshee, brandishing a knife above her head, Fallon grinned malevolently as she rushed at Theodosia, poised to strike!

"Wha—" said Theodosia, stunned, terrified out of her mind, and backpedaling like crazy as she tried desperately to scramble from Fallon's reach. "You!"

"Yes, me," breathed Fallon in a hoarse, harsh voice as she swung her knife at Theodosia.

Theodosia jumped back again, caught her heel in a jagged crack, kicked out of her shoes, then backed away slowly. As if retreating from a rabid animal.

But Fallon was out for blood. She darted forward, swinging her knife back and forth in a wide arc.

"Stop it," said Theodosia, gasping for breath. "You don't have to do this."

"But I do." Fallon grinned. All reason and logic had seemingly evaporated from her brain. Now she was just a stone-cold killer.

Backing across the patio, extending her hands in a pleading gesture, Theodosia felt her hip touch the back of a wrought-iron chair. Scurrying around the table, she tried to put some sort of barrier between her and Fallon.

"Why?" asked Theodosia. "Why your sister?" If she could keep Fallon talking, maybe she could also attract someone's attention.

"Not sister," spat out Fallon. "Not even blood. I was the adopted one. Never pretty enough, never good enough, never smart enough."

"You know that's not true!" said Theodosia.

"I saw the pity on their faces," cried Fallon.

"Not pity, love," said Theodosia.

"And they never even *told* me," shrieked Fallon. "Everyone keeping the big, bad secret."

"I'm sure no one wanted to intentionally hurt you," said Theodosia.

"Never fitting in," spat Fallon, lunging around the table.

Theodosia skittered away, desperately hoping to seek refuge inside, but Fallon doggedly stalked her in a darkly comic duck-and-hide ballet that took them whirling and dashing around the entire patio.

"Help!" Theodosia shrieked. "Somebody help me! Police! Fire!" she called out. Dashing and dodging, she pleaded for help that never seemed to materialize. Backed up against the large food table now, not much room to maneuver, Theodosia reached out and snatched Drayton's candelabra. Champagne flutes wobbled, then crashed on cement, shards flying everywhere as Theodosia thrust her makeshift weapon at Fallon, trying bravely to deflect her jabs. But the candelabra was heavy and clumsy, and all Theodosia could achieve were a few weak parries against Fallon's deadly blade.

"Nobody's going to help you," crooned Fallon in a low, strangled voice. "You're mine now, you meddling pest!"

"That's what you think," grunted Theodosia. Gathering

her strength, she swung the candelabra with all her might, connecting hard with both the knife and Fallon's hand.

"Oww!" howled Fallon. But she was still crazy and quick. Charging Theodosia in an all-out push, she thrust and jabbed and threatened, finally backing her up against the edge of the pond. No place to go.

Knowing she was in serious danger, Theodosia tried to feint to one side, but stumbled and lost her balance.

Fast as a snapping turtle, Fallon was on top of Theodosia, shoving her backward into the pond, pushing her head underwater.

Struggling frantically, Theodosia opened her mouth and screamed an underwater protest. Bubbles streamed from her nose and mouth, her cry echoed hollowly.

Still no one came.

Gazing up through thrashing water, Theodosia saw Fallon's arm raised high above her head, ready to bring the knife down in a final coup de grâce. Realizing she was still clinging to the candelabra, she thrust it once again at Fallon! This time she made contact with a dull clunk, causing the blade to tumble from Fallon's hand.

Still peering up through the water, Theodosia was stunned to see the knife zip past her, then tumble harmlessly to the murky bottom of the pool.

Fallon had lost her weapon, but she was still driven for vengeance. As Theodosia bobbed up for air, Fallon wrapped both hands around her throat, squeezing hard, shoving her below the surface again in an attempt to strangle her!

Dropping the candelabra, Theodosia's hands flew up to pry Fallon's hands from her neck. But, caught in a murderous fervor, Fallon maintained her deathlike grip!

Arching her back, Theodosia fought harder as she realized her air supply was running out.

Not good, this is not good! Gotta make something happen!

But Fallon was crazed and crazed people often possess superhuman strength.

Theodosia's lungs burned like fire and her arms flailed helplessly, batting against the rocky edge of the pool, scraping nails and fingertips.

If only she could get a better grip! Grab onto the rocks and heave herself upward!

Fighting with renewed energy, Theodosia twisted and turned and struggled to get her legs under her, then fought to push up. It worked. Sort of. Theodosia gasped a tiny sip of air as she floundered mightily, her left hand scrabbling across rock again. And just as she was pushed under a third time, her fingers touched . . . metal.

Metal? My misplaced lighter? Has to be.

Keeping that thought as a homing beacon, Theodosia struggled harder, straining to grab the lighter. But even though her fingers touched cool metal again, she couldn't grab hold. It was just out of reach!

Thrashing and wrenching her head to the left, Theodosia made slight contact with Fallon's right wrist.

Should I? Has to be done.

And bit down hard.

She heard Fallon's shriek, felt the woman's grip loosen just slightly. And made a final effort to grab the lighter.

Got it!

And just as everything faded black before Theodosia's eyes, just as her ears pounded like a million cannons firing, her index finger pushed down on the lighter's button.

She felt the click rather than heard it. But just knowing she had a weapon renewed Theodosia's resolve.

Taking a wild guess, what might be her only guess, Theodosia jabbed the flaming lighter at Fallon. Hoping, praying, she'd somehow make contact.

Staring upward, as if in a dream, Theodosia saw the

lighter with its small, wavering flame and what appeared to be her disembodied hand.

Then slowly, amazingly, a ring of fire seemed to dance and grow and shimmer above her. And Theodosia suddenly realized she'd set Fallon's skirt on fire!

A bloodcurdling scream rent the air. Fallon's hands clenched reflexively around Theodosia's neck, then slipped blessedly off.

Driving herself upward with the aid of her legs, drawing in blessed deep gluts of air, Theodosia flew out of the water like a seal heaving itself onto a rocky beach.

And beheld a scene as bizarre as any from Dante's *Inferno*.

Fallon, her skirt a flaming pinwheel, whirled and twirled her way across the patio like a drunken fire dancer. Frantic and frenzied, batting at the flames, high-pitched screams roiled from her in a death cry.

As Fallon's shrieks rent the air, curious, horrified guests cautiously opened the French doors to poke their heads out and see what was happening!

Theodosia, still gasping, pulled herself upright and watched in shock. Like a whirling dervish, Fallon crashed from one table to another, knocking over candles, setting white linen tablecloths on fire.

Dear lord, thought Theodosia, *this whole place might go up in flames!*

"Call the fire department!" yelped Drayton, as he ran out, balancing a tray of hors d'oeuvres.

"Somebody help her!" screamed Haley, standing stock-still, gripping a large silver teapot.

Theodosia sprinted for Haley, ripped the teapot from her hands, and lunged at Fallon. Splashing her head to toe with Russian Caravan tea, she managed to douse the flames.

30

❧

So much for the party on the patio.

Poor Drayton had to pull himself together and deliver yet another speech. This one was considerably more somber and apologetic than the first, but carefully diffused the situation. The upshot of his words were—there'd been an unfortunate fire on the patio. No one was seriously injured, but could you all kindly exit via the main hallway so the fire department, ambulance workers, and police officers could do their job. So sorry the cocktail party had to be called off.

Once Drayton and Timothy Neville had managed to beat back all the curious guests and send them packing, they collapsed in heaps at one of the tables.

"The woman . . ." said Timothy, looking grim. "Fallon."

"Dispatched in an ambulance," said Tidwell, who had somehow found his way back to the Heritage Society and was now seated next to Theodosia, watching her carefully. "With police guard."

"Is she okay?" asked Theodosia.

"Medics thought so," replied Tidwell.

"Are *you* okay?" Drayton asked Theodosia, peering across the table at her. She was thoroughly drenched and had accepted Tidwell's jacket to wear. It billowed around her like a circus tent.

"I think so," Theodosia murmured. But she was searching for answers, too. "Any idea on Fallon's backstory?" she asked Tidwell. "What might have turned her into such a raving maniac?"

"Best as we can determine," said Tidwell, "Fallon's been having trouble all her life. Trouble in school, in and out of a couple of private clinics, taking serious doses of antidepressants."

"Even though she had a loving family," murmured Theodosia.

"It wasn't until Jack Brux called me a couple of hours ago that I strung it all together," said Tidwell.

"Strung what together?" asked Drayton.

"Fallon was adopted," said Theodosia.

"What!" exclaimed Drayton. "I never knew that!"

"Brux finally pieced a couple of those documents together," said Tidwell. "The ones that had been ripped to shreds."

"Family records?" guessed Theodosia. She was beginning to get a clearer picture.

Tidwell nodded. "Obviously they were records where not a single mention of her was made."

"Fallon could have harbored feelings of anger and frustration that festered for years," said Drayton. "And seeing her nonheritage in black and white tipped her over the edge."

"Poor Sophie," said Theodosia.

Drayton nodded. "In a way she lost two daughters."

Theodosia turned toward Tidwell, suddenly angry. "But you *knew* about Fallon's mental state. And you'd just found out about the documents! So why didn't you warn me about her?"

"Because I had no idea she'd *be* here!" Tidwell shouted

back. "After we picked up the crazy perfume ladies, I was going to issue a warrant for Fallon's arrest. Show up at her house, take her into custody quietly."

"But she was here," said Drayton.

"Mmm," said Theodosia, her anger starting to retreat. "And then I had to open my big mouth and tell her how close we were to catching Daria's killer."

"Because we were," put in Haley. "Weren't we?"

"But I set Fallon off," said Theodosia. "Maybe she would have gone quietly with Tidwell if I hadn't suggested I was hot on the trail. Maybe she would have confessed of her own volition, helped put things right."

Timothy Neville suddenly put his head in his hands. "No, this was my fault. I almost got you killed, dear lady," he said mournfully to Theodosia. "Calling the shop. Borrowing that map."

"Don't lose too much sleep over it," Tidwell told him. "Truth be told, Theodosia enjoys plunking herself in the middle of a crisis. Any crisis."

"Don't say that," said Drayton, rushing to defend her. "Theodosia was only trying to help."

"And now things are a mess," said a glum Timothy Neville. He looked around the patio. "This place is a mess."

"Look at the bright side," suggested Haley. "Daria's killer has been caught. And this has to have been one of the craziest, most memorable evenings the Heritage Society ever had. I'll bet this helps pull in new members like crazy."

"You really think so?" asked Timothy, in disbelief.

Haley winked at Drayton. "Oh sure. Wouldn't you agree, Drayton?"

"I'm sure there'll be fascinating stories making the rounds," allowed Drayton.

"Huh," said Timothy, noticing the food trays Drayton and Haley had brought out. "So what are we going to do with all this food?"

"And champagne," said Drayton. "Don't forget all those cases of champagne."

A sudden pop sounded directly behind them. They all turned and were startled to see Bill Glass holding up a large green bottle. White froth gushed from it, spilling onto the patio. "Did I miss the party?" he asked. Delaine's sister, Nadine, hung on his arm, staring up with love in her eyes.

"I'd say you *are* the party," murmured Drayton.

Jumping up, Haley grabbed champagne flutes for everyone and quickly passed them around. Bill Glass, already in an effusive mood, followed her around the table, happily filling each person's glass with the bubbling amber liquid.

"How about a toast?" proposed Haley.

"Do you think it's appropriate?" asked Drayton.

Theodosia thought for a minute, then smiled. "I have one that might be." They all lifted their glasses high and clinked them together as she recited: "Lord, grant us all a good long life for you are surely knowing, that earth has angels all too few while heaven's overflowing."

FAVORITE RECIPES FROM
The Indigo Tea Shop

Haley's Vagabond Vegetable Soup

2 Tbsp. olive oil
1 cup onion, chopped
¼ cup celery, chopped
¼ cup pepper (green or red), chopped
1 cup sweet potatoes, diced and peeled
1 tsp. paprika
1 tsp. dried basil
1 tsp. salt
½ tsp. pepper
1 bay leaf
1½ cups chicken stock
1 tomato, chopped
¾ cup cooked garbanzo beans

HEAT olive oil in skillet, then sauté onion, celery, pepper, and sweet potatoes for 4 to 5 minutes. Add paprika, basil, salt, pepper, and bay leaf, then mix. Add in chicken stock, cover, and simmer over low heat for 20 minutes. Add

tomato and garbanzo beans to the soup and simmer for an
additional 10 minutes. Makes 4 to 5 servings.

Pecan Pie Muffins

    1 cup brown sugar, packed
    ½ cup flour
    1 cup pecans, chopped
    ¼ tsp. cinnamon
    2 eggs
    ½ cup butter, melted

COMBINE brown sugar, flour, pecans, and cinnamon in
mixing bowl. Beat eggs well, then stir in melted butter.
Add egg and butter mixture to dry mixture, stirring until
moistened. Spoon batter into foil baking cups that have
been greased, filling about ⅔ full. Bake at 350 degrees for
20 to 25 minutes or until done. Remove from pan and cool
on wire rack. Yields about 8 or 9 muffins.

Hawaiian Tea Sandwiches

    1 cup sugar
    2 cups crushed pineapple, drained
    1 cup walnuts or pecans, chopped
    1 pkg. cream cheese (8 oz.) softened
    2 to 3 Tbsp. cream
    Bread, very thinly sliced

COMBINE sugar and pineapple in saucepan and bring to a boil, stirring constantly. Cool, then stir in nuts. Mash cream cheese with fork and add enough cream to create a good spreading consistency. Combine cream cheese with pineapple mixture. Spread mixture on thin bread and top with another slice. Trim off crusts and cut into triangles or finger sandwiches. Serve immediately.

Smoked Salmon Florets

> Toast rounds
> Chive cream cheese
> 6 strips smoked salmon (lox, the cold smoked variety)

SPREAD toast rounds with cream cheese. Trim smoked salmon into narrow strips and roll until it resembles a flower. Perch atop toast round and add a snip or two of fresh chive.

Almond Devonshire Cream

> 4 ounces cream cheese, softened
> ¼ cup sour cream
> 2 Tbsp. sugar
> ½ tsp. almond extract

MIX all ingredients together until smooth and creamy.

Timothy's Toll House Cookie Bars

1 cup butter
½ cup brown sugar, packed
½ cup sugar, granulated
1 egg yolk
1 tsp. vanilla
2 cups flour
10 oz. chocolate chips
1 cup walnuts, chopped

CREAM butter, both sugars, egg yolk, and vanilla. Stir in flour and mix well. Spread mixture on greased cookie sheet, forming a thin layer of cookie.

Bake at 350 degrees for 15 to 20 minutes. Melt chocolate chips in double boiler or microwave and spread gently over sheet of warm cookies. Sprinkle walnuts on and press them in firmly. Cut into bars while still warm. Serve when chocolate is hard.

Chutney and Cheddar Tea Sandwiches

½ cup chutney
2 cups sharp cheddar, grated coarsely
½ cup sour cream
3 oz. cream cheese, softened
Salt and pepper to taste
12 slices bread, very thin-sliced

STIR together chutney, cheddar cheese, sour cream, and cream cheese. Add salt and pepper to taste. Spread filling on bread to make 6 full sandwiches, then cut into small sandwich rounds—or trim off crusts and cut into triangles.

Pimento and Walnut Tea Sandwiches

½ cup pimentos, chopped
½ cup walnuts, chopped
4 oz. cream cheese
½ cup mayonnaise

MIX together and add salt and pepper to taste. Makes enough filling for 12 tea sandwiches.

Charleston Breakfast Casserole

1 ½ cups croutons
¼ cup butter, melted
1 cup cheddar cheese, grated
3 eggs
1 cup milk
¼ cup red pepper, diced
2 tsp. prepared mustard
6 slices bacon, fried

GREASE 8-inch-by-8-inch baking dish and fill with croutons. Drizzle with melted butter, then sprinkle with cheddar cheese. Crack eggs into bowl and whisk, breaking up yolks. Add milk, red peppers, and mustard, then beat until well combined. Pour over crouton mixture and sprinkle with crumbled bacon. Bake in 325 degree oven for 40 minutes. Let stand 10 minutes before serving. Serves 4.

Frogmore Stew

    1 gallon water
    1½ Tbsp. Old Bay Seasoning (or other prepared seafood
        seasoning)
    1 lb. spicy link sausage, cut into 2-inch pieces
    1 onion, medium size, chopped
    6 ears sweet corn, broken into smaller pieces
    2 lbs. raw shrimp

BOIL water in large stockpot and add seasoning. Add sausage and onion and boil for 5 minutes. Toss in the corn and boil for another 5 minutes. Now add the shrimp and boil for an additional 3 minutes. Drain and serve immediately with chunks of hearty bread. Serves 4 to 5.

Butterscotch Scones

    2 cups all-purpose flour
    ⅓ cup brown sugar, packed
    1 Tbsp. baking powder
    ½ tsp. salt
    ½ cup butter, cut into pieces

½ cup cream, very cold
1 egg
1 cup butterscotch chips

SIFT flour, brown sugar, baking powder, and salt into
medium bowl. Add in butter and stir or rub with fingers
until consistency of coarse meal. Whisk together cream and
egg, then add to butter/flour mixture and stir with fork.
Add butterscotch chips. Drop dough onto lightly greased
baking sheet. Bake at 400 degrees for 20 minutes or until
scones are golden brown.

TEA TIME TIPS FROM
Laura Childs

Silver Screen Tea

Dig out your movie magazines and dress like your favorite silver screen star!

Set your table with white roses in silver vases, your best silver and china, tall candles, and a killer cake displayed on a cake stand. Serve crab salad sandwiches on tiny baguette slices and cream cheese and watercress tea sandwiches. Entertain guests with a classic black-and-white movie—*Casablanca* anyone? Serve a flavorful, full bodied Assam.

Croquet Tea

When warm weather rolls around, dust off your croquet set and invite the ladies outside for tea. Wear your white dresses or white polo shirts and skirts. Serve finger sandwiches of crab salad, shredded carrot and cheddar cheese, and pineapple cream cheese. Iced sweet tea would be perfect, but think outside the box (or teabag) with iced raspberry or sweet plum tea.

Mad Hatter Tea

Encourage all your tea guests to bring their favorite beads, feathers, ribbon, vintage pins, etc. Then you provide some wide-brimmed straw hats from the craft store to decorate. Of course, you'll also have to have some extra ribbons, feathers, glue, and doodads available, along with plenty of tea time treats. Think mushroom quiche, cream scones, and Earl Grey tea.

Tea in the Cotswolds

Turn your kitchen or dining room into a storybook English cottage. Set your table with a blue-and-white-checkered tablecloth, then add white crocks of flowers or lavender. Serve asparagus spears rolled up in ham, cream cheese with English chutney, and fresh-baked scones in wicker baskets. Make sure you have plenty of lemon curd and Devonshire cream on hand. Serve English breakfast tea or tippy Yunnan in extra-large cups.

Springtime Tea

Choose plates, cups, and saucers with a floral or vine motif. Carry on the theme with a floral tablecloth and buckets of flowers. Serve sliced strawberries and cream cheese on nut bread, cucumber sandwiches with cream cheese and chives, and a salad of mixed greens with edible flowers.

Delight your guests with pitchers of sweet tea, steaming pots of Darjeeling, and classical music, such as Mozart's *The Magic Flute*.

Romance Novel Tea

If your friends enjoy a good bodice buster now and again, why not entertain them with a Romance Novel Tea! Make your table as romantic as possible with crystal vases filled with roses, candles, and cushy pillows in chairs that are draped in afghans. Stack romance novels in the center of the table and make Xerox copies of covers of romance novels for place mats. Serve ham and apricot pinwheels, popovers stuffed with chicken salad, biscotti, and pound cake with raspberry sauce. Serve a tea reminiscent of romance, too, like passion fruit, lemon verbena, or Egyptian chamomile.

Low-Carb Tea

If your friends are counting carbs, that's no reason to skimp on the tea goodies. Think ham roll-ups spread with light cream cheese and apricot preserves, deviled eggs, chicken salad on low-carb bread, crab salad in lettuce cups, and chocolate-dipped strawberries. Splurge on the tea with lemon Gunpowder or a fancy Formosan oolong.

TEA CRAFTING

Teacup Candles

It's simple to make you own teacup candles. Start by selecting a pretty teacup and saucer, then epoxy them together. Add a wick, pour in melted wax, add a few drops of scented oil, and let stand until your wax hardens.

Make Your Own Rose-Flavored Tea

Strip rose petals from a rose bouquet or from rosebushes in your own garden, then dry the petals very well. When they are dry and crumbly, simply add a few petals to your favorite tin of black tea. After a few days, the rose petals will impart a rosy flavor and fragrance.

TEA RESOURCES

TEA PUBLICATIONS

Tea: A Magazine—Quarterly magazine about tea as a beverage and its cultural significance in the arts and society. (www.teamag.com)

Tea Poetry—Book compiled and published by Pearl Dexter, editor of *Tea: A Magazine*. (www.teamag.com)

Tea Time—Luscious magazine profiling tea and tea lore. Filled with glossy photos and wonderful recipes. (www.teatimemagazine.com)

Southern Lady—From the publishers of *Tea Time* with a focus on people and places in the South as well as wonderful tea time recipes. (www.southernladymagazine.com)

The Tea House Times—Go to www.teahousetimes.com for subscription information and dozens of links to tea shops, purveyors of tea, gift shops, and tea events.

Victoria—Articles and pictorials on homes, home design, and tea. (www.victoriamag.com)

The Gilded Lily—Publication from the Ladies Tea Guild. (www.glily.com)

Tea in Texas—Highlighting Texas tea rooms and tea events. (www.teaintexas.com)

Fresh Cup Magazine—For tea and coffee professionals. (www.freshcup.com)

TEA WEBSITES AND BLOGS

Teamap.com—Directory of hundreds of tea shops in the U.S. and Canada.

GreatTearoomsofAmerica.com—Excellent tea shop guide.

TeaRadio.com—Listen to guests share personal tea journeys.

Cookingwithideas.typepad.com—Recipes and book reviews for the bibliochef.

Cuppatea4sheri.blogspot.com—Amazing recipes.

Theladiestea.com—Networking platform for women.

Jennybakes.com—Fabulous recipes from a real made-from-scratch baker.

Bigelowtea.com—Website for the Charleston Tea Plantation, the oldest tea plantation in the United States. Order their fine black tea, too!

Teanmystery.com—Tea shop, books, gifts, and gift baskets.

Allteapots.com—Teapots from around the world.

Thechurchmouse.com—Gift shop that carries tea produced by the Fairhope Tea Plantation in Fairhope, Alabama.

Fireflyvodka.com—South Carolina purveyors of Sweet Tea vodka, Raspberry Tea vodka, Peach Tea vodka and more. Just visiting this website is a trip in itself!

Teasquared.blogspot.com—Fun blog about tea, tea shops, tea musing.

Bernideensteatimeblog.blogspot.com—Tea, baking, decorations, and gardening.

Tealoversroom.com—California tea rooms, Teacasts, links.

Teapages.blogspot.com—All things tea.

Big Island Tea—Organic artisan tea from Hawaii. (www.bigislandtea.com)

Sakuma Brothers Farm—This tea garden just outside Burlington, WA, has been growing white and green tea for ten years. (www.sakumamarket.com)

Baking.about.com—Carroll Pellegrinelli writes a terrific baking blog complete with recipes and photo instructions.

PURVEYORS OF FINE TEA
Adagio.com
Harney.com
Stashtea.com
Republicoftea.com
Bigelowtea.com

Teasource.com
Celestialseasonings.com
Goldenmoontea.com
Uptontea.com
Oliverstea.com

Turn the page for a preview of Laura Childs's next
Scrapbooking Mystery . . .

SKELETON LETTERS

Available in paperback from Berkley Prime Crime!

1

"Spooky," said *Carmela* as she stepped into the dark interior of St. Tristan's Church. It was an historic pile of stones tucked discreetly into New Orleans's freewheeling French Quarter. Dim overhead lights spilled muddy puddles of light down the center aisle. An ornate wooden altar with a large gold cross and tabernacle flanked by two red lamps loomed at the far end. Tucked down both sides of the church were small chapels and prayer nooks where flickering vigil lights cast dancing shadows across the faces of peeling, painted statues, giving them an uncanny animated look. All around were the rustlings of unseen people as beads rattled, doors closed softly, and footsteps whispered on slate floors. Choir practice had just concluded, and it felt like the final notes of "Abide With Me" were still hanging thick in the air.

Blinking rapidly, Carmela fought to adjust her eyes to take in the vaulted arches, dark confessionals, and gigantic pipe organ that all seemed to impart an air of monastic seclusion and deep solemnity. "It's almost like something

out of *Phantom of the Opera*," she murmured to her friend
Ava, who was a step behind, juggling a large hand-lettered
poster.

"Or *The Hunchback of Notre Dame*," Ava offered. "You
remember that poor, twisted creature scrabbling around in
the bell tower . . . ?"

"I remember," said Carmela, and wished she hadn't. St.
Tristan's had a bell tower, too. A Romanesque structure with
ancient bronze bells that clanged out their soliloquy above
the French Quarter three times a day.

"Still," said Ava, gazing about with an almost beatific
expression on her face, "I love it here. It's particularly meaningful now that I'm volunteering with the Angel Auxiliary."

Carmela, a youthful blond of not-quite-thirty, directed
a skeptical sideways glance at her best friend, whose
va-va-voom figure was sheathed in tight black leather slacks
and a plunging yellow T-shirt with a sparkling court jester
motif on the front. She herself was dressed in Republican
beige and had worn sensible, low-heeled shoes. True, Carmela
was lovely in her own right, with a peaches-and-cream complexion, blue-gray eyes that mirrored the color of the Gulf
of Mexico, and a certain air of barely contained mirth and
energy. And, on certain occasions, generally a fancy Mardi
Gras ball, Carmela flung caution to the wind and jacked her
five-foot-six-inch frame up onto tottering four-inch-high sti-
lettos to hang out with the tall gals. And the tall guys. Still,
the fact remained . . . when Ava strutted her stuff with the
assurance of a peacock, Carmela sometimes felt like a little
brown wren.

Got to ratchet up the sizzle, Carmela told herself. *Buy a Won-
derbra or a purple teddy. Spritz on a little Chanel No. 5. Keep that
boyfriend of mine on his toes. But maybe I shouldn't think about all
that . . . in church.*

"People don't realize," said Ava, dipping two fingers into
a marble holy water font, crossing herself, then turning

innocent, practically guileless eyes on Carmela, "that I'm a very strict Catholic."

"Really." Carmela's tone was purposefully flat. No question intended, no judgment made. Just a bushel basket full of curiosity. Like . . . had the church elders ever dug into Ava's background? Did they know she was the proprietor of the Juju Voodoo shop? Carmela thought not. But, seriously, what *was* the harm in a voodoo shop owner working as a docent in church? Nothing, really. And if your undies were in a twist, well, then you should string a holy medal around your neck, whisper an extra prayer, and grab a handful of ashes if you could find them. Because Ava was Ava, a retired beauty queen who partied her brains out and was known to enjoy a romantic fling or two. Or eight or nine.

"It's so peaceful in here," said Ava as they slipped silently up a side aisle and stopped in front of a low wooden table scattered with books, hymnals, and pamphlets. "And I can't thank you enough for hand-lettering this poster." She reached behind the table, slid out a wooden easel, and plunked the poster onto it. "A perfect display," she declared.

Carmela pushed aside a hunk of artfully chunked and skunked hair and directed a smile at Ava. "Always glad to help out." She'd been brushing up on her calligraphy like crazy anyway, gearing up for an upcoming seminar at her scrapbook shop, Memory Mine.

Ava set about straightening the little stacks of pamphlets, while Carmela gazed up at a stained glass window that depicted a tall, stern-looking angel cradling a lamb. What should have been resplendent panes of red, blue, and yellow glass, with thin November sunlight streaming through, only looked dull and muted today. Rain poured down outside, as it had for the past three days, encasing the entire city in a soggy, gray, amorphous cloud. Even in here, Carmela could hear rain drumming the roof and gurgling down drain spouts. For a moment, Carmela wondered if, way at the tippy-top of the roofline, St. Tristan's might not have gargoyle drain spouts, much like the great churches of Europe.

And why not? This was an old church built at the turn of the century—not this century, but two gone past—by the hands of the same type of good and God-fearing men who'd supervised construction of landmark cathedrals and abbeys. Using the tried-and-true Romanesque plan of long nave and short transept, they'd built this fine edifice, established an adjoining graveyard, and buried their noteworthy followers in crypts beneath the floor.

A sudden soft *clunk* focused Carmela's eyes on a nearby confessional. Was someone in there? A penitent and priest, conferring over some sins that required forgiveness?

Had those purple velvet draperies stirred just a touch? Or was someone else padding about the church? There'd been a sense of emptiness in St. Tristan's, the rustlings and bustlings of a few minutes earlier seemed to have faded away. And yet . . .

Carmela touched a hand to Ava's shoulder. "I think we should . . ."

Like ragged metal scraping metal, a bloodcurdling scream suddenly ripped through the church. It rose in ghastly screeches, spiraling into a high-pitched shriek.

Ava spun around and caught the eyes of a startled Carmela. Then both women whirled in tight circles, fearful, searching, trying to ascertain where that ungodly scream was coming from.

Ava lifted a hand and pointed across the church. "There!"

Squinting through the darkness, Carmela saw two figures locked in a rough-and-tumble embrace.

"No!" came another piercing scream. Now it was distinctly a woman's scream, a woman who was terrified. "Not the . . ." came her words, then she broke off in an agonized keening.

Carmela dashed forward a dozen steps, then pulled up

quickly. What was going on? Should she get involved? Was it a robbery of some sort? Was there even anything here to steal?

She was about to leap forward, try to thwart whatever was happening, when Ava suddenly grasped her arm.

"Be careful!" Ava hissed.

Then the woman across the way moaned low and deep.

Ava quickly touched a hand to her mouth. "I think she's . . ."

Carmela saw a swirl of brown robe as a cloaked figure forced a smaller figure to its knees. A flash of silver shone in the hooded figure's hands, then a four-foot-high statue teetered precariously and toppled from its perch. The woman dropped like a dead weight to the floor as chunks of plaster burst everywhere, knocking over candles and spewing rivulets of hot wax. Then the figure in the hooded robe leapt away and seemed to melt into darkness.

Carmela and Ava dashed between pews toward the small altar where the woman lay like a tossed rag doll.

"Call 911!" Carmela shrilled. Ava fumbled frantically in her velvet hobo bag for her cell phone as Carmela sprinted into a turn, smacking her left hip against a wooden pillar. Without breaking stride, she cartwheeled her way to the wounded woman.

"Oh no!" Carmela's eyes widened in disbelief.

There, splayed out in front of the small altar like a sacrificial offering, was Byrle Coopersmith, one of her scrapbooking regulars!

What? Byrle? Her mind could barely grasp this.

Ava careened to a stop behind Carmela, immediately recognized Byrle, and shrieked at the top of her lungs, "Dear Lord, it's Byrle! It's Byrle!" She gibbered for another couple of seconds, then caught herself and said, in trembling tones. "What *happened*?"

Carmela was already on her hands and knees. "Knocked

unconscious, anyway," she said, tersely. Byrle's head was bleeding profusely, her neck was ringed with purple splotches—almost like fingerprint impressions—and her eyes had rolled so far back in her head Carmela could see only the whites. Worst of all, Byrle didn't seem to be breathing.

"Do something!" Ava implored. "Maybe . . . chest compressions?"

Carmela nodded with the mechanical movement of a bobblehead doll. She lay her hands flat against Byrle's chest and tried to dredge up every morsel of know-how she had regarding CPR and chest compressions.

"Breathe," Carmela willed, as she pressed her fingers against Byrle's chest, up, down, up, down, working to establish a rhythm, trying to stimulate her heart and force some air into her lungs. "Come on, honey, you can do it!" she cried to the woman who was quickly turning a terrifying shade of blue. "You *know* you can!"

"Help her!" Ava implored. She squeezed her hands open and shut, as if working in concert with Carmela's efforts.

Carmela's knees were scraped raw, but she continued to work on Byrle. "Ambulance coming?" she asked. She was filled with panic and starting to tire.

"On its way," said Ava.

"Can you . . . ?" Push, push, pump, push. "Can you . . . spell me for a couple of minutes?" Carmela asked.

"Oooh!" Ava wrapped her arms tightly around herself.

"Never mind," said Carmela, trying to wipe her damp face on her sleeve. She renewed her efforts even as her back muscles burned, shouting out, "Come on, *breathe*!"

"Anything?" wailed Ava, as Carmela, resolutely but with hope failing, continued to pump, pump, pump.

"Doggone," Carmela muttered through clenched teeth. The poor dear wasn't responding at all.

She was too far gone and, undoubtedly, in the Lord's

hands now. As well-intentioned as Carmela had been, she was no miracle worker.

Byrle Coopersmith, their friend and fellow scrapbooker, who'd not long ago bought a pack of pink mulberry paper, lay lifeless on the cold, hard floor of St. Tristan's.

2

❧

"Blunt force trauma."

Carmela stared into the earnest brown eyes of the young detective who had arrived amidst a blat of sirens and a brace of uniformed officers. Another shocking intrusion into what had been an oasis of calm and contemplative spirituality.

"What?" Carmela asked in a hoarse whisper. Had she really heard Detective Bobby Gallant correctly?

"From the statue," Gallant told her, giving a downward bob of his head. He was young and earnest-looking with dark curly hair and hazel eyes. Because of the cool weather he was dressed in a black leather jacket and chinos.

Ava, who was hovering directly behind Carmela, increased her vise-like grip on her friend's shoulder. "The killer smacked Byrle over the head with St. Sebastian," Ava sobbed, trying to be helpful, but failing miserably.

"Saint . . . ?" Carmela began, as Ava suddenly released her hold and pointed toward the flagstone floor, where shards of plaster lay scattered. A three-foot-high statue, the one Ava had positively ID'd as St. Sebastian, lay face down. Most of its head was missing. Pulverized from the blow, she supposed.

Byrle's body lay prostrate at the foot of the saint's altar, where she'd fallen, looking like some kind of unholy martyr who'd given life and limb for the church. And, in a way, she had.

Carmela let loose a deep and shaky sigh. She knew she had to get a grip and try to pull it together. After all, she'd been a sort of witness. So maybe she could be of some assistance in the investigation? On the other hand . . .

Making a half spin so she faced Bobby Gallant, Carmela said, "We need Babcock on this." Her words came out a little more hoarse and a little more demanding than she'd actually intended.

Gallant barely acknowledged her statement concerning his boss. "I'm the one who got the call out," he murmured.

"The thing is," Carmela said, gesturing toward Byrle's lifeless body, "we know her. She's a friend."

"From Memory Mine," Ava added. "Carmela's scrapbook shop."

"I'm very sorry to hear that," said Gallant. And this time he did sound sorry.

"So we need to do everything in our power," Carmela gulped, "to find whoever did this."

"Which is exactly what I intend to do," said Gallant. He glanced around and noticed a uniformed officer standing off to the side, staring at Byrle's dead body. "Slovey!" he barked. "Get something to cover her up!"

Slovey seemed suddenly unhappy. "What do you want me to use?" he asked.

Color bloomed on Gallant's face. "I don't care," he snapped. "Use your own jacket if you have to!"

"This isn't happening," Carmela murmured to Ava. Holding on to each other, they staggered over to the row of church

pews that faced the small altar and collapsed together on the hard seat. There, they huddled like lost souls, trying to make sense of it all. At the same time, like some bizarre soap opera, the beginnings of the police investigation played out right before their eyes.

The crime scene techs arrived, set up enough lights to make it look like a movie set, and began to photograph Byrle's body as well as the damaged saint statue and everything else within a twenty-foot radius.

Uniformed officers were given assignments and hastily dispatched to interview possible witnesses and take statements.

And finally, two EMTs arrived with a clanking gurney to carry Byrle away. Probably, Carmela decided, they were going to transport her to the city morgue. And wasn't that a grim thought!

"Babcock should be here," Ava said in a low voice. "Working this case."

Edgar Babcock, homicide detective first class of the New Orleans Police Department, was, to put it rather indelicately, Carmela's main squeeze. As Carmela had wrangled through her divorce from Shamus, the two had gazed longingly at each other. When Carmela finally separated from her philandering rat fink husband, she and Babcock finally started seeing each other. And now that Carmela's divorce was signed, sealed, and delivered, they were most definitely an item.

"Don't worry," said Carmela, "I'm going to call Babcock." She hesitated. "But Gallant does seem to be doing a credible job."

"Credible is only good when it comes to talking heads on TV," said Ava. "For this investigation we need a grade A detective."

"Sshhh," said Carmela. Gallant was suddenly headed straight toward them.

Stepping lightly, Gallant slid into the pew directly ahead of them, settled on the creaky seat, and swiveled to face them. Only then did Carmela notice the tiredness and deep concern that were etched in his face.

"Something tells me this isn't the only case you're handling," Carmela said.

Gallant shook his head. "Two drive-bys last night and a floater in the river."

"Tough job," said Ava.

"Tough city," said Gallant.

"What . . . what's happening now?" asked Carmela.

"Well," said Gallant, "we've got the church and outside area pretty much cordoned off and my officers are interviewing everyone who was hanging around the church. Plus, we're canvassing the neighborhood."

"I think some people left before you got here," said Ava.

Gallant leaned forward. "Did you get a look at them?"

Ava shook her head. "Not really. It was more like hearing them." She looked suddenly thoughtful. "You know how when you're in church you're *aware* of people nearby, you hear their voices and shufflings and such, but you don't really look at them?"

"I suppose," said Gallant. He seemed keenly disappointed that Ava wasn't able to give him a complete description. He directed his gaze at Carmela. "You said earlier that you thought the killer was wearing a brown robe?"

"He definitely was," said Carmela. "Like a monk's robe. Dark brown with a deep cowl and hood."

"With a white rope knotted around his waist," Ava added.

"There's a bunch of those robes hanging in the back room on a row of hooks," Gallant told them.

"That's a problem," said Carmela. "It means anybody could have grabbed one and threw it on."

Gallant shifted on the uncomfortably hard pew. "What's the story with the garden and graveyard outside—all the digging and the stakes and ropes and things? Either of you know?"

"It's an archaeology dig," Ava told him. "Been going on for almost four months now."

"Do you know who's in charge of it?" asked Gallant.

Ava shrugged.

"I think it's the State Archaeology Board," said Carmela. "With assistance from students at Tulane." She paused. "At least that's what the article in the *Times-Picayune* said."

Gallant jotted something in his notebook. "They find anything?"

"Ten feet down," said Ava, "they discovered the ruins of the original church. The one Pere Etienne founded back in 1782." Pere Etienne had been a Capuchin monk who'd been a much beloved figure due to his tireless work with the sick and the poor.

Gallant looked mildly interested. "Ruins, huh. Anything else?"

"They also unearthed an antique silver and gold crucifix," said Ava, "believed to have been the personal crucifix of Pere Etienne."

"Which was stolen during the murder," Carmela said suddenly, almost as an afterthought.

Gallant reared back. "What? A crucifix was stolen?"

"From the saint's altar," said Ava. "Where Byrle was killed."

"I think," said Carmela, "that Byrle struggled with her killer to try to wrest the crucifix back from him."

"Why didn't you mention this sooner?" Gallant demanded.

"Because," said Carmela, "We thought it was more important for you to dispatch your men immediately to hunt down suspects."

Gallant stroked his chin with his hand. "So a robbery and a murder. I wonder . . . was this crucifix terribly valuable?"

"Byrle thought so," said Carmela. "After all, she gave her life for it."

BE SURE TO WATCH FOR

Bedeviled Eggs

THE NEXT CACKLEBERRY CLUB MYSTERY
BY LAURA CHILDS

When a dead body turns up on a Quilt Trail, Suzanne searches for clues as she gets drawn into dirty politics, a prison break, rescued dogs, and a spookier than usual Halloween.

FIND OUT MORE ABOUT THE AUTHOR

AND HER MYSTERIES AT

WWW.LAURACHILDS.COM

SAVOR THE LATEST FROM
NEW YORK TIMES BESTSELLING AUTHOR
LAURA CHILDS

SCONES & BONES
• A Tea Shop Mystery •

Indigo Tea Shop owner Theodosia Browning is lured
into attending the Heritage Society's Pirates and
Plunder party. But when a history intern is found
murdered—and an antique diamond skull gets plundered in the process—Theodosia knows she'll have to
whet her investigative skills to find the killer among
a raft of suspects.

penguin.com